K.M. GOLLAND
Book 4 in The Temptation Series

First Published 2014
Third Australian Paperback Edition 2018
ISBN 978 148924826 8

ATTRACTION
© 2014 by K.M. Golland
Australian Copyright 2014
New Zealand Copyright 2014

Published by
Mira
An imprint of Harlequin Enterprises (Australia) Pty Ltd.
Level 13, 201 Elizabeth St
Sydney NSW 2000
AUSTRALIA

MIX
Paper from
responsible sources
FSC   FSC® C001695
www.fsc.org

Printed and bound in Australia by McPherson's Printing Group

Attraction

ABOUT THE AUTHOR

'I am an author. I am married. I am a mother of two adorable little people. I'm a bookworm, craftworm, movieworm, and sportsworm. I'm also a self-confessed shopaholic, tea-aholic, car-aholic, and choc-aholic.'

Born and raised in Melbourne, Australia, K.M. Golland studied law and worked as a conveyancer before putting her career on hold to raise her children. She then traded her legal work for her love of writing and found her dream career.

*For my readers and fans who requested Carly's voice.
I question your sanity.*

PROLOGUE

Have you ever thought that you knew exactly where your life was headed? Knew what you would be doing and who you would be doing it with? Well, I did. I had my life somewhat mapped out in my head. My life was going to be free. Free from obstructions, free from drama and free from anchors that tied me to anyone or anything. Yep, I was an anchorless ship on her maiden voyage that never ended.

I was going to sail through life on a continuous journey of good times, fashion and fun. I was carefree, fat-free, child-free and fancy-free. I had good health, good family and friends, good shoes and a good arse! My life was good. Uncomplicated.

That was until I met Derek.

Firefighter Derek. Drop-dead gorgeous Derek. Blue-eyed, dirty-talking, cocky-as-hell Derek. He was the sweetest man I'd ever met and the one person to completely change my infinite voyage of freedom.

He was my iceberg.

CHAPTER

1

If you watch the second hand on a clock closely, you will see it pause then tick backward. Sometimes it even skips forward then bloody backward again. Don't believe me? Watch one, I dare you. Watch it like a hawk, just like I did every day at 3.15 p.m.

EVERY. DAY.

I'm not ashamed of being able to tell you every detail about the clock in my office. It's round, white, and it has a black circular edge. It has three hands and twelve numbers on it. It's quite simply plain and ugly and it taunts me on a daily basis.

Rolling my neck from side to side, I attempted to rid my body of the built-up tension that primary school students placed on it. I groaned and flinched as a cracking noise sounded from my neck, the sound alone indicating that I was in need of an appointment with my super-sexy chiropractor, also known as Give-Us-A-Crack Jack. *Mm, Jack … the things that man does with his hands.*

I removed the pervy smile from my face that said 'Yes, I'm currently daydreaming about being fucked' and, with an additional grizzle and gloomy moan, shrugged my shoulders and focussed on the remainder of my day.

It wasn't lost on me that I sound like a whinging, whining cat, and I knew that my job as the school receptionist was not the worst job in the world. I knew it because my room-mate, Libby — or Miss Hanson as she is known to her grade three students — has a cousin who drives to numerous public places, such as shopping centres and offices, and replaces those sanitary bins that sit in the corner of a ladies toilet cubicle.

Now that's a bad job!

And an old school friend of Lexi's and mine, who befriended us on Facebook, well ... he cleans those whack-off rooms in sex shops. *Yuck! Grossest job ever!* So, no, my job wasn't yuck or bad; it was just really draining and sucked the absolute life out of me. Why? One word: children. Curious, over-enthusiastic, loud and inquisitive children. They were the bane of my existence.

Stretching my fingers over my computer keyboard, I again watched as that bloody second hand on the clock played its evil trick on me. I had a dream once, a horrible, horrible dream that bordered on nightmare. I dreamed that the ghastly timepiece had a face ... a real face, a human face. It wasn't even hot or sexy; it was the face of a geeky guy and it talked to me, teasing and taunting as the seconds counted down to the final school bell for the day. 'Ten more seconds to go, Carly,' geeky clock-man had said. 'No, make that eleven seconds, also known as

660 billion nanoseconds. Oh, pardon me, I do stand corrected, there's ten seconds left. Aw, now it's twelve.' *Fuck off, geeky clock-man.*

'Miss Henkley?' a timid voice sounded from somewhere in my vicinity, snapping me out of my recollection.

Looking up, I spotted seven-year-old Ellie Lake, standing in front of my reception counter. We had a small footstool on the ground for short students, and Ellie, being one of them, was propped on top of it, peering at me.

'Yes, Ellie?' I replied with my pleasant hurry-up-and-get-out-of-my-face voice.

'I'm this week's bell monitor,' she advised proudly. *Ooh, lucky you!*

Almost instantly, the song 'Ring my Bell' by Collette played in my head, throwing me back into the 1980s: spandex, acid-wash denim and fluorescent pink and yellow hair scrunchies. *God, I need a night at the Metro.*

'Excellent,' I replied, a bit too sarcastically, while plastering on a faux smile.

Ellie was none the wiser.

'Come around here, Ellie, and I'll show you what to do.'

She jumped off the step, skipped past the reception window and came through my office door. Her ridiculous enthusiasm to press a button which inevitably sounded the last school bell of the day made me smile — children are such strange creatures.

'Okay, so when the clock says 3.20 p.m. exactly, you press this button right here,' I explained, pointing to the circular red button. 'Three times, like this: One. Two. Three.'

Unfortunately, I had to be precise with my instructions, making sure I clearly exaggerated the pause between each push. Last week, Jet Bradley — aged eight — decided that he would try to be the fastest bell-button pusher in history. OneTwoThree — no pauses. So to avoid a similar scenario — because superfast bell-button pushers were not what we were after as bell monitors — I reiterated the tempo of the push. *Somebody please kill me now.*

Thank everything in the world that is wonderful, though, because tomorrow is Saturday, which means no school and more importantly, no school children. Tomorrow was the beginning of the school holidays. Oh, and it was also my best friend Alexis' birthday.

Lexi and I have been friends for as long as we could remember, both of us having first met each other at the age of four when Mum and Dad bought the property next to her parents' farm in Shepparton. Mr and Mrs Blaxlo — also known as Graeme and Maryann — owned twenty-eight hectares of land which they used to farm beef cattle, whereas our farm was a little smaller and contained sheep: smelly, ugly, boring sheep.

Now, I wouldn't call myself an animal hater. In fact, I liked most animals. I even have a Mexican walking fish named Rico and an eight-month-old golden retriever named Sasha. I just didn't like cows, cats, mice, spiders or sheep ... especially sheep. *Baa, baa, fucking baa.*

Alexis — my partner in crime for the past thirty-one years — was having a birthday party at her extremely wealthy, and sexy as hell, boyfriend's penthouse apartment the following night. Apparently also her apartment, too. She moved in with Mr Sex-on-a-stick Bryce Clark a couple of months back after she found out her husband of twelve years — Rick 'arsehole' Summers — had cheated on her and spawned a love child he just recently found out about. *Who needs* Days of Our Lives *when I have Days of Alexis' Life?*

Jokes aside, though, their separation and the revelation of Rick's past was heartbreaking for Lexi. Luckily, Alexis had Bryce with her every step of the way to pick up the pieces of her broken heart. And not only did he pick them up, he forged the pieces together like a Herculean god, building a new heart for Alexis that he decided was his sole mission in life to look after and protect.

Hmm ... thinking of Herculean gods, might have to download the movie 300 *tonight and get my fix of triple-chocolate swirl ice cream and Gerard Butler. Damn, that Scotsman is fine.*

'One. Two. Three,' Ellie quietly chanted while waiting for the time to tick over.

Subduing a smile, I returned to thinking about my best friend's crazy-as-fuck life. You see, Lexi and Rick have two children: Nate, aged nine, and Charlotte, aged six. As I've said, children are the bane of my existence, but Nate and Charli are the exception. I love those two gorgeous twerps like they are my own. *My own? Ha, never! Carly Josephine Henkley is never having children. Not until sheep fly ... fly the fuck off, that is.*

Before Lexi found out about Rick's infidelity, she'd fairly recently gone back to work after staying at home and raising Nate and Charli for nine years. All well and good ... until she fell in love with her obscenely rich and sizzling-hot boss, Bryce Clark, and he just as madly, if not more so, fell in love with her.

The whirlwind that has been their romance could only be rivalled by the one that swept Dorothy's house from Kansas. But as explained by Alexis, it was as though the two of them were woven from the same cloth: made for each other, a romance written in the stars. And I couldn't say that I disagreed with her. Their connection was undeniably perfect ... akin to chocolate and peanut butter, or lamb and mint sauce. *Mm ... lamb and mint sauce. That's dinner sorted.* What? I may not like sheep, but I am more than happy to eat them.

Ellie shuffled impatiently, eyeing the taunting clock as the seconds ticked down, the anxious wait to perform her duty painted across her little face. I was of half a mind to ask if the second hand jumped back and forth for her as it did for me, but I didn't. Instead, I started to arrange the individual class folders in a pile, ready for me to input the day's final attendance record into my computer.

As I sat down on my seat and smoothed my black pencil-pleat skirt down my thighs, I noticed that my fingernails needed a new coat of polish. *Shit! Mental note: don't forget to prettify my digits before the party.* One of my cardinal rules — known as Carly's Cardinals — was that, as a female, one's nails should always look stunning. They should be pretty and intimidatingly scary, all at the same time. Not to mention that I couldn't possibly go to Lexi's party without fingernails that could stop traffic. Surely Bryce had hot friends ... wealthy friends, friends that came from the same planet as him. I'm guessing Krypton. Surely he was not the only super-sexy, smart, obscenely handsome, successful businessman in Melbourne. Odds were, he wasn't.

That was why my nails had to be smokin' hot and enticing enough to have one of his friends want nothing more than for me to drag them down his back in a moment of ecstasy. *Well, that's my plan, anyway.*

I once read in *Cosmopolitan* magazine that men notice women's nails because they fantasise about being scratched by them. I also read that men like hosiery because they think women who wear hosiery also wear a sexy garter belt. Oh, and men like long hair because they want to grab hold of it while they fuck you from behind. *Okay, so the magazine didn't say that. I just know that for a fact.*

Regardless of what men like, I keep up my appearance for myself. I like my long ash-blonde hair. I like to wear the latest fashion. And I like to adorn my face in MAC and L'Oréal. *Because I'm worth it.*

I giggled to myself. I loved those ads.

'Is it time yet?' Ellie asked, her finger hovering nervously over the button.

I looked up at the clock and took note of the time. *Urgh ... I wish it was.* 'No, one more minute,' I informed her.

She bopped her head eagerly. 'Okay.'

God, I can't wait for tomorrow. I hadn't seen Lexi since she fled to her parents' farm, soon after finding out about Rick's infidelity; at the same time she also found out that Bryce had paid Rick five million dollars to allow Alexis to spend a week with him — 'him' being Bryce. *I told you, Days of Alexis' Life.*

Apparently, Bryce discovered that Rick had had an affair. He'd also discovered that Rick was desperate for money, so Bryce offered the five mil to Rick for him to come clean to Alexis, which inevitably sent her directly into Bryce's waiting arms. *Fucking genius if you ask me, although I never told Lexi that.*

Despite my appreciation of Bryce's ingenuity, I still fretted over Lexi being in the middle of a love triangle to end all love triangles and that her marriage was in disarray. She had always been grounded, content and settled, having been with Rick since the age of seventeen. So I was concerned when her life went to shit, and not only because she found out that her husband was a cheating arse-wipe, but because she also had a charming, hot-as-hell wealthy man pursuing her relentlessly at the same time.

As exciting as that concept sounded, it had worried me. Lexi was not used to so much drama. It wasn't until I saw her and Bryce together that I realised he was her saving grace — they just clicked.

Ding. Ding. Ding. The bell sounded and Ellie turned to me with an expression that sought approval. I gave her a thumbs-up and sent her on her way.

''Bye, Miss Henkley. Have a good weekend.'

'You, too, Ellie,' I replied, watching her smile as she skipped out the door with her schoolbag, which was nearly bigger than she was.

With the end of my working week behind me, and the ringing bell prompting a huge smile to form on my face, I casually leaned back in my chair, putting my hands behind my head and spinning in a 360° twirl.

TGIF!

CHAPTER

2

The following day, I drove my Suzuki Swift Sport — known as Suzi — toward the waiting valet attendant at City Towers, which was Bryce's hotel. He owned the entire City Towers Entertainment Complex, which comprised three hotels plus a shopping and entertainment precinct. According to Alexis, his company — Clark Incorporated — had many hotels worldwide. She'd told me that she tried not to think about it all too much because it freaked her out. Personally, I thought she was bloody crazy. She was shacked up with one of the wealthiest and sexiest men on the face of the earth. What's not to think about?

Stepping out of the car, I handed my keys to the waiting attendant.

'Thank you, ma'am,' he said with a courteous smile. I checked him out for the slightest of seconds, taking in his baby-cute face. *Na, too young.*

Continuing toward the lobby, I stopped and craned my neck, looking up at the forty-three storey building towering over me while shielding my eyes from the rays of sunlight that shone through the overhead glass awning. I had been here numerous times, but never to the penthouse apartment. And I had never used the hotel's valet service before. I felt a bit spesh.

Last week Bryce had sent me a text message explaining that he was organising a birthday party for Alexis and I was invited to help celebrate. Of course I would help celebrate. Lexi and I had been at each other's birthday parties every year since we were four years old, birthday number six being one of our finest celebrations. I'm not sure whose idea it was — probably mine, seeing as it involved getting naked — but we had decided that games such as pass the parcel and pin the tail on the donkey were boring, opting to strip off our clothes and roll around in the grass and mud instead. *What better way to spend one's birthday in none other than one's birthday suit, right?*

I wished I had thought of that particular excuse at age six, because 'mud feels good between my toes' and 'Alexis told me to do it' did not cut it in the face of my mother's questioning. Let's just say that we put our clothes back on after Mum and Maryann gave us an eardrum scolding. They also took incriminating photographs which reared their ugly heads at both of our twenty-first birthday parties.

Making my way to the reception desk after a bellboy kindly received my funky Kate Hill overnight bag, I stopped at the counter and was greeted by a vivacious young man.

'Good afternoon, ma'am. How can I help you today?' he asked with a courteous yet chirpy tone.

'Hi. My name is Carly Henkley. I'm checking in as one of the guests attending Alexis Summers' birthday party.'

'Oh, you're Carls. Alexis has told me all about you,' he said with a mischievous grin, shedding his professionalism like a snakeskin.

I narrowed my eyes, spying his identification badge and taking note of his name. 'Liam,' I said as I met his eyes, 'Alexis is full of shit ... unless what she has told you is all good and nothing but good.'

Liam smiled and leaned to the side, placing one elbow on top of his counter. He quickly scanned the room and then lowered his voice. 'Don't tell her I said this, but she mentioned once that you reminded her of a horny Barbie doll on crack.'

Slapping my hand to my chest exaggeratedly, I feigned insult at Lexi's almost-accurate description. 'Me ... a Barbie doll? These are real, my friend. AND ... I don't do drugs. Drugs are bad. I learned that in school,' I replied while cupping my double D-sized breasts and hoisting them up.

Just as I performed my self-grope, a hot businessman walked through the foyer. Liam and I followed his toned arse as it teased us with its perky deliciousness.

'You must love your job,' I said with a jealous tone, my head tilted to one side, hands still cupping my breasts, and eyes still glued to hot businessman's butt.

'Uh huh,' Liam drawled.

'What room is he in?' I asked, still fixated on the way his trousers gently caressed the skin under them.

'Hopefully mine.'

My eyes snapped back to Liam's. 'Don't tell me a hot little sex toy like yourself is single?'

'Sadly, yes,' he replied as he broke free of his smut-stare and began to type on his computer keyboard.

'Really?' I asked excitedly.

'Yes,' he deadpanned.

'Hmm.'

Liam's lips pursed, and he raised his eyebrow. 'What's "hmm" mean?'

Smiling conceitedly, I assessed my fingernails. 'It means I have a friend of a friend. How old are you?'

'Depends, is this friend of a friend decent?'

'Yes,' I said with absolute certainty.

He lowered his voice. 'Is he out? As in "Mum and Dad know I blow guys"?'

I cracked up laughing. 'Oh, I like you, Liam.'

'What's not to like?' he said with a wink as he handed me a room card.

Poking out my tongue, I snatched the card from his hand. 'The SpongeBob SquarePants jocks you are probably wearing. Later,' I said with a wink.

'Have fun at Lexi's party, Barbie,' he called out.

''Bye, SpongeBob,' I said as I waved my hand over my shoulder at him, smiling at the thought of possibly setting him up with Brooke's — also known as Miss Lewis to her grade one students — room-mate's brother. Somehow I think they would work.

* * *

As I stepped into the elevator, I retrieved my phone from my handbag, realising I forgot to remind Libby that she was in charge of feeding Sasha and Rico for the night. Rico, my Mexican walking fish, was king of his tank. I loved him.

Libby answered her phone after two rings. 'What did you forget?' she asked in a condescending tone.

Her question offended me. Well, not really. I forgot shit all the time, hence the phone call. 'You're feedin' Sasha and Rico tonight,' I informed her.

'Who says I'm gonna be home?' she replied haughtily.

'You'll be home.'

'Will not.'

'Will so.'

The line was silent for a moment.

'Lib, you got a date?' I asked, teasingly. *She so hasn't.* Lib was a couch dweller and a bedroom hermit. She ventured out for shopping and the occasional walk with Sasha. If I was lucky, I'd get her to come dancing with me, which was pretty much never.

'What if I have?' she stuttered.

'I'd tell you to shave and wear sexy underwear. Oh, and don't go down on him on the first date. It's unlady-like and you, Lib, are a lady.'

'You're disgusting,' she responded, 'and fine, I'll be home.'

'Thanks, love you.'

Making a kiss sound at my phone, I disconnected and smiled at the fact I could read her like a book. I then glanced at the elderly couple standing beside me. Wifey was glaring at me with a contorted face, her expression indicating that I smelled of dog shit. Hubby, on the other hand, clearly thought I rocked, his expression an impressed smile.

'Blow jobs are for special men,' I informed them. 'They need to prove themselves first.'

The elevator dinged and they both exited the cart, wifey shooting out as if she were about to run a race against Usain Bolt. As the doors closed tight again, I let out a giggle. *I am so bad. Although I bet hubby gets a bit tonight.* That was my good deed done for the day.

* * *

The elevator cart took me to the thirty-third floor. *Nice! I'm staying in a suite on the thirty-third level of City Towers. Lexi, Lexi, Lexi, you really have secured yourself Mr Prince Charming.*

Shaking my head, I smiled happily for my best friend. She deserved happiness with Bryce. Although the strange thing was that I — together with everyone else in her life, including Lex herself — believed she was happy with Rick. That's why, when she told me about his secret affair, I could hardly believe it. Of course, I did believe she was telling me the truth, it was just ... he always seemed to have idolised her.

From the moment they hooked up at our year eleven formal, there was no separating them. It was Lexi and Rick, Rick and Lexi. They were engaged by age twenty-two and married by age twenty-three. She gave birth to Nate at age twenty-six, and Charli three years later. Then, out of the blue, it was finished: the end. Rick had made the biggest mistake of his life and as soon as Alexis informed me of what he'd done I knew he was screwed, even if Lex hadn't known that for herself. You see, I knew Lex. I knew her better than she knew herself. I also knew that although she was one of the strongest people I had ever come across, there was one thing that could always crack her: betrayal.

The thing about my Lexi was that she bounced back. Talk about bouncing ... she was like Pooh Bear's pal, Tigger! That girl bounced right into Bryce's arms and has stayed there ever since, quite happily. *Hmm ... Mr Bryce Clark.* Now, I know I shouldn't inwardly salivate at the thought of him, but fuck, it was pretty much impossible not to and I'm sure Lex wouldn't mind. Actually, I'm certain she wouldn't mind, because she would then rub it in by telling me that while I fantasised about his hard luscious cock, she was the one who had it in her mouth. I knew this because she had said it ... more than once.

Swiping my card through the slot at the door, I heard it beep then click open. Almost instantly, I was faced with a ceiling-to-floor window which had beige, sheer curtains hanging at either end. The room was huge and looked as though it had never been touched, the linen on the bed ultra-white and crisp. I noticed a card sitting in the centre of the pillows, my name clearly visible on the exterior.

Snatching it up eagerly, I unfolded it and read:

Carly, please enjoy your stay. If there is anything at all that you require, press 1 on the in-house phone and ask for Abigail. Help yourself to the minibar, and feel free to order room service. I've also arranged for you to use the hotel's spa if you so desire. Party starts at 7 p.m. See you then — Bryce

Holy fucking shitballs! Free minibar ... sweet!

Skipping and twirling over to the fridge, I opened it up. I loved mini things; mini cheese, miniskirts, and mini people. But most of all, I LOVED mini alcohol.

Reaching in, I grabbed a teeny tiny bottle of vodka and knocked it back while doing a little dance. Then, without hesitation, I dived back in the fridge and retrieved the mini bottle of champagne. *Pop!* Swigging it from the bottle, I got even more excited when I spotted the mini tube of Pringles. *Mini-gasm!*

Placing the bottle of champers on the bedside table, I jumped on the bed just as there was a knock at the door. I scooted off the bed and made my way to the door, opening it without even looking.

'Ms Henkley, your bag,' the bellboy informed.

'Thank you,' I replied, reaching out to take it from him.

Bellboy subtly snatched it back. 'I'll just put it in your room for you,' he politely explained, nodding his head in the direction of the interior of my room. I turned slightly and looked over my shoulder to where he was indicating, thinking it was kind of strange. My bag was not the size of the Titanic — more a gondola — and I was quite capable of carrying it myself.

Before I was able to just accept my bag at the door, the bellboy slid past and placed it down on the wardrobe shelf.

'Oh,' I said awkwardly, not used to the flamboyance, 'thanks.'

He smiled genuinely. 'You're welcome.'

'Um ... would you like a tip?' I went to grab my purse from within my handbag.

He let out a mild laugh. 'No, I'm just doing my job.'

'Oh, well, I know your boss. What's your name? I'll name-drop you,' I explained, waggling my eyebrows.

'That's not necessary,' he chuckled. 'Can I help you with anything else, Ms Henkley?'

Stepping forward, I tilted his name badge up. 'No. Thank you, Ben. You're a sweetie.'

He nodded, smiled meekly and exited the room.

Walking back to the bed with a happy swagger, I flopped down on it, grabbed my phone and my mini tube of Pringles then dialled Alexis.

'I don't know what to wear,' she blurted out as soon as the phone call connected. No greeting or words of endearment.

'Want me to come up and help you pick? I've just arrived,' I offered.

She sighed. 'Na, it's okay. I'll stew on it for a while. And anyway, Mum and Dad will be here shortly. I need to have a chat to them about something before everyone gets here.'

'Sounds serious,' I said, mumbling as my Pringle was assassinated by my teeth.

'Are you going to use the spa?' she asked, her deliberate attempt to change the subject obvious. 'Bryce said that he left a note for you, telling you to indulge. You really should. The girls at the spa downstairs are fabulous.'

'Yeah, I think I might. Do they do waxing? I need to wax. I could currently audition for a part in *Gorillas in the Mist*.'

Alexis let out a laugh. 'Yuck! Yes, yes they do. Go and de-fuzz, you dirty bitch. I'll see you later.'

'Later. Oh, and tell Bryce to give bellboy-Ben a raise.'

'Bellboy-Ben?' she queried.

'Yes. Later, whore.'

I hung up quickly before she could launch a verbal attack on me. She hated it when I called her a whore, which I had been doing ever since we were sixteen years old. Why? Because I could.

CHAPTER

3

Covered in a white fluffy robe, I happily floated into my room. I was now fuzz-free, dead-flaky-skin-free and free from any tension after the best massage in history. For the past two and a half hours, I'd been pampered and preened, and if I weren't already swooning over Bryce, I most definitely was now. *Wow! Lexi, you lucky bitch.*

Still in my dreamy, satiated condition, I decided to have a shower and then get ready for the night ahead. I planned on having a big night: letting my ash-blonde hair down and celebrating to the fullest extent with Lexi. Well ... technically, I didn't know how I was going to wear my hair yet. That dire decision required more brainpower than I currently had in my spa-inebriated condition.

I'd chosen my new, dark green, mid-thigh length, one-shoulder cocktail dress, the deep verdant shade high-lighting my emerald eyes. I love green. It's the colour of mint. I also love the taste of mint. Mint toothpaste. Mint gum. Mint sauce. *Mm... mint sauce.* Still undecided on my hair status, I decided to shoot Lexi a quick text for her advice:

Hair ... up or down? — Carls

She replied instantly:

Dress ... long or short? — Alexis

What a stupid question? Does she not know me at all? I was just about to type her an insulting reply when another text appeared on my phone:

Sorry, of course it's short. What was I thinking? Wear it down & give it a loose curl — Alexis

I laughed at her response. Taking back my prior thought, I typed a reply:

This is Y I love U. C U in an hour — Carls

I knew she'd respond, because Lexi always had to have the last word and, like clockwork, my phone beeped once more.

More like 2 hours ... if your hair isn't already done — Alexis

Shaking my head in amusement, I continued to play with her. I knew I shouldn't bait her as it was her birthday after all. But fuck, she was so much fun to taunt.

Whore — Carls

Bitch — Alexis

Pre-divorcee — Carls

Spinster — Alexis

Bitch! Smiling, because Lexi gives as good as she gets, I left my goading at that and scrolled through my playlist to find some Gaga, thinking I would 'Marry the Night'.

Just as I was about to set my phone down, another text message sounded:

I love U — Alexis

I chose not to respond, letting her have the last word as always. I am such a good freakin' friend.

* * *

As the doors opened to the penthouse floor, I was greeted by someone I could only assume was a member of the hotel's staff, an usher of some kind.

'Good evening, ma'am,' he politely addressed me with a nod of the head. *Oh, he's cute.*

I took in his puppy dog, brown eyes. 'Why, hello there,' I drawled.

'Just this way, ma'am ... right through this door.' He gestured for me to follow him.

'Please, don't call me ma'am. That's for women, post-menopause,' I said playfully as I nudged him with my shoulder.

He gave away a small half-grin, but remained completely professional, opening the door to the apartment and stepping aside for me to enter.

'Later,' I said with a wink, stepping backward through the threshold while keeping my gaze on his puppy dog eyes. 'I'll save you a drink.'

He nodded once more, although I sensed it was more of an acknowledgement, rather than an acceptance, of my invitation. I inwardly giggled, then turned around to spot Lexi in Bryce's arms, both of them standing in the middle of what could only be described as a palace. The place was huge, the decor contemporary: white, navy, and silver furnishings.

'Well, fu—'

I just was about to finish my sentence using my favourite bomb of vocabulary when I noticed Nate and Charli out of the corner of my eye, '— out,' I quickly offered, displaying my best 'oops' face to Alexis and hoping my quick exchange covered my initial slip. 'Far out, far freakin' out. This place is incredible.'

Lexi walked up to me and enveloped me in hug. 'Hey, Carls.'

'This place is amazeballs, Lexi!' I murmured, continuing to examine the extravagance over her shoulder.

She shook her head which made me smile. I knew how much she loved my lingo.

'Yeah, it's not a bad little place to live, eh?' she said with a shy smile.

'Pfft, yeah, you could say that,' I replied, then held her at arm's-length to get a better look after not having seen her for months.

Looking intently into her eyes, I instantly picked up on something she was withholding. She could never get away with lying to me. Even when we were young, when she'd sworn black and blue that she hadn't arranged a wedding for me and Kyle Payne. Granted, we were ten years old at the time.

I recalled the altercation. 'Alexis,' my ten-year-old self had said, with my blushing-red cheeks. 'Kyle Payne-in-the-butt just said that he and I are getting married tomorrow. He said that he will make me very happy. Do you know anything about this?'

Now, before I continue with this story, let me clue you in on something. The first sign that Alexis is lying is that she tilts her head to the side very slightly. If you are not looking for this particular movement, you'll miss it. The next sign is the avoid-eye-contact-at-all-costs trick, followed by a pause as her mind quickly conjures up her lame excuse. I remember that when I'd asked her about my pending nuptials with Kyle, she'd performed these telltale signs just beautifully. She'd said, 'What?', followed by the head tilt and a piercing stare toward something beyond my head. Next was the pause and finally, the lie: 'No. I don't know anything about it. It was probably Hannah.' *Busted! Liar!*

Knowing that she would eventually give her current secret away, I smiled at her. 'You look amazing. Shacking up with a rich studmuffin does wonders for you. Speaking of the sexy studmuffin, I need to formally thank him for his hospitality.'

I gently placed my hands on her shoulders and moved her aside, clearing a path to Bryce. He gave me one of those killer smirks that Alexis was always telling me about. I could definitely see what the fuss was over — his smirk warmed my Carly-cave.

'As long as you only thank him, Carls. That studmuffin belongs to me,' Lexi said in a firm but loving voice.

'Not until there's an engagement ring on your finger,' I replied smugly. *That's it! That's her secret.* 'Wait!' I turned back to face her. 'Show me your hand. Is that why you are looking so good?'

She rolled her eyes at me. 'No! There is no engagement ring on my finger.'

'There will be soon,' Bryce confidently stated.

Alexis froze and gave him a did-you-just-say-that look. He just smirked his smirky goodness in response. I smiled at them then continued toward Bryce, wrapping my arms around him. 'Thank you,' I said, seizing the opportunity to feel him up by squeezing his biceps.

'You're welcome, Carly,' he replied with a deep chuckle. *God, this man is sexy.*

Pouting, I reluctantly let him go and made my way back to where Lexi was standing. 'So! Lexi, the soon-to-be bigamist,' I stated, deliberately baiting her.

'I am not a fucking soon-to-be bigamist,' she snapped back at me.

'Mum!' Charlotte exclaimed, waltzing toward us and looking like a beautiful princess in her pink chiffon dress. 'You just f-bombed. You know the rules, now I get to bomb you.'

'Um, I know, Charlotte,' Lexi replied, with a quiver to her voice, 'but you can't bomb me. Not now.' *Oh, she is so definitely hiding something from me.*

'A rule is a rule, Mum,' Charlotte categorically declared, placing her hands upon her hips for emphasis.

I tended to agree.

'Charli, you can't,' Alexis ground out through her teeth, exaggerating the *can't* bit. 'You could hurt me. You don't want to *hurt* me, do you?' *Whaaa—? This is hilarious. Kudos to Charli for riling up her mum like this. Normally it's me doin' the riling.*

Smiling like the drama-greedy girl that I am, I was close to asking for a bowl of popcorn and taking up a seat.

Charlotte dropped her hands from where they sat on her hips as something seemed to dawn on her. 'Oh, I could hurt the baby,' she blurted, while slapping her hand to her head. 'Okay, Mum, I'll let you off this time.' She walked over to where I was standing — in shock, mind you — and gave me a hug. 'Hi, Aunty Carls.'

I couldn't help but stare at Lexi, my mouth wide open, a smile forcing its way to the surface of my face. Charli wrapped her arms around me, so I gave her a half-arsed squeeze, not really paying much attention to the little secret-shouter. 'You're pregnant?' I asked Alexis, completely stunned by the revelation.

'Yes, I am,' Lexi sighed in surrender before turning to her daughter. 'Charlotte, please don't tell anyone else. Bryce and I want to make it a surprise and tell everyone later tonight.'

Charli wrinkled her nose apologetically, then dropped her head. 'Oh, sorry, Mum.'

'It's okay, sweetheart. But don't tell anyone else, all right?'

'Okay,' Charli said, happily skipping out of the room, the bomb she had just dropped already forgotten.

Lexi watched her leave, then slowly shook her head from side to side before turning back to face me. 'Yes,' she answered as she placed her hand on her stomach and smiled. 'Bryce planted his seed.'

He walked up behind her and positioned his hands on her shoulders. 'What can I say, I like gardening,' he explained, his expression confident.

Alexis laughed and leaned back into him, she really did seem happy.

'Wow ... that's ... wow! I'm assuming it wasn't planned,' I offered, giving her a hesitant glance. 'Or was it?'

She closed her eyes for the briefest of moments. 'No. It definitely wasn't planned.'

Bryce shifted his gaze to look at Lexi, displaying nothing but love and adoration. It really was quite obvious just how much he truly loved her.

'So you're both happy?' I asked.

They answered simultaneously, just like fucking Tweedledum and Tweedledee. 'Of course we are.'

Amused by their cuteness, I smiled and shook my head. 'Well, in that case, congratulations.'

With impeccable timing, a waiter appeared next to us with glasses of champagne on a tray. I grabbed two of them and went to hand one to Lex, pausing when I realised that she shouldn't drink any alcohol. *Oh, this is gonna be great!* The last time Lex was pregnant and off alcohol, she sulked like a baby when I teased her with my many glasses of wine.

'Uh-uh,' Bryce affirmed, grabbing a glass of a slightly pink concoction which also sat upon the tray. 'You, my love, get this one.' He handed her the drink. 'The pink glasses are yours. The waitstaff have been briefed and know only to give you those ones.'

She screwed up her nose, taking a sniff of the contents. 'You've got to be kidding me. What is it?'

Before he could answer, the door buzzer sounded. Bryce turned and moved off to greet the arriving guests, calling back over his shoulder: 'No. I'm not kidding. I never kid where you are concerned. You, my love, are drinking non-alcoholic rosé tonight.'

I shrugged in mock sympathy and, rather than put one of the two glasses back on the tray, teasingly took sips from them both. 'Suffer,' I added with a childish grin. *I know, I'm a bitch, but hey, what are friends for?* Lexi fired me a squinty-eyed look in return. She was good at those. I, on the other hand, poked out my tongue.

The newly arrived guests caught my attention as they walked in, my gaze instantly shifting from Alexis to the three super-hot guys, one in particular sparking waves of excitement to flow through me. *Holy fuck! Who is that?* I'd hoped Bryce would have spunky friends, but shit, this guy was fucking gorgeous.

He gave Bryce a manly slap on the back, and the smile that beamed from his face was enough to nearly make my underwear go Carly-cave diving. *Oh. My. God!*

I couldn't seem to tear my eyes away from the spunk-rat. I took in his shaved head that still had just enough hair to give him a sexy rugged look. He was wearing a black leather jacket over a tight white t-shirt and, even though I was halfway across the room, I could tell by the way the material clung to his chest that his many muscles were screaming to be explored by my tongue.

My eyes dropped further down his body, spying light denim jeans which were riding low on his hips. *Holy mother of vaginal spasms, those hips would fit perfectly in between my legs.* I mentally took some measurements.

Unfortunately, I couldn't see his arse from my current standing position, but I was quite certain it was an arse that deserved nothing but a tight squeeze.

Barely able to swallow my champagne, I took in the sight of his ink, which disappeared under the neckline of his t-shirt. And it was that small hint of artwork that sent my hormones on a hormonal-bender.

Not knowing whether or not I had been ogling him like a lovesick schoolgirl, I quickly found concealment behind my champagne glass, because we all know a see-through flute made of crystal and no bigger than your hand provides ample camouflage. *Carly, you idiotic fool.*

'Who the fuck is that sex-on-a-stick?' I whispered, peeking over the rim of my glass before taking an inconspicuous sip.

Alexis followed my line of sight then leaned in and answered. 'That is Derek, Bryce's best mate. He's also the lead singer of the band. He was at the pub in Shepparton, remember? You know, when the band played "November Rain" and Bryce performed the guitar solos for me.'

'Is that him? Oh my god! He looks different,' I whisper-squealed.

'You were slightly occupied with the barman, Carls. Plus Derek has shaved his head since then. Maybe that's why you don't recognise him.'

'Fuck, Lexi, he is beyond hot. His hotness factor is through the bloody roof.' *That is actually an enormous understatement. This man is F.I.N.E.-fine. Very fucking fine.*

She laughed at me as though she was privy to information that I was not. 'It's funny you should say that, because he is a firefighter.'

Grabbing hold of her arm to prevent myself from melting into a puddle of my own drool, I dramatically pleaded, 'Please tell me he's single, Alexis, because I have a fucking ferocious fire in between my legs that he needs to put out.'

She cracked up laughing. 'Yes, Carls, he is single ... as far as I know.'

Halle-freakin'-lujah.

Bryce, Derek and the other two hotty-hotcakes made their way over to where Lexi and I were standing. As they approached, I squeezed Alexis' arm tightly. 'Quick! Quick! My vagina is burning, please *come* to my rescue,' I said theatrically under my breath, clearly enunciating my double meaning of the word come.

Alexis laughed then added just as quietly, 'Mr Firefighter Derek, please douse my friend's fiery hole with your fire hose. Nobody likes a burnt burger.'

I almost spat out the champagne I had only just seconds ago taken into my mouth and, with great difficulty, we managed to subdue ourselves and act like the adults that we were by the time the men reached us.

Securing Alexis by placing his arm around her waist, Bryce introduced the man candies. 'Alexis, you remember Derek, Will and Matt?'

'Yes, of course I do. It's nice to see you again. Thanks for *coming*,' Alexis answered, very subtly emphasising her last spoken word.

I couldn't help giggling. I was already in that type of mood and the champers was not helping.

'Happy birthday, Alexis,' Derek said, his voice rolling through me like a sex express train. He handed her a small package and gave me a quick smile before focussing his attention back to Lex. *Fuck me!* No, I really mean it. *Derek, sexy firefighter, please fuck me now.*

'You really shouldn't have,' Lexi said sheepishly, clearly embarrassed. She was never a fan of birthday presents.

Derek shot her another smile, a smile that somehow had an invisible line directly to my Carly-cave, my cave waking up and blessing me with an aroused tingle.

I not so subtly cleared my throat, not waiting any longer for Lex to introduce us. *My god! Talk about fail with the wingwoman duties. She should've done it by now.*

'Is it your birthday, Lexi?' I asked, feigning ignorance. 'Because I didn't get you jack shit.' Mind you, my statement was both confident and truthful. I honestly didn't get her anything, my presence being present enough.

Lexi gently shoved my shoulder. 'Sorry, this rude bitch here is my best friend, Carly. Carly, this is Will, Matt and Derek. They are Bryce's friends and members of the band he plays in.'

'Yes, I know. I saw you guys in Shepparton. You were fantastic.' I pointed my glass at Derek. 'And you have a voice to die for.' *And a body, and eyes, and lips, and ... let's face it ... you are just completely to die for.*

A seductive smile crept in at the corners of his mouth and, just as he was about to say thank you — or quite possibly, let me stick my tongue down your throat, Carly — Alexis offered her gratitude.

'I love it! Thank you.' She held up a CD which belonged to the band. 'You didn't tell me you had a CD,' she said to Bryce.

'We've only just recently produced it. It appears you would be one of the first to own a copy,' he answered, proudly.

'Oh, lucky me,' she replied excitedly. 'Can you all sign it?'

'I think track four already has your name on it,' Matt advised her, as he helped himself to a beer from the tray a waiter before us was balancing.

Alexis shot him a confused expression. 'A track that has my name on it?'

Before anyone could answer, the buzzer to the door sounded again, and this time, the people entering seemed to be a never-ending stream.

'Sorry, guys,' Bryce interrupted. 'I need to steal this beautiful woman and greet our arriving guests.'

We smiled as he whisked Alexis away, his playful demeanour eliciting a loving giggle from her mouth.

'So, Carly,' Derek said as he turned to face me, 'I'm a little concerned.'

'Why?' I stammered, unsure as to why he would be worried.

'Because, according to you, if I talk to you and you hear my voice, you could quite possibly die.' He lifted one eyebrow and took a swig of his beer.

Oh, god. Did I really say that?

CHAPTER

4

I was normally confident around men, probably too confident if I'm completely honest. My confidence, however, had absolutely nothing to do with how I felt about myself, or how I looked for that matter. Yes, I looked pretty bloody good, being fortunate enough to eat whatever I wanted and never worry about my dress size. But my good genes and luck where my looks were concerned weren't what gave me the poise and prowess to own a room when I walked into it. No, my confidence was more to do with the fact that I always felt on top of the game, in control of my life and any situation. Especially where men were concerned.

So the feeling of helplessness I was now experiencing — the result of one sentence spoken by Derek — was unfamiliar, strange and unsettling, and I didn't like it. I didn't like it one bit.

Mustering my semblance of Carly-is-the-shit, I placed my index and middle finger against my wrist. 'Nope,' I teased, with a slight shake of the head, pausing for effect. 'There's no need to worry. I feel a pulse. I'm still alive. It must only be when you sing.'

'Damn!' Will laughed while slapping Derek on the back. 'Talk about being shot down in a blaze of glory. Carly, I think I love you.'

The mention of the word 'blaze' had me giggling again, until Derek leaned in and started singing the opening line to the Bon Jovi song. The intense look in his eyes and the sexiness of his voice had me catching my breath.

Unable to help myself, I stared at his lips as if they were moving in slow motion, soon finding myself entranced by his sultry tone. His face was so close to mine that if I wanted to, I could stick my tongue out and lick the side of it. I actually did want to ... desperately.

A faint smell of beer gently wafted across my face. Normally, beer-breath would have me dry-retching, but the warm air that was lightly skating across the surface of my lips was about the yummiest thing I had experienced since my mini-tube of Pringles earlier in the day.

Just as I was about to drag my tongue across the tasty singing morsel in front of me, I was snapped out of my daze by the sensation of his palm pressed flat against my back, his other hand now comfortably splayed across my waist and his ear gently resting against my chest.

'I'm not sure I can hear her heartbeat,' he explained to Will.

Derek's fingers very subtly brushed over the dark green material covering my lower abdomen, the sensation exciting me. I honestly didn't want him to move, but I also couldn't allow the impression that I was easily turned into a puppet. Carly Henkley was no Pinocchio.

'Let's just say your performance gave me a heart murmur. That's all. You'll have to do a little better than that to stop my heart completely,' I compromised, giving an awkward but cocky smile.

He released me and took a small step back, a stern but mischievous look upon his face. 'Who said I wanted to I stop it? I prefer things pumping.'

'On that note, I'm heading into the cave,' Matt declared. 'You guys coming or what?'

My brain seemed to only decipher two words from that last exchange; pumping and cave. And I couldn't help but now visualise Derek doing just that; pumping my cave.

'Can you play eight-ball, Carly?' he asked, snapping me out of my head-porn.

'Can a dog lick his own balls?' I blurted out.

For the love of fuck, Carly. Filter, where is your filter?

'I'll take that as a yes,' he said with a laugh and pointed his beer in the direction the other guys went. 'After you, then.'

Nodding my head in acceptance, I led the way — finally leading something — and snatched up another two glasses of champagne from a passing waiter. I was almost certain I would require them both.

* * *

Entering a room that looked a little like a recording studio mashed together with a dude hangout, I found myself being handed a pool cue by Derek. I was still in a daze, feeling slightly unnerved and unsettled. Something that never EVER happened to me.

Taking the cue from him, I smiled and once again gave myself a mental bitch-slap. *Carly Josephine Henkley, what the hell is wrong with you? He is just a walking penis, a walking, talking, singing man-toy.*

I turned my back to him and reached for the block of blue chalk sitting on the rack fixed to the wall. As I chalked the tip of my cue and blew off the excess residue, I continued to give myself a silent pep talk. *Right, you've got this. You own a vagina, and a good one at that. You've spent many a night at the local pub playing eight-ball. And anyway, I'm sure Derek won't mind you bending over the pool table and enticing him with your size ten arse.*

'You want to break?' Derek asked.

'Sure,' I said confidently, still not facing him, 'unless you do?'

'No. Ladies before gentlemen,' he replied, his tone laced with cheeky provocation.

Rolling my eyes at his obnoxiousness — because, let's face it, no one likes to break the first time — I spun around. 'Who says I'm a la—'

He'd removed his jacket and the sight of him in his white tee stole the words from my mouth. His skin was the tone of caramel, to the point where I wanted to trail my tongue up his bicep, just to make sure he was not made of the sweet treat. And speaking of biceps, holy fucking muscle merriment ... those bumps and grooves were giving me vertigo.

I soon realised I was standing there, clasping the pool cue in a death grip, my mouth wide open with unfinished words. '—dy ... lady. Who says I'm a lady?' I barely voiced, finishing my sentence.

'Well, you sure as hell look like one,' he stated, perched on a stool, his eyebrow raised in amusement.

I tore my eyes away from his t-shirt snug chest and leaned forward across the table, preparing to take my shot. 'Well, I'm not,' I declared, concentrating on the trajectory of my cue. 'I chew gum, I drink beer and I eat pizza while sitting on my couch,' I explained as I slammed the pool cue into the white ball, sending it hurtling into the triangular arrangement.

Balls scattered in all directions as I straightened up.

'I read books instead of balancing them on my head,' I continued. 'My favourite word is fuck and I prefer my legs open. Clearly, I am not a lady.' I bent down to take my next shot, smiling at the fact that I had sunk a ball. Looking up before playing it, I locked my eyes on Derek who seemed to have *his* fixed on my cleavage. 'Looks like I have the big balls and you have the small ones,' I informed, snapping his attention to my mouth.

Suddenly, Will performed a rimshot, sounding a sting to punctuate my joke. Derek glared at him, placed his beer on the edge of the table and stood beside me, pretending to focus on the shot I was about to make. The heat from his body, which was subtly pressed against my side, along with the scent of his aftershave, worked to conspire against me, resulting in my aim being slightly off. I missed sinking a ball which was probably more sinkable than the *Titanic*.

Derek took the cue stick from my hands. 'The only small balls here, baby, are the ones on the table,' he said matter-of-factly, before lowering himself to take his shot.

Two of his balls found pockets quite easily. I was unfazed by this, more stunned at the way he had just called me 'baby'.

Snatching up his beer, I stole a swig to moisten my now parched mouth before setting it back down. 'Well, that remains to be seen.'

He looked at his beer bottle for the smallest of seconds then up at me. The hooded expression on his face had me clenching my legs together. *Oh, sweet fuck of all fucks that are downright hot, hard and sweaty. I want this man. I want this walking, fuckable man-caramel.*

Just as I was about to quite possibly turn Alexis' birthday party into the hottest live porn show on earth, Mr Sexy Brycealicious walked into the room. 'Watch him like a hawk, Carly. The dickhead cheats,' he informed.

Without removing my stare from Caramello Koala, I once again lifted his beer bottle to my lips and voiced, with more implication than mere words, 'I am watching him like a hawk.'

Derek inclined his head to the side slightly, then appeared to rein in a smug smile before taking another shot, which resulted in the sinking of his ball but also pocketing one of mine.

Smiling at his misfortune, I snatched the cue from his hands. 'Thank you.'

'Don't tell me you are taking it easy on her, mate,' Bryce queried while handing Derek a new beer.

Derek accepted the bottle from Bryce. 'What can I say, I am a gentleman.'

'You'd better not be taking it easy,' I snapped. 'I'm quite capable of beating you without your chivalrous bullshit.'

'I'm sure you are,' he said, without much conviction.

You arrogant ferret fucker. Time to put my many years of Thursday night billiards at the local pub to use.

I quickly surveyed the table, deciding on a shot which would hopefully pot one ball and then set up another three.

'Twelve ball, top right pocket,' I announced as I bent down and cued the white — said twelve ball falling neatly into the projected pocket. 'Fifteen ball, middle left,' I continued, as I walked around to the opposite side of the table. That ball, too, fell into the suggested pocket.

By that stage, Will and Matt had made their way over and were now standing next to Bryce and Derek. 'Apparently we need a lifeguard,' Will stated, 'there's a shark in the room.'

I smiled at Will and winked. 'Well, it so happens that I've been called Jaws before, but for an entirely different reason.'

Derek laughed. Bryce just shook his head.

Putting my serious game face back on, I continued to clean up the table. 'Nine ball, top left.'

I was pretty sure the nine ball would be my last pocketed ball as there were no clear shots remaining, so instead I set up another ball for my next shot then happily placed the cue in Derek's hands. 'Here you go, *gentleman*. Knock yourself out.'

He didn't move right away, just sat perched on the stool with me standing in front of him practically wedged between his legs, both of us still holding onto the cue. Our positions were like that of a Mexican standoff.

Before either one of us could surrender our stance, Bryce interrupted. 'As much as I would love to see Carly wipe the table clean with you, Derek, I need to go find the love of my life.'

'That ain't gonna happen,' Derek retorted before pushing up off his stool. He placed his hands on my shoulders and gently moved me aside before taking the pool cue from me. The sudden move surprised and excited me.

Before he took his next shot, he added a few words without looking at me. 'Just so you know, Jaws, I eat flake for breakfast.'

I couldn't help laughing. Mind you, I was more than happy for him to dine on me for breakfast. It was, after all, the most important meal of the day. 'Are you saying you want to eat me?' I asked nonchalantly.

As my question hung in the air, Derek miscued the ball and unintentionally set up my next move. Biting my lip to refrain from laughing at my cheap shot, I walked right up to him and reclaimed the cue.

Just as he was about to say something, Nate burst into the room. I had to turn my head away from Derek in order to give Nate my attention.

'Mum and Bryce are cutting the cake and making a speech. They want everyone out in the lounge area,' he announced with excitement.

Turning back to face Derek, I found that he had been staring at my neck, his eyes still lingering on the spot that was now tingling with a yearning only his lips could cure.

'We can finish this later,' he suggested in a low voice.

I took a deep breath, needing oxygen to prevent from fainting. 'No. I can finish it now.' Then, slowly turning around, I bent over the table, gently pressing my arse into his groin at the same time, and played my shot. I could've sworn I felt his cock move within his pants as he remained steadfast, not moving from his position behind me.

Standing up again, I watched as the ball I had just played easily found its way into a pocket, together with the ball I had strategically set up, leaving only the black ball remaining.

Just as I was about to move and reposition myself, I felt his warm breath caress my ear. 'If you miss, I get to take you out on a date,' he murmured.

His close proximity and the feel of his body pressed against my back sent tingles bursting across the surface of my skin. 'And if I sink it?' I asked, barely able to voice the words.

'You can take me out on a date,' he suggested.

Stepping away from him, I smiled and walked to the opposite side of the table, the white and black ball lined up beautifully before me. 'If I sink it, I will give you my number,' I compromised and, knowing with one hundred percent certainty that the eight ball would find the net, I leaned forward and played the shot.

CHAPTER
5

I'd left Derek standing in the man cave after successfully blindsiding him with my eight-ball prowess. It felt good, really good, having been able to secure the upper hand — the way it should be.

After living in a semi-rural town for the better part of my life, I was able to acquire certain skills. One skill was not turning the local wildlife into roadkill during late-night drives home. Knowledge and constant participation in billiards was another. Playing eight-ball was the only 'cool' thing young adults could do on their Thursday and Friday nights in Shepparton. Mind you, it also helped that back then I'd dated the local pub owner's son on and off for a year. So I was forever passing time with a cue in my hand.

* * *

Everyone had started to gather around the lounge area which was decorated with large silver and blue helium balloons. There were bunches of roses everywhere, some bunches a vivid shade of blue. At first, I thought they were fake, but it wasn't until I leaned in and sniffed their beautiful aroma that I realised they were real. *Wow! Blue roses! I bet if Alexis asked for an Oompa-Loompa, Bryce would be able to get her one.*

'So, are you going to give me your phone number?'

Startled, I turned around and found Derek standing behind me, holding out a glass of champagne.

'Thank you,' I accepted happily, taking it from him and smiling politely. 'And ... maybe.'

'Maybe? That wasn't the deal,' he protested.

'Well, Derek, I don't know anything about you. I don't give out my phone number willy-nilly, you know.'

'Ah, but if you gave me your phone number, it would allow you to get to know me better. That's what swapping phone numbers is about,' he explained, his tone awash with a cheeky enlightenment.

Honestly, I was in total agreement, and more than happy to share my digits with him. As I reached into my bra to pluck out my phone, Bryce demanded the room's attention with a repetitive tap on his glass. 'Firstly, I just want to thank you all for coming today, to celebrate Alexis' birthday. We both really appreciate you all taking the time to share this evening with us.'

Bryce took a deep breath, then looked to his glass momentarily. 'Look ... I'll start by addressing the elephant in the room by saying that it is no secret Alexis and I found each other under somewhat controversial circumstances.' He glanced at Alexis and I sensed a minuscule tinge of guilt.

Alexis winked at him, encouraging him to continue. I smiled.

My friend had an uncanny ability to make those around her feel at ease, to be comfortable and to be themselves.

Bryce smiled at her lovingly, then continued. 'Controversial or not, the truest crime of all would have been to ignore true love. From the moment I laid eyes on this beautiful woman standing next to me, my heart decided to once again function as it was designed to. And, if I'm going to be completely honest, the feeling that came over me shortly after meeting her for the first time shocked the shit out of me.'

Derek and I chuckled simultaneously. He looked in my direction and I met his gaze before we both awkwardly smiled and consumed our drinks. *Fuck me, he is one sensational looking man.* I couldn't help but take in more of his ink now that his jacket was off and he was standing so close to me, providing a better view. The design was one of those tribal-looking tattoos with black, sharp sleek lines covering a good part of his arm.

'You like tatts?' he asked, his voice barely above a whisper.

Diverting my attention from his delicious bicep, I focussed in on his equally delicious face. 'Huh?'

'Tattoos, do you like them? You look as though you want to lick mine,' he said with a smirk and a quick flick of his eyebrow.

Oh, I do. I do want to lick it. And I really want to see if you taste like caramel.

'Yes, I do like them,' I whispered, embarrassed I'd been busted ogling. I then returned my attention back to Bryce and Alexis, my cheeks now a little heated.

'... and there are also times in life when you have to ignore the morality of the problem that faces you and go with your heart,' Bryce explained, before facing Alexis who now had tears streaming down her face. 'Because at the end of the day, your heart is what truly makes you happy. And Alexis is my heart, entirely.'

While my heart pounded vigorously in my chest, I watched as Bryce tenderly wiped Alexis' tears from her cheek. There was a part of me that desperately wanted what the two of them had; true, undeniable love, a connection so deep it was bottomless and a family to call my own. But I knew that would never happen.

The day my aunty died giving birth was the day I decided I did not want to have kids. My aunty was the closest thing I had to a sibling; she was like my big sister. Then, out of nowhere and at the most exciting point in her life, my aunty and her baby were gone. It destroyed me and any hope I ever had of starting a family. I just couldn't bring myself to even go there.

Sucking in a deep breath and willing the pain of her memory to go into hiding again, I brought myself back to the events unfolding before me and smiled at Alexis who had spotted me in amongst her family and guests. I was genuinely happy for her and the new path her life was taking. She deserved all the happiness she was now bathed in, because she had to break through the barriers of hurt and deceit in order to get to it.

'Wow!' she choked out, 'I can't really top that can —'

'Yes, you can,' Bryce interrupted, a huge grin plastering his face.

The overjoyed and excited beam that radiated from him indicated he was referring to their surprise news. This must have been the point at which they planned to drop their baby bomb.

Alexis nodded and continued. 'As most of you are aware, I have recently had to fight for a reprieve during a very wounding, lightless time in my life, yet it was a fight worth winning, because the path that lies ahead of me now, at age thirty-six, is the most exciting path I will ever walk. It's a path I plan on taking with you, with my two beautiful children, with this wonderful amazing man who I now know to be my soul mate … and with our precious little miracle who is growing strong as each day goes by,' she said as she gently caressed her belly.

'No shit!' Derek said beside me, his broad smile indicating he was happy for his best mate. Seeing the disbelief radiate from him was endearing.

'I'm going to be a dad,' Bryce announced to the room. He picked up Charli and sat her on his hip while Alexis reached for Nate. 'We are going to be a family.' Bryce raised his glass toward his family and friends. 'To a life of fulfilment.'

Everyone joined him and Alexis in a toast. A toast to … well … happiness, I guess.

* * *

Family members immediately enveloped Bryce and Alexis shortly after the toast and the cutting of the cake, a cake I wanted to desperately sink my teeth into. *OMG! That thing is huge!* I loved cake but couldn't bake the damn things even if I tried. Turning out a deliciously warm, fluffy moist cake was not something I was exceptional at. Cooking was definitely not my forte, but that didn't mean I didn't try.

Before my aunty passed away, she always offered her two cents worth every chance that she got. There was one particular time where I'd had to produce a painting for school. I'd given up before starting the task, hell-bent on the 'I *can't* do it' reaction. I remember her saying to me, 'Try, Carly', to which I'd responded with an exasperated, 'That's it? That's all you're going to say? That doesn't help.' She'd then said, 'It really is that simple. If you try and fail you still succeed, for succeeding in failure is still a success.'

My aunty was optimistic and smart, and like Alexis, she was a combination of a best friend and the sister I never had.

'That was a surprise,' Derek exclaimed, once again bringing me back to the moment. 'Good on them. They both deserve to be happy, and Alexis makes Bryce very happy. I've never seen him like this before.'

'I agree. Lexi deserves a man who will treat her right, especially after what her husband did.' When no one was watching, apart from Derek, I stole a raspberry from the top of the cake. 'So ... how long have you and Bryce been friends?' I mumbled as I popped it into my mouth.

He watched my actions with an amused smile on his face. 'Since high school.'

'Nice.' I covertly snuck another raspberry and, this time, peeled off a shard of white chocolate.

Derek stifled a laugh. 'How 'bout you and Alexis?'

'Since we were four,' I mumbled again as I consumed the stolen cake topping. 'We were neighbours for eighteen years, right up until Alexis moved out to live with Rick and I moved to Melbourne.'

Derek nodded as if he were interested in what I was saying but, like all men, he was probably more concerned with what size my tits were and if they were real or not. I put that theory to the test by deliberately licking the icing off my fingers.

'Whereabouts in Melbourne do you live?' he asked with an awkward shuffle of his feet.

I couldn't help but bite the inside of my mouth and smile — I bet he just formed wood. His attempts to feign interest in order to get inside my pants were exceedingly obvious, but also terribly cute. 'Epping,' I answered.

'I live in Richmond.'

'Huh. So what do you do?' I asked, pretending to be none the wiser when, truth be told, I wanted nothing more than to see him douse my fiery hole with his man-hose.

'I'm a senior firefighter with the MFB,' Derek answered with a tinge of pride.

My eyes widened mischievously. 'That's hot!'

He raised his eyebrow at me.

'What?' I giggled, deliberately touching his arm. 'That was good.'

'It was lame,' he countered.

'It was not. Pick-up lines are lame. That was puntastic.'

'Puntastic?' he queried, shaking his head in amusement. 'Pick-up lines are not lame. Some are actually quite good.'

'Oh yeah, name one,' I probed.

'Is that a mirror in your pocket? Because I can see myself in your pants.'

'Please,' I groaned, 'that was terrible.'

'Okay, how about ... I lost my number, can I have yours?'

Looking down at my hand, I checked that my nail polish was pristine, all the while pretending I was bored. 'So original.'

'You smell like trash. May I take you out?' he offered before taking a swig of his beer.

I had to laugh at that one. 'Not bad. Although, telling me I stink is going to get you nowhere.'

'So saying, "Did you fart? Because you just blew me away," won't work either, huh?' he asked with a smile.

This time I cracked up laughing and clutched at my abdomen. 'No.'

'Okay, I've got one.' Derek placed his empty beer bottle down on the coffee table then turned back to me, a renewed sense of adventure animating his face. 'How about: I may not go down in history, but I'll go down on you.'

That particular pick-up line certainly got my attention, so much so that I ceased my laughing almost immediately. 'Um ... meh,' I offered, shrugging my shoulders.

'Gee, you're brutal,' he joked.

Before I was able to reply, Alexis distracted me as she casually walked past en route to the waiter. She was humming a tune that at first I couldn't quite make out. It was not until she started singing while she made her way to where Tash, Lil, Steph and Jade were standing, and trying to look inconspicuous, that I figured out it was the lyrics to 'All Fired Up' by Pat Benatar.

Bitch!

Derek seemed to be none the wiser and signalled me to lean toward him with a come hither motion. 'How about this?' he said in a low husky voice. 'I just made you come with one finger. Imagine what I can do with two?'

My mouth dropped open at the very thought of coming on his fingers. I wanted to come and I wanted him to make me do it.

Right at that very moment, Tash walked past singing 'Light My Fire' by The Doors, while slapping her hairy lady-pie like a fucking lunatic. Alexis cracked up laughing in response, so I shot her a what-the-fuck look and then quickly focussed my attention back on Derek.

'That one was a little better,' I choked out, clearing my throat, 'but it appears you will have eight other fingers that are just sitting around and doing nothing.'

'Trust me, Carly,' Derek said with a seductive glint, 'they wouldn't be doing nothing.'

My Carly-cave came to life and my vagina-bats started fluttering around. *Holy finger-fuck, he's gone and rendered me speechless again.*

Out of nowhere, Alexis, Tash, Lil, Steph and Jade started belting out 'Girl On Fire' by Alicia Keys and, unlike before, their subtlety had now flown out the window. If that wasn't bad enough, a tapping noise sounded from my right so I turned slightly in that direction to find Will drumming on the bar top with a couple of forks, assisting their sudden flash mob performance. The entire scene before me was ridiculous. Not only was my fiery hole still on fire with singed crispy vagina-bats, my head was now ablaze and ready to explode.

Alexis Elizabeth Summers, I am going to kill you.

Grabbing the bridge of my nose, I closed my eyes in the hope that when I looked again my idiot friends would have gone away.

'What are they doing?' Derek asked.

Opening my eyes at this point in time and explaining what Alexis and the girls were trying to achieve was the last thing I wanted to do. But standing in the middle of the lounge pretending I was invisible with Derek beside me was not an option either.

'They are digging themselves a grave,' I responded quietly.

'What?' he asked, raising his voice over their incessant howling.

'I think they are starting their own rave,' I said.

He gave them all an incredulous look. 'Interesting. Do they always do this?'

'Kind of.'

Derek laughed. 'God help Bryce.'

More like god help Alexis. Preggers or not, whoreasaurus is going down.

After the girls finished serenading the room with their vocal performance, I launched a heated glare in their direction. Alexis winked then made her way toward Bryce.

'So ... what do you do with yourself, Carly?' Derek asked as he reached out and grabbed two macaroons from a passing waiter.

It's called masturbation, Derek. And it's much more fun with a Lelo and a Tumblr account.

Realising that he was not referring to my self-pleasure methods, instead inquiring as to what my job description was, I belatedly said, 'Um ... I'm the receptionist at Yellow Bark Primary School.'

He handed me one of the macaroons and popped the other into his mouth. 'Sweet,' he mumbled. 'So you like kids?'

Hell no. 'Sure, who doesn't like kids?' I murmured with a laugh that lacked certitude before biting down on the circular treat he had gifted me.

'True, kids are a lot of fun.'

Fun, my arse. They are highly annoying disease-spreading critters. And they never shut up.

Derek took a long drink as if to wash down the mouthful of macaroon, or quite possibly wash away the conversation we were having. He suddenly appeared a little nervous.

Wanting to change the subject, because kids are not a subject I like to discuss when away from work, I asked him about his family. 'So, do you have any siblings?'

'Yeah, a brother,' he replied curtly. His clipped tone caught me off-guard and created an awkward atmosphere in the small space around us.

'Older or younger?' I hesitantly asked.

'Older.'

If 'fucking awkward' was a body of water, we'd both be swimming in it now. So I gave him an unsure smile then looked down at my feet. It was obvious I'd hit a raw nerve.

Now finding our situation highly uncomfortable, I opted to take my leave and get some space, not to mention attempt Alexis' demise. 'Will you excuse me for a moment? I need to have a word with Lexi.'

'Of course,' he replied, seemingly apologetic.

I was not quite sure — being a little puzzled myself — but I sensed he had become disappointed. So I offered him a small apologetic smile of my own and made my way toward Alexis.

As the distance between Lexi and I reduced, I screwed my face up in aggravation and pointed my finger at her. 'You are hilarious,' I bit out, sarcastically.

She covered her mouth for the smallest of seconds to subdue a laugh. 'I know.'

'No. That wasn't funny. I was so fucking embarrassed.'

'Relax. He had no idea.'

'Who had no idea?' Bryce asked.

'Derek,' we both answered.

Bryce looked over at his mate, confusion evident on his face. 'What does he have no idea about?'

Alexis jumped in before I even had a chance. 'He has no idea Carly has a burnt burger.' She burst into laughter.

I closed my eyes momentarily. 'You're a bitch, Alexis Summers.'

'No, I'm not, Carly Henkley. Your burger is burnt and you need it put out, I was simply trying to begin that process.'

'I can put out my own burger, thanks,' I responded through gritted teeth, practically hissing like a snake.

Bryce took a step back, hands up in surrender. 'I'm not fucking sure if you are talking about a barbeque or something entirely different. Either way, I don't want to know about Carly's burger, so please excuse me.' He headed toward the other men in the room.

'There is nothing wrong with my burger, Bryce,' I called out after him. 'Just so you know, it's a good burger.'

Let's just get that shit straight, right now! My burger is a masterpiece.

'Carly!' Alexis chided playfully, hitting me on the arm. 'Don't offer your burger to my man.'

'Why? Is he a vegetarian?'

'No! God, no!' she laughed, 'The man is a carnivore through and through.'

I watched as she bit her lip and blushed. 'I hate you, you know,' I said with an envious smile.

She flicked her eyebrows up once. 'You should. Every woman should. I've scored big-time.'

'Good. I'm glad you know it, hon.'

'Oh, trust me, Carls. I know it all right.'

* * *

I chose not to stick around much longer despite the fact I'd planned to have a big night. Quite frankly, I was exhausted after the week I'd had at work. Plus the mood between Derek and I seemed to have lost its spark around the same time I asked him about his family. He still requested my phone number, which I gave him, but I was pretty sure he was only doing it to be polite.

I'm not going to lie and say I didn't care, or that I wasn't bitterly disappointed. In fact, I was kind of devastated that things had gone sour so quickly. Initially, I'd felt that the two of us connected in a way that I had never experienced before. He seemed fun and free spirited, like I was, and I thought that the two of us could have had a bit of fun together with no strings attached. I got the impression he was a fan, like me, of no strings relationships — he just seemed the type.

Yawning, I rather sullenly made my way back to my suite, depressed thoughts of what could have been filtering through my head.

Oh, well ... knock me down and I'll get the fuck back up again. I always do.

CHAPTER

6

The next morning, I decided to lap up the luxury of my hotel suite. Why not? It was not every day that a girl like me got to enjoy spoils as a result of her best friend snagging a billionaire. It was also my way of cheering myself up after Derek's obvious fob off.

As I sat in the bathtub, which was big enough to accommodate the entire Brady Bunch, I couldn't help but think of the caramel firefighter. Maybe he was intimidated by a woman who knew what she wanted and was not afraid to ask. Or maybe he preferred the quiet type who sat, obeyed and worshipped. If that was the case, then I wished him good luck. I was not the worshipping, shut-up-and-look-pretty type. And I definitely did not obey.

Dwelling on females who had those particular attributes, I was reminded of my baby girl, Sasha. My playful, loving, golden retriever who I really needed to go home to and take for a walk.

Sighing in a lacklustre fashion, I dragged my wrinkly prune-like body out of the bath and prepared to head home.

* * *

As I walked through the door of my house, I heard the unmistakable sound of Sasha's feet skidding along the polished floorboards, the scratchy skitter of her toenails tapping on the hard surface beneath her. Her muscular body was not yet in my line of vision, but from past experience, I knew she was hurtling my way as fast as her legs would carry her.

Having no choice, I dropped my bag and braced for the impending impact.

When she turned the corner, her back-end apparently didn't get the memo to change direction as it failed to follow her body's lead and, because of this, she lost balance — like she always did — and skidded on her arse for a few feet. The sight of her ungraceful approach had me laughing but she recovered quickly and picked up her pace.

This was the part I always watched in what seemed like slow motion with the tune from *Chariots of Fire* playing in my head. Her golden floppy ears flapped simultaneously with the skin of her face, showing me what looked like a doggy smile every alternate second. And her long shaggy fur flailed with the breeze she was creating as she prepared to launch herself into my arms.

Sasha was only eight months old, but despite that, she still weighed a tonne.

'Sasha! Slow down ... argh!'

I squatted just enough so that when she jumped, I could roll backward with her atop me. This was a practised art.

Straightaway I felt her warm textured tongue lap at my face and smelled her disgusting doggy breath. 'You've just eaten a Schmackos, haven't you?' I asked in a voice that resembled Scooby Doo.

Sasha barked in response.

'Did you miss me?'

She barked again, and this time went to town on my face, licking with frenzied desperation.

'Sasha, stop it,' I laughed. 'Get off, you big woolly mammoth.' I rolled her off and proceeded to stand, brushing away the fur she so easily transferred.

'Where's Elmo?' I asked enthusiastically, distracting her from trying another kissathon by asking her to retrieve her favourite toy.

Continuing to brush the bits of fur off my pants, I moved into the house while singing out to Libby, 'Honey, I'm home.'

'Excellent! The toilet needs scrubbing. And guess what? It's your turn,' Libby responded from the direction of the kitchen, her voice awash with pure sarcasm.

'Lib. Elizabeth. Libido. Labia,' I announced, entering the room and catching her eye-roll. 'You know I don't do toilets.'

'I know you don't do toilets, but you're going to because I'm not doing it any more.'

I placed my handbag down on the kitchen counter and took a seat on one of our white shabby-chic styled bar stools. Our house was cute; a typical girl's space, I guess. It was always neat and tidy — thanks to Lib — and had a feminine touch everywhere you looked. From the vase of flowers on the dining table, to the pile of magazines on the edge of the benchtop and the framed pictures of French monuments hanging on the walls. Lib's and my home was our little sanctuary, and although I loved it, I hated cleaning it.

'I'm fairly certain we've had this conversation before. In fact, I'm positive. You said you'd clean the loo if I cleaned the floors.'

The ding of the microwave sounded. Libby stepped in front of it and opened the door. 'Yes, but have you cleaned the floors?' she asked as she removed what looked like leftover pasta. It smelled bloody divine.

'I have.'

'When, last year?' she retorted.

Just as Lib put the Tupperware container on the bench and stirred the contents with a fork, Sasha nudged my leg. The soft sensation on my skin drew my attention. I looked down and found her toy, Elmo, dangling from her mouth.

'Good girl,' I cooed quietly and patted her head. Then, giving my attention back to Lib, I continued to lie. 'No. I cleaned them last week.'

'I call bullshit,' Libby coughed, trying to camouflage her sarcasm.

My ginger-topped petite friend turned around and opened the fridge door, and even though Lib fell into the fanta-pants category, I could vouch for her being one of the cute ones. In my mind, redheads like Annie, Ginger

Meggs and Jessica Rabbit — *I don't care how big Jessica's boobs are, she is* not *hot* — aren't in any way cute.

Lib was a walking contradiction; petite with a bold attitude, pretty with an ugly bite when needed. She was an intelligent and beautiful pocket-rocket who packed a punch. I adored her.

While Lib's back was turned, I took the opportunity to dig into her pasta dish.

'Nothing to say?' she questioned as she bent over and sought her item.

I always had *something* to say, but speaking at this point in time would reveal that my mouth was full of food and, seeing as hers was the only food in my vicinity, I chose to keep quiet and continue to devilishly consume her lunch.

She scoffed at me. 'Well that's a first. Carly at a loss for words. Where's the bloody parmesan cheese?'

'I don't know,' I mumbled and quickly shovelled in another mouthful.

Lib turned around, displaying a puzzled expression, but soon became aware that I was stealing her pasta. 'Hey! Nick off. Get your own.'

She snatched it away from me just as my mobile sounded from within my handbag. I reached across the bench and pulled it out to find a text message from an unknown number. Curious, I tapped to open it up:

Carly, it's Derek. I just wanted to apologise for last night. I'm sure I came across as a prick when you asked about my family. It's a long story, but I'd really like to meet up and explain — Derek

The message had me a little bemused. *Why would he want to explain?* His family and his privacy were his to keep just that ... private. He didn't owe me any explanation.

Opting not to respond straightaway — because I've watched *He's Just Not That Into You* — I headed to my room to change and get ready to take Sasha for a walk.

* * *

Sasha loved the park. She also loved to chase things: birds, kids and balls to name a few. Picking up a stick, I threw it for her to retrieve and watched as she bounded off excitedly. The cold air was brisk and stinging my nose. I was thankful I'd chosen to rug up in my thermals, even though they were hideous.

'Good girl, Sashy,' I praised as she returned and dropped the stick at my feet. I picked it up and threw it again, being the first to admit that I'm not Sporty Spice. My aim and throwing ability are laughable, but Sasha never seemed to mind. In fact, she happily brought back whatever I threw so that I could do it again for her. Either she thought I was king-shit of stick throwing, or she wanted me to practise as much as possible because she believed that I sucked. Oh well, I guess we'll never know. Thank goodness dogs could not talk.

While Sasha stopped to take a dump, I pulled my phone out of my pocket. Derek's text had still gone unanswered and that was because I did not know how to respond. For some reason, he seemed to be unlike the many other guys I'd hooked up with in the past, and I didn't know why. Sure, he looked like the yummiest thing I could ever put in my mouth. And yes, his voice had the ability to render me stupid, but that didn't explain why I was hesitant to act either way.

Perhaps I was afraid that if I did respond and openly acknowledge that I liked him and would love to meet up, only for him to let me down, I'd be devastated more than I'd care to admit. But the alternative of fobbing him off, only for him to take it on the chin and not push to see me again would be equally as devastating. *Damn! This is why I'm happily single and unattached. Fuck, fun and fuck off. Those are the three actions I live by. And I live by them for this reason.*

I hit reply and sent a text back.

Hi, No need to explain. I had no right to pry — Carly

After pressing Send, my stomach dropped. *Carly, that response was pathetic.*

I mentally berated myself then looked up from my phone to see Sasha leave a nice pile of dog shit on the ground. *Urgh!* I hated picking it up with a baggie. Shovels I could handle, but only just; baggies, not so much.

Glancing around, I spotted some kids tossing a ball to each other. *Perfect!*

'Hey!' I called out and motioned them to come closer. Both boys jogged to where I was standing. They looked to be maybe twelve or thirteen years old.

'Want to earn ten dollars?' I asked, plastering as much enthusiasm over my face as humanly possible.

'Sure,' one of them replied.

'I'm not getting in your car,' the other stated. Clearly, he was smart and, clearly, his mum had taught him well.

'No, no. There'll be no getting in my car,' I reassured him. 'I need a little help. You see, I'm allergic to dog poo —' *no, not really* '— and my golden retriever Sasha just dropped one over there,' I said, while screwing up my nose and pointing. 'If one of you picks it up with this bag, I'll give you ten dollars.'

Both boys wrinkled their nose. *Shit! They ain't gonna take the bait. And they are far too young to flash my boobs to.*

'Twenty,' offered smart boy.

'Twenty?' I screeched in response.

He tossed his ball in the air and caught it in a show of teenage cockiness. 'Yep. Take it or leave it.'

I'm bloody inclined to do just that ... leave the steaming pile of shit on the ground. But I know better. I was taught to clean up after myself, or convince someone else to do it for me.

Huffing in surrender, I narrowed my eyes at the clever kid and handed him the baggie. 'Fine, twenty. And you'd better spend it wisely.'

As the two extortionists headed off, my phone beeped again. I pulled it out to find another text from Derek.

Okay, but I'd really like to catch up sometime. I'm heading interstate for work. I will be gone for a couple of weeks. Maybe when I get back? — Derek

Reading what he'd written, a small smile started to creep in at the corners of my mouth. But I stopped it before it spread any further. *Carly, is he really someone you want to fuck around?* Normally I would not hesitate with an answer, but there was just something different about Derek.

My phone beeped again.

Maybe I'm going about this wrong. What about this? Baby, I'm a firefighter. I find 'em hot and leave 'em wet. I hope you like being damp — Derek

OMG! I covered my face with my free hand and laughed before responding.

Do firefighters study Pick-up Lines 101? — Carly

Again, his response came through rather quickly.

Sure, I'll go with that. So, can I take you out and make you damp when I'm back in Melbourne? — Derek

My heart rate increased as I contemplated my answer. *Yes or no? Yes or no?* It really shouldn't be this hard a decision.

I bit my fingernail then typed my answer.

Yes — Carly

Good. Make sure you have a towel — Derek

'Shit!' I said out loud.

'Yes, here's your shit. Now hand over the cash,' a voice said in response.

I looked up to find smart kid dangling the baggie which now contained Sasha's turd. He was offering it to me and, with his other hand out, it was clear I had to pay up.

Ahh ... shiit!

* * *

For the week that followed, I popped in and out of work sporadically. It was school holidays so I was not required to be there daily, but had to perform some admin work in preparation for the following semester.

So for the holiday period my timetable was flexible and, because of that, I found myself to be Libby's slave, subjected to her threats of having to clean the floors in our house.

Just as I was about to switch on the vacuum, my phone rang.

I smiled at the perfectly timed interruption. Lib, on the other hand, just shook her head from her seated position at the dining table. She was planning the first week of term three's tasks. 'Don't think you are getting out of vacuuming,' she grumbled without looking up from her laptop screen.

'Of course not,' I responded before answering my phone. It was Lexi. 'What up, Duffy?' I said with a proud smile.

There was a short pause before she answered. 'Not up the duff any more, hon. I lost the baby.'

My breath caught and my chest panged. Slowly, I lowered myself to sit on the couch, gripping the light brown cushion as I came to rest. I wanted nothing more than to apologise for my highly inappropriate words, but I was too ashamed and disgusted with myself to even speak.

Unable to control my emotions, I let out a sob as tears wet my cheeks.

'Carls? You there?' she said softly.

'Uh huh,' I choked out, trying to avoid making her aware of my emotional state.

'You all right?'

Am I *all right?* I said in disbelief, then sniffed. 'I just shamefully make a joke about you being pregnant when you're no longer pregnant, and you ask if *I'm* all right? What's fucking wrong with this picture?' I spat out angrily. I was so furious with my lack of decorum.

'Carls,' she sighed, 'how were you to know?'

I knew she was trying to make me feel better. It was what Alexis did. She was forever attempting to make people feel comfortable in their own skin, and pushing aside her feelings was her way of trying to make me feel better. Even though I was an inconsiderate bitch.

'It doesn't matter,' I said bitterly. 'I'm a bitch, a horrible best friend.'

'You are not ... well ... you are a bitch, but you are definitely not a horrible best friend,' she said with a sad laugh.

'Yeah? Well, I disagree. So what happened, Lex? Do you want to talk about it?'

'Sure. There's not much to say really. I fell down the stairs, broke my ankle and miscarried,' she explained a little tersely.

I gripped at my chest. 'Jesus, fuck! When did this happen?'

'Monday, just past. I was in hospital pretty much all last week.'

Shooting up from the couch, I began to make my way to my room to grab my car keys. 'Right, I'm coming over there.' My eyes met Libby's and her eyebrows rose. She had closed her laptop and was now completely focussed on my conversation.

'No. I actually just want to be with Bryce, Carls. But thank you.'

Turning back around and pacing toward the window, I placed my hand on my forehead. 'Oh, poor Bryce. He was really looking forward to being a dad. How is he?'

'He's coping. Anyway, hon, as you can imagine, I need to call a few people, and next on my list is Tash. I will need a moment to prepare myself, so I'd better get going.'

I laughed mildly, trying to lighten the mood for Alexis' sake. Ringing family and friends with this news must be absolutely dreadful for her. 'I understand. Okay, if you need me for anything, please call. I love you, you know,' I whispered quietly.

'I do know. I love you too. 'Bye.'

As we disconnected our call, I let the tears fall freely. *Poor Lexi. Poor Bryce.* Hearing about people losing their baby always ripped me to shreds. But hearing that my best friend, my ally, my sister from another mother, had lost her child made my heart crumble to pieces.

This traumatic event, Alexis and Bryce's traumatic event, had now reinforced the fact that I would NEVER EVER have children of my own.

CHAPTER

7

Two weeks had passed since I'd made that horrid inconsiderate slip of the tongue to Alexis, and I wanted to prove, if not to my friends then at least to myself, that I could be a better friend. That night, when Alexis had told me about her miscarriage, I organised a bunch of flowers to be sent to the apartment. I couldn't take back what I had said, but I was a girl, and I knew all too well that flowers always made the biggest of fuck-ups seem not so bad. Plus Alexis loved flowers and, regardless of whether she'd accepted my apology or not, I wanted her to have pretty buds of colour to look at and find some form of comfort in.

During our telephone conversation, she'd asked to be left alone; to be given time with Bryce to grieve. And as much as it damn near killed me, I respected her request. I wanted nothing more than to take her out — broken foot or no broken foot — plaster her with alcohol and make her forget what had happened. But I knew deep down that it would not benefit her in the long run, nor was it a permanent fix. Not that there could be a permanent fix for what she had lost.

So instead I gave her space, knowing, like so many times before, that she would call upon me when she needed me — it was how we rolled. What she didn't know was that her request for solitude had an expiration date. She had one month, one month before I tracked her down.

* * *

For the duration of term three at Yellow Bark Primary School, the curriculum's focus was on emergency situations. I had arranged for members of the police force, fire brigade, ambulance and SES to visit the school in the coming weeks in order to educate the children through demonstrations and impart information on what to do in the case of an emergency.

Also, as part of Emergency Education Month, the staff had to participate in a first aid refresher course. Pressing Send, I forwarded a memo to the teaching staff's email accounts, reminding them of the course and that it was compulsory to attend.

Before I was able to move on to my next task for the day, my phone beeped indicating a message.

Back in Melbourne. Ready for a soaking? — Derek

His messages had a tendency to catch me off-guard, but to be honest, for the past couple of weeks, I hadn't really given the sexy firefighter much thought. I'd been depressed and moping around after Lexi revealed her bad news. Then I'd had my new Carly-is-the-best-friend-you-can-have makeover and had been busy pulling my weight around the house ever since. Not to mention the enormous workload that came with the start of a school term.

Feeling in a daring mood, I figured I'd give him a run for his money. At Lexi's party, he seemed to like that.

I'm not the moist type — Carly

Almost instantly, a response came through.

Trust me, I can make you wet — Derek

Fuck me stupid. He is already on his way to making that *happen.* Going by one of Carly's Cardinals — 'Do not let penises have the upper hand' — I opted to be brazen rather than modest. *Who am I kidding? Modesty is not a part of my repertoire.*

Oh, yeah? How exactly? — Carly

Again, faster than Quick Draw McGraw, he drew one out and fired it back at me.

I have a hose — Derek

Oh, and how I want to see this hose, touch this hose and douse my fiery hole with it. Caramello Koala had me hook line and sinker and I couldn't help but play with him.

It must be a pretty good hose — Carly

It's the best. But there's only one way for you to find out — Derek

Let me guess. You'll need to use it on me — Carly

That's the plan — Derek

Closing my eyes, I struggled to maintain my composure for what I was about to type.

I like your plan — Carly

You free tomorrow night? — Derek

Sweet baby cheeses, yes! But no. OMG! I need to de-fuzz. I need a colonic irrigation. I need to sharpen my nails. I need to strengthen my facial muscles.

Yes — Carly

Oh shit. Oh shit. Oh shit.

Sweet. I'll pick you up at six. What's your address? — Derek

As I pressed Send and forwarded my address to Derek, a timid voice captured my attention. 'Miss Henkley, I don't feel very well.'

I looked up to find a rather sickly-looking Samuel Barker — aged six. To say he was many shades of green did not do his complexion justice; he was as emerald as the city of Oz. *Eww, I hate this part of my job. I hate vomit ... and sneezing ... and snot ... and toileting accidents.*

'Samuel, do you feel like you want to throw up?' I asked quickly.

He nodded gingerly. 'Yes.'

Standing up at the speed of light, I pushed my chair back. Every fibre in me wanted to scream, *RUN! RUN THE FUCK TO THE TOILET!* But I didn't. I knew very well that I was required to remain calm, although calm in this situation went against my better judgement — that kid needed to haul arse to the dunny and fast. 'Well, quickly go to the sick bay toilet. I'll be right behind you,' I informed him.

He moved off the step and hurriedly made his way to the bathroom and, just as he bent over the bowl, a spew-nami hurtled from his mouth.

I held my breath and pulled a face that probably had me looking like a pufferfish. Then, gently rubbing his back, I comforted him as he continued to vomit. 'It's all right, mate. Get it all out. You'll feel so much better.'

Fuck me, this better not be gastro.

* * *

What's that saying ... famous last words, or put the mockers on something? Well, whatever the saying is, it fucking happened. Yes, Samuel's spewnami was the result of gastroenteritis, which also resulted in me getting gastroenteritis, which in turn meant my Derek-hose-sampling never occurred.

The morning of our date night — if that's what we were to have — I got struck down with the highly contagious bug. I'd had to text Derek and tell him I needed a raincheck. Unfortunately, I got the impression he hadn't believed me. It was now four days later and still not one text from him.

The relentless stomach bug spread right through the school faculty. Mind you, given that Lib and I lived together, it was inevitable that she, too, would contract the virus.

I'd been vomiting on and off for days and was only just now able to keep my food down. Lib, however, was still in the stages of everything-is-gonna-come-up.

As she walked into the lounge room wearing her pink fluffy slippers, Tweety Bird flannel PJs and carrying a bottle of water, I felt her pain. I'd gained enough energy to shower and do my hair. Lib, on the other hand, looked like a walking troll doll, her red hair somehow defying gravity.

'Feelin' any better?' I asked from my curled position on the couch.

She flopped down beside me and commandeered the other end of the seat, resting her feet against mine. 'No.'

Adjusting my blanket, I spread it out so that it covered her as well. 'You contracted it roughly a day after me, so you should start to improve tomorrow.'

'I hope so,' she groaned. 'I've got so much stuff to get through in preparation for the emergency services members who are visiting early next week.'

I flicked the channel of the TV, searching for something decent. 'Can you not ask the substitute to get started with it?'

'Of course, and she will. I just had some special activities that I wanted to do with my kids.'

Lib loved being a teacher. LOVED it. She was forever going far beyond the call of duty and what was expected of her. I didn't get it ... not that I really needed to.

'Being sick sucks,' I said resolutely. 'I had a hot date planned the other night which I had to cancel. And, to top it off, he is a firefighter. Lib, my vagina is a blaze and I wanted him to put it out with his fire hose.'

She raised her eyebrow, then scowled and rubbed her tummy. Knowing these signs, I calculated in my head that she had less than five minutes before she was blowing chunks again.

'Where'd you meet him?' Lib asked before taking what looked like a laboured sip of her water.

'You want me to get you anything, a dry cracker?' I suggested. 'It may make you feel a little better.'

She shook her head. 'No thanks, it will barely see my oesophagus. I don't want to waste a good cracker.'

I let out a small giggle. Lib was the biggest tight-arse I had ever come across. She wasted nothing. 'You need to eat something. You can't just rely on water.'

She groaned. 'Do we have any more of those Hydralyte ice blocks? I'll suck on one of those.'

I stood up. 'Hang on. I'll check the freezer.'

Shuffling into the kitchen in my moccasins and yellow duck PJs, I opened the freezer and searched for the hydrating ice stick.

'So, where'd you meet this fireman?' Lib called out from the other room.

'He's Alexis' boyfriend's best friend,' I shouted back, delving into the depths of the freezer.

Managing to find the ice treat for her, I snipped the plastic top off and wrapped it in a paper towel. *I'm such a good fucking friend.*

Just as I was about to head back into the lounge, Sasha barked from her position outside and not so subtly scratched the glass sliding door with her paw. I opened it and let her in. 'Who's a good girl?' I praised in my Scooby Doo voice.

She wagged her tail and gave me a smile — at least, it looked like a smile — then proceeded into the lounge. I followed her and handed Libby the ice block. 'Here. This will at least hydrate you.'

'Thanks. So ... tell me more about this firefighter. Is he hot?'

I laughed. Hearing Derek referred to as hot would always make me laugh. 'God, yes! Seriously, Lib, he is the hottest guy I have ever seen.'

She bit down on the ice block then made a holy-shit-that-is-cold face. 'Nice! So when are you seeing him next?'

'I don't know,' I answered sullenly.

'What do you mean you don't know?'

'I mean that when I texted him and told him I had gastro, I don't think he believed me. He didn't ask when I was free again.'

'So text him back and ask when he is free,' she suggested, as if it were that simple. It wasn't. There was a process, an unwritten law on how these first dates were handled. He was meant to chase me. Not the other way around.

'Elizabeth,' I sternly remarked, 'with all due respect, when was the last time you dated?'

'What's that got to do with it?' she griped.

'A shitload. You don't chase the guy before the first date.' I rolled my eyes at her. 'Everyone knows that. He has to chase you.'

'Who says?' she mildly groaned, clenching her tummy.

I flicked my eyes in her direction and gave her a questioning glare. 'You gonna be sick? If you're gonna be sick, fuck off. This is my favourite blanket.'

Lib closed her eyes momentarily, then opened them again. 'I'm good. I've got this. I am a strong woman who is in charge of her body. I say what it does and doesn't do.'

Looking at her as if she had grown a second head, or was about to wrench off her bra and set fire to it in our living room, I asked her what verbal diarrhoea was spilling from her mouth. 'What the king fuck of Fucktown have you been reading?'

'None of your business. Just know that it works. I'm in charge and ruler of my destiny.'

'You're a ruler of looneyville. Where all loonies liaise and sprout utter looneyness.'

Before I was able to hold my intervention in order to pull Lib out from her obvious descent into cray cray country, Sasha happily placed her head in Libby's lap and presented her with a dead bird.

'Oh my god! What is that? Get it off me. Is that a bird?' Libby screamed.

She leapt off the couch, flinging the mangled bird carcass in my direction.

'Argh! Don't throw it at me,' I screamed back, while throwing my legs up in the air in defence and looking somewhat like a beetle trying to get itself upright.

I was quickly tangled in my blanket, still performing the beetle dance. 'Where is it? Lib, for the love of god, where the hell is it?'

Peeking out from underneath the corner of my blanket, I observed Lib standing there with her hand over her mouth, eyelids tightly closed and shaking her head. It was written all over her face that in mere seconds she was going to throw up again.

Sasha's wagging tail, repeatedly tapping the side of the couch, grabbed our attention. We glanced in her direction. What I thought earlier on was Sasha smiling at me had been one hundred percent correct. Because there, standing happily on four legs, was my dog with the dead bird half hanging out of her smiling mouth.

'Ugh, I'm gonna be sick,' Lib said, running off at rapid speed.

'Sasha! Out! Go! Get outside,' I yelled at her.

She gave me a look that said what-did-I-do-wrong, then drooped her head and made her way to the back door.

* * *

After a week's absence, Lib and I returned to work, having recovered from our spate of gastro, although both of us felt a little seedy for the duration of the work week. You'd think that after working around children our immune systems would be invulnerable. They weren't. Well, at least mine wasn't. I was forever coming down with every germ, bug and infection that these fucklets felt necessary to share with me.

Now over a week later, things had returned to normal.

'What the hairy spider has he written?' I mumbled to myself as I tried to decipher the principal's notes for the weekly newsletter I was typing up. 'The prep students can write neater than this.'

'Excuse me, ma'am, but I'm here to put out your fire.'

Unsure that I'd heard what I thought I'd just heard, I looked up at the person standing on the other side of the counter.

I blinked a few times as if my eyes were deceiving me, then realised Derek was leaning toward me and was only centimetres away. He was wearing a tight-fitting navy t-shirt with the Metropolitan Fire Brigade emblem on it. He was also sporting a devilishly sexy grin on his face.

Holy fuckalicious firefighter!

CHAPTER

8

I stood upright and looked to my left then to my right as if I were about to cross a fucking road. 'What the crap? What are you doing here?' I asked, shocked but equally excited to see him.

'Easy, princess, I'm here for the Fire Ed program,' he answered. *Princess ... really?*

'Oh, of course you are,' I laughed awkwardly when, to be honest, I was a little disappointed that he wasn't here to see me. *And on a side note: if I were a 'princess' where is my fucking tiara?*

Plastering on a faux smile, I remained composed. 'A coincidence perhaps?'

'You could say that,' he replied with a cocky grin that had the ability to render me his slave and perform a sexual extravaganza for him. *Holy clit jitters. How does he do that?*

'Um ... just give me a second and I'll escort you and the truck through the gate to the oval area where you can set yourselves up.'

As I turned to make my way out of my office, feeling like a complete and utter fool, Libby walked in with her head down, her attention focussed solely on the paperwork she was reading. 'What time are the fire brigade due?' she asked without raising her head.

'They're here,' I replied through my clenched teeth.

At that point she looked up and spotted Derek standing in the office reception area. Her jaw dropped open and she turned the shade of her hair — bright red! 'Oh. That's ... great!'

Trying to retain my calm professional manner, I walked past her. 'Can you man the office for a minute while I show the MFB where they can set up?'

By that point, I was still standing behind the doorframe and out of Derek's sight, but I was, however, in Libby's line of vision.

'Sure,' she said with an unsure smile as she glanced at Derek, then back to me.

When her eyes met mine again, I performed a few indistinguishable hand gestures and mouthed the words, 'That's Derek, that's the firefighter', while overly accentuating my finger-pointing in his direction.

It took her a couple of seconds to figure out what I was getting at, but when she did, her face morphed into an unusually large smile ... even for Libby.

Stepping up to the counter, she offered her hand. 'Sorry, I'm Ms Elizabeth Hanson ... or Libby, when my class isn't listening,' she babbled, her flushed cheeks now downgraded from Elmo-red to Miss Piggy-pink. *OMG! Lib, you little flirt.*

'Senior Officer King ... or firefighter Derek, when your class is listening,' he smiled with a wink while shaking her hand. *Fucking man-whore!*

I shook my head, rolled my eyes and walked around to where he stood, fully kitted out in his uniform. The sheer magnitude of his sexiness nearly had me grabbing at the reception counter for stability. *My god, I love a man in uniform. I mean, seriously, how hot are firefighters, military officers, policemen, Batman, Thor? Wait a minute, does Thor wear a uniform? Pfft, who the fuck cares, he's hot!* Anyway, my point is a man in uniform screamed sexy. It screamed, 'I am one fuckable piece of man candy, put me in your mouth and suck me.'

As I fantasised about consuming Senior Officer King, my eyes travelled the length of his yellow coloured protective pants which were held up by red braces. Surely it was a crime of some sort that those braces were currently functional. I wanted nothing more than for those protective pants to just drop to the floor in a pool of material around his booted ankles. His presence alone made me weak at the knees and slightly giddy.

Derek began to take steps toward me and I noticed that his mouth was moving, but the words he was speaking were not registering. I honestly felt as though I was in a fog, a trance of some kind.

'Carly, are you all right?' he said as he gently placed his hands on my shoulders. He squatted and lowered himself to my eye level.

I could see the concern in his eyes. 'What? I'm fine. Sorry, I'm fine,' I stuttered, apologetically.

Derek tilted his head slightly, indicating that he thought my explanation was bogus. 'Are you sure? You looked as though you were about to faint.'

'Yes, I'm fine. I'm just a little woozy. My appetite has not yet returned,' I flippantly remarked.

Technically, that statement held some truth. The 'some truth' being the woozy part, because my appetite had returned tenfold. No, I was woozy because he was standing before me in his firefighter uniform and it was making me light-headed.

'Do you two know each other?' Libby asked, with a smile only I could see the meaning behind.

Still standing there with Derek's hands on my shoulders, I became aware he was staring at me. I very quickly glared at Libby. 'Yes, we've met before.'

Derek leaned in closer and pierced me with his baby blue eyes. The close proximity of his head and the intense stare he placed upon me stole the air from my lungs.

'Is it on vacation?' he asked, his expression dead serious, his eyes continuing to peruse my facial features.

I gave him a crooked smile and answered with great difficulty, my response a challenge due to noticing that his gaze kept returning to my lips. 'Is what on vacation?'

'Your appetite,' he responded, still displaying a stoic mask.

'No. Why would it be on vacation?'

'Because you said it hadn't yet returned,' he smiled. 'I was just wondering where it had gone.'

Our conversation was cray cray; appetites taking holidays. I mean, who talked about that shit? Regardless, I wasn't in the least bit interested in our discussion, instead being more fascinated by the way his nostrils flared as he breathed heavily.

'I ... I had a bad case of gastro and haven't been eating properly since,' I stuttered.

Derek leaned back, affording me my personal space again, yet he kept his hands on my shoulders. 'So you weren't spinning me some bullshit lie to get out of our date?'

'Language! You're in a primary school,' I scolded him.

He flexed his fingers. 'Shit, sorry.'

'No, I wasn't. I was genuinely crook. And anyway,' I offered, shrugging out of his grasp because his fingers were causing heat waves to roll through me, 'if I didn't want to go out with you,' I mumbled, heading to the reception counter and stepping up onto the small platform to lean over and reach for the keys to the gate, all the while gifting him a nice view of my arse, 'I would've just come right out and said it.'

Turning back around, I shot him an exaggerated smile, then leapt off the step with the elegant grace a dancer would possess. As I passed him en route to the door, I stopped and finished what I had to say. 'I'm open, honest and tell it like it is. Take me or leave me.' Holding my arm out, I gestured for him to exit. 'After you, Officer King.'

Derek clicked his jaw from side to side and placed one of his hands in his trouser pocket, then casually strolled past me to walk out the door, and as if my eyes were on autopilot they followed that man's toned firm arse until it was no longer in sight.

* * *

For the hour that followed, I sat anxiously at my desk, desperately wanting to go outside and perve on Derek. So when Brooke casually strolled into my office and said she'd been informed by Libby that Officer Hotstuff was my soon-to-be new fuck-friend so I could go outside for the next demo because her grade one class was having their library session and she would cover for me, I couldn't have been happier.

'Thank you, Brooke. And just for the record, I never said he was to be my new "fuck-friend",' I said quietly, making sure no little ears were close by.

Tightening her blonde ponytail, she rolled her eyes. 'Carly, please, I know you. I've known you for years. And I've just seen his ... um ... exterior. Plus, Lib said you both know each other and that you were only seconds away from getting it on in this very office.'

'We were not!'

'Sure,' she drawled.

I narrowed my eyes at her as I stood up from my seat. 'Changing the subject ... Lance's brother, he is still single?'

Brooke picked up one of my fancy pens and gave it a critical once-over while answering nonchalantly. 'Yeah. Why?'

'I met someone a few weeks ago who might be a great match.'

'When are you going to learn to stay out of setting people up?'

'What? I'm a human cupid,' I smiled proudly.

'So be your own human cupid.'

Ignoring her stab at me, because she knows I'm one to avoid commitment on any level, I continued with my original plan. 'As I was saying, I met a guy called Liam. He works with my best friend, Alexis. He's single, cute and strictly dickly. I told him about Lance's bro and he seemed interested.'

Brooke shrugged her shoulders. 'Okay, I'll have a chat to him.'

'Sweet! Later,' I said, blowing her a kiss and making my way outside.

* * *

Walking toward the demonstration, I took in the sight of Derek addressing the prep students. He had their unequivocal attention, their wide eyes glued to every movement that he made.

'So repeat after me. Stop, drop, cover. And if your clothes are on fire what do you do?' he asked while putting his hand to his ear, ready for them to shout the answer.

'ROLL!' they enthusiastically screamed.

'Yes, roll. But only if your clothes are on fire.' Derek leaned back against the truck and raised one foot, balancing it against the tyre. He then crossed his arms in front of him and shook his head from side to side. 'You kids are pretty smart. I bet you are all smarter than me.'

Most of them shouted, 'No', the exception being Tanner Morgan — aged five. 'My dad is smarter than you,' Tanner bellowed.

I had to bite my lip to refrain from laughing. Sally — or Ms Taylor as she is known to her prep grade students — stepped forward. She was clearly embarrassed, blushing profusely as she tried to hush Tanner.

'Oh yeah?' Derek asked. 'Is your dad a rocket scientist?'

'No. He is a policeman, and policemen are way better than firemen,' Tanner answered resolutely.

It was obvious by the way Derek quickly looked to the ground that he was trying not to laugh. 'Really? Why are they better?'

'Tanner!' Sally warned.

Tanner totally ignored his teacher. 'Because policemen have guns and you have stupid fire hoses,' he responded.

'Stupid? This is not stupid,' Derek announced as he whipped out a hose. Honestly, I'd much prefer he whip out the hose in his pants. But hey, there's a time and place for that, and it certainly wasn't here ...

Instead, he was handed a hose by one of the other firefighters.

'This is an attack hose,' he explained with a melodramatic tone.

All the kids — even Tanner — ooh'd and ah'd.

'Is it heavy?' one of them asked.

'Can you blow a hole in someone's gut?' said another.

'Can you drink from it?'

'Whoa! Remember, if you have a question, please raise your hand,' Derek instructed kindly.

As I watched him interact with the kids, it was apparent that he had paternal qualities. He was cool, calm and collected, and he appeared to enjoy their annoying and, at times, non-compliant nature. He seemed, quite simply, tolerant — which was something I was not. My tolerance, where young humans were concerned, was zero ... nil ... nada. That didn't mean I treated them badly though. I didn't treat anyone badly. Regardless of whether I was fond of a person or not, I always showed them respect. Respect is the easiest thing to give, yet the hardest to be earned.

Ding! Ding! Ding!

The sound of the school bell broke my inner musings about Derek and children. *Thank Christ for that! Why my mind is pondering that topic is beyond me.*

Taking a few steps closer to him, he noticed my approach and looked up. A small group of children were saying their goodbyes when he excused himself and instructed them to hurry and catch up with the rest of their class.

'I hope you got all that?' he said with sincerity.

Got all what? Is he asking if I spotted that he is great with kids, or that he has a massive hose?

'Got what?' I asked hesitantly.

'What to do in an emergency.'

I rolled my eyes at him. 'I know what to do in the case of an emergency.'

'Really? Where's the safe point at your home?'

'Easy, by the letterbox.'

'How often do you change your smoke detector batteries?'

'At the beginning of daylight saving.'

'Good,' he praised. 'So, Carly, I know that you said your appetite had not yet returned, but I'm hungry. I want to eat and I want to eat with you.'

'Um ... well, I'm just about to go on my lunchbreak. There's a cafe down the road that has great sandwiches. We could —'

'Perfect. Just give me a minute,' he said before turning and jogging toward his two colleagues.

I watched as he — I assumed — filled them in on his lunch plans. One of them looked in my direction and shook his head in amused disbelief, before saying, 'I don't know how you do it.'

I furrowed my brow.

* * *

We walked the short distance to the cafe and secured a table.

'What can I get you both?' the waitress politely asked.

Derek motioned for me to answer first. 'Ladies before gentlemen,' he said with a smirk.

'I thought we'd established that I'm not a lady,' I replied.

'No. You inferred that you weren't. You are yet to prove it.'

I handed my menu to the waitress and ordered the roast lamb sandwich and an OJ, then leaned back in my chair and laid my napkin across my lap. 'And how would you like me to prove it?'

'I'm sure you mentioned something about preferring your legs open,' he stated, then turned to the waitress. 'I'll have the turkey and cranberry sandwich and a bottle of Coke, please.'

The poor thing was already blushing as she jotted down his order, her eyes quickly flicking from her note-pad to Derek's uniform-covered chest. 'Thank you,' she said hastily and fumbled with the menu when Derek handed it to her. 'I'll be back in a minute with your drinks.'

Leaning forward, I opted to give him a dose of his own medicine and get up close and personal. 'Yes, I did mention that. And I still go by it. I've had more fun with them open as opposed to them closed.'

Derek swallowed heavily, the muscles in his neck tensing with the motion. 'I bet you have. So ... are we going to reschedule our date?'

Relaxing a little, I moved back to a comfortable position on my chair and rested my elbows on the table. 'Maybe.'

'Why maybe?'

'Because, according to you, you owe me an apology,' I smiled sweetly.

Just as the waitress arrived with our drinks, Derek leaned back and put his hands behind his head. He thanked her, then waited for her departure. 'Look, Carly, I'm sorry for being so short with you at Alexis' birthday when you mentioned my fami—'

I interrupted, because I didn't feel he should have to justify himself where his family was concerned, regardless of the clipped way he had spoken that day. 'You don't have to explain about your —'

'Yes, I do,' he butted in. 'I do, because I want you to understand that I was not trying to push you away. I enjoyed spending time with you that night. And the way I ended things was a fucking disgrace.'

'You're overreacting,' I offered, before sipping my OJ through the straw.

Derek tipped his drink bottle back and began to skoll the contents. Instantly, I became entranced by the way his throat muscles worked as he swallowed. I said a little prayer in the hope he would spill some of it so I could launch myself over the table and lick the drip from his neck.

Unfortunately, my prayers went unanswered and his drinking ability was almost perfect.

'My father is an arsehole of epic proportions and my brother likes to suck up to him and make accusations. I don't like either of them,' he explained, placing his bottle on the table.

I nodded. I didn't want to add anything that might imply he should continue with his private confession. This really was none of my business.

'Have you heard of King Logistics?' he asked, rocking his chair back to rest on two legs instead of four.

'The freight company?'

'Yep, that's the one. Well, that's the family business. The one my father wanted me to run with my twin brother,' Derek explained.

Oh, sweet lord of all things duplicated. He's a twin.

Before I could answer, the waitress returned with our sandwiches. We thanked her before she made herself scarce.

'I take it you do not want to co-run the business,' I replied as I lifted the lid of my sandwich to check the contents.

Stupid bloody yuppy cafe. How many times have I told these morons to put in mint sauce? Who the hell eats lamb without mint sauce? It's sacrilege.

I harrumphed, closed the lid and scanned the cafe for the waitress, flagging her down. She quickly made her way toward me. 'Yes? Can I help you with something?'

'Can you please get David to put in some mint sauce? Tell him it's Carly's sandwich. He'll know who I am.'

She apologised. 'Sorry, I'm new here. I didn't know.'

'It's fine. Chef David knows I cannot possibly eat a roast lamb sandwich without mint sauce.' I smiled, handing her my plate.

She laughed. 'Sure, I'll remember that.'

Taking the dish from my hands, the waitress then headed toward the kitchen, only to return moments later. 'On behalf of Chef David, here is your mint sauce sandwich with a side of lamb,' she said, wrinkling her nose.

'Hey, don't knock it until you try it,' I encouraged.

She laughed. 'Was there anything else?'

I shook my head. 'No, thank you.'

As I bit into my sandwich, humming with delight at the tangy zest of the mint sauce connecting with my tongue, I noticed Derek's amused face.

'What?' I mumbled around my mouthful.

'That's disgusting.'

I swallowed. 'How can you say it's disgusting if you haven't tried it?'

'I don't want to try it.'

'Well, good, that's your loss then. And anyway, I wouldn't share even if you begged me to. I *do not* share mint sauce.'

'I'm sure I could get you to share if I really wanted you to,' he said arrogantly before biting into his own sandwich.

Pausing with mine only centimetres from my open mouth, I snapped my jaw shut and glared at him. *You cocky cock popsicle.*

'Derek, let me fill you in on something. The only time I will share mint sauce with you is if you licked it off my tongue, and even then you would have to lick it hard.'

Derek swallowed his mouthful and rocked his chair forward with a thump. 'Baby,' he said while leaning forward and grabbing the back of my neck, 'there's only one way I lick, and it ain't soft.'

He then pulled me forward to meet his mouth.

CHAPTER

9

The kiss caught me off-guard, but holy hot vagina spasms, the taste of Derek's tongue mixed with the mint sauce was by far the tastiest thing I've ever had in my mouth. And without sounding like a slutsky, I've had a few tasty morsels in that orifice during my lifetime.

Derek's tongue was warm, wet, hard and controlling, his lips firm but soft all at once. With the loss of control over my voice box, I moaned as he brushed his fingers over my neck. The way his mouth skilfully dominated mine was both divine and aggravating. *Carly Henkley is not one to be dominated.*

Releasing me gently, a stark contrast to the way he captured me, I had to admit that both comparisons melded flawlessly together, the kiss pure perfection. *Goddamn it, no!*

'I believe in compromise, Carly,' he said as he pulled away and sat back in his seat. 'You shared your mint sauce the way you wanted to share it, and I proved I could make you do it.'

What? You stuck-up, egotistical, game-playing egghead.

Embarrassed at being played by him, I stood up in a fit of anger, tossed my napkin on my plate and proceeded to exit the cafe. As I wrenched open the door, not only did the stupid bell on top of it jingle and piss me off further — because I hate those stupid things — but I also spotted Vice Principal Sidebottom with her critical stare. *Argh! Just what I need, a Sidebottom grilling when the lunch hour finishes.*

Feeling hurt — a feeling I was not used to because of the protective wall I had built around myself — I stormed along the footpath which led back to the school, wanting to get far away from Dickhead Derek and his dickhead games. I didn't appreciate being treated like a pawn. I hated pawns and I fucking hated chess ... last time I checked, castles were stationary. They're not supposed to move. Stupid game.

'Carly! Carly, wait!

My pace quickened when I heard Derek calling from behind. I was no martial artist, but I would sure as hell dig my shellac nails into his cheeks if I needed to, not to mention perform the trachea-jab self-defence move that Lexi showed me a couple of months back.

'Carly, hold up,' Derek said as he grabbed my arm.

I wrenched it free and kept walking. 'Don't fucking bother.'

'Wait! What did I do?' he asked with a tone of surprise.

Stopping, I spun around and glared at him. 'I'm not a toy, Derek. I don't like to be played with just so you can get your kicks and prove a point.' I turned and began walking again, feeling tears start to pool in the corners of my eyes. *Oh, no you don't. I am not going to cry. Screw him.*

'Carly wait! I didn't mean —'

'You didn't mean what?' I interrupted, turning to face him once again. 'To kiss me in a public place just so you could demonstrate some form of male chauvinistic dominance?'

Stepping forward, I poked my finger at him to make a point. 'I may not be the settling down and marrying type. I may not be the type you want to take home to meet your mum. Hell, I may not even be the relationship type, full stop. But I can tell you what type I am. I'm the don't-fuck-around-with-me type. The don't-use-and-abuse-me type. The —'

Before I could cement just the type of person I was, Derek grabbed my face and kissed me once more, backing me up until I was pressed against a telephone pole.

My hands found his head and slid on the short stubble that was his hair. As our tongues ardently fought with one another's and our lips competed for the upper hand, I was unable to help myself, gently digging my nails into his scalp and slowly dragging them down until I found his neck and shoulders.

I pushed him back, needing to catch my breath and bearings. 'Stop. Don't. I can't.'

'Carly, I wasn't playing with you in the cafe. I wanted to kiss you ... I want to kiss you,' he said as he leaned forward and seized my mouth for the third time in less than ten minutes.

I tried desperately not to welcome the intrusion when, truth be told, the intrusion was more like a welcome guest. A guest that I wanted to show some hospitality to even though my head was telling me not to. It was screaming: *Don't give in to him. He has the capacity to break your heart.*

I'd come to the conclusion a long time ago that if I never handed a man my heart in its entirety, it would never be rendered vulnerable enough to break. I was the keeper of my heart. No one else.

Pulling back slightly, my lips left his, but lingered just long enough for one last featherlight kiss. They were traitors, wanting the soft caress of his mouth when they knew it would only leave me in turmoil.

Derek searched my eyes when I parted from him completely. 'You don't believe me, do you?' he asked, the question more of a statement.

'No, I don't,' I answered honestly.

'Tell me what I have to do to prove to you that I'm not fooling around?'

'I don't know, Derek. I don't know what to tell you. I ... I ... I'm not used to this,' I answered painfully, my body slumping and my head dropping in surrender.

Raising his arm to rest it on the pole above my head, he relaxed his posture and leaned into me, lifting my chin with his hand. 'You're not used to what?'

'This,' I gestured between us with my hand.

'What? Attraction?' he offered with a smile.

Yes, attraction, undeniable attraction. I am utterly attracted to Derek. That's all.

I nodded.

'So you do like me,' he said with a boyish grin.

I shoved his shoulder light-heartedly. 'Shut up! You know I do.'

'No, I don't. I honestly thought you stood me up when you cancelled our date.'

'I didn't stand you up. I was really sick. I promise.'

He touched my lip just lightly. 'I know that now.'

The question, with regards to the supposed happen-stance of our meeting today, sat on the tip of my tongue, when Ms Sidebottom walked past, clearly taking note of both my and Derek's positions against the pole.

Her expression was one of disdain. 'Miss Henkley, need I remind you that you are in view of the students currently playing on the school grounds.'

'No, Ms Sidebottom. I was just —'

'In the middle of a demonstration,' Derek interrupted, not bothering to look in my vice principal's direction.

'Demonstration?' she asked, incredulously.

'Yes,' he replied, pushing off the pole with his arm and stepping toward her.

Her eyes widened in surprise as he approached her.

'I was explaining to Miss Henkley the effects of smoke inhalation. Do you know what smoke inhalation injury is?' he asked, his voice low and seductively suggestive.

'Of course I do,' she stuttered, feigning insult.

Derek nodded as if for her to continue. 'Well?'

'It is the effects of breathing in smoke from a fire,' she answered haughtily.

'To put it mildly, yes,' he said, moving closer to her yet again. 'But to put it more accurately, it is injury caused when inhaling or being exposed to hot gaseous products of combustion.'

Derek spilled the informative words from his mouth like a song without the need of a tune. His aura was one of pure sexual intoxication.

I watched with amused curiosity as Ms Sidebottom submitted to Derek's instruction as if she were a cobra being charmed with a pungi.

Derek continued: 'The hot smoke can injure or kill through a combination of thermal damage, poisoning and pulmonary irritation and swelling. This is caused by carbon monoxide, cyanide and other combustible products,' he explained and then stopped.

Ms Sidebottom waited for him to continue, but Derek just stood there and put his hands in his pockets before rocking back on his heels. 'That is what I was demonstrating.'

Realising that his 'demonstration of a demonstration' was done, she took a step back and gave us both a faux smile. 'Right ... well ... thank you very much for that information. But maybe the demonstration could be done elsewhere in future,' she said, as she stepped around Derek and made her way back to the school.

When Ms Sidebottom was out of earshot, I let out a laugh. 'I can't believe you just seduced my vice principal.'

'Seduced? That was not seduction, Carly. I can show you sed—'

I ignored his seductive intent and butted in. 'Then what the hell was that?' I asked bewildered, and with my hands gestured to the space they had occupied.

'A distraction.' Derek grinned mischievously, then sauntered closer.

I put out my hand and held him at bay. 'No.'

His tongue darted out of his mouth and traced his bottom lip. 'Why?'

'Because you're a terrible kisser,' I explained, lying through my teeth.

He smiled and pushed his stone-hard chest into my hand, the force buckling my arm. 'Then help me improve.'

Before I could rebut any further, Derek's tongue was exploring my mouth once again, his strokes slow, tender and utterly delicious. I melted into the kiss. I couldn't help it. It was a meltworthy exchange.

After what seemed like a lifetime in pash-paradise, he pulled away. 'Was that better?'

'No. You need so much more practise,' I slurred, still in a euphoric state.

'Well, that being the case, our date is now Friday night.'

'I'm busy,' I lied, breathing heavily as I stared into eyes that were the sky's mirror.

'Carly,' he said in a stern voice. 'I'm fucking taking you out this Friday night and putting my mouth to further use. Don't argue with me.'

I didn't argue. How could I?

* * *

Friday came round rather quickly, and I soon found myself trying to come up with an excuse to cancel. 'What if I told him I had perma-crabs?' I explained to Lib.

'Perma-crabs? What's that?' she asked, her tone and lack of interest in what I was saying clear from her decision not to make eye contact with me. Lib was completely engrossed in my *Shop Til You Drop* magazine, both she and Sasha comfortably splayed across my bed.

Standing in front of my full-length mirror, I frustratedly adjusted my black leather skirt which came to mid-thigh. 'A permanent case of crabs.'

Lib lifted her head with a dumbfounded expression. 'You are such an idiot. And you are your own worst enemy, you know.' She returned her gaze back to the magazine and flipped the page angrily.

Sighing, I sat on the bed next to her. 'I'm getting those,' I said sulkily as I pointed to a pair of Iron Fist heels. 'I ordered them yesterday.'

She smiled, but didn't look up at me. 'They are hot! They'll suit you.'

'Hmm,' I mumbled, as I twisted a ring on my finger.

Libby closed the magazine and gave me her full attention. 'Okay, Carls, what's wrong?'

'Nothing.'

'Don't lie. You're not very good at it.'

'I'm not lying.'

'You are the queen of equivocation.'

'Don't use your namby-pamby teacher vocab on me.'

'Look,' Lib said with an aggravated sigh, 'you can either tell me what's wrong and get it off your chest in the hope I can help, or you can continue to sulk and wallow in your own pathetic self-pity. It's your call.'

Dramatically flopping onto the bed, I was ambushed by Sasha as she seized the opportunity to lick my ear. 'Sasha! Stop it.' I pushed her back to a safe distance and scratched her belly in order to keep her wayward tongue at bay.

'So now you're going to use evasion tactics are you, and not answer my question?' Libby asked.

'I'm not deliberately trying to evade your question. I don't know what's wrong.'

'You're sceptical about Derek. Why? He seemed nice enough.'

'I never said I was sceptical.'

'Queen of equivocation, enough said,' Libby stated smugly as she rested her head in her hands.

A frustrated groan escaped my mouth. 'I like him, all right.'

'Aaand ... you didn't like any of the copious other men you have dated?'

Sitting up again, I shot her a distasteful glare. 'You make me sound like a whore. I'm not a whore, Lib. I'm just not fond of tying myself down to someone.'

'So what's different? Who said you have to tie yourself down to the firefighter?'

'No one. I don't.'

'So what's the problem then?'

'He's different.'

'How?' Lib was firing questions at me left, right and centre, backing me into that proverbial corner that no one wanted to be in.

'He gives me heart palpitations, all right? I lose my sense of control when I'm around him. I don't like it.'

She rolled onto her side and smiled emphatically. 'Carly has a big girl crush.'

'So.'

'So, it's good. First there's a crush, then comes love,' she said before laughing and continuing, 'then comes marriage. Then comes a baby in a baby carriage,' Libby sang, replicating the young girls in the yard at school.

'Ha ha, you're so funny,' I spat sarcastically, huffing as I stood up. 'You suck. Now get out, so I can finish getting ready.

She laughed and hummed the stupid taunting tune as she exited my room.

* * *

I spent the next hour conducting my own inner personal call to arms. The mission: reiterate that I was thirty-five, mature and not in the least bit like a school girl with a crush. Yes, I was unequivocally attracted to Derek. And yes, he kind of made me weak at the knees, but that was it. I was now of the mindset that he was just simply fucking sexy on an epic scale. And it was that total sex appeal that wreaked havoc upon my usual demonstrative self. I was going to have fun with him like I had with all the other guys I dated. He. Was. No. Different.

Pinning the final tendril of loose hair to the top of my head, I assessed myself in the mirror as I mentally repeated that mission to myself, hoping the repetition would actually have me believing it. My white Wayne Cooper tail blouse sat effortlessly over my black leather skirt. And my eyes, as per usual, were a seductive smoky grey. As I pulled on my black patent five-inch heels, there was a knock at the door.

'I'll get it!' I shouted to Lib who probably had no plans of lifting her arse from the couch anyway.

I quickly shuffled along the hallway and past the lounge when Lib let out a long whistle. Halting in my tracks, I back-stepped until I was standing at the doorway. 'Behave,' I warned.

'Since when do I not?'

'You have your moments,' I reminded her.

A knock sounded again.

'You'd better get that,' she chorused in a provocative singsong voice.

Stomping out of the room like a toddler, I made my way to the front door and yanked it open. 'Hi —'

Sweet mother of twat tingles. The gush of air from the door's movement, or his aftershave or the sexual magnetic field that was radiating from his body, nearly had me stumbling backward. The man before me screamed intense eroticism.

Derek was standing on the front doorstep wearing a white shirt and black jeans, a pair of mirrored aviators a seductive screen for his eyes. 'Hey,' he said with an upward nod.

Mouth, tongue, vocal cords, teeth ... for fuck's sake, work in unison, please! I tried to speak, to say the simple word he greeted me with in return, but I failed on all counts. I could only comprehend that he reminded me of Maverick from *Top Gun*.

The sound of skittering paws on hardwood flooring broke my Kenny Loggins head-karaoke.

Spinning around to where the approaching noise was coming from, I spotted Sasha barrelling toward us. 'Oh, no! Sasha, no, stop!' I yelled, finally finding my voice.

Sasha did what Sasha always did when the front door to Libby's and my house opened — she jumped on whoever walked through it.

I couldn't stop her. It was either put myself in between her and Derek and ruin my outfit, or let her clean him up.

I opted for the latter.

'Look out!' I screeched.

Sasha launched herself at Derek and, to my surprise, he caught her quite happily.

'Whoa! Who's this?' he laughed as she tried to lick his face.

'This is my golden retriever, Sasha. I'm so sorry.'

Looping my fingers around her collar, I guided her back to ground level with Derek's help, then awkwardly led her down the hallway and out the back door. 'Naughty girl, Sasha. No Schmackos for you. Did you hear that, Lib?' I shouted. 'No Schmackos for Sasha.'

'Whatever,' Libby called back.

Sliding the back door closed, I turned around to find Derek a mere metre away from me, aviators now hanging from the dip of his shirt.

'I must admit that when I planned for a cute blonde to jump me and lick my face, I was expecting it to be you.'

I swallowed, then, remembering my pep talk from earlier, sucked in a confident breath and stepped up against him, pushing my breasts into his chest. 'The night is still young.'

CHAPTER

10

Derek pierced me with wanting eyes, a renewed sense of challenge sparkling from them. I tilted my chin up and invited his kiss with the slight opening of my mouth. Before he lowered his lips to mine, he smiled ever so slightly, that gesture enough to weaken my knees.

I slumped into him, grabbed the collar of his shirt with both my hands and wrenched him forward, confidence growing within me as we explored each other's mouths with our tongues. *Fuck, he tastes good, even minus the mint sauce.*

His ability to make just a simple kiss an exquisite experience both excited and worried me. I could indulge in his kiss and get lost for days.

Suddenly distracted by Sasha's barking and continuous scratching of the glass door, I broke free from Derek and glared at her. *Sasha, you little pussy blocker.*

'She needs training,' he said with a nod toward my insolent puppy.

'I know,' I groaned. 'I've been lazy and just never arranged it. I should really look into it though.'

He turned back to face me with a knowing smile. 'Yeah, that might be a good idea. I know someone, if it helps.'

I shrugged my shoulders; 'Sure.' Although I didn't want to owe him any favours.

Wanting to change the subject, I wriggled out of his arms and walked to the kitchen bench where my purse sat. 'So where are you taking me?'

'Dinner and movies,' he said with a waggle of his eyebrows. Then he led me from the room.

* * *

When Derek advised that we were going to 'dinner and movies', I half expected a ritzy Michelin-starred restaurant and a gold class cinema experience. What I didn't expect, though, was TGI Friday's and the local movie theatre.

'Have you ever had the Jack Daniels steak?' he asked excitedly while rubbing his hands together after we were seated.

I smiled at his cuteness. 'No.'

'Don't tell me you are one of those salad and water type girls,' he added, a hint of aloofness in his tone.

Picking up my menu, I began to scan the choices. 'There's a salad and water type of girl?' I questioned, pretending to be curious. I knew what he was insinuating.

He nodded. 'Yes.'

'And you have a problem with that "type" of girl,' I asked, emphasising the *type* bit and raising my eyebrows accusingly.

He held up his hands in surrender. 'Hey, don't get me wrong. I'm all for watching what you eat and looking after yourself, but avoiding one of life's pleasures and not tasting great food for fear of gaining a little weight, to me, is lame.'

'Hmm ...' I mumbled still reading my menu, not giving away my thoughts on the topic. I wanted to make him fret.

'What does hmm mean?'

'Um ... I think it's contemplation,' I answered, keeping my eyes on the menu and desperately trying not to laugh.

When the only thing that ensued was silence, I couldn't help myself and looked up, finding sex-on-a-stick harbouring a stubborn scowl. 'It means I completely agree with you ... to an extent,' I laughed.

'To an extent —' he asked with a puzzled expression.

'Are you ready to order?' a waitress asked, interrupting with a smile that didn't quite hide her desire to go home.

Derek looked to me as if to ask if I was, in fact, ready. I smiled and indicated that he go first. 'Gentlemen before ladies,' I said under my breath.

He coughed and then looked toward the waitress. 'Sure, I'll have the Jack Daniels steak, medium rare, and a pot of VB, thanks.'

The waitress jotted it down on her pad then turned to me.

'And I'll have the Jack Daniels burger and a Corona, thanks,' I replied, snapping my menu shut and handing it to her.

'You sure you can eat all that?' Derek asked, his tone lacking confidence.

I can eat a fucking cow mounted on a horse and covered in mint sauce. And even then I'd want dessert. 'On second thoughts,' I said to the waitress, but keeping my eyes fixed solely on Derek, 'I'll have the Ultimate Jack Daniels burger, thanks.'

'Not a problem,' the waitress sniggered, then walked away.

'If you're trying to impress me, Carly, I'm flattered. But you don't need to. I'm already extremely impressed,' he advised, his eyes raking over the parts of my body he could see.

'You are such a cocky fucker. I'm not trying to impress you one bit. I've told you this before and I'll say it again, this is me. Take me or leave me. End of.'

'Oh, I'll take you all right,' he said, leaning forward across the table. 'And when I do, your body won't function for days afterward. Every sensation you feel from then on in will remind you of what I did, how I did it and how much you fucking loved it.'

I forced myself to swallow and felt my nipples tingle in response to his promise. My Carly-cave also clenched and burned with need. *Extinguish. Extinguish my fiery hole, goddamn it.*

'Well, senior firefighter King, you have just set the bar very high. Don't let me down.'

He sat back in his chair and crossed his arms over his chest, an expression of pure satisfaction rolling from him. 'I won't.'

'Here you go,' the waitress said as she placed our drinks down. 'Your meals won't be much longer.'

We both nodded our thanks.

'So, what movie do you want to see?' Derek asked as he swigged his beer.

Shit! I don't know. I don't do scary movies where things jump out at you. I can't handle that crap. 'Um ... I'm really not fussed. You pick,' I smiled, hoping for a miracle that he loved romantic comedy.

* * *

Why the fuck did I tell him he could choose the movie? I mean seriously, how stupid could I be? After both thoroughly enjoying our TGI Friday's dinner, and after proving that I was not a 'salad and water' type of girl, we headed to the movies. Derek had chosen *Species of the Night* and so far I had witnessed crazy motherfuckers hiding in the back seat of unsuspecting victims' cars, along with them springing up out of nowhere on deserted roads in the middle of the night. Oh, and don't get me started on the fucking cats that would jump out from behind doors, behind sofas and within the confines of a closet.

My stomach was beyond knotted ... it was twisting and churning, and I was on the verge of either vomiting or passing out.

'You all right?' he asked curiously while offering me some popcorn.

I shook my head at his offering then bit my lip. 'Uh huh.'

'You don't look it,' he mumbled through a mouthful.

'I'm fine,' I choked out. *So not fine. So. Not. Fine.*

'Carly, you're as white as a ghost.'

Closing my eyes, I breathed in deeply through my nose and let out my confession. 'I don't like scary movies. I don't do creepy shit. It terrifies me.'

'Jesus!' he whispered. 'Why didn't you say something?' Derek put the popcorn down and turned toward me.

I shut my eyes, finally blocking out the giant screen in front of me. It helped. 'Because I wanted you to see the movie that you wanted to see.'

'You're so fucking adorable, you know that?' he said, his breath caressing my cheek. His sudden closeness startled me, prompting me to open my eyes. 'Keep them closed, baby. I know something that will help distract you.'

The fact he called me baby — which I was beginning to like — together with what he planned on doing to distract me, made me gasp. My chest began to rise and fall rapidly and, as I waited for him to do something, I pressed my lips together quite hard with anticipation.

Suddenly, I felt Derek's hand gently caress the skin of my leg just above my knee. His touch on that spot made me flinch.

'Sh ...' he whispered, 'just keep them closed.'

'What, my eyes or my legs?' I breathed out, opening my eyes and closing my legs. I turned my head from side to side in order to see if anyone was watching. They

weren't and, thankfully, we had no other people sharing the same row of seats, nor was there anyone directly
behind or in front of us. In the scheme of things, our
position was somewhat private.

'Baby, close your eyes and open your legs,' Derek
instructed, this time with a firmer tone.

I turned to face him and noticed him adjust the prominent hard-on within his jeans. The sight had me biting
my lower lip.

He darted forward and sucked my lip into his mouth
while forcing my legs apart with his hand. 'Open your
legs and close your eyes,' he repeated with a slight mum-
ble before releasing my lip and kissing my eyelids, the
action forcing them closed.

Oh, shit!

Hesitantly, I complied and relaxed my legs while
tightly squeezing my eyes shut.

Derek's hand began to move up my thigh in a tor-
tuously slow motion. 'Relax,' he murmured. *Relax?* You
fucking relax. 'Are you wearing underwear?' he murmured again.

'Of course I am,' I chided quietly. 'Who the fuck
doesn't wear underwear to the movies?'

He chuckled. 'Me.'

'What? Are you serious?'

His hot breath filtered into my ear. 'I'm always serious.'
Fuck me, he's commando! Commando Caramello Koala.

The thought of his cock pressing hard against the
denim of his jeans made me groan ever so slightly. I
wanted to touch it. I wanted to feel the silky skin of his

shaft glide along the palm of my hand as I pumped him. I wanted to see the head of his cock glisten with desire. I wanted HIM.

'Your nipples are hard,' he stated quietly before pressing his mouth against my blouse. The material of my bra was only thin, which meant I could feel the warmth and moisture from his tongue as he sucked at my breast.

'Oh, god!' I moaned, arching into him.

He bit me gently then pulled away, which was when I noticed that his hand had found the seam of my underwear. Slowly, he slid his finger underneath and gently stroked the sensitive skin around my clit. My jaw fell open.

'Jesus fucking Christ, you shave,' he groaned against my neck.

'Yes,' I panted, 'I don't like vajungles.'

Derek let out a loud laugh which prompted me to open my eyes. 'What?'

He shook his head with amusement and then kissed me passionately. As his tongue fondled my own, his finger twitched fervently. The quick flick against my clit had me closing my eyes and dropping my head back on the seat once again.

'Your pussy feels amazing, Carly. I can't wait to have it on my face and surrounding my cock,' he whispered as he slid two fingers inside me.

Words, sounds, anything coherent escaped me in that moment. I was completely overcome with the sensation he was gifting me. And it was a gift. What we were doing in the cinema was by far one of the most rewarding sexual experiences I'd had. And I was certainly no prude.

Slowly, he slid his fingers out, then back in. Out, then back in. I couldn't help myself and rocked against his hand.

'Fuck,' he ground out. 'Come on me, baby.'

'No,' I protested with as much enthusiasm as a wet sponge.

He nipped at the skin of my neck then said with a harsh rasp, 'You're not going to get a choice.'

His sliding motion increased in pace while his thumb rubbed against my clit. The pressure he applied was perfect. Not hard and not pansy-soft either.

As he rubbed and probed insistently, my head flushed with heat and the muscles in my lower abdomen and inner thighs contracted. The sensational tingling intensified, and I had to raise my hips from the seat and dig my nails into the armrests as my orgasm washed over me.

Opening my mouth, I breathed in and out ardently, trying to regain my composure. Derek's mouth gently grazed my collarbone before he dragged his lips higher and whispered in my ear. 'You fucking rock.'

I let out a laugh of relief and opened my eyes, blinking to regain my vision. As I began to decipher my surroundings once again, Derek dragged his finger from within my pussy and placed it in his mouth.

I smiled. 'No. You fucking rock.'

* * *

We never watched the end of the film, instead kissing in the darkness of the movie theatre as if we were a couple of horny teenagers. It was strangely sweet.

Soon after, Derek drove me home where we continued to taste one another's mouths on my front doorstep.

'So,' I purred coyly, but with a hint of sexy innuendo, 'do you want to come in?'

'I want to come in *you*,' he mumbled as his lips teased my neck and ear lobe.

The state of bliss that he cast upon me was both good and bad, bad being the words that had a tendency to uncontrollably tumble out of my mouth. 'I want you to douse my fiery hol—' I heard myself begin to say when the front door was wrenched opened behind us.

'I've been trying to ring you for the past twenty minutes,' Libby said desperately.

'Oh, sorry,' I responded, a little stunned. 'My phone must still be on silent from when we were in the cinema.'

Taking in her distraught face, my stomach began to butterfly. 'Why, what's wrong?'

'It's Sasha. Something's not right,' she replied, a little panicked.

'What?' I pulled myself free of Derek and pushed past Libby. 'Where? Where is she?'

'She's in the lounge room,' Lib called out, following behind me, Derek close behind her.

As I turned the corner, my heart constricted when I spotted Sasha lying on her stomach on the floor. She stood up when she saw me, and straightaway I noticed her twitching.

'Sashy, what's wrong, sweetie?' I said as I dropped to my knees and patted her head. She was frothing at the mouth and clearly distressed.

Derek squatted down beside me and placed his hands on either side of Sasha's face. He then scooped her into his arms. 'I'd say she's ingested something. She needs a vet. Now! Carly, reach into my back pocket and take out my phone,' he said as he stood up.

I did and then followed him. 'Where are we going? What are you doing?' I asked in a panic, tears welling in my eyes.

'Activate the phone. We're taking her to the vet. Elizabeth, what has she eaten?' he asked Lib as we hurried down the hallway.

'She didn't eat her dinner after I took her for a walk,' Libby explained. 'So nothing.'

I swiped the screen on Derek's phone. 'What's your password?'

'Sixty-nine, sixty-nine.'

If I weren't scared out of my mind, I would've rolled my eyes at him.

'Go to contacts and find Layla,' he instructed. 'What about during the walk? Did she eat anything then?' he continued to ask Lib.

Before I knew it, we were outside, standing next to his Ranger.

'I ... I ... I don't know,' Libby stuttered. 'She was fine. I'm sorry, Carly. I was just about to call the vet when —'

'Not now, Lib. It's fine,' I said, my tone unintentionally clipped.

Although having difficulty seeing from the tears welling in my eyes, I scrolled down his list of contacts until I found Layla. 'Okay, I've found her, Derek.'

'Dial her number and press speaker,' he instructed.

I did as I was told and climbed into the front seat of his car, holding the phone in the air for him to speak. He placed Sasha on my lap as the call connected.

'Derek, long time no hear. To what do I owe the pleasure?' a woman's voice sounded from the speaker of his phone.

He took it from my hand. 'Layla, I need a favour,' he said loudly. 'Can you open up the surgery for an emergency, please?'

'Um ... yeah. What's the problem?' she asked.

'I'm bringing in a ...' he paused, 'a friend's golden retriever pup. I think she's eaten poison. Quite possibly snail pellets or rodent poison.' He leaned forward and wiped a tear from my cheek then closed the door.

Looking down at Sasha, I took note of her body violently twitching. Her breathing was frantic, and I could no longer hold myself together. 'It's okay, baby girl. What did you eat? This is all because I said no Schmackos, isn't it?'

My trembling hand gently caressed her fur. She looked so ... so hyperactive yet scared.

Derek opened the driver's side door and hoisted himself into the seat. 'She's meeting us there. The veterinary surgery is only twenty minutes away.'

I nodded and looked back down at Sasha, blocking out everything around me. It was just me and her.

* * *

We pulled up to the veterinary clinic. Derek quickly made his way around the front of the car, opened my door, and then lifted Sasha into his arms. I climbed out of the car and took his keys which were dangling from his finger, and then locked the car door before both of us raced up the ramp.

'Press the button on the wall, Carly,' he said, pointing to a red knob with his head.

I quickly slammed my hand into it which then inevitably sounded an alarm tone.

A petite mousey-brown brunette rushed toward the glass door. 'Hey, what do we have here?' she asked, looking from Sasha to Derek to me.

I stumbled on my words at first. 'Um ... this is my eight-month-old golden retriever, Sasha. We came home and she was like this.'

Layla assessed Sasha from within Derek's arms. 'Did she eat snail pellets?'

'I don't know. My room-mate took her for a walk and said that not long after they returned home, she started twitching and drooling.'

'Okay, let's get some apomorphine into her to make her vomit. Follow me,' she said with a smile.

Why do they always smile? It doesn't bloody help. Clearly my dog is horribly ill. I'm not going to fucking smile.

Layla led Derek and I into a surgical room and then disappeared to get the apple morphine, or whatever the hell it was bloody called.

'Did you eat snail pellets, Sashy?' I asked, resting my head on hers.

Suddenly, I felt Derek's hand rub my back soothingly. 'She'll be all right, Carly.'

I didn't look up as tears formed in my eyes. 'How can you be sure? You can't.'

He stepped closer, put his arm around my shoulder, and pulled me into him, all the while patting Sasha. 'No, but there's nothing wrong with being positive.'

'All right,' Layla announced clearly as she entered the room again, 'I'm going to inject Sasha with this medicine which will make her vomit and remove the toxin from her stomach, okay?'

I nodded.

'Now hold her head, because it will sting a little and she may want to get away from me.'

Doing as instructed, I wrapped my arms around Sasha's head as if I was giving her a cuddle. She whined a little, but then sparked up with even more excitement as soon as the injection was done. She was kind of a little crazy.

'Okay, let's just clip this leash to her collar and take her outside. The medicine should make her sick soon enough.'

Layla led Sasha out to the courtyard behind the clinic with me and Derek in tow. 'And now we wait,' she explained with an apologetic smile while still holding onto Sasha's leash.

'What if it's not snail pellets?' I asked, concerned.

'I'm fairly sure it is ... I'm sorry, I didn't get your name before?' Layla asked with an inquisitive look.

'Carly. My name is Carly.'

'Sorry, Carly. I'm fairly sure it's metaldehyde poisoning which is the lethal toxin in snail pellets. Sasha's symptoms are a clear indication of it.'

'Oh, okay ... and this will make her vomit it up and she'll be fine?'

'This will force her to empty her stomach, yes. But we will also give her activated charcoal, orally, which will bind any excess toxins she has already digested so that she can pass it in the form of a stool.'

I nodded again and carefully watched Sasha. She was beginning to whine more obviously now.

'So, Derek,' Layla said from her squatted position next to Sasha, 'how have you been?' She gave him a look that made me feel there was a hidden question behind it. I got the sense they knew each other well.

'I've been great, thanks. And you?' he answered, while clicking his jaw from side to side.

I may not have known Derek for long, but in the short time I have known him, I'd figured out that when he was aggravated he would perform this movement.

'Things are good. We miss you, you know,' she said sadly. *I knew it!*

All of a sudden, you could cut the air with a knife. No one seemed to want to break the silence that ensued, except for Sasha, who began retching over and over until she finally threw up.

Layla inspected the vomit and stood up quickly, stretching as she went. 'Yep, snail pellets.'

To me, the pile of sick looked like brown mush. *Yuck! I'll take her word for it.*

* * *

Sasha vomited a few more times, then was given the charcoal substance. She was definitely *not* a fan of that stuff and shook her head violently, flicking some of the residue on Derek, Layla and I.

Layla had looked at my blouse sympathetically, informing me it would more than likely stain. I figured that at some point I would mourn my desecrated top, but for now I was just happy that Sasha was okay.

Before we left the clinic, I thanked Layla profusely for not only curing Sasha, but for taking time out from her personal life and rushing to the rescue. She said it was her job, but I sensed it was more to do with Derek, which she kind of confirmed when she said goodbye to him and touched his cheek.

Seeing that intimate gesture made me feel ill, although I was pretty sure my feeling sickly was more to do with the drama of the night. Derek's past girlfriends were none of my business.

* * *

When we returned to the house, Lib came rushing out to the car. She was clearly distraught over what had happened, and even had the remnants of a cry-sesh.

'What happened? Is Sasha okay?' she asked as she opened the passenger side door of Derek's car.

By that stage, Sasha had almost returned to her vibrant, mischievous self — almost.

'She's fine, but when you took her for a walk she must have eaten snail pellets at some point.'

Lib shrugged her shoulders regretfully and put both her hands on either side of Sasha's face. 'I honestly can't say that I saw her do it. The only possible time she might've eaten them was when she stuck her head in Mrs Robins' garden for a sniff around.'

'That was probably it,' I sighed and passed Sasha's leash to Lib.

Sasha jumped from my lap and Lib happily took her inside.

By that stage, Derek had exited the car and was by my door as I slid out of my seat.

Turning back around to snatch up my purse, I noticed the mess of dog hair Sasha had left behind. 'Oh my god, Derek, I'm so sorry. What a mess.'

I leaned into the car and began scooping up the hair; the fact of the matter is I'd need a freakin' vacuum.

'Carly,' he said as he leaned over me and placed his hand on mine to stop its movement. 'Leave it. I'll get it cleaned tomorrow. Come on, it's late. You have had a shit of a night. Let's go inside.'

He was right. Our night had turned into an emotional mess.

Dropping my head against his shoulder, I sighed with exhaustion. 'I'm sorry our date was ruined.'

He chuckled lightly and kissed the top of my head. 'Baby, I got to feel you, taste you and see your vulnerable side. Our date was anything but ruined.'

OMG! This man is going to crush my heart.

CHAPTER
11

Derek didn't stay long after we'd gone back inside. He'd been terribly sweet, making sure both Sasha and I — and even Lib — were all right. He'd left me with a kiss that I still felt on my lips even as my head hit the pillow. But as my head did hit the pillow, I couldn't stop myself from wondering who Layla really was and what she had meant to Derek.

Those thoughts still plagued my mind the following day as I made myself breakfast: a choc peanut butter Pop-Tart. *Yum!*

'Why aren't you the size of an African elephant?' Libby asked as she spooned her muesli into her mouth.

I shrugged my shoulders and drank some milk. 'Because I was blessed with the ability to put many things in my mouth and not worry about the consequences,' I mumbled with a smug grin as I swallowed my mouthful.

Libby raised an eyebrow sceptically. 'Yeah, well, some things have a tendency to catch up to us. Roles can reverse.'

'You need a penis in your vagina,' I said with assurance as I placed my plate in the sink.

She tutted and returned to her cereal. 'Sex is not the answer to everything, Carly.'

Turning around to face her, I placed my hands on top of the bench. 'Yes, it is.'

'No, it's not. It doesn't answer unanswered questions.'

'What questions are you trying to answer, Lib? Sex is sex. You open your legs and enjoy yourself. Why does it have to be more complicated than that?'

'Obviously, you don't appreciate the act of lovemaking,' she retorted.

'Oh, I appreciate it all right. I appreciate it right down to the point where I'm screaming a name and digging my fingers into something,' I slurred, pretending to have inner visions of doing just that.

She placed her spoon in the bowl and put on her ace-card face. 'Okay, tell me something. Have you ever had sex with someone you have been in love with?'

I smiled at her attempt to sway me toward her side of the argument. 'No.'

'Then I rest my case. When you have, we'll revisit this discussion,' she said conceitedly.

'Whatevs,' I responded unperturbed. 'See you later. I'm off to have coffee with Lexi.'

Grabbing my purse, I headed out the door, hiding the fact that I was now curious about the different acts of sex. *Surely there isn't that big a difference?*

* * *

When I'd arranged to catch up with Alexis, she'd asked to meet at Gloria Jean's. Why? I'll never bloody know. She lived at the most prestigious hotel complex in Melbourne and was happily screwing the owner's brains out. He was, in turn, quite happy to give her whatever she wanted. If she wanted her own private high tea in a ritzy suite, she could have it. But instead, she chose to sit in Gloria Jean's with everyone else in the damn place. She was nuts!

When I walked into the coffee shop, I found her sitting on a couch in the far corner of the cafe, her leg propped up on a seat. She was flicking through her phone when she looked up and noticed me.

'Hi,' she greeted and went to stand up.

'Hey, sit your arse down. I don't want you falling and breaking your other leg,' I teased as I gave her a quick peck on the cheek.

She grumbled. 'I'm not an invalid.'

'You sure 'bout that?' I goaded.

Narrowing her eyes at me, she picked up her hot white chocolate. 'Fuck you.'

'I see you didn't wait to order,' I said playfully. *I probably wouldn't have either.* 'Give me a sec and I'll organise my coffee.'

'I've already done it for you,' she explained as she nodded to the perky blonde barista.

Relief flooded me as I took in her happy aura. To be completely honest, I wasn't sure what to expect where her temperament was concerned. On the phone, when I told her I wanted to see her and that she'd had enough time to herself, she sounded fine. But with everything she had been through, I just couldn't be sure. I didn't know whether to metaphorically tiptoe on eggshells or interact like we usually did. So to find her — for the most part — appearing her usual self, was such a relief.

Sitting down, I took hold of both her hands. 'So, how are you, truthfully? No fucking lies or pretences. This is *you* and *me*. I want to know it straight up.'

'Carls, I'm fine. Life moves on. Will my heart forever be incomplete? Yes. That cannot and will not change. Nobody can bring my baby back and, because of that, I will forever mourn my loss. But I will do it in a healthy manner. I'd rather focus on what makes me happy, rather than what makes me sad.'

'I don't know how you do it,' I said quietly, trying not to choke on my words.

She laughed mildly. 'I could say neither do I, but I've come to realise that we just simply ... do. We do all we can do. It's basic survival.'

'Yeah, well some people survive better than others,' I added, as the barista placed my coffee before me.

'Thank you, Stacey,' Alexis said politely.

The young blonde smiled. 'You're welcome, Ms Summers.'

As I watched her return to her duties, I gave Lexi a cocky grin. 'You're a fucking socialite, you know that?'

'Bite me, bitch. Okay, change of subject, hmm. How about Derek?'

'What about him?' I bit out, harshly. *Shit! What has he told her? And why would he tell her? Unless he told Bryce and Bryce told her.*

'Geez! Settle, petal. I was just going to ask you what happened at my birthday party. The two of you seemed to spend a lot of the night together. You appeared to hit it off.'

Phew. 'Yes and no,' I said dismissively, inwardly sighing with relief.

'That's not what it looked like to me. It looked as if your fiery hole would see his extinguisher.' Alexis pursed her lips together to try and prevent an outburst of laughter.

'Sorry to burst your perverted bubble, but there's nothing to say,' I explained flippantly, deciding that playing none-the-wiser was my best option at this point. If possible I did not want Alexis knowing about Derek and me, whatever Derek and I were. Hell, I didn't even know what we were.

'Come on. There's got to be *something* to say,' she probed, her face glowing with mischief.

I couldn't help smiling, it was so nice to see her happy and being ... well ... Lexi. 'He fucking sang to me.'

'What?' she squealed, nearly spilling her drink. 'When?'

'At the beginning of the night, shortly after you and Bryce left us. I'd made a stupid remark about his voice being to die for and Derek, being a bit of a smartarse, wanted to call my bluff. So he sang Bon fucking Jovi.'

'Oh my god! Really? How sweet.'

'Yeah, it definitely added to the heat already blazing in my snatch.'

Alexis laughed and nearly snorted her white chocolate. 'Only you, Carls. Only you.'

I gave her a wink. 'So, apart from hobbling around on those crutches, what else have you been doing?'

'To be honest, not a whole lot. I'm bored shitless. I've been having physiotherapy sessions, and every now and again I go for a short hobble around the precinct. Apart from that, I read. And I've been getting guitar —' she cut herself off and turned a nice shade of rose.

'You've been getting guitar what?' I asked curiously.

'I've been getting guitar solos played to me by Bryce,' she explained, her weird expression confusing me.

'Do you think he'd play a solo for me?' I asked teasingly.

She glared half-heartedly. 'No! Hey, changing the subject again, can I tell you something in confidence?'

'Of course, you know I'm tight-lipped.'

Alexis cracked up laughing, spraying her white chocolate over the table and me.

I was far from impressed as I slowly wiped it from my face while displaying an artificial smile.

'You ...?' she asked incredulously, still giggling. 'I don't know which set of your lips you are referring to, but both are far from tight-lipped.'

Biting the inside of my mouth, I gave her a don't-mess-with-me look.

She fired back a go-on-I-dare-you-to-deny-it look.

No more words were said about the issue.

'So, as I was saying, I have something to tell you that I need you to swear you won't repeat. It involves Bryce's cousin, Gareth.'

My eyes widened. 'Did he try to fuck you?'

'Carls! No! No, he's sick.'

'Sick as in ... bletch, puke? Or sick as in twisted motherfucker?'

'Neither. Sick as in mentally ill. He suffers from Dissociative Identity Disorder,' she whispered, looking around the cafe unobtrusively.

I leaned toward her and narrowed the space between us. 'As in multiple personalities?'

'Yeah, it's really quite sad. We went to the cemetery just the other day, as it was the anniversary of the accident that claimed the lives of Bryce's parents and brother. It was also the accident that resulted in Gareth's illness. Anyway, we went to the cemetery to pay our respects and the emotion of the visit triggered one of Gareth's alters to appear. Carls, it was so strange to interact with a man whose persona was that of an elderly woman.'

I sat back in my seat and drank the final mouthful of my coffee. 'Woman? Are you for real?'

'I'm serious, her name is Deirdre. He has another alter who I have met, his name is Scott. Scott can be a nasty piece of work though. I can't stand him. He sets off my alarm bells.'

Noticing her distressed appearance, which was rare for Lex, I touched her hand to gain her full attention. 'Why? What has he done?'

'He's threatened me many times. How can I put this?' she said as she took a deep breath and looked at our hands. 'He is in love with Bryce and sees me as a threat.'

Holy fucking dramaville.

I shook my head and went to speak but decided just to keep shaking my head instead. I was at a loss for words.

'I know. It's such a mammoth thing to fathom let alone be around. But I'm trying. I have to. He is a big part of Bryce and Lucy's lives,' she said sadly.

'Well, yes, but never ignore your gut instinct. If you are wary of him, always be on high alert. Our senses tell us things daily, we just don't always listen to them.'

Smiling, Alexis shifted her position, which I'm guessing was to make her leg more comfortable. 'When did you become all-wise and stuff?' she asked.

I shrugged. 'I don't know. I don't even know why or how that came out of my mouth,' I joked, when, in all seriousness, it was another thing my aunty had instilled in me before she died.

Lexi and I sat and chatted for a while longer, catching up on the minor details of each other's lives. It was hard not to tell her about Derek, but I'd managed to steer clear of any part of the conversation that would inevitably lead to letting the cat out of the bag.

Stretching, Lex proceeded to awkwardly stand up. 'Want to come up to the apartment? The kids will be back from Rick's soon.'

'Na, I can't. I've got some grocery shopping to do with Lib. I'm under strict orders not to try and skip it this time. Damn she's a ballbreaker. I'd hate to be dating her,' I explained, somewhat annoyed.

Lexi laughed as she hobbled out of the shop. 'Apart from lezzie love, you kind of already are.'

I wrinkled my nose. *Fuck, she has a point. Lib has me under her thumb. When the hell did that happen?*

'Okay. I guess I'll see you when I see you then,' Alexis said with a pouty face.

I gave her a tight squeeze. 'Like always, love you. Take care of yourself.'

She pulled away from me. 'I'm trying, and you too. Go and have sex or something. I'm guessing it has been a while because you haven't relayed any details.'

I groaned. 'Don't remind me.'

* * *

After I left Alexis, I quickly detoured past the City Towers lobby to tell Liam I'd probably found him a fuck buddy.

'Barbie! Great to see you again,' he said boldly as I approached his desk.

With a sassy and dramatic flick of my hair for affect, I then propped my head in my hands and rested my elbows on the counter. 'SpongeBob. How's it hangin'?'

Liam lowered his voice. 'That's all it does. Hang,' he sulked.

'Not for long, lover boy,' I said with excited enthusiasm.

He narrowed his eyes at me. 'What do you mean?

I scrolled through my phone until I found the details of Brooke's husband's brother. 'Carly has found you a new play-friend. His name is Jeremy and he's twenty-seven. Here are his details.' I handed my phone to Liam and watched his face stretch into curious amusement.

'Ooh, he has Facebook. I need a pic,' he said excitedly as he pulled out his phone and started transferring the information.

As Liam handed me back my phone, a young couple approached the desk. Stepping aside, I blew him a kiss and told him to let me know how it all went. He nodded quickly in response, then switched to his professional front office manner, just like a chameleon would change its appearance.

* * *

During my drive home, the Bluetooth in Suzi activated and answered my ringing phone. I loved my Suzi. She's an awesome car: sexy, smart, petite and red. Suzi was a vixen.

'Hello,' I answered, still bopping along to 'Undressed' by Kim Cesarion, which had now been muted due to the incoming call.

'Hey, gorgeous, been thinking 'bout me?' Derek asked, his voice filtering through Suzi's speakers and exciting every pore of my body.

My car rolled to a stop at a set of lights. 'Well, that depends, have you been thinking about me?' I asked, losing the battle not to smile.

'Constantly. I want your wet pussy on the tips of my fingers again,' he stated rather loudly, also informing the occupant of the car beside me, as both our car windows were down. I gave the middle-aged dude a proud smile.

Turning back to face my centre console, I rifled through it and dug out my packet of mints. 'Then, yes, I have been thinking about you,' I said smugly as I popped one into my mouth.

'And ...'

'And I would like to see if your tongue is as good as your fingers,' I answered, unfazed by the obvious eavesdropper next to me.

'All my body parts work in unison, baby,' he said with a husky tone that held promise of what he'd just said.

I swallowed heavily. 'I bet they do.'

Derek chuckled and the sound made me feel warm and fuzzy. *What the fuck? He freakin' laughed ... laughed. Carly, get a grip.*

'So, how's Sasha?' he asked.

The traffic light turned green, so I continued ahead. 'She was fine this morning, thank god. Again, thank you so much for what you did last night.'

'No sweat. Speaking of last night, I enjoyed our date. But I'm curious. Did I prove to you that I wasn't mucking around?'

I could hear the sincerity in his voice, but at the same time, a petite brunette named Layla disturbed my thoughts. Over the course of the night and morning thus far, I'd tried to deny the obvious. But a fool is made by ignorance and a refusal to acknowledge what is clearly in front of them; the evidence in this case being the blatant green-eyed monster I was morphing into.

'Maybe,' I said honestly.

'Maybe?' he asked, his tone slightly dumbfounded.

'Yes. I need more than one date for you to prove that you aren't only trying to get in my pants.'

'But I am trying to get in your pants,' he joked.

Sighing, I couldn't help, but smile. 'You know what I mean. I still don't know you, and you still don't know me.'

'What do you want to know?'

His forwardness caught me off-guard, and I stuttered, 'I ... I don't know.'

'Okay, how 'bout ... my name is Derek Ian King. I'm aptly nicknamed Dik because I have an enormous one and know how to use it. I *want* to use it with you.

'I'm thirty-six years of age, never married, never engaged. I extinguish fires, sing songs and play sports. I leave the toilet seat up and don't wash dishes. I snore, but will fuck you so goddamn hard that you will be unconscious from exhaustion and won't hear it. Anything else?' he asked with nonchalance as if that last piece of information didn't parch my mouth.

Realising that I just had to come out and say it, I closed my eyes for the briefest of seconds, then let it roll from my tongue. 'Are you seeing anyone else, because although I'm not seeking commitment, I won't be someone's side dish?'

'No, Carly,' he said with clear annoyance, 'I'm not seeing anyone else. Where'd that come from?'

'What about Layla?' I asked curiously.

'What about Layla?' he snapped.

The sudden angry tone in his voice warned me off. It was clear she represented a sore spot for him.

Screwing up my face in irritation over my stupid probing, I chose to let it go. 'Never mind.'

'What. About. Layla?' he repeated again, speaking each word slowly to enunciate the question he clearly wanted an answer to.

'It's nothing,' I dismissed. 'You just seemed close, like you shared a past. It was obvious she wanted you.'

'You don't know what you're talking about,' he advised, seeming frustrated.

Derek's blatant disregard for my justified curiosity pissed me off. 'You know what? You are right. I don't know, which is why I'm fucking asking in the first place. But seeing as you turn into a prick each time I ask a personal question, I can't help but get the impression you are either full of shit, or don't give a fat rat's arse as to whether we take this any further or not. So, Dik, I have to say that I agree with you. You certainly live up to your name.'

Pressing end on the LCD panel in my car, I disconnected the call and took a few deep breaths in order to calm my thumping heart. *Arsehole!*

'Undressed' instantly resumed playing through my speakers, and I mockingly laughed at the irony when, truth be told, laughing was the last thing I wanted to do.

Derek

'Fuck! Motherfucking fuck!' I cursed to my phone before throwing it on the pile of clothes on the floor by my locker. Sitting on the bench seat with nothing but my towel wrapped around my waist, I dropped my head in my hands and inwardly berated Carly. *Why the hell does she have to ask the wrong fucking questions?* The woman infuriated me, but at the exact same time managed to send my dick into a state of desperation. It, too, was desperate to feel the warmth of her pussy, like that of my fingers.

'Shit!' I cursed, realising I was too harsh with her. It wasn't like her observations were entirely false. Layla and I had known each other for quite some time.

'Fucking Layla,' I groaned as I took a deep breath.

'Is that her name?' Brad asked as he walked into the locker room, ready to start his shift just as mine was finishing. 'Nice, mate, real fucking nice piece of arse she is.'

'If you are referring to Carly from Yellow Bark Primary School, then no, her name is not Layla.'

'Hang on. You got two on the go? Fuck me,' he chuckled. 'What happened to a brother sharing?'

Brad turned his back to me and shoved his bag in his locker just as I stood up and opened mine, reaching in for my t-shirt.

'I haven't got two on the go, and after the phone call I just had I'll be lucky to have one,' I griped.

'Shame, the blonde was fucking hot. And those tits? Couldn't keep my eyes off them while you were keeping the kiddies busy.'

Hearing him talk about Carly in that way riled me, especially knowing he'd been staring at her tits. 'Carly,' I snapped at him. 'Her name is Carly, and I'm well aware of how hot she is.'

'So what happened?' he asked after closing the door to his locker.

'She asks too many fucking questions, that's what happened. Questions I don't want to answer.'

'Ahhh,' Brad said, drawing the word out. 'She one of those all-looks-no-brains types?'

I shook my head at him. Brad was a dick. He treated women like toys to fuck and then chuck. But out in the field, in amongst flames that licked your skin with a fierce burn, flames that wanted to incinerate you into nothing but a pile of dust, well ... I wouldn't want anyone else beside me. Brad might be an arsehole where chicks are concerned, but he is one of the best firefighters I've ever worked with.

'No, she's not that type. She's smart and quick and feisty as hell,' I answered, irritated that I was even having this discussion with him.

'Then what's wrong with her? Dead lay?' he asked as he unlaced his boots.

Stepping into my jeans, I didn't answer him while I pulled them on, not bothering with underwear. *Unnecessary items of clothing, anyway.*

'That's it, isn't it? Bad fucking lay. Such a shame, man, with a body like that she ought to know how to use it.'

'Brad, shut the fuck up,' I snapped, slamming my locker door closed before picking up my phone and dirty uniform. 'You don't know shit.'

'Easy! Dude, whatever it is that's up with this Carly has sure got you in a mood. Best you get that shit out of your head before next week. You don't want to head into training with pussy problems clouding your brain.'

Fuck, he's right. That was the last thing I needed. But trying to clear Carly out of my head was near impossible. She's a work of fucking art; the most beautiful thing I've ever seen.

That long blonde hair that I just want to wrap around my hand and fucking pull. If I'd been face to face with her during the spat we just had, I would've been hard pressed not to tug her pretty hair while nipping biting her wordy fucking tongue. And don't get me started on that tongue. *Fuck me.* That tongue of hers not only captured mine when we kissed, but it also captured every fucking nerve ending I possessed. Then there were her brilliant green eyes and smile, both of them working together like some kind of voodoo magic.

'I'm tellin' ya, Derek. Clear your head. You've four days to rid it of big-tits blondie —'

'Brad,' I sternly warned him, 'I'd be very careful what you say about Carly, because if I hear you mention her tits again, I'll knock you the fuck out.'

The dickhead doesn't even raise his head while he unlaces his other boot. 'Whatever. Just get your head clear,' he advised as he stood and made his way out of the room.

Hearing the door close behind him — and when I was alone once more — I fisted the locker door beside me. 'Argh!' I growled with a guttural roar. *What is it about her that has me so whipped?* Yeah, she was the hottest thing

I'd ever seen. And yeah, she had tits that could make a grown man give up beer just to breastfeed, but fuck ... she got me so easily wound up. She was feisty and mouthy. But she was also shy and sweet. *Sweet? Fuck ... the taste of her on my finger was sweeter than fucking sugar.*

I remembered back to the other night when I had her panting and coming apart on my hand at the movies. How terrified she was watching the movie, but then how quickly I was able to take that terror away with just the simple twitch and slide of my fingers. Seeing how she reacted so easily to my touch was an indescribable feeling. I've never had a woman comply so naturally.

Don't get me wrong, I've had my fair share of women unashamedly throw themselves at me. I've also had my fair share of women come apart on my hand, or underneath me. But not like that. Not like Carly had with her hard-peaked nipples pressing against her shirt, begging to be licked, sucked and bitten; not like Carly with her plump fuckable lips and hands so tense they were tearing into the arms of the cinema seat.

Just thinking about it has my dick dancing against the denim of my jeans. *What the hell do I do? I don't normally chase. I never have. I've never seen the point of it. Chasing means they are either too high maintenance, or just not that into you. Is Carly not that into me? No, she fucking is, I can tell. Is she high maintenance? Hell, yes.*

I chuckled to myself, thinking of Carly and her impeccable physique. *She looks high maintenance, but she's not. Not deep down.* It didn't bother her one iota that we went to TGI Friday's and to the local cinema; she didn't complain. She was also down to earth and fragile when Sasha was sick. *No, Carly is not high maintenance. She might pretend to be, but she's not.*

That's it! She's blooding bluffing. Well ... I call her bluff. I call her pretence to be hard, unfazed, controlled and dominant. It was obvious she used those attributes as a shield of protection from hurt and betrayal. But I could tell that underneath her hard exterior, there was a fragile woman in need of a man to take the place of that shield. A man who would protect her whether she wanted him to or not. A man who would step up and prove to her that she actually needed him. *Do I want to be that man?* 'Shit!' I mumbled as I shoved my clothes into my bag and pulled my runners on. I think I did. She had a vulnerability that I wanted to protect. Not to mention I could not get her out of my mind. The way she smiled so easily, even when trying not to. Her surrender when I push all the right buttons. She had a pull; a lure, hooking and towing me along. I wanted her like I'd never wanted a woman before. And that's just it ... she made me want. *Really* want.

Looking at my phone, I debated whether or not to call her back. I wanted to make it right again and explain who Layla was and what she meant to me, but then thought better of it. *No, Brad is right. I need to leave it go for a few days and clear my head.* Too much was at stake where the next few weeks were concerned.

Putting my phone in my pocket, I walked out through the garage and waved to the guys, before pulling my helmet over my head and starting my girl with a roar. As her engine purred invitingly, I kicked up the stand and took off. I needed air ... the open road. I needed a fucking breather.

CHAPTER
12

Standing in my kitchen with flour smeared upon my nose, I glanced around me and took in what could be described as my fridge and pantry having thrown up everywhere. The place was a mess; an abomination to say the least. Then again, it was a result of my hard work and effort where baking was concerned, so it pleased me all the same.

Happily applying that thinking in order to ignore the obvious disaster zone before me, I satisfactorily nudged the oven door shut with my hip. Tash, Lil, Jade, Steph, Jen and I were due to head over to Bryce's apartment later in the evening to surprise Alexis. He had called me during the week, explaining that Lexi had been a little sulky because she was sick of feeling useless. He'd also informed me that she didn't want to go out anywhere, because apparently her moon boot made her feel as though she should audition for a part in *Iron Man*.

Personally, I thought she was being a sooky sooky la la and could totally rock a sexy superheroine, moon boot and all.

As I was cleaning away the leftover ingredients from the best lemon-lime meringue cake to ever be produced — because I knew it was her absolute favourite cake — my thoughts drifted to Derek. Just the idea that I could bump into him in mere hours had me a little on edge. I hadn't seen him since our first and, as it so happened, last date. I also hadn't spoken to him after verbally biting his head off during our last phone call.

It had been six weeks since then. SIX WEEKS! And during those six weeks, I'd sulked, gotten angry and swept our entire fling under the rug. I'd even tried to take out my sexual frustration on a cute twenty-some-thing-year-old who I'd met at the local pub. Fortunately — and for the first time in my life — I'd abandoned that rebound fuck for lack of enthusiasm, in the end just not having been up to it.

A few days after that last horrid phone conversation with Derek, he had sent a text, saying sorry. He'd also explained that he was due to participate in some form of training program for a few weeks which would inevitably keep him tied up, but that I could call him. I didn't ... call him that is. I wanted to, but I didn't. In the end, I chose not to for fear that I had already grown far too attached to him. When all was said and done, I was too scared to deal with those particular feelings, but more so, what they obviously meant.

I'd been on one date with him, *one* date, and had almost turned into some kind of green-eyed monster. That just wasn't me. Carly Henkley was no Hulk.

The obvious signs that I had been losing control of my sense of independence, and the ability to live my life with my feelings undamaged, had been right in front of me. But because I was as stubborn as they come — and had sensed I felt something different where Derek was concerned — I chose to ignore those signs and ended up getting hurt anyway. When I thought back on the situation, I couldn't help but ask myself this: was what Derek and I shared solely attraction or quite possibly something more? Regardless, it didn't really matter. Derek and I are nothing, and six weeks without so much as a word to one another was a clear indication of that.

'Okay, whip four egg whites together, gradually adding one cup of caster sugar until thick, stiff and glossy,' I said to myself as I read the recipe out loud. You'd think that I'd know how to bake this cake with my eyes closed after the excessive number of times Lex and I have made it. But, like I've said before, cooking is not my forte; neither was paying attention while Lex did the actual baking.

'Carly! What did you do, have a food fight with yourself?' Libby screeched as she walked into the room.

Rolling my eyes at her over-dramatic assessment of the sight before her, I switched on the handheld mixer to whip the egg whites — and to drown out any further whining from her.

'Oh, please,' I shouted over the loud hum, 'it's not that bad.'

'Not that bad?' she questioned, her face expressing disbelief. 'Do you have cake batter in your eyes? Surely you have cake batter in your eyes?'

Wiping the back of my hand across said eyes, I gave her an enthusiastic smile. 'Nope.'

'I'm not cleaning up this mess,' she stated emphatically, while placing her bag down.

'I didn't ask you to,' I retorted.

Continuing to beat the mixture for a few minutes longer, I watched the clear gooey egg whites transform into white fluffy meringue and, still raising my voice loud enough for her to hear, I asked Libby what her plans were for the evening. 'So ... what ya doin' tonight? Want to come to Lexi's cheer-the-fuck-up party?'

'Her what?' Lib shouted.

I turned off the mixer, unplugged the detachable whisk beaters and offered one to Lib. She happily accepted and both of us stood there licking the meringue mixture as if we were a couple of kids.

'Her cheer-the-fuck-up party,' I mumbled as my tongue twisted in between the metal prongs. 'She's still hobbling around in her moon boot and needs some cheering up. She refuses to go out anywhere so we are bringing the party to her.'

'Ah ... good idea,' Lib mumbled back. 'I'd love to come, but it's Mum's birthday dinner tonight.'

'Bugger,' I slurred as my tongue twisted and turned.

Lib glanced around, visibly cringing at my mess. 'So what are you making?'

'Lemon-lime meringue cake, Lexi's favourite. It's that one food item that always makes her feel better.'

'Sounds yum,' Lib said with a smile, before indicating I hand over my well-licked beater. I obliged and passed it to her so that she could place them both in the sink. She then picked up the sponge and began to wipe the benchtop. *Whaa? Does she not realise she is doing what she said she wouldn't — cleaning up?* I decided not to make her aware of this particular fault in her genetic make-up.

'Lib,' I questioned hesitantly, but wanting the conversation to remain flowing in the hope that it would continue to distract her from thinking about her cleaning efforts, 'when was the last time you and I went out for drinks somewhere?'

She stopped her circular wiping motion and looked up at me. *Damn it. Don't stop cleaning.* 'Um ... I don't know. Why?'

'Because it's been a while,' I said quickly, hoping she would return to her wiping unawares. 'And, anyway, I think both you and I need to scope out some local talent.'

Libby turned around and rested her arse against the kitchen counter. 'You know what? I think you are right. I think I need to get out, get in amongst the crowd again.'

Okay, who is this person and what has she done with Lib?

Putting my hands into the oven gloves, I proceeded to pull the cake out from the oven.

'Mm ... smells good,' Lib purred.

It did smell good — *thank fuck* — but it didn't look good. *Shit! It has a dip. It's not supposed to have a fucking dip.*

Placing it down on the wire rack which sat atop the bench, I sighed with frustration. 'Why the change of heart? I thought you didn't like fishing for men.'

Libby looked down at her hands which were fiddling in front of her. 'Because I'm sick of waiting for Prince Charming to come find me. He's not doing a very good job of it.'

I tilted my head to the side and gave her a pouty sympathetic smile. 'Maybe he just needs a GPS.'

'Pfft, maybe, but either way, I'm sick of waiting. I'm going to be my own Prince Charm—'

'You're what? Are you turning lezzie?' I asked with amused playfulness.

'No! I'm going to find my own man. Where does it say that he has to find me? Oh, I know where ... in those stupid fairytale books I've been reading all my life. That's where.'

Libby was one of *those* girls. You know, the ones who love Disney princesses and the whole concept of being swept off your feet by a knight in shining armour and blah, blah, blah-bibbity blah. That notion always made me gag and shake my head with annoyance.

'Okay, tell me what's happened and where my roommate formerly known as The Libby Mermaid is?'

'She's gone,' she said resolutely as she rinsed the sponge in the sink ready to use for another wipe down.

'This has something to do with that self-help book you're reading, doesn't it?' I asked as I closely inspected my dippy cake.

Quickly turning her back to me, she opened the dishwasher door. 'It's not the book, Carls. I've just come to realise that life is not a fairytale, and that the man of my dreams is not out there searching for me.'

'Hmm ...' I contemplated, having known this concept all along. But hearing it from Lib was a little unnerving. I couldn't help but feel saddened for her, as though she had lost faith in the magic of life's possibilities, yet I didn't have that faith to begin with. *God, I'm such a hypocrite.*

'Hmm ... what?' she asked, as she started packing my dirty dishes away.

Feeling guilty, I just couldn't let her clean up any longer. She was clearly having one of those my-head-is-so-fucked-up days. 'Lib, sweetie, you're cleaning up my mess. Here, I'll do that,' I said with a smile as I took the dirty mixing bowl from her hands.

She snatched it back and smiled in return as if she was aware she had been cleaning up all along. 'I always clean your mess, Carly. What are friends for?'

Shaking my head at her, I reached into the drawer, found the spatula and began to spread the meringue mixture onto my depressed cake. 'We are going to find our men, Lib,' I told her with as much assurance as possible. 'And when we do, we will be in control.' I stood upright, as if to prepare for the speech of a lifetime and continued. 'Do you want to know why?'

She shrugged her shoulders and held back an unsure grin.

Pointing the spatula at her, I enlightened Lib with the most valuable piece of information a woman could be privy to. 'Because vaginas rule the world.'

* * *

Bryce had arranged for Danny — his chauffeur — to collect me and the other girls and drive us to the apartment in his limousine. All six of us were armed with a cheer-the-fuck-up item for Lexi: Tash, a copy of *Dirty Dancing* on DVD; Lil, a big bunch of brightly coloured roses; Jade, the board game Celebrity Head; Steph, her pedicure set; Jen, her Michael Jackson *Thriller* CD; and me with the best-disguised cake in the world.

'Oh no,' Steph gasped right before I pushed the buzzer to the apartment.

Jade touched her shoulder. 'What?'

'We forgot balloons.'

'Thank Christ for that,' Tash pointed out, a disgusted look upon her face.

Steph glared at her. 'We should have bought balloons. Every party needs balloons.'

'No, it fucking doesn't,' Tash reaffirmed as I pressed the button and stood back.

Moments later, Bryce opened the door, smiled and ushered us in. 'Ladies.'

'Nobody puts Alexis in the corner,' Tash dramatically stated as she presented Lex with the DVD and kissed her on the cheek.

'Wha—' Lexi stuttered, her mouth agape and eyes open wide.

Giggling, I approached my best friend of thirty-plus years, the look upon her face a beautiful sight. I loved moments like these when she was stunned stupid.

Wanting to quickly offload my cake-atastrophe, I plonked it in her hands and kissed her forehead before heading straight for Bryce, this little action now being one of my new favourite moves.

'Mr Clark, as always, it is a pleasure to see you,' I said before giving him a tight squeeze. My forwardness never seemed to bother him, or Lexi, for that matter.

As I squeezed Brycealicious, the rest of the girls filtered into the apartment and greeted Lex with their gifts.

'This is your official cheer-the-fuck-up-party, luv,' Lil announced to Alexis while handing her the bunch of roses. 'You didn't want to go out dancing, so we have come to you.'

Jen giggled and waved her Michael Jackson *Thriller* CD in the air.

'What? When? Who?' Alexis finally spoke, her three words clear and concise.

All of us pointed to Bryce who then strode toward Lexi and grabbed her face with his hands, directing his lips to hers. She fell into the kiss, heavily, greedily and completely mesmerised, so much so that her walking stick fell to the floor.

Holding out the hand which held my cake, she indicated that someone ought to take it from her. I did, which was when she put her newly-freed hand around Bryce's neck and threaded her fingers through his hair.

'Get a room,' Tash groaned.

'No, this is hot,' Steph replied.

'Where's the fucking popcorn?' Jade asked.

'I'm getting a drink,' Lil declared.

'I miss my husband,' Jen sighed.

'Fuck, I want to join in,' I added.

Both of them ignored us, totally engrossed in one another's arms. 'I love you so much,' Alexis whispered against Bryce's lips.

'The feeling is mutual, my love. Now have a great night. Relax, drink, drool over Patrick Swayze. Just this once though,' he smirked.

'Don't you worry, he's got nothing on you. I've seen you dance ... in next to nothing, remember?' Lexi playfully added, raising her eyebrow seductively at him. *Dance, in next to nothing? Why have I not been informed of this until now?*

'What. The. Fuck!' Steph screeched. 'He dances ... too? Alexis, I officially hate you. H.A.T.E. you.'

'I'll see you later,' Bryce said, giving her one last kiss before making his way to the door. 'Have fun, ladies.'

As I watched their interaction and then him leaving, I became aware of the many different emotions I was feeling. The pit of my stomach was churning with a strange sensation of grief and yet admiration. Quite frankly, my emotions were all over the place.

Jen encouragingly threaded her arm through Lexi's and led her to the lounge. 'Come on you. It's party time.'

We sat down and, not long afterward, dove straight into watching *Dirty Dancing* while eating the delicious tapas that Bryce had arranged from one of the restaurants at City Towers.

After the movie finished, Jade excitedly pulled out Celebrity Head. I, however, took the opportunity to prettify my toe digits with Steph's pedicure set. They needed a new coat of love.

'Alexis Elizabeth Summers, get your head out of cloud-Clark and pay attention,' Tash snapped.

'What? Sorry,' she apologised while adjusting her Celebrity Head headband and taking a swig of her gin. 'Is it my turn?'

'Yes!' we barked at her.

'Okay, geez! Um, am I male?'

'Sometimes I think you are,' Tash added sarcastically. I tried not to laugh.

Lexi retaliated by launching a cushion at her.

'Yes, Lex, you are a male,' Lil clarified.

'Am I fucking hot?'

'Yes,' Steph said resolutely.

Lil's jaw dropped and her eyes widened. 'Are you serious? No, Lex, he is not.'

I agreed with Lil, but didn't say anything, opting to return to concentrating on my nail polish skills. It was a fine art and deserved my complete attention.

'Yes, he is,' Steph corrected her. 'Don't tell me you wouldn't want that between your legs.'

'No, I wouldn't,' Lil responded flatly.

'You're a lesbian, aren't you? Admit it, I'm totally fine with it, Lil. I love lesbians.'

Alexis and I both laughed at Steph's ability to deliberately bait Lil, but Lil ignored the stab and picked up her beer bottle, wrapping her lips around it suggestively and taking a drink. 'So am I fucking hot or not?' Lex shouted over the top of the two of them.

Jade blew at her toes, which she'd just painted with polish. 'Debatable. Ask another question.'

'Am I an actor?'

'Yes. A very fucking good actor, in more ways than one,' Jen said, as a hint of anger crept across her face.

'Do I have a big cock?' Lex asked as she appeared to try and swallow her gin around a pending laugh.

'Yes,' Steph said, appearing to be daydreaming of his big cock.

Lil gagged. 'Bet you it's tiny.'

'His hands are huge. Enough said,' Steph scowled.

'That's a fucking myth,' Lil bit back.

'Alexis! Stop thinking about wrapping your lips around Bryce's man-rod,' Tash chastised, her hands dramatically placed on her hips.

'Why? It's a pretty good man-rod,' she giggled.

'How good is it?' Steph asked eagerly.

'Oh ... real good.'

I looked up to see Lex raise her eyebrows and open her mouth suggestively.

'I knew it. I knew you swallowed,' I piped up, pointing my nail polish brush at her.

'So do you. And again, for the record, you can stop telling me all about it,' she stated, trying to pretend she was offended. But I knew better.

'Well, yeah, of course I do. It's full of protein, you know,' I smiled devilishly.

Jen shivered, 'Na, yuck. I'd rather eat a friggin' egg.'

We all looked at Jen and burst into laughter.

'What?' she said defensively. 'I would. Hang on a minute, do you all swallow?'

What a stupid question. Doesn't everybody? The girls searched each other's eyes with sly smiles on their faces, no one giving anything away, except for Tash, her lips beginning to purse.

Lex pointed at her. 'Tash, you little whoreasaurus, you swallow too.'

Tash rolled her eyes. 'Alexis, how old are you?'

'About as old as you,' she drunk-giggled.

'Lexi, can you please pull yourself together and ask another fucking question or I'm quitting this stupid game,' Lil threatened.

'All right, all right. Have I been in a lot of blockbusters?'

'Yep,' we all answered.

'Well, if they are blockbusters, I'm guessing they are action movies.'

'Yep,' we all answered again.

Lexi seemed to ponder for a while before the light bulb in her head switched on. 'Will he "be back"?' she said in the most pathetic Austrian accent I had ever heard.

Steph rolled her eyes. 'Yes,' she groaned.

'Does he say, "It's not a tumour" really well?' Lex asked, again in her horrible Austrian accent.

Jen cracked up laughing. 'You suck.'

Happy-dancing and bum-wiggling in her seat, Lexi beamed as she revealed her answer. 'Am I Arnold Swarzaschnitzel?'

Tash laughed and gave Lex a knowing smile while the rest of the girls sat with a dumbfounded expression.

'Don't you mean Schwarzenegger?' Jade asked.

Tash giggled. 'She can't say Schwarzenegger, so she says Swarzaschnitzel.'

'She can't say parallelogram, either,' I chimed in, now finished with my sexy toes.

'Say it,' Steph prompted.

'No!' Lexi stubbornly replied.

'Say it!' we all begged.

'Urgh! Fine,' she sighed frustratingly. 'Pall ... arello ... agram,' she mumbled.

We burst into hysterics, it really did sound funny.

'That's gold, Lex. Say it again, please,' Jade pleaded.

'Fuck off,' she giggled.

Jumping up with enthusiasm, Tash bounced on the spot. 'Okay, this game sucks. Let's dance.' She grabbed Jen's Michael Jackson CD and turned in a 360° spin. 'Where's the CD player?'

'Ooh, in here, follow me,' Lexi answered like a naughty kid as she excitedly pushed herself up from the chair and limped to the man-cave.

Before opening the door, she turned around. 'This room is known as the man-cave,' she slurred, and sniggered. 'It's where men do manly things.'

I knew all too well what was behind those doors. It was the place where I showed Derek a part of the real me the night of Lexi's party. It was also where we flirted considerably with each other.

Alexis opened the door and we all filed in. 'Don't touch the instruments,' she ordered.

Steph pouted. 'Aw, you're no fun.'

'Awesome, a pool table! Rack 'em up, bitches,' Tash hollered as she frisbee'd the CD to Jen.

I glanced at the pool table, not wanting to go near it. My emotions were already festering within me and I couldn't explain why. *What the fuck is wrong with me tonight? I'm all over the place; happy, sad, hot and cold. Oh, my, god! Am I menopausal? Shit! Can you go through menopause at age thirty-five? Does this mean I won't be horny any more?* The howl of a wolf sounded through the speakers around the room, snapping me out of my climacteric terror. The beats of *Thriller* ensued, together with a whistle from Lil. Tash and Lex instantly started jerking their shoulders as if they had an involuntary twitch, both of them taking slow steps toward each other. And I must say that Alexis' limp actually complemented her zombie impersonation. It made me laugh.

One minute we were casually standing around the man-cave, the next we were possessed by Michael Jackson's zombies. It was crazy, but I loved it. This was the stupid kind of fun us girls had together. It didn't matter how old we were, or what we did for a living. We were just completely comfortable with one another and, as a result, our inhibitions went out the window.

Jen let out an MJ holler and threw her hands up in the air, dangling them like claws, and Jade and Lil then proceeded to stomp around the room with me and Tash joining in.

I was happily twitching my shoulder, rocking the shit out of the song and putting a zombie to shame, when I turned around and locked eyes with Derek. *Well, fuck me stupid.*

Absolutely fucking mortified did not even begin to describe what I felt at that moment and, having no other choice than to initially smile sheepishly like an idiot, I turned back around and pretended he was not in the room and had not just caught me dancing like a freak.

Please don't come over here. Please don't come over he—

'Will you twitch like that when my cock is inside you?' he asked, his voice low, his warm breath cascading over my ear and neck.

I didn't turn around, instead continuing to slowly move to the music while he stood behind me.

'Hello, Derek. Long time no see or hear,' I said bitterly.

Why I was bitter was beyond me. I was the one who didn't call him. Plus we'd barely gotten to know each other before whatever it was we'd established had ended. One thing was for sure ... he made me so fucking confused, which was probably why I was angry with him. God I hated drama kings. I was more of a what-you-see-is-what-you-get kind of girl, and I wanted that in the man I screwed ... minus the girl part.

'Carly, we need to talk,' he said quietly, as he gently moved a piece of hair away from my neck.

The second I felt his finger on my skin, I jumped and spun around. 'No, we don't. Six weeks is a long time to get over whatever it was that happened back then. It's all good, Derek. We don't owe each other anything,' I explained, then smiled contemptuously before stepping aside and making my way to the bathroom.

I needed air — or a vibrator — or perhaps just a moment to calm my raging fiery hole. Apparently it never got the memo that firefighter Derek was a topsy-turvy arsehole.

CHAPTER
13

My plans to hastily go to the second floor guest bathroom were halted when Derek slid his hand in between the closing doors of the elevator cart.

'What are you doing?' I asked angrily.

He stepped inside, stopping just shy of where I was standing with my back pressed against the far wall of the elevator. The doors closed slowly behind him, thwarting my escape.

'We need to talk,' he said sternly, the look on his face one not to be argued with.

'Why? What's the point?'

'Because I want to set the record straight,' he said with determination. 'I never got the chance and that was partly my fault.'

I sighed, but at the same time let out the breath I had been holding. I didn't want him to see the emotional havoc his presence caused me. 'I need to pee, Derek.'

'You pee, I'll talk,' he offered, flashing me a cocky smile.

I raised an eyebrow at him. 'Fine, if you must,' I said with frustration as I fisted the level two button. 'Talk, but again, there really is no need. You don't have to explain anything.'

'Layla is my sister-in-law,' he said quickly. 'She is married to my brother who I no longer speak to, nor want to speak to.'

Oh, shit! Did I jump to the wrong conclusion or what? Chancing a quick glance from the corner of my eye, I spied Derek gauging my reaction. When I didn't say anything — because I felt like an absolutely stupid bitch — he continued. 'Layla has been lobbying for me and my brother to "kiss and make up" for quite some time. She loves Sean and wants us to play happy families.'

The ding of the elevator indicated that we'd arrived at the second floor, followed by the opening of the doors. I stepped out and made my way to the guest bedroom, Derek following closely behind me. 'When you insinuated that she was a past girlfriend, it pissed me off.'

Stopping, I turned around and nearly bumped into him. 'I'm sorry, I didn't mean —'

Derek captured me in his arms and pressed me up against the wall. 'It pissed me off that your first thought was that I had fucked her. I hate how you see me as some kind of bloke who likes to fuck around, Carly. I'm not that bloke.'

His sudden closeness, his firm body pressed against me, and his face mere centimetres from mine, had intensified my heart rate. My chest rose and fell as I looked into his bright blue eyes, breathed in his fresh aftershave tinged with beer scent, and felt the heat radiating from him. 'Yes,' I said honestly. 'I do get that impression.'

Derek's gaze dropped so that he was looking at his feet, his jaw also working from side to side, displaying his obvious disappointment. 'Why?' he murmured.

'I don't know. I guess that "type of bloke" is what I'm used to,' I said quietly, as I watched his brow crease. 'Look, I'm sorry. I don't mean to offend you. And I'm sorry I jumped to the wrong conclusion about Layla. I don't know what else to say. I don't know you well enough to trust you, and every time I ask you a personal question you shut me down.'

He tilted his head back up and searched my eyes pleadingly. 'I want you. I want to be with you, whether it's for an hour, a night, weeks or months. I want to get to know you and you to know me. If these past six weeks have taught me anything, it's that I want to be around you in any way that I can.'

'But you keep —'

He put his finger on my lips, stopping me from speaking further. 'I'm going to be completely honest, and after that, you can pee and give me your answer, okay?'

Nodding while his finger still hung from my lips, I uncontrollably grazed my tongue over it, relishing his salty taste.

He groaned ever so lightly, then continued. 'Weeks ago, outside that cafe when you said you may not be the relationship type, I honestly couldn't have been more fucking relieved. I'm not the relationship type either. But that doesn't mean I go sticking my dick in anything and everything. What it means is that I have not found anyone remotely interesting enough to want to spend continuous time with. Until you.

'I don't know what it is between us, but whatever it is, I want more,' he said with assurance as he removed his finger and replaced it with his lips.

Derek thrust his tongue into my mouth, my lips parting obediently and submitting to his control. His tongue repeatedly swept across mine with long powerful strokes while his grip on the back of my head tightened.

Finding his hips with my hands, I pulled him to me, feeling his hard erection press into the base of my belly. My breasts ached for some attention of their own and, as if reading my mind, both his hands found them, greedily massaging and squeezing them with fervour.

'Oh, fuck,' I moaned around his tongue as he continued to dominate me against the wall.

He broke free from my mouth and kissed my neck before yanking down my top and bra, releasing my tits. They bounced receptively.

'Fuck,' he ground out as he captured them in his hands. The look on his face as he stared at my chest was one of both pained restraint and ravenous hunger. As his hands cupped my flesh, the pressure he applied was strong, but at the same time, tender. It was just the way I liked it.

He leaned forward and licked my nipple with one long slow stroke then switched and repeated his tongue lash on the other one. He was voracious and utterly hot.

'Carls,' Lexi called out, 'where are you?'

'Shit!' I murmured and shoved Derek from my chest before pulling up my top and walking over to the balustrade. I looked down into the lounge area to find Lexi by the sofa, balancing on one foot. 'I'm up here.'

She looked up. 'What are you doing?'

'Looking for your vibrator! What do you think I'm doing? I'm going to the friggin' toilet,' I admonished. Suddenly, I felt Derek nipping at my denim covered arse. I tried to subtly kick him away.

'Well, hurry up. And have you seen Derek? Bryce wants to run some band stuff by him.'

'No —' I began to say, just as Derek crawled around to the front of me and pressed his back against the balustrade wall, purposely aligning his head with my pussy. Slowly, he started to undo the buttons of my jeans.

I almost choked as I covered my mouth with my hand and whispered. 'What are you doing?'

'What does it look like I'm doing? I vaguely recall you saying that you wanted to know if my tongue was as good as my fingers,' he whispered back. 'So you are about to find out.'

Thank god the top of the plaster balustrade wall was level to just under my breasts, because the next thing I knew, he had yanked my jeans down to my ankles, baring me completely.

'Jesus fucking Christ, that looks nice,' he growl-whispered before placing his hands on my arse cheeks and pressing me to his face.

I yelped at his ferociousness. *Yes, friggin' yelped like a puppy.*

'Did you hear me?' Lexi called out again, this time sounding a little irritated.

Derek dragged his tongue across my clit in one long swipe, prompting me to quietly moan and step out of one leg of my jeans in order to spread wider for him.

'Yes, sorry. I don't know where he is. I think he went out on the balcony to order something to eat.'

'Oh, I'm fucking eating all right,' he mumbled into me, the vibrations of his words igniting my clit.

'Okay, well hurry up. And if you see him on your way down, tell him to get his arse back in here.'

'Sure,' I replied, barely able to speak through the waves of pleasure his tongue and mouth were giving me. 'When I see him going down, I'll tell — what?' I mumbled, fucking confused and slightly disorientated.

'Are you all right?' Lexi called back.

'Yes, I'm fine,' I corrected myself, giving her a reassuring smile.

With a sceptical expression on her face, she nodded and limped back into the man-cave.

'Oh god,' I breathed out, dropping my head forward and gripping the balustrade railing with renewed force.

Derek slid two fingers inside me, gently pumping them in and out as he licked and sucked at my clit. My natural reaction was to mount his fucking face and thrash my hips into him. I wanted nothing more than to ride that cocky, sexy mouth of his.

Separating his glistening mouth from me, he looked up with a satisfied expression. 'Fuck, you taste good.'

Almost instantly, he was back in between my legs, alternating between relentless quick flicks of his tongue, to slow tortuous lashes and the sucking of my clit into his mouth. Each time I predicted his next move he'd do the opposite and heighten my approaching climax.

'Are you going to come on my face?' he murmured.

'Do you want me to?' I asked huskily, my breathing ragged and laboured.

'Of course I fucking want you to,' he growled, while plunging his fingers in deep and scissoring them gently.

In that moment I saw stars and fireworks and all things fiery and bright as my orgasm exploded and sent shock-waves right through me. My pussy clenched around his fingers, gripping and clamping them within me. My thighs clenched and I buckled, collapsing onto his lap.

Shuddering momentarily, I bit my lip and silenced the cries of pleasure. The restraint it took to refrain from screaming out his name was pure agony, but I managed it and once again found my semblance of normal.

As I stared up at him, his heavy-lidded lust-filled expression took my breath away.

'Baby, I can't wait to be buried inside you when you do that again,' he said with a smile before lifting me upward to kiss him.

In all honesty, I couldn't wait either.

* * *

After cleaning myself up and finally peeing, I made my way out of the bathroom to find Derek sitting on the edge of the bed.

He looked up and smiled as I walked toward him. 'Well, so what's your answer?'

Stopping so that I was standing in between his legs, I placed my hands on either side of his face. 'What answer?'

'Carly, I left you alone for six weeks when you didn't respond to my messages. I don't want to leave you alone any more. I want more of this.' He gestured to the both us. 'I want more of you. Do you want more of me?'

I could see the desperate plea in his eyes and it both frightened and excited me. Telling him I wanted the same, meant I was quite possibly agreeing to a relationship. A relationship both of us admitted to not wanting or being any good at. Did this mean we were doomed before we even started?

'Don't think. Just answer. Yes or no. Do you want me or not?'

I leaned down and licked from his collarbone to his Adam's apple. 'Yes, I want you.'

I winked and walked out of the room.

* * *

For the hour that followed, the men performed a couple of impromptu jam sessions. Watching Derek sing and play the guitar was my new aphrodisiac. The man was the epitome of sexy and smooth when he communicated through song. Every part of his body spoke erotically to me in one way or another, whether it was the way he strummed the strings of his guitar, or the way he mouthed the microphone, or even the way his stare inflamed my core when he held a note. His voice was sensual and raw, and it rolled from his mouth with superb control.

'Do you still have a fiery hole?' Tash asked quietly as she sat down on the couch beside me.

Tearing my eyes away from Derek, I felt my cheeks redden as I answered her. 'It's a fucking inferno. I swear the man is going to incinerate me. You wait. You'll walk into a room and there will be nothing left but a pile of ash. That will be me.'

She laughed and nudged me with her shoulder. 'Why are you holding back? That's not like you.'

'Who said I'm holding back?'

'Carly, if it were any other man, you'd be dry-humping his leg right about now.'

True! I don't mind a decent dry-humping.

'Okay,' I conceded with a roll of my eyes, 'what if I said that it was time for me to grow up and take things slow?'

She laughed and pointed at me. 'Ha! I'd say you were full of shit.'

'Tash, I'm serious.'

'Carls, you don't know how to be serious.'

'Neither do you,' I retorted.

'I don't have to. I'm married. Dean knew what he was getting himself into before he said I do.'

I swirled my hand at her, emphasising the bird I was flipping. 'Whatever.'

'Yep, real grown up,' she winked.

'Look, Tash,' I squealed excitedly, pointing above her, 'a balloon!'

She screamed and spun around, swatting at nothing but air.

I cracked up laughing and fell back on the couch. *Take that, bitch-flaps.*

When she realised there was no big scary balloon hovering above her, she glared at me. 'Oh you'll keep, kittykat.'

Still laughing, I meowed for her. Tash then turned and headed back to where Lexi was perched on Bryce's knee.

'Do you purr as well?' Derek whispered in my ear, his warm breath paralysing my vocal chords.

I tilted back and stared at his upside-down face, finding him leaning over the couch. 'Do what you did before and I'll make whatever animal noise you want,' I replied quietly.

'Just so you know, baby, you're sleeping in my room tonight.'

A ghost of a smile played at the corners of my mouth. 'Who said anything about sleeping?'

Derek clicked his jaw from side to side and stood upright before swigging his beer and piercing me with a heated stare. That one look spoke many things. It said I was going to get fucked. Fucked hard and for however long he wanted to fuck me.

Oh ... fuck!

* * *

Hours later, when everyone was leaving the apartment to go to the rooms that Bryce had arranged, Lex pulled me aside. 'So, Carly Josephine Henkley, is your fiery hole about to be put out?'

I smiled at her, but at the same time expressed my trepidation. 'Lex, he is so putting a scorching heat between my legs, it is not funny.'

'Need I remind you that he is a firefighter ... let the guy put it out. Apparently, that's what he's good at.'

'I'm terrified,' I whispered.

She whispered back. 'What the fuck? Carly does not get terrified. Why is Carly terrified?'

Continuing the whispered conversation, now referring to myself in the third person, I answered, 'Because Carly really fucking likes Derek.'

She dropped her hands to hold mine by our sides inconspicuously. 'Oh, Carls, that's great. Do you want to know a secret?'

'What?'

'He likes you, too,' she whispered with an impish grin.

'How the —' I blurted out, then looked around sheepishly and continued in a more quieter tone, 'fuck do you know?'

She leaned in and kissed my forehead. 'Because he told me.' Alexis then turned my shoulders around and playfully smacked me on the butt, ushering me out the door.

As the door closed behind me, I tentatively took steps until I was through the foyer. Derek was waiting for me, a smug but eager grin on his face.

'You told Lexi that you liked me?' I asked incredulously. 'What else have you told her?'

'Whoa. What's the problem?' he chuckled.

'I ... I ...' I stuttered, not really sure what the problem was. 'I don't know. I guess she just caught me off-guard when she mentioned that you'd talked to her.' I narrowed my eyes at him. 'When did you tell her?'

Derek slid his arm across my shoulder and pulled me to him. 'I've been giving her guitar lessons behind Bryce's back for a couple of months,' he explained quietly. 'Come on and I'll explain it on the way.'

* * *

Derek filled me in on his and Alexis' secret meetings, meetings where he taught her to play the guitar so that she could surprise Bryce and play for him. The idea was genius and if anyone could learn the guitar in a short space of time, it was Lexi. She was naturally talented at many things ... except realising that she was naturally talented was a talent that evaded her.

'I can't believe she didn't tell me? We tell each other everything,' I said sombrely as we exited the elevator cart.

Derek turned his head and gave me an are-you-listening-to-yourself look.

I furrowed my brow. 'What?'

'Have you told her about us?' he asked, clearly already knowing the answer.

Crossing my arms over my chest, we walked down the passageway. 'That's different.'

'How?' he questioned, stopping me outside his room. *His room! Shit! We are about to enter his room and have sex. My fiery hole is about to be extinguished.*

'Um ... because I wasn't sure there was an "us", so why bother her with something that may not have been,' I answered.

He tilted my chin up and looked intently into my eyes. 'There's an "us",' he stated definitively.

The honesty that radiated from him as I stood there and stared had me stunned into silence. Deep down, I knew there was an 'us', whatever 'us' was. Maybe 'us' was the chemistry we created. *Doesn't a chemical reaction need its own chemical symbol? Yes, I think it does.* From now on, 'Dc' will be the reactive substance that crackles in the air when Derek (D) and Carly (c) lock eyes on one another.

'Carly. Carly!' Derek said, snapping me out of my impromptu science lesson.

'Yeah?'

'Are you coming in, or are you going to stay out in the passageway all night?'

Turning my head from side to side and taking in that, yes, I was still standing outside his room and that he was standing in it, I quickly stepped over the threshold of the door and closed it behind me.

I'd barely made it to the main area of the room before Derek was stalking toward me. 'You ready to feel me for days afterwards?'

Hell, yes! I want your hose. I want it to squirt me.

'You could be setting yourself up for failure, you know,' I said quickly before his lips prevented any further words from escaping.

Derek grabbed my face and thrust his tongue into my mouth, the abrupt and possessive action shocking me to the point of dropping my purse. I ran my hands up his chest and rested them on his shoulders, which was when he placed his hands on my arse and lifted me up. Instinctively, I wrapped my legs around his waist and crisscrossed my ankles just above his arse.

I moaned with pleasure when he vigorously squeezed my cheeks, forcing me to separate my mouth from his and drop my head back. Instantly, his mouth claimed the exposed skin of my neck, kissing, sucking and nipping.

'You smell so fucking good,' he murmured against me.

'Daisy,' I murmured back.

'What's Daisy?' he asked as he continued to kiss, making his journey down toward my cleavage.

'It's why I smell good,' I gasped, sucking in air as he dipped his tongue in between my breasts. 'It's my perfume.'

Derek hoisted me up so that my chest was at the same height as his mouth, my pussy now pressed into his ribs. 'Take it off,' he growled, nodding toward my top. 'I've got you.'

I let go of his shoulders and pulled my top over my head.

'And the bra,' he instructed as he eyed my flesh with a lust-filled expression.

Reaching behind me, I unclipped my black lace balconette bra and pulled it off my shoulders. Before I had any time to adjust to the sudden change of temperature, Derek's lips were tugging on my perked nipple.

'Oh god,' I cried out as I clenched my fingers into his shirt.

He hummed as he teased my sensitive peak, then let go and dragged his tongue from just above my navel to in between my breasts in one long delicious swipe. Eye-fucking me devilishly, he then circled each nipple before sucking them back into his mouth.

Being licked in that fashion while taking in his amorous stare just about sent my pussy into party mode. I swear she even blew on a party-blower. *Is that possible? I wonder if my pussy can really blow on a party-blower.*

Derek's pager sounded, bringing my attention back to the moment. 'Fuck!' he shouted, and shot me an apology-ridden look. 'I'm sorry. I have to check it.'

I smoothed my hands down the sides of his face and smiled. 'Don't be. I should go freshen up anyway.'

Unwrapping my legs from around him, he helped me slide down his torso, then pulled his pager from his pocket. 'Shit! I gotta ring the station,' he bit out and started tapping on his phone.

'I'll be right back,' I mouthed as I picked up my purse and pointed toward the bathroom.

Derek winked and gave what could only be described as an I-know-you-fucking-will look.

Smiling, but also completely wired over what we had just been doing and what we would be doing next, I made my way into the bathroom.

Okay, okay, okay. I need to pee and then clean. I danced and jiggled with excitement at the thought of dousing my fiery hole with Derek's hose. *Derek's hose. OMFG! I'm about to see Derek's hose.*

Pulling my pants down, I sat on the toilet and relieved myself while salaciously contemplating the cock I was about to see, devour and fuck deliriously. I reached for the toilet paper and looked down to wipe.

'You've got to be fucking kidding me! You. Have. Got. To. Be. Fucking. KIDDING ME!' I yelled. 'Fuck, fuck, fuck, fuck, fuuuuuuck. Fuck a duck. Fuck a truck. Fuck a duck on a truck. Fuck a fucking duck driving a truck.'

'Carly, you all right?' Derek asked from his position on the other side of the bathroom door, his voice full of concern.

'Of course,' I laughed sweetly while looking to the roof and shaking my head in disagreement. 'Never better.'

'Okay, juuuust checking. Now hurry the fuck up and get that pussy of yours out here. I'm hungry.'

I slumped forward and rested my head in my hands. *Fuck. I hate periods ... period.*

CHAPTER

14

Why? Why me? Is it God's plan to have my hole burning for all eternity? Is my punishment for being a bad girl to have singed crispy vagina bats nesting in my Carly-cave for as long as I shall live? And even then, I will no doubt end up having singed crispy vagina ghost-bats in the afterlife.

I let out a strangled cry and shook my head, which was still held in the palms of my hands.

I know! Head job! Springing my head back up, a renewed sense of venture washed through me. *I will blow his fucking mind! I will suck that hose of his until it squirts me in the eye. Okay, maybe not in the eye, that shit stings, but I will suck the living fuck out of him.*

Reaching into my purse, I pulled out my tampon and took care of business while performing my pre-blow job exercises, stretching my mouth and enunciating the alphabet.

'Aay, Beee, Ceee, D ... d ... deee, eee —'

'You coming out or what? My balls are about as blue as Papa Smurf's,' Derek called from the next room.

I scrunched my face in disgust — a visual of Papa Smurf's nuggets now in my head — but focussed and continued with my exercises anyway. 'Ffff, Geee ... Yeah, just a minute,' I called back. 'Aahch, I, Jay, K ... Kay, Ell, Em, En, Oooo ...' I stopped and held the O. It was, after all, the most important of pre-blow job exercise letters. 'Oooo ...'

Looking at myself in the mirror, I took note that I resembled a fish, a cute little blowfish. I giggled at my own silliness and touched up my lipstick — because we all know that red lips wrapped around a cock is about as sexy as it gets. *Okay, Carly, this is it. Go suck that sexy motherfucker.* Nodding to myself, I opened the door and stepped into the room with cocksure confidence.

Derek was sitting on the edge of the bed, socks and shoes removed. He seemed agitated, but over-keen at the same time. 'Baby, I'm dying here. What took you so long?'

I didn't give him the courtesy of a reply, instead prowling toward him with a promising yet passionate smile, only to stop when I reached the spot in between his legs.

Reaching out, I placed my finger on his lips to shush him. He went to speak but I shook my head slowly, eyeing him ferociously.

Kneeling down before him, I slowly began to unbutton his jeans. 'Stand up,' I commanded, my voice not one to be argued with.

He licked his bottom lip and rose so that I could pull down his jeans and underwear. As I slid them over the top of his cock, it sprang free and nearly poked me in the eye. *Holy fucking shitballs! Talk about Cockasaurus Rex!*

I swallowed heavily, unable to get over just how well-endowed he actually was. His hose was huge, deserving of its own postcode. *Shit! I should've exercised for longer. That thing is gonna give me facial cramps.*

I could honestly say that it was the prettiest cock I had ever seen. And mark my words, cocks can be pretty. If they can be ugly, then they can sure as hell be pretty as well.

'You just gonna stare at it, baby?' Derek asked, his voice low and sexy as hell.

'I could,' I answered, choking on the imaginary cotton lodged in my throat. 'It's pretty.'

He shook his head at me and pointed to his dick. 'This ain't pretty. A man's cock is never pretty.'

'Yes, it is. It's pretty fucking superb.'

A conceited smile spread across his gorgeous face as he wrapped his hand around the base of his cock, palming his length slowly and enticing me to do more than just stare. I wanted to do more. Oh boy, did I want to do more. But watching him slowly glide his hand up and down his incredible length was so erotic and just as rewarding.

I licked my lips, shuffled forward on my knees and placed my hands on his bare firm arse, gripping it forcefully and pulling him toward me. The taut hard muscle beneath my hand heightened the frenzied need within me.

Derek positioned the shiny head of his cock at the entrance to my mouth, prompting me to open up and gently sweep my tongue over it, teasing him as I delicately swirled.

He hissed and pushed his pelvis a little closer, wanting to take control, but I was hell-bent on not conceding and dodged my head to the side, flashing him a dominant and smug grin. I then licked from his crown all the way down to his manscaped base, the salty taste of his skin a pleasure to digest.

The fact he pruned and took care of his man-area did not surprise me; he just seemed that type of guy. And anyway, you could always pick a manscaper versus a pube-activist. And Derek was no pube-activist. Personally, I appreciated good hygiene where the genital region was concerned. And I'm sure I speak for most women when I say that none of us want a mouthful of short and curlys.

Releasing my hands from his tense cheeks, I reached forward and took hold of his cock while placing my other hand on his balls. Gently, I caressed them with my fingertips, kneading the soft bumpy flesh. With my other hand, I gripped his shaft tighter and proceeded to move his skin up and down before leaning forward and engulfing him completely.

'Fuck,' Derek moaned and placed his hands on my head almost instantly, flexing his fingers into my scalp.

My smile encircled his cock, as I glanced up to spy him looking down at me, his heavy-lidded expression exciting, yet tormenting at the same time. I wanted all of him, but knew that was not going to happen and although I was thoroughly enjoying giving him head, the fact we could not have sex afterward was pure torture.

I bobbed up and down a couple of times, relishing the warmth and taste of his skin before releasing him from my mouth. 'Take your shirt off. I want to see that chest of yours,' I demanded, before running my tongue back over his crown to be rewarded with a bead of pre-come.

He reached behind his shoulders and grabbed the collar of his t-shirt, pulling it over his head while gently bucking into my mouth.

I paused. *Oh. My. God!*

The sight of his bare chest etched with black ink made my jaw drop open with his cock teetering on my bottom lip. Derek's pecs, shoulders and abdomen were simply stunning ... and caramel; golden and oozing deliciousness. The bumps, the grooves, the dips and ... the V! I closed my eyes momentarily and had a silent Vgasm. *Oh, sweet Vgasm.*

Giggling greedily, I opened my eyes and clamped back down on his dick, all of a sudden wanting nothing more than to clamber on top of him and touch every single part of his body. I wanted to run my hands up and down his chest, his shoulders, his arms, his legs. EVERYWHERE! I was a voracious and frenzied ball of hormones ready to explode.

'Fuck, baby. Stop looking at me like that, or I'll shoot my load right now.'

I groaned at the sound of his desperation and took him in deeper, his cock hitting the back of my throat. I prided myself on my oral skills; I was a 'head' honcho.

'That's it,' Derek said abruptly and went to withdraw from my mouth.

I panicked and grabbed him, forcing him to stay.

'Carly, let me go. I want to fuck you now!'

'... ou an't,' I mumbled, pumping him vigorously with my hand.

'What do you mean I can't? I fucking well can. Just watch me,' he retorted.

Releasing his cock from my mouth with a 'pop', I palmed it slowly and gave him a sympathetic look. 'I'm surfing the crimson wave.'

He gave me a dumbfounded look in return. 'You're what?'

'You know ... code red, kitty has a nose bleed?'

'What the fuck are you talking about?'

Rolling my eyes at him, I gripped his shaft in frustration, my grip probably a little harder that what it should've been. 'I have my period, dummy.'

Realisation dawned on his now-distraught face. 'You serious?'

'Yep,' I nodded sadly, then with a devious smile continued, 'so I suggest you place your hands back on my head and let me suck you dry.'

With a sexy smile, he lifted one shoulder and cocked his head to the side. 'Well, when you say it like that ...'

Dragging my tongue up his length, I happily sucked him back into my mouth, taking him deep until he was coming against the back of my throat with an animalistic growl that vibrated right through me. *Oh, sweet fuck, this man is sexy.*

Derek reached down and placed a finger under my chin, directing me to stand in front of him. I complied, which was when he seized my mouth and wrapped one arm around my back and the other under my legs, lifting me into his arms.

'What are you doing?' I giggled.

'Taking you to bed. I'm not finished with you yet.'

He gently laid me down on the crisp white linen of the suite's king-sized bed and then crawled up and over me, placing a soft kiss to my forehead, my nose, my lips and my neck. I hummed my appreciation, closing my eyes and savouring his attentive lips.

My moment of appreciative bliss came to an abrupt halt when Derek began to unbutton my jeans. 'Don't,' I blurted, stopping his hands with my own and propping myself up on my elbows. 'I don't do red-sex.'

He raised an eyebrow then shook his head with amusement. 'I don't do it, either, baby, but that doesn't mean I'm going to let you sleep in your jeans.'

Relaxing, I nodded. 'Good,' then lay back down and let Derek remove my pants.

'Your body is gorgeous, Carly,' he said with an appreciate smile as he slowly ran his hands up the outer sides of my legs. 'Do you work-out?'

Do I work-out? Pfft, I work out how not to work-out. That's how Carly works out. 'No. I don't. I'm just lucky.'

He laughed and shuffled up my body to straddle my hips and then began to blissfully knead my breasts, his masterful hands working my chest in a tantalising fashion. I closed my eyes, arched my back and threw my hands above my head, reaching to grab hold of the edge of the mattress.

'I swear to fucking god that these tits are the nicest I've ever seen,' he praised.

Opening one eye, I couldn't help smiling boldly. 'Really?'

'Oh, yeah.'

'The nicest you've ever seen?' I asked with a seductive, yet overjoyed drawl.

He nodded and leaned forward to take my nipple into his mouth. 'Definitely the nicest,' he mumbled.

I laughed and closed my eyes once more, realising that non-sex was not all that bad when it was with Derek.

* * *

The next morning I woke to the smell of coffee and bacon. It was definitely a good smell to wake up to, but even better was the sight of Derek wandering around the room in nothing but a towel hanging dangerously low on his waist. *Fall, goddamn it. Slip. Untie. Unravel and drift to the floor.* Willing the towel's descent with every bit of mental telepathy I could conjure, I soon gave up with an inward grumble of disappointment when it didn't budge.

Instead I took a moment to admire him in the sunlight, filtering through the window of the thirty-fourth floor suite we were occupying. His body was simply perfect: his chest, arms and abdomen rippled with taut muscles. I knew that firefighters had to be fit, carrying around heavy equipment and climbing stairs and shit, but fuck me, he certainly looked after himself.

'Hungry?' he asked, breaking my perve-sesh.

Quickly wiping my eyes to insinuate I was just waking up and not eye-fucking him instead, I sat up and stretched. 'Yeah, smells good.'

'I figured you'd be good with bacon, considering you aren't one of those "salad and water girls" that we talked about,' he playfully explained.

'Bring it on! I love a good pork in the morning,' I blurted out as I climbed off the bed.

'Well, this is as good as it's going to get today. But next time, I promise your morning pork will be a hell of a lot better.'

Sidling up to Derek, I wrapped my arms around his waist and kissed his lips. 'Mm ... thank you. This is perfect.'

He gestured for me to sit down on the tub chair where I settled with one foot on the edge and leaned forward to rest upon my leg. I had only my black lace, boy-leg panties on and nothing up top, being comfortable with my body and not afraid to show it. Another of Carly's cardinals was: if you've got it, flaunt it. And I sure as hell had it.

'You cold?' Derek asked.

I bit down on my bacon. 'No. Why?' I mumbled curiously.

He nodded toward my peaked nipples.

'These?' I queried, looking down and tweaking them. 'Oh, they are always like this.'

'Always?' he asked, nearly choking on his coffee.

'Yep, I'm in a constant state of arousal,' I smiled jokingly, winking at him seductively.

He let out a mild laugh, but kept eyeing my breasts with a heated expression. 'So ... got any plans for today?'

Leaning back, I spread my arms across the back of the chair, poking out my chest for his entertainment. Then, gathering my hair into a ponytail within my hand, I answered casually, 'No, not really. I was just going to lounge around and utilise this fine establishment.'

His eyes widened at my now prominent display. 'Do you like footy?' he ground out, still staring at my breasts.

'Yes, I've followed Essendon all my life. Lexi and I are Bombers crazy.'

A sly smile spread across his face. 'Excellent! Hurry up and eat then. You now have plans.'

* * *

Just under two hours later, Derek and I were seated on the ground level of the MCG, watching the players of both the Essendon and Collingwood Football Clubs undergo their pre-match practice and warm-up. The stadium surrounding us was enormous and filling quickly as people scrambled along the aisles in order to find their seats.

'Here you go,' Derek said as he draped an Essendon Bombers scarf around my neck. 'Worst fifteen dollars spent in my life,' he joked. He also passed me a plastic cup of beer as he sat down next to me.

I laughed at his stab at my beloved team. 'Thanks. Your support of the Dons is very much appreciated.'

'You do realise you are going to get flogged today,' he added with an unapologetic tone. *Oh ... you have no idea how much I want to be flogged. And by you.*

'Don't be so sure,' I countered. 'You know ... that's the biggest problem with you Magpie supporters, you're all cocky fuckwits.'

Derek laughed and placed his arm around my shoulders. 'Baby, we have reason to be cocky. It's called fifteen premierships.'

'I'm sorry ... haven't we won more?' I asked carelessly, trying to hide my smug smile because I knew that we had.

He turned toward me slightly and raised an impressed eyebrow. 'Let's not go there, all right?'

I laughed again, his playful attempt to change the subject highly adorable. In true Magpie supporter style, the Bombers were a very touchy subject, the fierce rivalry between the two teams transferring to their supporters.

'So how does a small wager sound?' I suggested, while stealing a chip from the tray lying across his lap.

'You crazy?' he mockingly laughed, stealing it back from between my lips before I had a chance to completely consume it.

Narrowing my eyes at him, I stole another one and quickly shoved it in mouth. 'You scared?' I mumbled then nearly spat the chip out, instead opting to flap my hands in front of my face in an attempt to cool down the contents of my mouth. *Fuck, that was hot.*

'No. I'm more concerned for you in what will be inevitable failure,' he laughed, taking in my flappy idiocy.

'Pfft,' I responded, then shouted praise to my favourite player, Brent Stanton.

From out the corner of my eye, I noticed Derek shake his head with amused disapproval, so I deliberately kept my eyes focussed on the players and continued, 'You know what? I think you are just a pussy and don't like to lose.'

The siren sounded and both teams gathered in their respective circles, revving themselves up with last-minute game plans and advice before assuming their positions on the field. The crowd roared to life, and I sat up taller in my seat to gain a better view.

Derek leaned in and nuzzled my neck then whispered in my ear, 'You said that all wrong, baby. Let me rephrase it for you ... I don't lose and I like pussy, especially yours.' He gently licked the side of my neck then pulled away, shouting, 'Carn the pies!', leaving a cool sensitised trail behind.

* * *

After the game Derek drove me home, his demeanour relaxed and contentedly happy due to Collingwood winning by thirty-four points. He even attempted to cash in on the bet he never agreed to.

'So, what do I get?' he asked as we stood outside my house.

'You get nothing,' I exclaimed, stubbornly crossing my arms over my chest as I rested my arse against the front guard of Suzi.

Derek was standing opposite me, leaning his arse against his blue Ford Ranger, his hands in his pockets and feet crossed at the ankles. 'Bullshit! We had a wager.'

'Noooo ... I offered a wager at the beginning of the game and you, being a pussy, didn't take it.'

His sexy grin teased at the corners of his mouth. 'Say pussy again. I like it when you say pussy.'

I smiled and even blushed. 'Pussy.'

'Say, "Derek, when I'm no longer surfing the crimson wave, I want you to lick my pussy and then fuck it hard."'

Pushing off from Suzi and stalking toward him, I stopped when my chest brushed up against his. 'Derek, next week when we meet up again, I will let you lick my pussy until your tongue hurts. And then, I will ride your cock until the cows come home,' I whispered, before gently grazing his lips with my tongue.

As I walked toward my front door, he called out, 'You don't have cows.'

Raising my eyebrows suggestively, I answered, 'Exactly.'

* * *

The following week at work was business as usual, the normal boring day in, day out, clock-torment crap I had to forever deal with. If it weren't for the close friendships I had with the teachers, and if it weren't for bearing witness to the hilarious shit that kids sometimes do and say, I would be — at best — a friggin' nut case.

It was Friday afternoon and Lib, Brooke, Sally and I and a few of the other teachers were sitting around the tables in the staff room.

'So, to tie up Emergency Education Month before the end of the term, I asked the kids a partial question and they had to fill in the blank,' Lib said, obviously excited about the story she was telling. 'Some of the answers were hilarious. Want to hear?'

Sally leaned over and grabbed a handful of M&M's from the open packet which sat in the centre of the table. 'Yeah, shoot.'

'Okay, so I said, "Where there's smoke there's ..." and asked them to raise their hands with answers that I would then write down on the brainstorm board. Here are some of their responses: pollution, a smoker, a teepee, a cold morning, burnt toast, a bushfire and, of course, a fire.'

'Burnt toast?' Brooke laughed. 'Oh my god, I love it.'

Lib was shaking her head with a smile that showed admiration for her kids. 'I tell ya, trying to explain to Jet Bradley that our breath on a cold morning was not smoke was definitely a tough task.'

Trying to explain anything to Jet Bradley was a tough task. But before I could add to the conversation, my phone rang from within my handbag. I pulled it out to find Derek's name on my screen.

Instantly, I stood up and went to walk away for privacy.

'That wouldn't be the sexy-arse firefighter who is "not" your fuck-friend, now would it?' Brooke asked, a teasing smile on her face.

I glared at her and turned my back as I pushed through the double swinging doors and out of the room before hitting accept.

'Hey, what's up?' I asked as calmly as I possibly could. For some reason, I couldn't help sounding giddy whenever I bloody spoke or texted him.

'Hey, gorgeous. Bad news,' he said sullenly.

My stomach dropped and a sense of disappointment washed over me. We were due to meet up again tonight and, by the sound of his voice, that was not going to happen. 'Is everything all right?'

'No, not really. I, ah ... I have to go to Sydney for a while. It's family related. I could be gone for a week or maybe two.'

'Oh, when are you leaving?'

'Now! I'm at the airport. It's kind of urgent,' he said with an apologetic tone.

I waited for him to perhaps fill me in on exactly what was so urgent, but he didn't impart further. His reluctance to open up to me, yet again, was kind of devastating.

Sucking in a breath in order to sound nonchalant, I straightened my shoulders. 'Well, I hope you sort whatever it is out. Let me know when you're back, if you want to.'

'Carly,' he said firmly then paused, waiting for me to answer.

My shoulders lost their vigour and slumped. 'Yes?'

'Of course I want to. And I will, as soon as I touch down in Melbourne again. I have to leave. I have to do this.'

'What is "this", Derek?' I questioned sadly, knowing he was keeping something from me, the unknown acting like a silent noose.

'I can't get into it right now. But I will, eventually. I promise.'

I took a moment to deliberate whether I believed him or not. I wanted to. REALLY wanted to. But he made it difficult when he so easily shut me out or left me in the dark. I was not the nocturnal type; I liked the light. I liked clarification.

'Baby?'

Sighing, I answered. 'Yeah?'

'I'll be back as soon as I can. And when I am, we have some unfinished business to see to.'

Sighing again, I was no longer sure whether that unfinished business would ever be resolved.

CHAPTER

15

After ending my call with Derek, I was back in the realm of what-am-I-fucking-doing? A major part of me wanted to believe in him, have faith in him, and trust that what we had was real. But where my heart advocates, my mind guards, keeping me grounded, balanced and in control. I never let one dominate the other, and as much as I desperately wanted my heart to reign, I just could not bring myself to let that happen. I had to keep thinking that what Derek and I were embroiled in was fun and impetuous, and in no way serious. We were simply pleasure pals, fuck buddies — except we hadn't yet got to the 'fucking' part.

To be honest, if it were any other time, I would look at this situation and be highly embarrassed. We'd been 'not' seeing each other for nearly three months and hadn't even fucked. I mean, who did that? NOBODY!

'I need a night out,' I said to myself as I made my way back to the staff room. And I was going to drag Libby out with me whether she liked it or not.

Pushing the door open, I walked into the room. 'Right! Opals ... tonight, who's in?'

Brooke, Libby, Sally and George — known as Mr T to his grade six students (which makes me laugh because he is far from the boisterous man who is his namesake) — looked up.

'I'm in, sweetheart,' George offered, eagerly.

'You are too old. You are not invited,' I said, while poking my tongue out at him. 'And anyway, something tells me that were you to accompany us tonight, Mrs T would have your balls for breakfast.'

George not so subtly covered his package with his hands in a show of protection. 'Nobody is havin' my balls for breakfast, especially Mrs T. She can have porridge.'

I laughed and shook my head at him, then proceeded to sit my butt on the table. 'Brooke, Sally, you in?'

Lib stood up and took her coffee mug to the sink. 'I can't, Carls,' she said with a sympathetic smile.

'Lib, you don't have a choice.'

She spun around, displaying astonishment. 'Says who?'

'Me,' I answered, dismissing her constitutional right to decide for herself.

'Yeah, I'm in,' Sally said as she grabbed yet another handful of M&M's. I gave her a warning look, which prompted her to frown at me, and then watched as she hesitated for a moment, debating whether or not to put that handful of chocolate in her mouth.

Sally was mildly overweight, but was forever complaining about it and never doing anything to help her cause. She wasn't dealt the lucky hand that I was and could not eat whatever she wanted and, because of that, appointed me as her make-me-lose-weight bitch. It was one of my jobs to ensure she didn't eat foods that would go directly to her arse.

Quickly, and with a cheeky yet guilty smile, she shovelled them into her mouth.

'Sal!' I exclaimed.

'I'll work it off tonight on the dance floor, I promise.'

'Oh, I know you will,' I replied with a searing look that meant business.

'It's all right for you,' she whined, 'you can eat whatever you like and —'

Here we go again, blah, blah, blah-bibbity blah. I deliberately blocked out her you-suck-I'm-a-victim spiel. I'd heard it before.

'Okay, we'll taxi it from my joint,' I added. 'Brooke?'

'I'll let you know. I'll have to see what Lance is doin'. If he's busy then, yeah, I'm in.'

'No probs. Text me later on.' Pushing myself off the table, I picked up my handbag. 'Okay, you ready, Lib?' I asked, now full of excitement and adrenaline, ready for the girls' night out ahead.

'Wouldn't matter even if I weren't,' she grumbled. 'You'd leave without me.'

I shrugged my shoulders and winked at George. 'You snooze, you lose.'

* * *

Lib and I were in the car and heading home shortly after I said I was leaving. There was no time to waste and no room for mucking around. I had a canvas that needed painting, and I intended on painting it with my newest pink lipstick and blush.

'Why the urgency to go out?' Lib asked from her position in the passenger seat next to me.

'No urgency. I just want a night out with my friends,' I replied, hiding my real reason with a kick-arse lie, my real reason being the resulting hurt and feeling of disappointment caused by Derek.

'You seem to forget — even though I tell you all the time — that you are the world's worst liar.' *Damn it.*

Rolling my eyes, I chose to turn up the radio to block out her correct assessment. Lib, however, leaned forward and switched it off completely.

'That was Derek on the phone, wasn't it? What happened?'

'Nothing. He just said he's going away for a while, that's all,' I explained, attempting to appear unfazed.

She turned to face me. 'That's not all.'

'What are you, a mentalist?'

'Maybe?' she smiled smugly.

I quickly glared at her then returned my attention to the road. 'More like mental.'

'So ... Derek said he had to leave for a while and that it was over, yeah?' she asked with a tone that hinted she was baiting me.

'No!'

'Right ... so he said that he was leaving for an unknown stretch of time and that he wanted to try a long-distance relationship, but was not sure if it would work?'

I kept my stare straight ahead but narrowed my eyes and answered with a sneer. 'No!'

'Then what's the problem?' Libby groaned.

'He said he had to go to Sydney for "family" issues,' I snapped, emphasising the 'family' with one-handed quotation fingers. 'He didn't tell me any more.'

'So what's the problem?' Lib repeated, her eyes bugging out of her head in a sarcastic and childish manner.

'The part where he wouldn't tell me any more.'

'Maybe it's personal, or he's not even sure what that "any more" part is just yet. And maybe when he does, he'll let you know.'

'Or maybe he has a wife and kids up there and I'm his dirty little secret,' I added like an insolent child.

'Don't be so fucking stupid, Carly,' Libby growled.

I turned my head to face her, shocked by her sudden outburst. Libby rarely swore in anger at me. 'Whoa! Geez, I didn't know that my lovelife meant so much to you.'

'Yeah, well it shouldn't, because it obviously doesn't mean that much to you. You are forever sabotaging your own chance at happiness. Finally, a guy comes along who appears to mesh with you ... a guy that you are clearly smitten with, and yet you refuse to stop playing this what-we-have-is-nothing game.'

'I'm not playing games, Lib,' I admonished quietly.

'Then why are you building that wall of yours? For once, don't. Don't build it. Enter a relationship without the fucking wall.'

Glancing sideways at her yet again, I couldn't believe how worked up she was over this. There had to be something else festering within her mind. 'Now, how 'bout you tell me what's going on?' I asked, turning the tables and hopefully prompting her to spill.

'Nothing,' she huffed, then instantly changed her mind. 'Actually, I will. Here you are with a drop-dead gorgeous guy, and you choose to push him away. You do this ALL THE TIME. It's not fair. Where's my drop-dead gorgeous guy, the one that if he showed even the slightest bit of interest in me, like Derek shows you, I would certainly not push away?'

Feeling every kind of guilt, sadness and annoyance as a result of Libby's confession, I decided to enter silence territory. Silence territory was a safe place to venture into when one wanted to eat one's words. Apparently, Libby was word-hungry as well ... the rest of the drive home was uncommunicative.

* * *

Four hours later, Lib, Sal, Brooke and I were stepping through the doors of Opals, one of the nightclubs at City Towers. I'd texted Alexis to see if she wanted to head down from the penthouse and have some fun with us. She'd explained that she, Bryce and the kids were having a family games night, but would definitely be up for it next time.

Apparently, Brycealicious had kindly informed the club's security guard that we were his VIP guests and, therefore, were escorted to a roped off section near the stage. *Note to self: show Bryce some bicep-squeezing gratitude.*

'This is so awesome!' Sal beamed. 'How do you know the owner again? What's his name ... Bryce?'

Sally was happily sipping on her Cosmopolitan, her brown wavy hair pinned into a sexy mess of curls on top of her head. She had on a black and gold-speckled off-the-shoulder top, complementing her black dress pants, and her make-up was subtle and classy.

'He and my best friend Alexis are seeing each other. They live in the penthouse,' I explained.

Her eyes widened. 'No shit! Really?'

'Really!' I affirmed, before throwing back my Slippery Nipple shot.

'Are you going to pace yourself tonight, Carls?' Lib asked with a sceptical glare.

I smoothed down my black, sequined shift dress, which rested mid-thigh, deliberately focussing on the unnecessary smoothing when I answered. 'Probably not.'

Just as I was about to scoop up my second shot, a masculine hand darted out of nowhere and swiped it from my grasp. Shocked, I watched as the contents of the small glass disappeared into the mouth of Will.

'Mm ...' he murmured with a boyish grin. 'I love a good Slippery Nipple.'

I smiled brightly, happy to see him. I liked Will, he was good value. 'It just so happens that I like Slippery Nipples as well. And now you owe me one.'

'Carly, if it weren't for Derek beating me to a pulp, I'd totally give you one,' he smiled again, his rugged and unshaven face endearing.

Will had short, dark, tousled brown hair that housed a sparse but sexy hint of grey through it. His face was adorned with a light yet well-groomed beard and moustache, and his pouty lips rivalled Brad Pitt's.

'Sure,' I drawled cynically while waving down our waiter. 'I'm almost certain he wouldn't give a flying fuck.'

'Are you for real?' he scoffed.

Shooting him a quick sideways glance, I nodded. 'Well, yeah. He's never once hinted we are anything more than just extra-special friends,' I explained with a sprinkle of sarcasm as the waiter stopped next to me. 'I'll have four Slippery Nipples. What do you girls want?'

Up until that point, Lib, Brooke and Sal had been as quiet as mice and, as a result, I had only just realised that I hadn't introduced them to Will.

'Shit! Sorry! Will, these are my friends and work colleagues: Sally, Brooke and Labia,' I playfully joked, gesturing toward Lib. Her face blushed a nice shade of salmon.

'Labia,' he questioned with a seductive smile toward Lib. 'Doesn't get any sweeter than that.'

Lib's colouring went from salmon to tomato, which didn't really do her whole ensemble much justice: redheads donning a complexion of pinks and reds was not a good mix. 'It's Lib or Elizabeth,' she corrected while shooting me tiny Libby-daggers.

'I think I like Labia better,' Will said, his voice a little lower and suggestive this time around.

Lib then turned her visual daggers in the direction of Will, making him flinch.

'Geez,' he said in surrender, 'Lib or Elizabeth it is. So what would your royal highness like to drink?'

'Oh, please,' Lib said with obvious irritation, 'as if I haven't heard that before.' *Ooh ... Labia likes Willy! This could be interesting.* 'And anyway, I'm quite capable of getting my own drink —'

'Actually, they are on the house,' the waiter interrupted.

'Make that five Slippery Nipples and five Cum Shots,' I announced. 'And they are all for me.'

'Carly!' Lib scolded.

'Labia!' I mimicked her scold in return.

Will chuckled, then slapped the waiter on the back in a familiar manner. 'I'll have a Redheaded Leg Spreader.'

Sally gasped and looked at Lib who was statue-like.

'Is that a real drink?' I asked incredulously.

'Sure is,' Will smiled, his focus now solely on Lib. *Ooh ... Willy likes Labia. Excellent!*

'Ladies! Can I get either of you a drink as well?' the waiter asked Brooke, Sal and Lib, his patience visibly wavering.

Sal slurped the last of her Cosmo in the most unlady-like manner. 'Yep, one of these.'

'Make that two,' Brooke added.

Staring Will squarely in the eye, Lib added, 'I'll have a Maneater.'

And with that the waiter disappeared into the crowd only to return moments later with our drinks.

I lined up my shots and started knocking them back.

'You may want to pace yourself,' Will warned, a look of concerned curiosity marring his burly face.

'Yes, Dad,' I said sarcastically.

'Hey, Will!' a female voice called from behind us. Both Will and I turned to face her. 'Oh, hi, Carly, this is a nice surprise,' Lucy said when she recognised who I was. Lucy was Bryce's extremely intelligent sister. She also played alongside the boys in the band.

'Hey, how are you?' I smiled. 'Got the night off?'

'You mean from Alexander? Yeah, the crazy kid is upstairs with Bryce and Alexis. I think his presence helps them both ... strangely enough,' she said, mumbling that last bit to herself.

Sliding along the booth seat, I suggested she sit down. 'Would you like to join us?'

'Thanks. Maybe for just one drink, then I have to head back upstairs. Where's Matt?' Lucy asked Will.

Will shrugged his shoulders. 'Probably attached to some chick at the mouth.'

'Nothing new,' Lucy murmured.

'Hey, Lucy, these are my friends: Brooke, Sal and Lib —'

'Oh, thank you. Using my proper name now, are we?' Libby interrupted, her sarcasm dripping as smoothly as honey.

I poked my tongue out at her.

Lucy laughed. 'Hi, nice to meet you.'

'Lucy is Bryce's sister,' I explained to the girls.

They all sounded their comprehension with a long-winded, 'Ohhh'.

Remembering that Lucy was a lesbian, I picked up one of my shots and offered it to her. 'Would you like a Slippery Nipple?'

Will burst into laughter at the sight of Lucy's tickled expression.

I rolled my eyes at him, then smiled at Lucy. 'Well ... I could offer you the Cum Shot, but apparently you are not into that. So, naturally, I assumed you'd want the Nipple,' I retorted.

Nodding her head, she accepted the shot. 'Yes, you are right. I'd take a Slippery Nipple over a Cum Shot any day.'

'Fuck, this conversation is hot,' Will said eagerly, now leaning up against the pylon next to our booth.

Libby tutted with disgust. 'Come on, Sal, Brooke, let's go dance.'

The three of them stood and snaked their way through the crowd toward the dance floor.

'So, what's her deal?' Will asked seriously.

'She's a redhead,' I deadpanned.

'Besides her hot as fuck hair,' he said with a tone of desire while watching Lib dance. 'She got a man?'

'Nope.'

'She want one?'

'Yep.'

'Good to know,' he said before finishing his drink, pushing off from the pylon and making his way in the direction of my friends with the look only a hungry predator would possess.

'I hope you realise you just willingly tossed your friend to a wolf,' Lucy informed me with a knowing smile.

'I know. She needs to be chewed on for a bit.'

'Nice!' Lucy laughed and then reached over me to grab hold of another shot. 'Nipples come in pairs,' was all she said, her explanation quite satisfactory. 'So, how's things with you and Derek?'

I choked on the Cum Shot I was in the process of downing. 'What do you mean?'

'The two of you ... you're an item, right?'

I shook my head as I wiped my lips and chin. 'No, I don't think so.'

'Oh ... sorry. I just thought that from what he and Lex said — Sorry, it doesn't matter. Forget I said anything.'

Her reddened cheeks had me curious. 'We've been having some fun together, but that's all. And anyway, he's in Sydney for god knows how long.'

'Yes, I know. Once he has things sorted with his father, he'll be back,' Lucy said softly with a kind smile.

Why does she know about his trip to Sydney? And why does she know more than me?

I was aware of the fact that Lucy and Derek had known each other ever since they were kids. But what I wasn't aware of was just how close they were now ... obviously closer than I thought.

Plastering on an artificially-sweet smile, I downed the last of my shots. 'Right, let's dance!' I hollered, my tone a mix of anger and determination. Clearly, in the mind of Derek, I was only close enough to fuck around with, yet not be privy to important information regarding his life. Maybe I was expecting too much? I don't know. One minute, he was saying one thing and the next he wasn't backing it up. He gave me the impression he wanted 'more', but then again, that was probably the problem ... we weren't exclusive so why expect anything more.

With thoughts of retribution and a weird confused-clarity now swimming through my body with the alcohol, I tore my metaphorical blinkers off and expanded my peripheral vision to take in some sexy looking man-bait. I was done with Derek holding me at bay.

* * *

'What are you doing?' Libby said angrily as she pulled me away from a piece of Italian man-sausage.

'Dancing with ...?' I asked, gesturing to the sausage and raising my eyebrow in anticipation of his answer.

'Marco,' he responded with arrogance.

'Marco, I'm dancing with Marco,' I answered Lib. 'Want to join in?'

'No, you stupid cow, I don't. And I don't think Derek would like you dancing with him either.'

Italian man-sausage shook his head in frustration and then walked away.

'Lib, you just scared him off. I wanted to see the sausage's sausage,' I whined with a giggle-infused pout.

'What is wrong with you? What about Derek?'

'What about Derek?' I barked. 'He's in Sydney, and whatever it is that he is doing there, he obviously doesn't want me to know.'

Will stepped up beside me and handed me his phone. 'You may want to take this,' he said, with a look that spelled trouble.

'It's not my phone. My phone is here,' I explained while reaching into my bra to retrieve it. As I pulled it out, I noticed five missed calls and ten text messages from Derek.

Shit! 'Is that him?' I mouthed to Will, swaying slightly as a result of my intoxicated state and daringly high heels.

Sporting a shit-eating grin, he nodded his head slowly. I groaned and grabbed the phone. 'What's up?'

Derek's sexy but infuriated voice filled my ears and journeyed through my body in a tantalising manner. 'Baby, I'm fucking pissed.'

'So,' I slurred, 'so am I.'

'So? What the fuck is going on, Carly? I get a text from Will telling me that you're getting salsa lessons from a cock-happy Italian fucker at Opals. I thought you said no side dishes.'

'I did,' I quipped.

'So why you breakin' that rule?'

Guilt, frustration, anger and sadness washed over me like an emotional tsunami that forced the closing of my eyes and the intake of a deep breath. 'Because we aren't working, Derek.'

'Who says?' he asked angrily.

'Me.'

'Why?'

'Just wait a minute,' I scowled. 'I need to find some-where more quiet.'

I moved away from the crowd of people dancing around me and headed for a private, more quiet alcove in the club. 'Derek, I can't do this any more.'

'Why?'

I sighed defeatedly. 'Because I'm feeling things I'm not used to. Because I'm confused and I don't like it.'

'And ...' he asked, his tone now sounding perplexed.

'And it fucking frightens me, all right?' I blurted out.

'Baby?'

I didn't answer him. I was too confused, angry and wasted to speak.

'Baby?' he said a little more firmly.

'What?' I snapped quietly.

'Let me try this in a language we both speak so that you understand it loud and clear: "I'm not a photographer, but I can picture you and me together."'

I dropped my head back and let out a small laugh at his cheesy pick-up line.

'Your body is sixty-five percent water and I'm thirsty,' he continued.

'Derek, stop it,' I sighed with a sad smile, 'you are not helping,'

'Carly. You and me just "are", all right?'

'Are what?'

'We just ... "are".'

Understanding what he was getting at, I begged the question I'd been pondering. 'Are we?'

'Yes. No side dishes. Just us,' he said firmly.

'What are you saying?'

'You know what I'm saying. I'm making us official.'

'If we are official, then why won't you tell me why you are in Sydney?'

'I will,' he said on a loud exhalation of breath. 'But I want to do it face to face.'

'So why is it that Lucy knows?' I asked, unable to hide the accusation in my tone. *Damn it! This is not me. I'm not the jealous type.*

There was a pause on the line before he spoke again. 'Carly, Lucy and I have known each other for a long time.

We are close, as are Bryce and I. They know my family, and they know me.'

'That's just it, Derek. How am I supposed to get to know you if you won't let me?'

I could hear him let out yet another frustrated breath. 'I will let you.'

'When?'

Silence circled again, dashing my optimism that the two of us could work. 'Never mind. Look, I'll see you when you get back, whenever that will be.'

Just as I was about to end the call, Derek's voice raised to a desperate shout. 'Carly, my dad is sick. This shit is hard for me, all right? Please just give me time and let me explain on my own terms.'

I inwardly sighed with relief that he had finally opened up, even if it were only a little. Why was it so difficult for him to be candid, and for me to give him the benefit of the doubt? Why could I not embrace that what we shared was so much more than just surface attraction? Why was it so hard?

'Baby,' he asked softly, 'will you give me time?'

Surrendering to the supplication in his voice, I sighed. 'Okay.'

'Good, now get this into that pretty blonde head of yours. You and I "are", remember that. And if I get word that you are rubbing that sexy fucking body of yours against another man, shit, it ain't gonna be pretty.'

'Well, best you hurry up and get back here, because I like to dance and I like to dance dirty.'

'I can tell you now that when I get back, we won't be dancing.'

'We'll see about that, Dik,' I said, my cheeky smile audible through my words.

Derek chuckled deeply. 'You'll be getting dick, and plenty of it, don't you worry.' His promise and deep sounding amusement were the ignition to the fuse of my heart.

'I can't wait,' I choked out.

'Neither can I. Now go. Go and enjoy the rest of your night. I'll talk to you tomorrow. Oh, and Carly ...'

'Yeah?' I asked, expectation lacing my voice.

'I mean it, stay away from the Italian fucker. I'm not the sharing type, baby.'

I smiled at his possessive words. 'Neither am I.'

We disconnected the call, which was when the last few moments of our conversation finally sunk in. *Not the sharing type? We 'are'? Fuck the stars! I think Derek just officially became my boyfriend.*

CHAPTER
16

Derek had to remain in Sydney for the three weeks that followed our discussion that the two of us 'are'. I was still not sure what 'are' was. Okay, so I gathered 'we just are' meant we were officially together, and in youngster's terms, boyfriend and girlfriend. But the notion was still strange to me. Yes, I was thirty-five years old and acting like a pathetic adolescent. But the whole commitment thing was foreign territory for me. I'd never committed to anything or anyone in my life — apart from raising Sasha and Rico. Oh, and my joint tenancy lease with Libby. So I guess it was only natural that Derek and I being 'are' would take a while for me to get used to.

During our telephone conversations and text messages over the course of the past few weeks, Derek had opened up bit by bit on his own terms and explained that his dad had suffered a stroke many years ago.

He and his twin brother, Sean, had both been expected to take over the family business. Sean and their mother,

Loretta, had made the assumption that Derek would give up his career as a firefighter and co-run King Logistics. So when Derek explained that he had no intention whatsoever of doing that, the proverbial shit basically hit the fan.

Just the other night, after a session of scorchin' hot phone sex, Derek mentioned that he and his father had always gone head-to-head with respect to his chosen career path. He also explained that he'd very adamantly stood his ground and pursued the life that he wanted for himself and, because that was not the life his father wanted for him, they had become estranged.

After his father suffered the stroke, Derek's parents moved to Sydney to be closer to the country's leading neurologist. Sean remained in Melbourne and was appointed president of King Logistics by proxy. Unfortunately, and ever since, Derek's relationship with his entire family had become strained.

He'd told me that although he hated having to go to Sydney, because being around his family was incredibly hard, he still felt obligated to make sure his mother and father were coping after his father's most recent TIA — a Transient Ischaemic Attack, apparently. That devoted and caring side to him only further reinforced my feelings that if I'd had any doubts about his loyalty toward people he cared about, then those doubts were undeserved and disproved.

* * *

I'd received a text the previous night, prior to Derek boarding his flight. My plans were to drive to the airport and pick him up, but he'd explained that his flight was delayed and wasn't due to arrive at Tullamarine until the early hours of the morning. He didn't want me driving at such a dreadful hour and had told me he'd taxi it home and pick me up the following day, where he would take me to the gig that Live Trepidation were playing at a rooftop bar in the city.

So when I heard the engine of his Ranger pull up out the front of my house, the excited feeling he evoked in me was paradoxical: elated fear. I was excited at seeing him in the flesh after three weeks, but the thought of that terrified me. This would be our first reunion since declaring that we 'are'.

As I scooted along the hallway after hearing him knock, I took a few deep breaths before stopping and opening the door.

'Hi,' I said with a smile that stretched my skin, almost to the point of discomfort.

Derek was standing with hands behind his back, his expression mirroring my own, but in a more cool and controlled manner. 'Hi, gorgeous,' he replied, his smile drawing an unusual feeling from within. It was a feeling of infatuation, of weak knees and light-headedness.

I took in his tight grey t-shirt and black denim jeans, which were fastened with a thick, black leather belt. The whole I'm-a-sexy-rock-god ensemble was finished with a pair of heavy black boots.

Reaching out, I grabbed the collar of his t-shirt and aggressively pulled him to meet my lips. One of his hands instantly found my arse while the other gently slid up the back of my neck, stopping at the base of my skull. His touch sent a delightful shiver down my spine.

He pressed me into his hard warm body, and I moaned with pleasure at finally being able to feel and taste him again — he really was addictive.

'I've missed you,' I murmured honestly.

'Mm ... the feeling is mutual, baby,' he murmured in return, firmly flexing his fingers into my hair.

We continued to kiss each other hungrily while standing at the threshold to my house, neither of us wanting to separate from one another. So many emotions filled my being as we held each other tightly: desire, longing, fear, safety and an undeniable attraction. The physical allurement between us was acute.

I felt comforted and relieved, yet I also felt anxious and frenzied. One thing I no longer felt, as a result of our forced telecommunicated relationship and lack of physical interaction over the past three weeks, was reluctance. I was no longer reluctant where Derek was concerned. The hesitation and foreboding I experienced beforehand were now a thing of the past. It was time for me to see what was beyond attraction. It was time for me to accept that we 'are'.

'Want to come in?' I spoke breathlessly against his neck, releasing my lips from his and pressing them to his Adam's apple.

'Sure,' he answered with obvious lust-filled restraint. 'But first, I have a present for you.'

I looked up at him and smiled brightly. *Carly Josephine Henkley LOVES presents.* 'Ooh ... what is it?'

Derek released me from his grip and brought his hands in between our bodies.

Dangling off his finger and gently swaying before me was a white gift bag with a La Perla logo printed on it.

'La Perla?' I asked excitedly.

He just nodded, smiled and indicated with a twitch of his finger that I accept the bag from him.

'Where did you get this?'

'Airport. I'd always wondered why there would need to be a fancy lingerie shop at the airport. Now I know,' he said with cheeky raised eyebrow.

Eagerly, I slid the bag from his finger and peeked inside, moving the tissue paper to find a stunning piece of black and red lingerie. 'What is it?'

He stepped toward me, gently coaxing me into the house. 'It's what you will be wearing today, Carly. It's what I will be thinking about as I sing on that stage, and it's what I will quite fucking happily remove from you before we fuck later tonight.'

Stopping at the sound of the words he just spoke, my cheeks warmed and my pussy meowed. *Yes, it meowed like a hungry feline.* I smiled boldly and once again peeked into the bag before turning on my heels. 'Well, best I go put it on then.'

* * *

Not long after Derek arrived to pick me up, we'd had to leave so as not to be late to Live Trepidation's gig at Bar 22. Mind you, they'd be hard pressed starting proceedings without their lead singer.

I'd been to this particular venue before with Steph and Jade, as we all loved scoping out local bands. Funnily enough, we'd never previously come across Live T.

'Hey, Derek, glad to have you back,' Lucy said as we approached the stage upon arrival.

Lucy — together with Bryce, Will and Matt — was setting up for the gig. She gave him a tight hug and rubbed his back affectionately. Her reassuring gesture stirred my inner hulk, but I quickly put that to rest by reminding myself that Lucy was pussyfied and cock-resistant.

She pulled away from Derek and then gave me a quick hug in greeting as well. 'Nice to see you again, Carly.'

'You too,' I replied as we pulled apart. 'Derek, I'm just going to go and sit with Alexis and the kids, all right?'

He leaned over and gave me a quick peck on the lips before whispering in my ear, 'Don't forget, I'll be thinking about what's under those clothes the whole time I'm up there.'

I moved my lips to his ear while gently grazing my cheek to his. 'And I'll be thinking about how you will take it off me and what you will do afterward. Don't forget, you have set the bar high.'

He chuckled. 'Baby, my bar will be high, don't you worry.'

'I'm not,' I said sincerely, as I pulled away from him.

Now directing my attention to the rest of the band, I smiled and wished them well. 'Good luck, guys.'

'Don't need it,' Will replied arrogantly. 'Pure talent does not require luck.'

'True,' I yelled back as I walked away. 'But pure narcissism leads to nothing but fapping, so I hope you like self-service.'

Bryce laughed at my response. Will, on the other hand, asked what narcissism meant.

Winking at him, I then detoured to the bar to get myself a glass of wine before making my way over to where Alexis and the kids were sitting.

'Hey, bitch,' I greeted her as she picked at a loose thread on the red and white striped tub chair she was sitting on. Nate and Charlotte were also sitting in tub chairs positioned around a small wood-slatted table. They were both quietly playing their iPods.

'Hi, Carls,' she responded as she snapped out of her preoccupied state.

Straightaway, I sensed that she was agitated, but it wasn't in a way that had me worried. Instead, her nervous demeanour had me curious.

'Nice day, huh?'

She looked at me, but her eyes held no direct interest in what I was saying. 'Yeah, nice.'

'Summer, come at me,' I added eagerly as I sat down, scruffing Nate's hair in the process. 'How's it going, twerps?'

'I'm not a twerp, Aunty Carls,' Charlotte stated with absolute certainty.

'I beg to differ.'

She wrinkled her nose. 'What does that mean?'

'It means she still thinks we are twerps,' Nate added without taking his attention away from his iPod.

'That it does, and Mum agrees with me, don't ya, Lex?' I asked, wanting to bring their mother in on the fun. She didn't answer me, continuing to stare intently at the band who were just about finished with setting up. 'Alexis?' I asked again, this time raising my voice.

'Yeah, what?' she snapped.

'Are you all right? You've been off with the pixies ever since I arrived.'

'Sorry, I'm just ...' she leaned in closer to me, 'nervous.'

Alexis then slumped back in her seat with a terrified expression on her face.

'Why are you nervous?'

She quickly glanced at Charli and Nate who both had their heads down, attention fixed on their iPods. 'Derek has been teaching me how to play the guitar, and I'm going to surprise Bryce with a song. I'm freaking out. I've only been playing for a few months.'

'Fuck off!' I said out aloud, honestly surprised by her confession. I knew that she had been getting lessons, but had no idea that she'd planned to perform at one of the band's gigs.

Alexis glared at me, then subtly flicked her eyes in the kids direction. Both twerps hadn't even flinched.

'Are you for real? Oh, my god! That's awesome. So why are you nervous?' I asked with excitement, having not heard Lexi sing for years. She used to sing a lot when we were younger. Mind you, back then I found it annoying.

'Oh,' she deadpanned for the smallest of seconds, 'let me guess ... 'cause there's a whole rooftop full of freakin' strangers.'

I picked up my glass of wine and sipped it. 'Who cares?'

'I do!' she blurted out as she picked up hers, sipping it not quite as calmly as I had.

'Why? Who are you performing for? Them,' I gestured to the people slowly filling the space around us, 'or Bryce?'

She closed her eyes for the briefest of seconds and sucked in a deep breath. 'Bryce.'

'So just play it for him. Don't even acknowledge anyone else,' I explained before sipping my drink again.

Glancing up at the stage, I focussed my attention on Derek and his bent-over position. He was fiddling around with guitar amp cords and displaying his sexy as fuck arse for my enjoyment. 'We haven't had vanilla yet,' I regretfully confessed.

'Oh.' Lexi gave the kids another quick glance, checking to see if they were still occupied with their handheld devices and not catching on to the fact that their mother and I were now talking about sex. 'Why not? That's unlike you. You normally devour vanilla, then jump right into chocolate or even rocky road.'

'I do not,' I scoffed, blatantly lying. She knew me so well.

'Yes, you do. There're not many flavours you haven't tried.' *This is true.*

'I like strawberry, Aunty Carls. Do you like strawberry?' Charli asked, her eyes still figuratively glued to her screen.

Pressing my lips together to refrain from laughing, but also utilising my locked tight lips, I sounded an 'mm' noise before I was able to answer. 'Yes, Charli, I love strawberry. It's my favourite.'

'Mum, what's your favourite?'

Alexis turned a nice shade of flushed pink. 'I like vanilla with sprinkles and topping and chocolate chips,' she answered quickly.

'Yeah, me too,' Charli smiled. 'Can I have some now?'

This conversation had turned highly amusing. I was now revelling in the fact that Lexi had to somehow dig herself out of this double entendre styled discussion.

'What, Charli?' Lexi asked, appearing a little flustered. 'What do you want?'

'Ice cream.'

'Oh. Um ... sure.' She dug out her purse. 'Nate?'

'I'll have what she's having,' he replied unperturbed and, like Charli, not removing his eyes from the little screen before him. *This is the best doublespoken conversation ever.*

I couldn't help it and started laughing. It was no secret that I loved watching Alexis squirm during an awkward situation.

She glared playfully at me in return. 'Here, Charli, go up to the bistro desk over there and order two ice cream sundaes. Nate, go with her, please.'

When they were gone, Lexi turned to me, all serious like. 'Why haven't you fucked Derek yet? Carls, what's wrong with him?'

I shook my head, displaying my bewilderment. 'Nothing, it's not him. It's me.'

'What's wrong with you, then? Is your fiery hole singed?' she asked, nearly choking on the wine she had not long beforehand consumed.

I glared at her. 'You're such a bitch. No, I really like him and I don't want to screw this up,' I explained honestly.

Saying it out loud even surprised me.

Alexis pulled my hands into hers and squeezed them with reassurance. 'You're not going to screw this up, Carls,' she said quietly.

'How can you be so sure?' I groaned.

'Well, I can't, hon. But I know you, and you're awesome. Derek seems to like your awesomeness as well, so just be yourself and go with the flow. Don't try to change who you are.'

I sighed. 'It's not that simple.'

'Carly?' she questioned harshly.

'Yes,' I replied, deliberately lacing my tone with hostility.

'Do you want to fuck Derek?' *Of course I want to fucking fuck Derek. Who in their right mind wouldn't?*

Sighing at the thought that I would be doing just that by the end of this day, I answered. 'Yes.'

'Well, that's fucking great, because I want to fuck you, too,' Derek said as he stepped up beside me, a shit-eating grin on his face. 'How 'bout tonight? My house. I'll even cook you dinner first.'

I took in his knowing expression, his intent both terrifying and exciting me beyond anything else I had ever felt sexually.

Leaning closer he spoke quietly, his breath tickling my ear. 'I won't bite, Carls, unless you want me to.'

My eyes widened at the visual I was conjuring in my head of Derek sinking his teeth in my neck. I kind of had a thing for vampires, Damon Salvatore and Eric Northman my ultimate vamp porn.

'Sure,' I answered shakily.

'Good.' He stood back up with a satisfied yet cocky look on his face then turned to Lexi. 'Alexis, how are you feeling?'

'As nervous as fuck,' she answered, holding up her trembling hands as evidence.

'Don't be. The last time we rehearsed you were fine. I will pick up the chords if you falter. Now, Lucy is going to call Charli up on stage as soon as our set finishes, then you'll be next.'

'Okay,' she answered.

I was still staring intensely at Derek, eye-fucking him greedily, and mentally licking his caramel skin. He had flipped a switch and turned on my Carly-cave, triggering an excited tingle of anticipation deep in my core.

'Hope you like chicken. I make a mean satay,' Derek declared before placing a quick kiss on my lips. He then made his way back to the stage, not even giving me a chance to respond or kiss him back, or even cop a quick feel of his package.

Slowly settling my Derek-daze, I made eye contact with Lexi. 'I don't.'

'You don't what?' she asked with a confused expression.

'Like satay,' I admitted. 'But fuck! I'll eat it for him. I'll even eat it off him if he wants.'

Dropping my head to the table, I surrendered to the enormity that was Dik.

* * *

Derek owned the stage during the following set in a way that only a naturally sexy and talented lead singer could own it. It wasn't just the fact that his voice had sensual unadulterated sex with my eardrums. No, it was more than that. It was the way he caressed the mic stand and how he fingered the strings on his guitar. It was the way he made eye contact with the occupants of the room. And it was the way he articulated his connection to the lyrics; his inner emotions poured out of him in the form of intense facial expressions. It was clear he was a passionate person, dedicated to everything he put his time into and that was by far his sexiest trait. Well, that, and his caramel chest and Cockasaurus Rex.

'When do I get to sing?' Charli asked, excited and impatient.

'Derek said when they finish this first set of songs,' I explained. 'So what are you going to sing, Charli?'

'I'm going to sing "True Colours". Lucy has been helping me practise. I like that song because it's about rainbows.' *Um ... well, technically, twerp, it's about finding inner courage and being yourself, but I guess rainbows will do.*

The music died down and the band began to exit the stage, except for Lucy. 'Charlotte, would you like to come up here?' she voiced through the microphone.

Charli sprang up like a bloody jack-in-the-box and enthusiastically made her way up on stage.

'We have a very special guest here today to perform a song for you,' Lucy continued as she adjusted her seated position behind the keyboard. 'I'd like to introduce Miss Charlotte Summers. She is going to help me sing "True Colours" by Cyndi Lauper.'

Charli took a seat next to Lucy and moved the microphone down so that it was positioned perfectly in front of her mouth. 'Hi, everyone,' she said happily, addressing the room's occupants with confidence.

Lucy started playing the keyboards, and I couldn't help but notice how naturally beautiful she really was. I even decided that had I enjoyed a little lady-licking myself, I'd totally want in on her.

Charlotte was a natural performer and entertained everyone in the room with her happy aura, Lucy guiding her the entire time. As the song wound to a close and Lucy slowly pressed the final keys on the keyboard, the room erupted into a round of applause. Alexis and I both stood and clapped Charli's efforts. The twerp's innate talents were like her mother's.

'Thank you very much,' Charli said, positioning herself in the middle of the stage and curtsying before leaping to the ground happily.

Alexis walked toward her and knelt down, meeting her daughter halfway in order to give her a congratulatory hug. Lucy also stepped down from the stage and squatted next to them before she and Charli then made their way to where I now sat with the rest of the band, sans Derek.

Standing up slowly from her squatted position in front of the stage, I watched as Lexi nervously smoothed down her pink floral dress before greeting Derek and accepting the guitar he handed her. He gave her a friendly and reassuring wink then took a seat on a stool positioned next to hers.

'What's she doing?' Bryce asked, clearly confused.

'Just shut up and watch,' Lucy replied with a conceited smile.

'Yeah, it's a secret,' Charli added.

'Hello, everyone, my name is Alexis and I have to let you in on a little secret. You see, for the past few months, I have been learning to play the guitar for the sole purpose of performing here today as a surprise for someone who means the world to me. This special someone and I suffered a great tragedy recently, and in the midst of that tragedy, I came to realise that I couldn't live without him. He always finds ways to support and give me everything that I could possibly want or need. So I wanted to give him something back, something only I could give him. Bryce, this is from me to you.'

'You've got to be bloody shittin' me,' he said as he muffled his mouth with his hand. 'How the hell did I not know about this?'

Lexi started strumming the guitar, Derek joining in and playing his part alongside her. I watched in awe as she began singing and inwardly admired her courage. Not wanting to openly admit it to her before because she was having her mini-breakdown, but fucked if I would *ever* do anything even remotely like what she was doing now. I'd seriously pee my pants.

Before too long, and as if able to wield a spell on all around her, Alexis had captivated the room's occupants, everyone hanging on every note that she sang and every move that she and Derek made. Even I was entranced and astonished by how brilliantly she played the guitar.

Alexis stepped from the stool she had been seated on and placed the guitar on top of it, opting to take the microphone with both hands and make her way toward our table, or more accurately, toward Bryce.

The chemistry and love between the both of them in that moment was immeasurable. The way they blocked out everyone else around them and focussed solely on each other was purely magical. It was what I wanted with Derek, that instant where no one else in the world other than the two of us existed.

In that moment, as if having been smacked across the head with a wake-up-and-seize-the-day bat, I realised that what Derek and I shared was not just attraction. It was a deep connection that, if he too felt the same way, meant it was quite possible we could have a future together.

Realising I'd just had an epiphany of sorts, I tore my eyes away from Alexis and Bryce and looked toward Derek, who was still perched on a stool on the stage. He was watching me intently as he played the guitar, his stare setting every nerve ending I possessed into an explosive state. The heat from his burning gaze had the ability to mentally strip each item of clothing from my body, stripping me down to my core.

I realised once again that he owned me. *What. The. Fuck?*

Alexis finished the song and then indulged in a near-porn session on Bryce's lap. I was almost at the point of covering both the twerp's eyes.

'You are incredible. I'm ... I'm just so ...' Bryce shook his head in awed shock. 'I ... thank you ...' he stuttered.

'You're welcome. Sometimes it's easier to hide something furtively than it is to hide it blatantly,' Alexis said softly to him with a sneaky smile.

'Nice work, Alexis,' Will added with a tilt of his beer in her direction. 'Now we can finally get rid of Derek.'

'I heard that, arsehole,' Derek answered as he stopped next to where Bryce and Alexis were seated.

Lexi climbed off of Bryce's lap and stood up, giving Derek a hug. 'Thank you so much,' she said appreciatively.

He chuckled at something she whispered in his ear and then pulled away. 'You did great.'

Her cheeks flushed with embarrassment. 'I did miss that chord.'

'What chord?' he said with a shrug of his shoulders, obviously trying to dismiss her mistake.

Bryce rose to his feet and shook Derek's hand. 'Thanks, mate, although I'm not sure what to think about you being able to spend so much time with my woman behind my back and without my knowledge.'

Derek patted Bryce on the back. 'You *should* be worried about that, mate,' he said playfully, before moving away and pulling up a chair next to me.

As he sat and turned in my direction, our eyes locked and something within us both ignited. I couldn't speak for him and guess what emotions he was feeling, but for me, my heart was pounding uncontrollably within my chest and I all of a sudden felt like crying. It was absolutely fucking insane.

CHAPTER
17

Derek, Bryce, Will, Matt and Lucy played the remainder of their gig, which gave me a chance to calm my farm. Coming to the realisation that you could quite possibly have found the one you want to share the rest of your life with was the most terrifying revelation ever. I shit you not. It was more terrifying than MAC going out of business or David Gandy quitting modelling.

Now that the gig was coming to a close, I found myself starting to think about my impending fuck-fest with Caramello Koala. Not to mention that I now wanted to become Mrs Caramello Koala in the distant, distant future. *Holy fucking shitballs. I want to be Mrs fucking Caramello Koala.*

'Ready to go?' Bryce asked, as he slid his hand across Alexis' back. *Shit! Shit! Shit! No!*

'No, Alexis and I need the ladies room,' I insisted, almost at the point of panic.

She gave me an unsure look then turned to Bryce. 'Be back in a minute. I'll meet you at the car, Apparently I need to pee.'

As we pushed through the door of the bathroom, she gave me a questioning stare. 'So why the last minute toilet trip?'

Not knowing how to divulge my life changing '*WTF?*' moment, I answered her flatly. 'Because I have a bladder to empty.'

'Why else?' she probed further.

Entering the toilet cubicle, I sighed, figuring that I should just come out with it. 'Because I'm still shitting bricks.'

'Literally or figuratively speaking, Carls? We are in the loo, remember?'

'Figuratively, you idiot! I'm terrified of having sex with Derek, and clearly he wants it ... tonight!' I put my head in my hands, elbows resting on my knees.

'Carls, for god's sake just screw the man. What is wrong with you? I've never seen you this apprehensive about intimacy, ever!' She flushed the toilet and I followed shortly after.

'I don't fucking know,' I groaned painfully. 'I hate this feeling. What ... the ... fuck is this feeling?' I demanded while we both stared at our reflections in the bathroom mirror.

'I think it's lurrrve,' she purred, moronically. *Love? Oh, you can fuck right off to Fucktown.*

'Pfft. It's not love. I barely know him,' I dismissed.

She flicked water at my head, getting my attention. 'You love him.'

'You're disgusting,' I replied, wiping it off.

'Well, you are falling for him at least. That's the only explanation.'

I looked back at my reflection in the mirror, knowing that she was speaking the god's honest truth. 'Urgh! You're right. I think I'm falling in love with him, and we haven't even had sex yet. This is insane.'

Alexis moved to the hand dryer, raising her voice over the loud hum. 'No, it's not. It's exciting and wonderful and the first time you have sex with him is going to be great.'

A smile teased at the corner of my mouth as I joined her to dry my hands.

'Go home, Carls. Shave your legs, arms, pussy and toes if you have to —'

'I don't have hairy toes. Who has hairy toes?' I rebuked.

'Shave whatever needs shaving, then moisturise and do all the fucked-up shit we think we have to do before we let a man see us naked. Then make sure you practise your alphabet to loosen the muscles in your face.' She started emphasising the letters 'A' and 'O' opening her mouth wide, suggestively. 'When was the last time you sucked cock? It's been a while, hasn't it? You would've told me otherwise.' *Oh, I've sucked cock, all right. And I owned that alphabet shit right there.*

'Fuck off,' I retorted, looking away and not wanting to insinuate the obvious ... which was that my mouth had already enjoyed some of Derek's cock. For once in my life

I didn't want to brag. And that, in itself, was strangely out of character.

'Yeah, I thought as much.'

'Well, I'm not telling you any more,' I said as I walked past her and pushed the door open to return to the rooftop.

'Oh, yes you will. I want a phone call first thing tomorrow morning.'

* * *

The atmosphere in the car during the drive to Derek's house was like nothing I had ever experienced before. My chest was heaving uncontrollably and my thighs were trembling as a result of my excited yet nervous anticipation. I was an emotional wreck at the thought of what was to come — that notion extremely foreign to me — for I knew what we shared was so much more.

'You're nervous, aren't you?' he asked, breaking the silence between us.

I opted to remain staring out of the window when I answered quietly. 'Just a little.'

'Why?' he asked, his soft, concerned voice filling my ears.

I turned to face him. 'To be honest, I'm not sure.'

'I know my cock is huge, baby, but I won't hurt you,' he said with a playful smile, quickly glancing at me.

Laughing, I could tell this was his way of easing my tension. 'I'm not afraid of your cock, Derek. I like your cock. In fact, I like it very much.'

'Then why are you nervous?' *Jesus, stop asking me that.*

Sighing, and continuing with my new-found Carly-speaks-the-truth quality, I answered honestly yet again. 'Because I don't do intimacy very well, I never have. How can I put this? I feel without feeling.'

Derek turned the corner and pulled up at a tiny-looking cottage with a picket fence. The quaint little house had me raising my eyebrow at him questioningly. 'That's ... cute,' I said, trying to hold in my impending laugh.

'Don't let the fence fool you,' he advised, nodding his head toward his house. 'My place is badarse.'

'Yeah, it looks it,' I said, clearly lacking sincerity while nodding and smiling, before reaching down and grabbing hold of my bag which sat at my feet. Derek climbed out of the truck, jogged round to my side of the car and opened the door for me.

Swivelling around to face him and thinking I was about to slide down from the seat until my feet hit the road, I was pleasantly surprised when he stepped up to me and opened my legs, slotting himself in between them.

He slowly ran his hands up the outside of my denim-covered thighs until he secured my arse and pulled me to his pelvis in a rough jerking motion. 'Stop with the nervous shit. There's nothing to be nervous about. I'm going to worship that pretty little body of yours with my own and I can tell you it's going to be fucking intimate. You will *feel* everything,' he said as he slowly thrust his hips against me.

My eyes fluttered and a small cry of pleasure whispered across my lips.

Derek leaned forward and brushed a wisp of my hair away from my face. 'After we are done, baby, then you can tell me whether you do intimacy or not, all right?'

I clenched my legs tightly around his hips and rubbed my pussy against him, desperately trying to relieve some of the ache my clit was harbouring. 'All right,' I said with a relieved smile. Then, slinging my bag over his shoulder and wrapping my arms around his neck, I motioned toward the house. 'Now how 'bout you show me your pretty little cottage and then fuck me inside it.'

He lifted me to him, provoking a small scream of excitement to escape my throat. 'How 'bout I fuck you first then show you around.'

Mashing my lips to his, I mumbled, 'Sounds like a plan.'

Derek carried me up the path and onto the small verandah, all the while plunging his tongue into my mouth. He fumbled with his key as he tried to unlock the door, cursing sweet words of frustration in the process.

It made me giggle.

After finally getting the door open, he stepped us into his narrow foyer where I dropped my bag behind him in order to run my hands up and over his closely shaved head. I loved the feel of his short hair stubble as it gently caressed the palm of my hands.

Pressing me up against the wall, he groaned with a desperate fierceness that rendered any control I'd previously held utterly useless. Then, pushing a code into the security panel beside my head, he continued to kiss me passionately.

The carnal desperation, desire and palpable need arising from him stripped me of oxygen. I separated my mouth from his and drew in some much needed air. My lips were plump, moist and buzzing with the after-effects of his divine oral assault.

Searching his eyes for the smallest of seconds, I could see — for the first time — his vulnerability. On the surface he may have displayed such brazen cockiness, but on the inside, he was just as nervous as me.

Leaning forward, I kissed him softly, changing the pace from frenzied to sensual. Then, sliding my hands down his back, I pulled his t-shirt free from his jeans and yanked it over his head.

Derek's smooth, muscled chest was a sight to behold and lock away for those lonely nights with just me and my Lelo. It truly was a piece of fapping-art.

Leaning down once again as he held me to the wall, I licked his pec and gently sucked his tense nipple into my mouth.

'Carly,' he warned with ardour, pulling me away from the wall with lightning speed.

We entered frenzied territory once more as I slid my tongue back into his mouth and held his head tightly. I couldn't get enough of all that he wanted to give me — I couldn't get enough of him.

He walked me along the hall until we made a turn into what I assumed was his bedroom. I didn't take much notice of my surroundings, for now was not the time. Instead, I became acutely aware of his mattress beneath me as he gently laid me down upon it.

Scooting backward as he crawled like a hungry animal above me, my entire body buzzed with a sexual depravation that I knew he would soon remedy.

'Stop,' he said firmly, halting my backward scooting.

I looked into his eyes, wondering what the hell we were stopping for and if I'd done something wrong. 'What —'

Slowly, he began to unbutton my shirt, each touch of his fingers to my skin like a searing knife, invisibly branding me.

With every button he undid, he would smooth open the shirt wider and wider until it fell completely open, exposing his La Perla gift.

'Fuck!' he ground out, taking in the black lace bustier with red ribbon detailing. With not as much composure as he'd just managed, he began unbuttoning my jeans and pulling them down, revealing the matching G-string, garter and stocking.

'Jesus fucking Christ!' he whispered.

I giggled and looked down upon my body. 'Yeah, I'm all right,' I said conceitedly.

'You are more than all right. You're gorgeous, Carly. But as hot as this looks on you, it's time for it to come off.'

'Like fun it is!' I said resolutely, kicking his hands away. 'This would have cost an absolute fortune. I'm not taking it off now. You are just going to have to fuck me while I'm in it.'

Derek's eyes widened at my stubborn stance, so I lazily let my legs fall apart, rewarding him with the view only an expensive crotchless G-string could give him.

He leered devilishly, then pulled me toward him in a swift movement that nearly stole my breath and, before I knew it, he had rolled us over until I was straddling his chest. 'Sit that pussy of yours on my face, now!' he demanded.

His insistent tone and greedy expression had me wet almost instantly and, not wanting to wait a second longer to feel that talented tongue of his slide over me, I crawled up and over his shoulders until my butt rested on his chest.

'Up,' he said, as he lifted my arse with both his hands, placing my pussy on his mouth.

'Oh, god!' I croaked, feeling his tongue caress me in a long, slow and tortuous sweep. As it glided over my wet skin, every nerve ending I possessed in that area woke and tingled exquisitely. The man and his ability to use that mouth muscle was beyond impressive. And again, without wanting to sound like a slutsky, I've had plenty of tongue-wielders to compare him to. My Carly-cave has seen its fair share of muff-divers.

Grabbing the top of the headboard for balance, I began to slowly move my hips against his face, heightening the sensation as I experienced the softness of his lips and tongue, the hardness of his nose and chin, and the roughness from his stubble. Every surface that my sensitive clit came into contact with mixed gloriously with his artistry: the way in which he alternated from lapping, to flicking, to sucking and then probing was a divine pleasure.

I murmured incoherently, the sounds leaving my mouth not legitimate words.

Derek flexed his fingers which were gripping my hips and rocked me a little harder and faster, intensifying the superb sensations I was feeling that were escalating me toward orgasm.

'Yes! Harder, faster,' I moaned, encouraging his efforts.

He increased his tongue's movement, flicking my clit with newfound intensity and, coupled with the amorous growl resonating from him, I climaxed and came on his face. 'Oh god!' I cried out. *Holy fucking face fuck.*

Finding just enough strength to lift my pussy from his damp face, I sat up, still gripping the headboard for stability. My head was bowed, my ability to formulate a rational thought nonexistent. But regardless of my disjointed and blissful state, I could still decipher the sound of him undoing his pants.

Turning around, I spied him reaching for a condom on the bedside table. And the thought of not being able to feel his naturally beautiful cock saddened me.

'I'm on the pill,' I said quietly. 'And ... I'm always safe. With ... with everyone else, that is.'

Desire yet caution flooded his chiselled features. 'Are you sure?'

'Yes, but only if you tell me that you are always safe as well?'

'Yes, always,' he admitted.

I nodded and crawled toward him, taking the foil packet from his hands and pulling him atop me as I fell back on the bed. The weight of him crushed me in a wonderful way ... his heat, his scent, his feel completely enveloping me.

Derek ran his hand down the side of my face while he kissed me sensually, its warm, calloused texture teasing my skin as he continued to drag it down my neck. He stopped its journey at my cleavage and then wrenched down my bustier and grabbed a handful of my tit. With a delectable squeeze, he separated his mouth from mine and pulled away to wrap his lips around my peaked nipple. 'Are you *feeling* this, baby?' he mumbled.

'Oh god, yes,' I breathed out.

Derek then let go of my breast and ran his hand down my side until he reached my pussy. Slowly, he plunged two fingers deep inside me.

'How 'bout this?' he asked as he licked my neck. 'Are you *feeling* this?'

I cried out again, 'Yes,' and closed my eyes.

Everything he did felt fucking amazing, which kind of confounded me. It wasn't as if I'd never been kissed, licked, sucked or fucked before. And it wasn't as if he were the porn king of Pound Town. Yet every kiss, every word and every touch he gave me was unlike anything I'd ever experienced.

My eyes jerked open when his fingers vacated me and I felt the crown of his dick press into my entrance.

'You ready for some Dik?' he asked smugly.

I let out a small giggle and nodded before biting my lower lip. Derek leaned forward and released it from within my teeth by sucking it into his mouth, all the while pushing his cock inside me.

'Oh. My. God!' I moaned through a wave of rapture. The feeling of him stretching and filling me was pure fucking bliss. I raised both legs and wrapped them around his back, locking them together and securing him to me.

Derek began to push against me with a slow deep rock of his hips, the depth he reached triggering my pussy to clench around him.

'Fuck, you feel good,' he murmured into my neck.

I gripped his shoulders tightly and rocked with him, enhancing every slide, push, pull and rub our bodies produced.

Lying there with Derek inside me felt like ecstasy, and I couldn't put my finger on exactly why that was. Yes, I was *feeling* — fuck, I was feeling every goddamned inch of him — but no, it was more than that. For the first time in my life I was connecting in every way to the man I was actually physically connecting with ... it was enlightening, albeit just a tad shocking.

'You *feeling* that, beautiful?' Derek asked as he peered deep into my eyes, into my soul.

The emotion within me started to bubble, so I nodded and closed my eyes to prevent the obvious moisture building behind them.

The soft brush of his lips against my eyelids provoked them to flutter open, coupled with his more incessant and stronger thrusts into me.

My breathing hiked, as did my rising orgasm, as I sank my fingernails into his shoulders.

'Fuck!' he groaned, tensing with the arching of his back. My pussy clenched his cock, gripping and milking him as he filled me. My fingernails scraped his shoulderblades and settled with a biting grip into his back as I, too, climaxed and came with a shudder.

What the fuck was that? I was in post-coital bliss, *feeling* everything he said I would. But I was also fighting an emotional wave of tears that were persistently trying to pool in my eyes. Recognising what I was experiencing, there was no possible way I could deny the bleeding obvious.

I was in love with Derek Ian King.

CHAPTER

18

Derek rolled off me not long after our breathing returned to normal and the emotion and effects of our sex-sesh subsided.

Positioning himself on his side, he propped his head up with his hand. 'I think it's safe to say that you just *did* intimate, Carly,' he said while teasing his finger over my lace nipple.

I looked up at the ceiling and tried to process that, for the first time in my life, I'd just had sex with someone I loved. 'Yes, I know,' I answered quietly.

'So, was it that bad?'

Snapping my attention away from the boring white ceiling, I turned to face him with an indignant look. 'No, of course not. It was great. Wonderful, in fact.'

'Well, just so you know and to reassure you further, I never have unprotected sex,' he said sincerely.

I nodded gratefully, but was uncertain as to why he decided to break that rule for me. 'Oh. So why did you do it this time ... with me?'

'Because you are different,' he responded quickly, shooting up from the bed and grabbing a pair of tracksuit pants. He pulled them on and walked back toward the bed, his deliberate intention to change the subject quite obvious. 'Right, I promised you satay. Are you hungry?'

A little taken aback by his response to my question and his subsequent Speedy Gonzales action, I answered, 'Yes.'

'Good, you can help me,' he said as he held out his hand.

I placed mine in his and gave him a sceptical look. 'Ah ... I'm not one to excel in the kitchen.'

Pulling me upright until I was standing flush with his chest, he smiled greedily and squeezed my arse. 'I find that hard to believe.'

* * *

'Sweet fucking Jesus, you weren't kidding, were you?' Derek asked accusingly, as he tried to stir the pot I had been in charge of. 'What the fuck did you do to the rice?'

Flustered, I stepped back from the stove and put my hands on my hips. 'I don't know! One minute there was water and the next it was gone!'

'That's because you've boiled the ever-loving shit out of it!'

'No. It's because your saucepan sucks ... literally. It sucked all the fucking water away.'

Derek laughed with a disbelieving tone. 'My saucepan did not suck the water, Carly.'

'Whatever! Someone or something did, because water just doesn't disappear into thin air.'

'Actually, it kind of ... never mind,' he said, smiling. 'Here, stir the sauce while I fix the rice. Don't stop stirring, okay?'

Widening my eyes at him in a show of impertinence, I once again positioned myself at the stove. 'Okay. Geez!'

As Derek began pouring boiling water from the kettle into the pot of gluggy rice, his sexy voice softly sounded throughout the kitchen. It was a surreal feeling to be standing there with him while he sang carelessly, but no matter how it felt, the unworried, relaxed and serene atmosphere he generated was very pleasant. I could honestly say I was thoroughly enjoying it.

The lyrics of 'Black', by Pearl Jam, filtered out of his mouth, mesmerising me with the smooth and sultry tone. And it was obvious that the ability to maintain such a melodious tune was effortless for him. The man had a gift. Well ... actually ... he had many gifts.

Realising that I was staring at the back of his head and in a Derek-sing-along fog, I returned my focus back to the satay sauce which had now escalated from a gentle simmer to a berserk boil. 'Shit!' I muttered quietly to myself.

I shot him a quick glance and noticed that he was looking over his shoulder in my direction. 'You didn't burn it, did you?'

Stirring the sauce frantically, I spotted bits of burnt residue surfacing, evidence of yet another kitchen fail. *Bugger, bugger, bugger.* 'No, I didn't,' I answered defensively.

'Baby,' Derek hummed against my ear, his hands sliding across my bustier-covered stomach. 'That black shit floating around in my sauce says otherwise.'

Startled, I jumped mildly, then melted into the virile man standing behind me. 'I did warn you that I sucked at cooking.'

Derek removed the pot from the stove and turned the gas switch off. 'Yes, you did, which begs the question, what else do you suck at?'

I giggled, savouring his lips on my neck. 'Is that a trick question?'

'No,' he chuckled. 'I want to know what else you are terrible at?'

I couldn't help rubbing my arse against his cock in an enticing manner. 'Not much. Well, there is one other thing I'm terrible at,' I answered as I turned back to face him with a mischievous smile.

'Yeah?' he whispered against my ear, his breath warm and inviting.

My eyelids fluttered uncontrollably. 'Yeah ... bowling.'

He chuckled before placing one of his hands on my hip and the other in between my shoulderblades. Then, gently, he pushed me forward so that I was bent over just slightly. My breathing spiked as he began to untie the ribbon which held my bustier together, but it was the feeling of his hard cock pressing into the apex of my arse which paused any further intake of air. *Holy fuck! I'm ready for round two and quite possibly rounds three and four soon afterward.* The sex drought I had experienced prior to this evening would no doubt go down in history as one of the longest ever endured and I intended to make up for it.

'Stand up and turn around,' he commanded, his voice now husky.

His sexy rasp added to my oxygen-depleted state, but I complied and straightened, only to find that my bustier was now loose enough to fall to the ground.

Derek smiled appreciatively as he took in my bare chest. 'Definitely the nicest set I've seen.'

'So you keep saying,' I answered, sliding my hands up my abdomen to give the 'nicest set' a tantalising squeeze.

He stepped forward, dipped his finger in the satay sauce and gently wiped it down my neck. The sensation was hot, but not enough to scald — it was an exquisite torture.

Derek then dropped his head and lapped up the sauce trail in one delicious swipe, all the while pinching my nipple with his thumb and forefinger. The way this man licked my skin was a sweet mixture of carnivorous need and sensual ownership.

Grabbing the saucepan, he knelt down before me and placed the pot on the floor next to him. He then looped his fingers into the waistband of my G-string and pulled them down my legs.

I stepped out of them, together with the bustier, and opened my stance for what I knew he had planned. With my hands behind me, braced on the edge of the stove, I was positioned and hankering for his tongue, fingers and lips.

Derek dipped his finger in the pot again and then teased me by swaying it in front of my face. 'Do you want some, baby?'

I smiled and nodded eagerly.

'What was that?' he questioned, turning his head and putting his hand to his ear. 'I can't quite hear you.' Derek then placed his finger in his mouth and pulled it out seductively while giving me a sexy wink.

You fucking twat-tease. 'Yes, you sexy piece of caramel.'

He let out a large belly laugh. 'Sexy piece of caramel?'

Frustrated, I squatted down and dipped my finger in the pot. Then, eye-fucking him heatedly, raised my finger to my mouth.

Derek grabbed my hand before I had the chance, wrapping his lips around my finger and licking it clean. Then, positioning my hands back on the edge of the stove top behind me, he let them go, leaned forward, and buried his head in between my legs.

'Oh ... god,' I moaned as he gently lapped at my pussy, his tongue's unhurried ability making me smile appreciatively. 'Do I taste better?' I asked, my voice low, but playful.

Closing his eyes, he nuzzled my clit and then pulled away. 'No.'

'What do you mean, no?' I exclaimed. 'What's wrong with my pussy? Why doesn't it taste better?' I asked with a new-found sense of anxiety.

I pushed his head away and squeezed my thighs together. Derek, on the other hand, wrenched his head from my grip and gently sank his teeth into my hip. The penetration was not painful, but it was enough to make me shriek and pull his hair. *Well, if he had any hair I would've been successful in pulling it.*

'Derek, what are you doing?'

'Don't ever stop me from eating your pussy,' he said, after releasing the skin on my hipbone, leaving a nice indent from his bite.

'You fucking bit me!'

Smiling devilishly, he placed a light kiss on the spot, soothing the area. 'Yes, I did.'

'You said you didn't bite,' I accused, while narrowing my eyes.

'I lied,' he admitted before giving me a cocky smile and attempting to part my legs again.

I clenched them tightly.

'Carly!' he warned sternly. 'Open your fucking legs.'

'No.'

'No?' he questioned, as he pulled them apart.

'Derek!' I squealed.

'Baby, shut up,' he interrupted. Quite rudely, I thought.

'Don't tell me to shut up,' I said, astounded.

'Sorry. Please refrain from speaking such utter shit so that I can go back to devouring your cunt,' he corrected himself.

My jaw dropped in shock, and then stayed that way when he once again buried his head between my legs and ferociously licked, sucked and nipped.

I cried out, gripping the bench for stability, his continuous motion skilfully tickling my clit. Derek's lust-filled eyes hungrily enflamed my core and, together, they both tipped me over the edge. 'Oh ... god ... fuck,' I mumbled incoherently.

Throwing my head back, I braced myself on the counter once more and closed my eyes, letting my orgasm roll through me. Every single nerve ending I possessed was alight, fizzling divinely as I slowly regained my sense of normalcy.

When I brought my head up from its slumped-back position and managed to pry my eyelids apart, I noticed Derek standing before me, tracksuit pants miraculously gone.

His cock was fully erect, pointing prominently at me, taunting me with a voiceless message to have a taste. As I stared at it ravenously, I mentally tied a napkin around my neck and licked my lips.

'Lay down,' I growled, pushing off from the stove and gently shoving him backward.

He obeyed, lay down, arrogantly put his hands behind his head and then waggled his eyebrows at me. 'Enjoy,' he said boastfully.

Kneeling down in between his legs, I leaned over and dipped my finger in the sauce then trailed it along one side of his 'V' muscle. As the heated substance touched his skin, he let out a harsh hiss. The sexy sound had me bending forward and looking up at him from underneath my lashes. 'Oh, I will, don't you worry.'

I opened my mouth and dragged my tongue along the line of sauce, performing a second pass in order to consume every skerrick of it. I then repeated the same action, wiping and licking sauce from the other half of his 'V'.

Watching as his cock bobbed eagerly under my chin, I took a hold of it and teased his tip with my tongue. He groaned quietly, his cock twitching within my grasp.

'Behave,' I said with a playful warning.

It twitched again, so, this time when I opened my mouth, I wrapped my lips around his crown and sucked on the smooth head, happily rubbing my lips all over it.

'Fuck, baby, we should try this with sauce more often,' he groaned. *Yes, we should. I love sauce, especially mint sauce. Oh, my fucking god! Derek's cock covered in mint sauce!*

Now running my tongue up and down his shaft, licking it with my incessant strokes, I mumbled my newfound fantasy. 'Uh uh. Ext ime, gona sped int auce on ur cock.'

'You're gonna what?' he asked with a laugh.

I lifted my head. 'I said, next time, I'm going to spread mint sauce on your cock.'

Derek sat up and leaned back on his elbows. 'Bullshit you are. Isn't that stuff made with vinegar ... and mint? It will fucking burn.'

'It will not, big baby,' I reassured him, dipping my finger back in the pot and trailing it along his inner thigh before running my tongue along his muscled leg.

Continuing to paint the satay sauce on his legs, chest and abdomen, I made my way up his torso, stopping at his pecs and neck, before wiping some more sauce on my lips and then mashing them to his.

Derek grabbed the back of my head — securing me to him — and plunged his tongue into my mouth, kissing me passionately and heightening the peanutty taste. He then flipped us over so that I was now lying on my back and he astride me.

As he leaned over to reach the pot, his cock teased my face. I sucked it back into my mouth and bobbed up and down hungrily.

'Jesus fucking Christ!' he groaned, while bracing his hands on the ground just above my head. 'You want me to fuck your face, don't you?' he asked as he started rocking his hips toward my head with a gentle assertiveness — his question more of a statement.

I watched the lower muscles of his abdomen flex and his eyelids close over as lust dominated him. Wanting to heighten his euphoric state, I reached up and cupped his balls in my hand while swallowing his slow, deep thrusts.

'Fuck!' He pulled out, dragging his heavy-weighted dick down my body before stopping and hovering over my hips. Derek then wiped some sauce down my neck and over my nipples, chasing it eagerly with his tongue.

By that point, we were both smeared quite extensively with the nutty mixture, and without taking a peek into the pot, I would have hazarded a guess and said that satay chicken was no longer an option for dinner.

I sat up and positioned myself on all fours before crawling toward him. 'Sit,' I commanded and waited for him to do so before straddling his lap.

Lifting up just slightly, I hovered over him so that he could position the head of his dick at my entrance and, when feeling his tip tickle my flesh, I lowered and engulfed him completely.

Derek placed his hands on my hips and assisted me with riding him. The thing was, I considered myself a fucking rodeo star. Therefore his assistance was not required. Over the past few months, I'd been deprived of sex and, because of that, was raring to go. I didn't need assistance. No, the only thing I needed was to make up for lost sexual time.

'Carly, Jesus, slow down,' he groaned, tightening his grip in order to slow my bouncing.

I reached over, grabbed the pot, plunged my hand into it and then smacked it against his chest, splattering sauce on his face and across my breasts. 'Don't tell me to slow down when I'm riding your cock,' I barked out, mimicking the tone of voice he used when warning me not to stop him from eating my pussy.

His eyes widened in surprise then glazed over with a boyish grin that spelled nothing but trouble. *Shit!*

Before I knew it, I had a handful of sauce mushed over my chest and neck. He even went so far as to dab some on my nose. Derek then swirled his finger around my nipple, collecting some of the sauce that had rested there and then stuck his finger in my mouth.

I bit down.

'Fuck,' he groaned, his groan a mixture of pain and desire.

He glared wildly at me then rubbed and squeezed my breasts firmly, almost to the point of pain, yet the smooth-slippery sensation his hands were producing erotically stimulated me toward climax instead.

'Oh, shit. Oh, fuck. Oh, god,' I moaned as my pussy clenched around his cock.

Derek then bucked into me and groaned ferociously before pulling my mouth to his and drinking any further screams of ecstasy.

Slumping over him like a rag doll, I rocked slowly as our orgasms subsided, our kiss now slow and sensual. I then mustered whatever energy I had left and pulled away from him, both of us smiling at one another.

'Holy fuck!' I said in wonderment.

'That was ... nuts!' he replied with a stupid grin.

I cracked up laughing and dabbed some sauce on his nose. 'We are so doing this with mint sauce.'

Derek secured me with one arm, braced himself against the kitchen cupboards and pulled himself to a standing position with me still attached his waist. 'Oh no, we are fucking not,' he said with conviction.

I giggled. *We so are!*

* * *

First port of call after satay-sex was the shower. Albeit hot, fun and exciting, it was exceedingly messy.

While I'd washed using Derek's masculine toiletries, he'd cleaned the kitchen and ordered a pizza.

'That's better,' I said as I walked toward him while drying my hair with a towel.

He stepped up to me and fiddled with a wet strand of my hair. 'I'm just going to have a shower. Make yourself at home. The pizza should be here soon.'

'Okay. Do you mind if I snoop?'

'Wouldn't that defeat the purpose of you snooping ... you know, me agreeing to it?'

'Go and have your shower,' I said playfully, pushing him in the direction of his bedroom, his peanut-encrusted back still deliciously enticing as he exited the room.

Once I was alone and Derek was happily singing in the shower, I had a chance to really inspect his house. Situated in Richmond, it embodied a Victorian style; it was small with heritage values. For a man, I must say, it was incredibly neat and tidy, but like Derek had said when we first pulled up outside, it was badarse.

The walls were painted light grey, the high ceiling and architraves white and elegant. The floorboards were stained with a light oak finish and the furniture was rugged, worn and screamed masculine. His couch was made of dark green leather and had a well-worn exterior. And, of course, his TV was huge and braced against the wall.

Beneath the TV was a lowline unit which had an Xbox and a rather extensive DVD and CD collection. There were also three guitars leaning up against the wall and, above them, a framed picture of Jimi Hendrix.

From what I had seen thus far, his house consisted of two bedrooms: his master bedroom and a spare bedroom which was also used for storage. He had one living area, one bathroom and toilet, a laundry and a dining and kitchen area. He also had a small alfresco courtyard out the back and a single garage. His cottage really was perfect for him.

Spying a motorcycle helmet on the floor beside the front door, I walked over to it and picked it up.

'When the roads aren't wet, I'll take you for a ride on the love of my life,' Derek said from behind me.

I spun around quickly to find him standing in the doorway of his bedroom, a towel hung low on his waist and his skin still delectably moist. What also became moist was the apex between my legs.

Placing the helmet back on the floor, I eyed him up and down as I prowled toward him. 'I'll tell you what. How 'bout I take you for another ride instead.'

'Baby, you seriously can't go aga—'

'Try me,' I challenged, a heated promise in my eyes.

Derek took in my determined expression and gestured me to enter his room. 'Just so you know, you will tire before I do.'

I stopped before I entered the room and poked my finger into the knot of his towel, unravelling it and setting his semi-hard cock free. 'Don't be so sure. I'm only just beginning to get warmed up.'

CHAPTER
19

After spending the weekend with Derek, holed up in his house and fucking like rabbits, I was thoroughly and deliciously tender in all the right places. He hadn't been lying when he said that I'd tire before him, although I did put up one hell of a fight. He even admitted to finally finding someone who could match his stamina.

Hearing him say that made me proud, honoured in fact, for my sexual skills and prowess were something I prided myself on. Between the sheets, I considered myself to be the female version of James Bond; the non-slutty Debbie from *Debbie Does Dallas*. I was a fornicating-fiend, a porn-professional, a sex-shark. I was fucking Jaws.

'Miss Henkley?' a small child of the female variety said as she climbed up on the step in front of my counter.

Looking up, I found Rani De Silva — aged six — standing before me. 'Yes, Rani.'

'What do I do with this?' she asked as she thrust her open hand at my face.

Her sudden movement and perplexed expression had me jumping back for fear of not knowing what the hell it was she planned on presenting me. One time, Simon Bains — aged nine — practically tossed a dead mouse on my desk. A. Dead. Fucking. Mouse.

Cautiously, I peered at her hand to find a small white tooth. *Eww.*

'It just fell out. What do I do with it?' she asked. *I don't fucking know. Who do I look like? The friggin' tooth fairy?*

Trying desperately not to appear completely grossed out, I grabbed a tissue and laid it out on the reception area. 'Place it in here,' I instructed her. 'Is this your first tooth to have fallen out, Rani?'

'Yes,' she explained with a pout. Rani then tipped her hand over the tissue and, you guessed it, the tooth rolled over the edge of the counter and onto my computer keyboard. *No! No, no, no, no, no! Eww! Yuck!*

I stared at the little white calcified nugget with disbelief then back at Rani who was trying to peer over the edge to see where it had landed. 'Where'd it go? Can you see it?' she asked, anxiously.

'Yes, it's just here.' *Shit! How am I going to do this?*

Spotting my tin of fancy pens from out the corner of my eye, I came up with the idea of using two of them like chopsticks. *Fucking genius.* 'Right, hang on a second,' I explained, psyching myself up for the challenge and selecting two of my funkiest fluorescent feather pens.

Positioning them in my fingers, I tapped the pen tips together — a little pre-testing exercise — then meticulously grasped the tooth as if I were playing a game of Operation.

Slowly, I swivelled and raised my arm, concentrating deeply on the task at hand and, just as I was about to lean forward and set the tooth down on the opened tissue, Lib appeared at my side. 'What are you doing?' she asked.

'Crap,' I exclaimed, jolting and flinging the tooth at her head.

She flinched in defence as it bounced off her cheek. 'Carly!'

'My tooth!' Rani cried.

Both Lib and I froze, not wanting to move in fear of stepping on the tooth and breaking it.

'Where'd it go?' I asked, twisting to look on the floor behind me.

'Over there,' Rani said, pointing to a white spot on the floor near the photocopier.

Libby walked over, bent down and picked it up. With. Her. Bare. Hands. She then placed it down on the tissue and wrapped it up tightly in the shape of a little square. I watched with curiosity as she tore off a piece of sticky tape and secured it, followed by a small piece of curling ribbon from the spindle on my shelf.

Lib secured the tooth in what turned out to look like a present, and then stuck a sticker on it. 'There you go, Rani. You can take that home and give it to the tooth fairy. She loves presents.'

Rani smiled brightly as she admired the tiny tissue-wrapped gift which was now in the palm of her hand. 'Thank you, Miss Hanson.'

'You're welcome. Make sure you put it in your pocket so that you don't lose it,' she called out as Rani skipped off. Lib then turned back to face me. 'What on earth were you doing?'

'You are disgusting,' I stated definitively, ignoring her question.

'Why?'

'Because you just picked it up ... with your fingers.'

'So!'

'So ... that is just disgusting. It's been in her mouth.'

'Um ... yeah,' Libby countered, pulling a 'der' face. 'I don't know what planet you are from, but here on Earth, teeth are normally found in one's mouth. And anyway, since when have you had an issue with anything oral?'

I hit her on the arm.

'Ouch! That hurt,' she whined.

'I don't have a problem with oral or oral-related things. I just don't like holding someone else's body parts in my hand,' I explained.

Libby raised her eyebrow questioningly at me. 'Really?'

'Okay, so some body parts are an exception, especially if they belong to Derek,' I explained, blushing.

'Did someone mention firefighter Derek's body parts?' Brooke asked as she walked into my office.

Before I could answer her, my phone sounded an incoming message. I fished it out of my bag to find it was from Derek. I swear the man is psychic.

I'm picking you up on the bike at 6 p.m. Wear something warm — Derek

The bike? His motorcycle? A passenger? Oh no. No, no, no. I quickly typed him a response.

No can do. I don't ride bitch — Carly

As always, his reply was instantaneous.

Are you fuckin' shittin' me? Why not? — Derek

Screwing up my face in vexation, I sighed, not wanting to answer him.

'Is that Derek?' Libby asked.

I looked up from my phone. 'Yeah.'

'What now? Why are you whining?' she questioned angrily.

Crossing my arms over my chest, I protested. 'I'm not whining. I didn't even say anything?'

'That,' she pointed to me, 'that is whining.'

I turned around, thinking she was pointing to someone or something behind me. 'What?'

'Your slumped position and sissy little sigh. What's that about?'

Letting out a breath in surrender, I squeezed my eyes shut and placed my phone on my desk. 'He wants me to ride bitch.'

'What?' Brooke asked.

'You know, ride bitch ... take me for a ride on his motorcycle,' I explained. 'I can't be a passenger. That's putting a lot of faith in the person driving.'

'How's that different from being a passenger in a car then?' Libby asked.

'Because a car has a roof, sides and a floor, you idiot,' I scowled.

She glared at me as my phone beeped again:

Do I need to ring you? — Derek

'Grrr,' I groaned and typed a message back.

No — Carly

Then answer me. Why not? Why can't I pick you up? — Derek

Before I could stall him any longer, my phone rang. Brooke giggled and grabbed the spare seat to sit on and get cosy. Lib just leaned back against my desk and crossed her arms in front of her.

Taking a deep breath and then exhaling, I pressed accept. 'Hi.'

'What the fuck, baby?' Derek asked, his voice calm, but questioning.

'I can't do it.'

'What?' he chuckled. 'Sit on the back of my bike? Are you for real?'

I placed my head in my hand and gritted my teeth. 'There's too much trust involved. I'm not ready.'

'You trusted me enough to go bare while we fucked all weekend, yet you can't trust me to ride my bike?'

My head shot up knowing that the girls would've heard that, but copped a whack from Lib in the process. *Bitch!* I glared at her and mouthed, 'What?'

She either mouthed 'No condom', or performed a fish impersonation. Either way, I ignored her.

'I can't talk about this right now,' I whispered into the phone.

'Fine, we'll talk about it after I've picked you up. Remember, wear something warm.'

'But Derek, I —'

Pulling the phone away from my ear, I confirmed what I'd suspected. 'He hung up on me,' I said, glancing up at Brooke and Libby with astonishment.

Brooke just shrugged her shoulders.

Libby performed her fish face again.

Jet Bradley walked in, sporting a bloody nose.

And I inwardly cursed every living male.

* * *

At six o'clock on the dot, I heard the roaring sound of a motorbike as it pulled up outside my house. I ran to the lounge room and jumped on the couch, leaning over the back of it to get a decent view out of the window.

Lib, too, jumped on it beside me. 'Oh, now that is hot! He is hot! Firefighter Derek and his motorcycle are scorchin' bloody hot!'

She was right. The sight of him swinging his leg over the back of the bike and taking his helmet off was akin to the hotness I would experience had someone struck a match and physically set my vagina alight.

'I suck his cock,' I blurted out, a salacious grin covering my face.

Lib burst out laughing and shoved my shoulder. 'Carly!'

'Well, I do, and I'm proud of it. Look at him. I get to drag my tongue all over that,' I said, pointing to Derek.

'Oh, I'd like to drag my tongue over that too,' Libby purred, practically drooling.

We were both perched on our funky turquoise suede couch, arms slumped over the backrest, gazing out the window while Derek began to undo his jacket.

Watching with gratification as the zip unfastened and the leather slid off his bicep-happy arms, I was unable to help myself and started humming the tune to 'You Can Leave Your Hat On' by Joe Cocker. Lib giggled and joined in, and we both perved appreciatively.

Before making his way to the door, he hung his jacket over his shoulder with his finger and secured his helmet under the other arm.

The rapping of his knuckles against solid wood sounded, prompting me to turn around and slump in my seat.

'Aren't you going to answer it?' Lib asked with a teasing smile.

'No. Probably not,' I answered stubbornly.

Lib turned around also and slumped next to me. 'Carly, I know you like to be in control of everything, but sometimes you just have to let go.'

'What are you talking about?' I asked with a shake of the head, although knowing exactly where she was headed.

'This has nothing to do with riding on his bike, does it?' she explained with a soft show of sincerity. 'You're scared of letting go of some of the control you have held for such a long time.'

'Letting go renders you vulnerable,' I said while fidgeting with the ruby ring that my aunty gave me. 'I don't do vulnerable.'

'Nobody *wants* to do vulnerable. But without vulnerable, we wouldn't have trust. And believe it or not, trust is a beautiful thing.'

'Not if it's broken,' I said, tears welling in my eyes.

She stood up, pulling me up with her. 'Well, that's the beauty of broken. Broken can be fixed.'

'Can it?' I asked as she gently pushed me toward the door. 'Not all things can be fixed.'

'Yes, they can. Some things just need more effort.'

Standing toe-to-toe with Lib, I gave her a grateful smile. She knew me well. Too well, if I was to be honest. Yes, I built walls around myself in order to protect my emotions, but she, along with Lexi, saw right through them. They were both immune to my barriers. I may not have openly admitted it, but I was so thankful that they knew how to break through.

'Carly, open the door, I know you're in there. I saw you through the window,' Derek called out from his position on the other side of the door.

I giggled and made my way to the door, squinting through the peephole. *Oh man, he is fine, even when distorted.*

'No. Go away,' I answered. 'I'll let you in when you return with the Ranger.'

'You've got two choices, baby. One: open the door and I'll reward you. Or two: force me to open it and get punished. Either way, I'm happy.'

'You wouldn't force my door open. And anyway, you can't. I have a deadlock.' *Ha, take that, you cocky cockfuck.*

'You seem to forget what I do for a living,' he retorted.

'Oh no, I don't. You douse fires with your big hose,' I said, trying not to laugh. Lib, however, snorted behind me. I turned to face her and poked out my tongue.

'I also break down doors in order to douse those fires.'
Oh, well shit! That's true.

'If you force your way into my house, Bucko, I guarantee you'll have to force your way between my legs as well, because I won't be letting you go there freely,' I stated, practically stomping my foot.

Derek laughed sadistically. 'That can be arranged.'

'I'm serious. Go home and come back with the truck, then I'll let you in.'

'Baby, I'm not leaving. I want to take you for a ride on my bike. Trust me, you'll enjoy it.'

There was that word again. *Trust.*

'Trust is varied, Derek. I *trust* that you will sing wonderfully when on stage. I *trust* that you will douse a fire with your hose. But I cannot *trust* you to keep me safe on the back of your bike. So, yes, while I trust you ... I don't. Now go and get your truck. And bring me back a peanut butter frappe from Max Brenner's while you are at it.'

I went to turn and high-five Lib when he spoke again. 'Are you finished?'

'Yes,' I giggled.

'So what are you saying ... you don't want to sit on my saddle?'

I scoffed with a smile and answered. 'No.'

Silence ensued for the smallest of seconds, so, in order to see what he was doing, I curiously stood on tiptoe and peered through the peephole again.

Derek was pacing back and forth across the front door-step, when suddenly he stopped and lifted his head as though a light bulb switched on. It was overly adorable.

'Come on, come check out my big unit.'

I laughed. 'How big is it?'

'You tell me.' Derek stepped up to the peephole and peered into it from his end. His magnified face had me laughing again. 'Baby, I want you to ride my bike. I want to feel you behind me, wrapped around me and clenching me tight. I promise I'll keep you safe.'

'Just ride his bike, Carly. Fuck! If you don't, then I will,' Lib groaned, then walked off to the kitchen.

Letting out a defeated breath, I grabbed the handle of the door and opened it. Derek took a second to look me up and down and then smiled, taking in my skinny jeans, black knee-high leather boots, thick cashmere sweater, scarf and leather jacket.

'You were always going to ride with me, weren't you?' he asked with a smile.

I grabbed the collar of his shirt and pulled him to me. 'No.'

'Sure. Whatever you say.'

Leaning forward, I brushed my lips to his. 'When it comes to riding, I'm always in charge. I ride how I want and when I want. And don't you forget it.'

* * *

I'm not submissive. I don't conform. I do what I want, not what someone else wants. I'm always in control.

'Oh, shit! Wait!' I said in a panic before Derek put my helmet on.

He ignored me, pushed it onto my head and opened the visor. 'What?'

'How will you hear me if I need to talk to you?'

'I won't. You will need to tap my leg three times if you want me to pull over.'

I nodded. 'Oh, okay.'

'Carly, don't nod. I'm trying to do your bloody helmet up,' he explained with a smidgen of frustration.

'Sorry.'

Derek placed his hands on the sides of my helmet and held my gaze. 'Hey, don't be nervous. Just remember what I told you: wait until I'm ready for you to get on the bike; never pull on my arms or shoulders; try not to bump my helmet with yours; lean into the corners with me; press your tits into my back; and hold the fuck on.'

'Okay,' I nodded again.

His face lit up with excitement. 'Good. You're gonna love it.'

'Don't bet on it,' I grumbled.

Winking before smacking my visor down, he added, 'We'll see.'

Derek mounted the bike and positioned himself before indicating I get on behind him. Placing my hand on his shoulder, I stepped up onto the peg and swung my leg over the bike, settling into his back and bearhugging him tightly. *Tits in the back. Tits in the back. Hold the fuck on.*

I tapped his abdomen twice — like he'd told me to — to indicate I was ready and, revving the engine a couple of times, he put the red Ducati Superbike into gear and took off.

Oh my god, I'm gonna die.

CHAPTER
20

Willpower is having the strength of will and determination to refrain from doing something difficult. It's the art of restraint, self-discipline and control. It's also the art form I had to draw upon in order to avoid shitting my pants as I endured moments of terror while riding bitch on Derek's bike.

If it weren't for the delectable fact that I could squeeze the sexy fucker with not only my arms but also my legs, I sure as hell would not be getting back on that two-wheeled machine of death. There was nothing super about a superbike.

Derek took me bowling, where I proved to him that I was just as dangerous with a ten-pound weighted ball containing three fingerholes as I was with a pot of boiling rice. And already, after just one game, I'd managed to break a nail, start the process of a nice purple bruise on my arse and fail in my attempt to rock a pair of hideous bowling shoes. I also knocked more pins down in the aisles beside me than I had in my own.

'Never again!' I stated resolutely, removing the maroon, navy and white block-styled bowling shoes from my feet with disgust. 'Seriously, who the fuck designed these?' I asked, presenting them to Derek. 'It's criminal.'

'Bowling is not supposed to be a fashion show,' he answered while tying up his black boots.

'Everything is supposed to be a fashion show,' I deadpanned.

'So, where do you want to go next?' he asked.

A small devious smile crept across my face. 'Coles.'

Derek paused in the zipping of his jacket and gave me an unsure look. 'Coles? What for?'

'I've run out of mint sauce,' I quickly explained.

'Fair enough,' he murmured. He went to go and take our bowling shoes back to the counter, but then turned back around to face me. 'Hang the fuck on, Carly, we've discussed this. I'm not rubbing mint sauce on my cock.'

'No, of course you are not. I am.'

Shaking his head, he walked away. 'Ain't gonna happen, baby.'

* * *

The second stint on the 'stupidbike' was not as bad as the first, albeit still scary as hell. As I clung to Derek like shit to a shovel, I noticed us cruise past the nearby Coles store. 'Hey,' I complained, my protest falling on deaf ears due to the fact he couldn't hear me.

I tapped his leg three times, but he ignored it and kept riding. So I tapped again, letting him know that I wanted to stop.

Derek pulled into a service lane and stopped outside a group of shops. He placed his feet down to balance the bike, lifted his visor and turned his head. 'What? Are you all right?'

I lifted my visor and glared at him. 'You drove past Coles.'

'You stopped me for that?' he asked with a trace of annoyance, yet a hint of smugness.

'Don't brush me off, Derek. I want mint sauce.'

'Get off the bike, Carly.'

'What?' I asked, shocked.

He chuckled. 'Get off the bike. We're here.'

Dumbfounded, I looked around, recognising the group of shops that we had parked in front of. There was a twenty-four hour gym, a wholesale food distributor and Sexyland.

Smiling boldly, I swung my leg over the bike and dismounted. 'Awesome!'

Derek kicked the stand down, removed his helmet, then wrapped his arm around my shoulder. 'Come on. Let's go shopping,' he said with an over-exaggerated thrill, mimicking a teenage girl.

I couldn't help but laugh.

As we walked into the store, we were greeted by a sales staff member. 'Good evening, welcome to Sexy— Carly! How you been, girl?' she exclaimed excitedly.

'Hey, Cynthia. Bit quiet tonight, huh?' I called back.

She sighed with disappointment. 'Yeah. Where are all the Carlys of the world?'

Leaning into my side, Derek whispered in my ear. 'I take it you've been here before.'

I glided my arm down his back and found the pocket of his jeans where I slid my hand in and happily squeezed his arse. 'This is my second home.'

'Who's the stud?' Cynthia asked, smiling impressively as she eye-fucked Derek.

'This is my piece of man-caramel, Derek. Derek, this is Cynthia, my friendly erotic object sales technician.'

'Nice to meet you, Derek. Is there anything in particular I can help you with tonight?' she asked.

'Yeah, Carly needs a substitute for mint sauce, something that won't burn my cock.'

I gasped and removed my hand from his arse-pocket, placing it on my hip. 'You sneaky little fuckcake.'

'Baby, I've told you before, I'm all about compromise.'

'We have mint flavoured oral gel,' Cynthia explained. 'I personally haven't tried it, but the raspberry flavour is nice.' She shrugged her shoulders.

Still glaring at Derek, I spoke in Cynthia's direction. 'Show me.'

'Just this way,' she instructed happily. 'Oh, Carls, I have to show you these nipple clamps. They came in last week. So good,' she rattled off as she led the way.

We stopped by a shelf of bottles, where Cynthia picked one up and handed it to me. 'Here, mint flavoured oral gel, *bon appétit.*'

I scrunched up my nose as I turned it around, scrutinising it disapprovingly. It looked minty, displayed a picture of a mint leaf and it was also green just like mint sauce.

Shrugging my shoulders, I decided to give it a try. 'Yeah, all right, I guess we can give it a go,' I said, turning to Derek but finding that I was talking to myself.

'Cockrings,' Cynthia informed. 'He's over at the cockrings. God, Carly, that man is a keeper.'

I passed the gel back to Cynthia and craned my neck to find him staring inquisitively at something before him — his perplexed expression making me giggle. Sauntering up behind him, I threaded my hands across his lower abdomen and dropped one of them for a quick grope.

Reaching forward with my other hand, I picked up one of the packets. 'You like Diablo, do you?'

'It's a fucking devil on a jelly-looking donut. And it goes around your cock like some piece of kinky jewellery,' he said, clearly impressed.

'I know. They're great. You want one?'

'Add it to the cart,' he said with a flick of his head. 'What else do you want?'

Laughing, I let him go and surveyed the shop. 'I think I have it all already.'

'Why does this not surprise me?' Derek stopped by the kink section and picked up a crop. 'You got one of these?'

'Yep.'

'Noted. How 'bout one of these?' he asked, picking up a flogger.

'Yep, but the tails on my one aren't that long,' I explained, running my fingers through the leather tassels.

'Here you go, Carls. Check these out,' Cynthia said, placing a packet of vibrating nipple clamps in my hand.

'There's no chain or wire. They run off batteries and have two different vibration settings.' She stepped back, displaying an impressed expression.

I pursed my lips in deliberation. 'They are a bit big. You couldn't wear them out and about.'

'Na, solely for home play.'

'How much?' I asked.

'$24.95. Honestly, they are a bargain at that price,' Cynthia said with a convincing smile.

I passed them back to her together with the cockring. 'Okay, you've never let me down before.'

'A cock moulding kit, really?' Derek asked, holding up a box.

'Yeah, they are very popular. That's a really a good one, too,' Cynthia advised while giving me a suggestive look. I caught her drift, but unfortunately, Derek did as well.

He put the box back on the shelf. 'No fucking way. Forget it. Okay, are we done? I think we are done.' Derek then walked over to the counter, ready to pay.

Cynthia giggled and started scanning our items. 'You got your loyalty card?' she asked me.

I fished through my purse, pulling out my loyalty card. I'm very fucking loyal. 'Yep, here you go.'

Cynthia scanned my card and happily handed it back. 'You have enough loyalty points to get the cock moulding kit if you'd like.'

'She's not getting the kit,' Derek stated absolutely.

'You can't tell me what I can and can't buy,' I retorted.

'Yeah? Well, whose cock are you going to mould? Not mine.'

I narrowed my eyes at him, then turned back to Cynthia.

'Don't worry,' she joked as she handed our items over in a plastic bag. 'I can always order one in if we run out.'

I winked at her. 'No worries, I'll keep that in mind.'

Derek thanked her and took the bag before I could grab it. 'No, you won't.'

* * *

As we walked in the front door of my house, Sasha, as per usual, came barrelling toward us.

'Sashy girl,' I squealed, squatting down ready for her assault.

Bracing for impact, I was shocked — and a little jealous — when my golden pup bypassed me completely, instead launching her fluffy arse into Derek's arms. *What the fuck?*

'Hello, my favourite blonde,' he said as she lashed him with her tongue.

I gave them both an are-you-fucking-kidding-me look.

Sasha ignored me but Derek corrected himself with a chuckle. 'Favourite four-legged blonde.'

'Sasha, you little traitor,' I said angrily. 'And you,' I pointed to Derek. 'I'll remember that.'

I stood back up and sulkily stomped into my room, swinging the door behind me and nearly collecting the two of them in the process.

'I think your mummy is a little jealous, Sasha,' he mumbled behind me. *Pfft, jealousy is for the insecure. I'm secure with all that is me.*

Making my way over to Rico's tank, I peered inside. 'My loyal and loving Mexican walking fish, how has your day been so far?' I asked with over-enthusiastic praise. 'Who's a cute axolotl?' I cooed. His red gills fanned and he smiled. *Yes, Rico smiles.*

Derek walked up behind me with Sasha still draped across his arms as if she belonged nowhere else.

I ignored them and grabbed Rico's food pellets, twisting the cap and tapping some into his tank. 'Are you hungry, buddy?

'You do realise you are talking to him like a baby, don't you?' Derek stated.

'Rico is my baby,' I snapped, stepping to the side and giving Derek the cold shoulder.

I watched via the reflection in the tank as he placed Sasha down on my bed and gave her a belly scratch, smiling cockily toward me while she lay there and lapped it up.

You arrogant arse!

Turning back around, I fired him another dirty look and then awkwardly removed my boots, hopping around the room like a moron due to forgetting to brace myself on something. After finally wrestling them off my feet, I tossed them into my wardrobe with a childish show of stubbornness.

'Problem?' he asked, amusement staining his face with satisfaction.

I wrenched down the zip of my jacket and widened my eyes. 'Nope.'

'I take it you always undress with such anger then?'

'Yep,' I mocked.

Locking my eyes on his, I belligerently unbuttoned my jeans and pulled them down, stepping out of them and kicking them into the corner of my room. I then sarcastically smiled at him and yanked off my socks.

Now standing before him in only my G-string and singlet top, I went to undo the braid in my hair.

'Leave it in,' he said harshly as his stare raked my body and inflamed the room.

My hands froze on the elastic band.

Derek slowly stood up and prowled toward me while taking off his jacket. The raw, vehemently hungry expression on his face had me taking backward steps until I was pressed against my wall.

He stopped, his tall robust frame towering above me. And with both hands, he grasped my singlet top and tore it right down the middle. 'I like pissed off, baby, because I can still fuck when I'm pissed off.'

Firmly grabbing my chin with his hand, he squished my cheeks before planting a forceful kiss on my lips.

I pulled back and slapped him across the face — hard. 'Derek! You just fucking ripped my top, you arrogant prick.'

Annoyed — but extremely aroused by his heated aggression — I pushed at his chest, but he didn't budge. Instead, he grabbed my G-string and tore that from me as well, leaving me standing there with ripped shreds of material hanging from my body.

'Stop it!' I yelled and went to slap him again.

Derek caught my wrist and his eyes blared sexual filth at me, sexual filth that had me suddenly feeling desperately dirty. *Oh ... my.*

'You want to play rough?' he asked, a hint of excitement breaking across his face.

'No. I don't want to play at all,' I said through gritted teeth, trying not to smile.

'I think you do.'

I leaned forward getting right up into his face. 'You are wrong.'

Derek dropped his other hand and plunged his finger into my pussy, the swift intrusion surprising me and making me gasp.

He slid it in and out a couple of times, teasing me before he pulled it out completely. Then, bringing it up to my face, he wiped my arousal across my lips. 'Clearly, I am not wrong.'

'Clearly, you're an arsehole,' I countered, licking my lips.

Derek inwardly growled and mashed his mouth to mine, kissing me passionately and lifting me up into his arms. I instantly wrapped my legs around his waist and ran my hand up the back of his head, digging my nails in hard with intent to punish.

'Fuck,' he roared while carrying me over to the bed and dropping me down on the mattress. 'Hands and knees,' he demanded. His tone was severe but also held a gentle caress, a promise that what I was about to experience would be a mixture of sensuality and ferocity.

I stared at him for a minute, his return gaze equally as fierce. Our battle of wills were pouring from the both of us and circling the air with crackling anticipation, our reactive chemical 'Dc' in full effect.

As I sat there debating his request and wondering whether or not to comply, I realised that today had been a day where I had freely — yet reluctantly — relinquished my control. I had stepped out from within my bubble of security and *trusted* him. I had let go ... and enjoyed it.

Deciding to continue that theme, I turned over and positioned myself on my hands and knees, baring my arse to him.

'Mm ... good girl,' he praised as he stepped up behind me.

'Don't fucking "good girl" me,' I bit out harshly, snapping my head around to fix him with my warning glare.

The loud, sharp sting of his hand connecting with my arse made me yelp, shocking me into silence. It also excited me no end. *Ooh, Mr Spanky Spankster with his big hose. Hello, Carly's wet dream.*

Feeling the confines of my bra loosen as he unclipped it and pushed the straps down my shoulders, my breasts hung freely and heavily before me.

Derek leaned over and cupped one aggressively before whispering into my ear. 'I'm gonna fuck you hard, baby. I hope you are ready.'

I heard the zipper of his jeans undo and felt his warm hard cock land with a light thud on my arse. The sensation and knowledge that he was almost inside me resulted in my back arching ever so slightly, my pussy now primed and waiting for his penetration.

The gentle tease and tickle of his fingertip as he slid it down the crevice of my arse made me shudder. But it was when he stopped its descent and slowly circled the entrance of my pussy before replacing with it the crown of his dick that had me quivering with delighted anticipation.

Derek eased himself in slowly, forcing a shallow moan to escape my throat. The feeling of him filling me completely was beyond wonderful — the man had a cock that touched all extremities.

Suddenly, my head was jerked back and an uncomfortable yet tantalising ache formed on my scalp.

'Oh fuck!' I cried out, my braid now wrapped around Derek's hand, my body now at his complete mercy.

Sounds of skin slapping skin soon dominated the room as Derek pounded my flesh with his own. His thrusts were hard, fast, relentless and brutal, and I fucking loved every second of it.

'Is that ... the ... best you can ... do?' I stuttered as my voice jerked with my body's movements.

'Not ... even ... fucking close,' he growled as he pistoned into me continuously. Bang. Bang. Bang.

Oh, my fucking GOD! The man was a machine, a relentless sexual engine running on endless fuel.

'Stomach,' he growled and secured both my arms to my back when I fell forward at his command.

Being restrained and completely helpless would normally have me feeling highly distressed, but slave to Derek's every control and whim was far from that regular feeling. Submitting to him just felt ... right.

His unyielding rhythm, the friction from his cock deliciously gliding against the walls of my pussy, and the sounds of sex hanging heavily in the air in the form of moaning, grunting and heavy breathing, all combined exquisitely to bring my orgasm screaming out of me. 'Oh ... god!'

Derek, too, erupted like a volcano, spilling into me, over me and consuming everything within and around me. 'Fuck, baby,' he groaned passionately as he collapsed onto my back.

His damp heavy frame stole whatever skerrick of energy I had left, rendering me limp. I was spent, taken, consumed and owned. I was absolutely fucked.

Derek and I fell asleep in a tangle of sweat-dampened limbs. His body engulfed mine, owned it ... he made me feel safe. My body was now his and not my own. Carly Henkley was no longer free.

CHAPTER
21

A couple of months went by and, during that time, Derek and I grew closer. Much closer. It was kind of weird in a non-weird kind of way. You see, the progression of our relationship happened naturally, which — for me — was just ... well, weird. Now don't get me wrong, what Derek and I shared was not always unicorns and rainbows. Most of the time it was Shetland ponies and shit-storms. But that was who we were. We fought each other, challenged each other and set each other straight. We comforted each other, complemented each other and drove one another insane. One thing for sure, Derek had been right ... he and I just 'are'.

We'd spent Christmas Eve with my parents. I'd even cooked. But it was nothing fancy. It also ended up being inedible. Derek was forced to show me his firefighting skills firsthand when I smoked out the kitchen and burnt the potatoes to the point where they resembled gorilla testicles. And not being one to want to eat food that looked like animal genitals, they were inevitably thrown away. I did, however — as a result — get to admire Derek in firefighter mode. And damn, the man was good at dousing fires. Needless to say, we ended up having to make an emergency dash to the local Red Rooster in order to pick up another cooked chook and some roast vegetables, reiterating another of Carly's Cardinals: thank fuck for takeaway.

Mum and Dad had been big fans of Derek, and what I thought would be a nightmarish and awkward occasion turned out to be relaxed and successful ... with exception of nearly burning down my house.

Dad had been non-stop with questions about the MFB and Mum was abnormally bubbly and attentive. In the past, my parents had never been that interested in my romantic life; then again, I'd never allowed it to be a topic of discussion. In hindsight, it was as if at one point we'd made a silent agreement not to mention who I dated and when. So I guess that introducing Derek to my parents, and in particular on Christmas day, was a novelty. It was also a huge step for me and one I'm glad I made.

In the lead up to Christmas, I'd asked Derek if he had wanted to fly to Sydney to see his parents, even offering to go along with him. But he had been dead against that idea, saying, 'I only go and see them if it's an emergency, Carly.' I'd replied with, 'You can't choose your family,' to which he responded, 'No, but that doesn't mean I have to put up with their fucking bullshit. Family will hurt you the most if you are not careful. They share the same blood, so they know how to make you bleed.' He'd then gotten angry and, for the first time in our relationship, I could see the pain he harboured where his family was concerned. I let it go after that, although it was definitely something I wanted to revisit. Family were unalterable, no matter how much we wished that were not the case at times.

One month had now passed since Christmas and nothing further had been said. I was not normally one to try and fix people or push onto them their damaged issues. People have to want to fix themselves and their broken surroundings before someone can assist them with it. If they didn't, repairs could not truly be made. That said, I found myself desperate to fix Derek's broken relationship with his family. I could tell the rift tore him apart, and to bear witness to that was killing me. It literally hurt my chest.

'Carly! Hurry the fuck up. We gotta go,' Derek bellowed from the lounge room.

Lucy had rung Derek a couple of days ago, explaining that Bryce and Alexis had gotten engaged during their trip to Italy and, as a surprise, she wanted to organise an impromptu engagement party and afternoon tea for when they arrived home.

Personally, I thought it was a shit idea. Knowing Alexis, she'd want nothing more than to take it easy and recover from jet lag so that she could be fresh and lively for when she saw Nate and Charlotte the following day. Coming home and hosting an apartment full of friends and family? I was fairly sure she'd hate it.

However, I'd learned very quickly that Lucy was a force to be reckoned with. Lucy, like her brother Bryce, got what she wanted. She was also very kind, sweet and highly knowledgeable. Without intending to, she intimidated me ... which never happened. I only ever felt what *I* wanted to feel. Nobody could force me otherwise. It was the one thing in life I controlled solely.

I had my iPod switched to random while in the bathroom doing my hair and make-up. Singing the lyrics to 'Sexual Healing' by Marvin Gaye, I ignored Derek's hassling from the other room. We had plenty of time. My make-up was complete and I just needed my lippy.

I stretched and opened the mirrored cabinet door in my bathroom. A couple of near-empty bottles of lotion fell out like they always did and, rather than throwing them away, I put them back in and dug deeper for my MAC Everyday Diva red lipstick while swaying my hips to Marvin's sexy song.

'Got it!' I said to myself with a victorious holler as I spotted the holy grail of lip wear and, twisting the lid off, started applying it to my lips as I closed the cabinet door.

'Jesus!' I yelled, startled by Derek's sudden appearance behind me. The shock of seeing him made me smear the lippy on my cheek. 'Now look what you've done!'

Derek chuckled and held his hands up in surrender. 'Sorry, here, I'll help you,' he said, grabbing the face washer and lifting it to my face.

'Back the fuck off!' I warned. 'Oh my god, you don't just wipe this with a damp face washer!' I said incredulously, pointing to the canvas that was my made-up face.

Stomping out of the bathroom, I retrieved my handbag and dug out my make-up remover tips. They were the one and only thing that could fix this epic disaster; they were my saving grace. 'Face washer? He's got to be kidding me.'

As I approached the bathroom again, I could hear Derek singing 'Sexual Healing,' which stopped me in my tracks. *Well, fuck me lyrically.* My lower abdominal muscles together with the walls of my pussy clenched at the sound of his verbal sensuality. Yes, they clenched ... just like that.

Hearing him sing that song was akin to my ears climaxing joyously, his voice as smooth as a silk scarf ... a baby's bottom ... a pane of fucking glass. And when the word *sexual* rolled from his mouth, I swear I almost rolled on the floor.

Being the happy voyeur that I was, I sleuthed my way closer to the door and snuck a little peek. Derek was resting his arse against the bathroom basin and fiddling with his phone. He had on a pair of dark denim jeans, black boots, white tee and his black leather jacket — the one he wore to Alexis' birthday party. He looked absolutely irresistible ... like pie with cream.

I stared at his mouth, taking pleasure in the way his lips were moving at a slow sensual pace, releasing melody and blessing me with intermittent glimpses of his silky soft tongue. I wanted to drink the words he sang; take them from his mouth with my own in a gentle kiss. *Who am I kidding? Gentle kiss my arse. I want to suck them right out of his mouth in a frenzied Carly-style attack.*

My sights slowly skated down his chin, stopping at his neck while it throbbed and tensed in creating song. I wanted to touch it, bite it and lick it all over.

At the request of getting up and making love tonight, I got an idea.

I grabbed the mint flavoured oral gel we'd bought at Sexyland from the top drawer of my dresser and put it in the pocket of my dress. I then stepped into the bathroom.

Derek looked up and his singing died off when he spotted the blaring heat in my gaze. *Try and fucking douse this inferno, you firemonkey.*

I strode toward him and smacked my lips to his, sliding my hands up his pecs as I licked the tongue that had just made hot love to my ears. My swift assault caught him off-guard at first, but he recovered and returned my intensity with a strong and passionate squeeze of my arse.

'You are one sexy fucker,' I rasped, separating my mouth from his and dragging it down his strong smooth neck. 'Keep singing,' I instructed as I dropped to my knees and undid his belt.

Derek stuttered at first, but picked up the lyrics while watching me release his cock into my hands. 'Jesus, Carly!'

'Sing!' I demanded.

I stroked my tongue up and down his firm, ridged length while he struggled with the fluency of the lyrics, mumbling words of sexual healing being good for him and it made him feel fine. It made me feel friggin' fine too, hearing him say that while I blew gently on the crown of his dick.

His head fell back, and the muscles in his neck flexed with a beautiful show of strength. 'Fuuuuuck!' he hissed.

The song stopped and so did he, prompting me to look up and glare at him angrily: 'ing! ucking ing!' I mumbled through a mouthful of penis.

'I can't reach the iPod,' he explained, straining as my tongue gently flicked his balls.

Sucking one into my mouth, I slowly let it out again. 'You're a singer, sing without the fucking music. I don't care. Just sing.'

His eyes flared with the challenge and he opened his mouth, releasing lyrics about a woman who'd been cooling and that he'd been drooling. Straightaway, I recognised that he'd begun to sing 'Whole Lotta Love' by Led Zeppelin.

I moaned and licked up his shaft before wrapping my mouth around him when he mentioned something about going down. As I deep-throated him, his head fell back in surrender, making me inwardly smile. There really was nothing better than watching a grown man come apart on the tip of your tongue. If he wanted a 'Whole Lotta Love', I was going to give it to him.

Reaching down, I took hold of the mint gel from my pocket and popped the lid. His head snapped forward at the sound, curious as to what I was doing. With a salacious glint streaming from my eyes, I squeezed a little on my outstretched tongue and then swirled it over his tip.

The minty flavour was present, but it was in no way a substitute for the real thing and, in that moment, I vowed I would, at some stage, put mint sauce on his dick.

Increasing the speed at which I slid him in and out of my mouth, I relaxed my jaw and let my lips glide along the masterpiece that was his cock. His heated length tensed within my hand, so I gripped tighter, glancing up and giving him a wicked grin.

He smiled at me, a smile that spoke of greed, but also appreciation. 'I can blow in you or on you. You pick,' he offered while gently dragging his finger down the side of my cheek. *Fuck me, this man screams sexy.* He also screamed dominance, carnality and a rawness dipped in sugar. The man was fucking rock candy.

Releasing him from within my mouth, I answered, 'In me,' and then stood up and positioned myself over the basin in an inviting manner by wiggling my arse with seductive intent.

Opening my legs, I flipped up the chiffon skirt of my dress and flashed him my lace-covered arse while speaking to his reflection in the mirror. 'I want it hard and fast. Don't even give me a chance to think. Do you think you can handle that?'

Without answering, he stepped up behind me and rubbed the head of his cock over my clit before pushing abruptly into my pussy, his eyes never leaving mine as he began to slide in and out at rapid speed.

I gripped the edge of the sink as the force of his thrusts propelled me forward.

'Hold the fuck on, baby,' he warned.

Placing my hand on the mirror, I braced myself. *Oh, my, god!* His unruly rhythm had me continuously slamming into bathroom cupboards which sat underneath the basin. I felt as though they would break at any moment. Either that or I would. My legs were aching, painful even, but the feeling of him pounding the ever-living fuck out of me had the magical ability to counteract with a pleasure so great that I wished it would never stop.

'Oh, fuck,' I screamed, 'fuck!'

Dropping my head, my back arched and I shuddered violently as my orgasm blasted through me like a freight train, forcing filthy uncontrollable grunts to leave my mouth. I loved it!

Derek then groaned harshly and filled me, strangled lyrics about wanting to be my back door man leaving his mouth.

I lifted my head to catch his reflection in the mirror and, breathing heavily, I asked, 'Do you just?'

My arse tensed with anticipation.

'It's not a matter of do I, Carly, it's a matter of when will I.'

He leaned over me and stuck his finger in my mouth, only to retract it and place it at the entrance of my arse, teasing it deliciously before sliding it in.

* * *

After cleaning ourselves up and then getting a lecture from Lib because we'd left the en suite door open and scared Sasha with our animalistic mating calls, we'd left for City Towers.

Upon exiting Bryce's private elevator car, we were met with a roomful of people.

'Oh, shit!' I whispered to Derek and, performing my best impression of a ventriloquist, continued, 'Lexi ain't gonna be happy about this.'

He draped his arm over my shoulder as we stepped into the room. 'Why?'

'Look at all these people! Would you want to come home to this after a fifty hour flight?'

'I think it's more like twenty hours in a private jet,' he answered, kissing the top of my head.

'Whatever. My point is you wouldn't want to come home to a place full of people after just getting engaged and probably shagging the entire twenty or fifty hour flight home.'

'Derek! Carly!' Lucy squealed happily. 'Thank goodness. God, I knew you were running late, but I didn't think it would be this late. They're almost here,' she said excitedly.

'How did you know we were running —'

'Sorry,' Derek butted in, 'you can blame Carly for that.'

I gave him a bite-me look in response. 'Well, maybe next time I'll keep my mouth closed and you can keep your dick in your pants,' I chided.

Lucy bit back a grin and jiggled Alexander who sat comfortably on her hip. He smiled at me so I smiled back. The next thing I knew, he was lunging toward me.

'Whoa, do you want to go to Carly, Al?' Lucy asked her infant son as she laughed but struggled with his shift of weight.

Oh no, no, no, noooooo. He lunged again and, unfortunately, this time I had no choice but to put my arms out and catch him. *Shit! Shit! What the hell do I do with it?*

No doubt resembling a stunned mullet, I stiffened and felt highly uncomfortable. I don't do kids, especially little ones with more drool outside of their mouth than in.

Derek chuckled while pretending to grab Alexander's nose. 'Stop looking at him as if he is about to grow another head.' *Well, fuck. He just might. These little things are unpredictable.*

'I'm not. He just surprised me, is all. Kids don't normally lunge at me like that,' I said with a faux smile as Alexander placed his wet soggy finger on my perfectly applied eyeshadow. *Get it off! Somebody take this thing, please!*

Just as I was about to hand him back to his mother, her phone beeped. '"They are here",' she read out loud. 'Oh my god, they are here! Everyone, take your places.' Lucy hurried off and, much to my disgust, left Alexander in my arms.

I turned back to Derek with what I can only imagine was a look of terror plastered on my face.

'Here, I'll take him,' he said, holding his arms out to Alexander. Al, once again like a monkey, leapt toward Derek.

'Hey, buddy, who's getting heavy now?' he asked while holding him above his head like an aeroplane.

Alexander squealed and laughed uncontrollably. And even though I did not relate to little humans all that much, their laughter was infectious.

Derek brought him back down only to place him on his shoulders and, instantly, Alexander smacked him on the head.

'Hey, Al, play the guitar, remember? Not the drums. Only tools like Will play the drums.'

'I heard that,' Will said to Derek as he sidled up beside me. 'Jaws, how they hangin'?'

'Hey, ease up. They don't hang, they sit,' I explained eloquently. 'I haven't entered the age of hanging tits yet.'

'No, you are quite right. They sure as hell don't hang,' Will stated, eyeing my chest.

'You have exactly half a friggin' second to find something else to look at, Will,' Derek cautioned in a tone that held a grave warning.

'Too late! Those,' he said, with a shit-eating grin while pointing his beer to my chest, 'are imprinted on my brain.'

'Un-friggin' imprint them now!' Derek stated in an icy tone.

Will tapped Derek on the head like a bongo, making Al do the same. 'No can do.'

I cracked up laughing, then pursed my lips while watching Derek struggle between a rock and a hard place. He could not do or say anything with Alexander on his shoulders.

Derek took in a deep breath. 'Later, mate. You and I are havin' words later.'

Will placed his hand on my shoulder and squeezed it teasingly, then smiled at Derek. 'Is that all?' he asked, deliberately provoking him. He then whispered into my ear. 'And you thought he wasn't serious about you.'

Just as Lucy called everyone to hush, I elbowed Will in the ribs, which made him grab at his abdomen before stumbling backward and heading toward where Matt was chatting to some brunette.

'Everyone shush,' Lucy called out. 'Bryce and Alexis are in the elevator. Get ready.'

Everyone ceased their discussions and waited patiently for the doors to open and, soon enough, the elevator pinged and they slid apart.

Bryce and Alexis stepped into the room, Bryce with his hand on Alexis' belly. '... And because you are carrying my —'

'Surprise!' we all shouted.

Both of them looked up, shock emanating from their faces. '... Baby,' Bryce stuttered, completing his sentence.

'Oh. My. God!' I gasped, smiling, but with a sense of unease.

'Shit!' Derek mumbled as Alexander bounced on his shoulders, making it a task for Derek to keep a hold of him. 'Bryce doesn't muck around, does he?'

Alexis stood frozen to the spot, mouth agape at the sight of all the smiling faces before her.

'You're pregnant again?' Lucy asked, appearing ready to burst at the seams with happiness.

Alexis — still in shock — just nodded, and both she and Bryce were then instantly swarmed by their families.

Turning toward Derek, I looked up at Alexander who was now scratching Derek's head.

'For f-f— sake, Al, stopping scratching,' he complained.

Looking from Alexander to Derek and then to Alexander again, the bond they seemed to share hit me with force. *Oh, hell. Derek would make a great father.* It was obvious that he was naturally paternal — it seeped from his pores.

'You didn't, mate?' he questioned nervously, while scrunching up his face in disgust. 'Shit, you did. You just drooled on my head, didn't you?'

I stretched up on my tiptoes to see the damage. 'Yep, he sure did. Consider your head the shiniest I've ever seen it,' I laughed.

'What are you doing up there?' Nic asked angrily as she approached Derek. Nic was Lucy's lesbian partner. Or was it wife? I'm fairly sure they were as married as lesbians could be in the state of Victoria. 'Come here,' she said, putting her arms up for Alexander.

'He's fine, I've got him,' Derek snapped. 'I know how to look after a baby, Nic. I'm not stupid.'

Nic scoffed. 'Some may disagree.'

'Hey!' I scowled, standing in front of Derek. 'What the hell crawled up your arse? The bitch brigade?'

Nic took a step back and glared in horror at me, then even more so at Derek before she walked off with Alexander.

'What's her problem?' I asked with disbelief.

'She's a man trapped in a woman's body,' he said quietly, firing daggers into the back of her head. 'I guess that would be enough to piss anyone off.'

As I watched Nic leave the room and Derek's gaze follow her, I sensed the two of them had history. Bad history.

Turning to him, I moved his chin with my finger, gaining his attention before kissing him briefly on the lips. 'I need a drink.'

'What about congratulating Bryce and Alexis?' he asked, giving me an uncertain look.

'They'll be busy with their families for a little while longer. I don't want to overwhelm them. Come on, let's get a drink and go outside for some air.'

* * *

After Derek and I had made our way out onto the balcony to get a drink, I found thoughts of how great he was with Alexander plaguing my mind. There was no doubt that I wanted a future with him; I'd never felt this way about anyone in my life. And although he had never mentioned it, I sensed he wanted a future with me too. But would he want a future with children? Children with me?

Oh fuck! Oh hell! I don't want children. I just don't.

Suddenly, Tash started belting out 'I Will Always Love You' from the movie *The Bodyguard*, snapping me out of my mental panic.

'That chick is crazy,' Derek said with a laugh, pulling me to his side before swigging his beer.

I shook my head and laughed. 'You have no idea the level of craziness Tash harbours.'

'Carly!' Alexis announced sternly, but with an undertone of playfulness as she approached us.

I gave her a wary look, glanced up at Derek then looked back toward her again. 'Alexis?'

'Hole status? Affirmative or negative?' she demanded.

Sweet fiery fucks. 'Affirmative,' I answered through gritted teeth.

Alexis raised an eyebrow. 'I thought as much.'

Bryce came up behind her and automatically threaded his hands across her belly. It made me flutter. *WTF?*

'Congrats, mate,' Derek offered, putting a hand out for Bryce to shake.

'Thanks,' he replied and shook it.

I gave Lexi a sly smile then quickly glanced toward Derek's package. She inconspicuously glanced at the men, then furrowed her brow at me, an interrogatory look on her face.

She then leaned forward and concentrated her eyes on mine, which were flicking back and forth from her to Derek's groin. I repeated that motion a couple of times, trying to insinuate that he was well-endowed.

Lexi smiled, realisation dawning on her face. She then looked around the outdoor area before settling her gaze on a cylinder candle.

Widening her eyes at me in question, she sought confirmation of a correct size comparison.

The candle was short and did not do Derek's hose justice, so I screwed up my face and shook my head as if to say no.

I controlled my eagerness to blurt it out while she bit her lip and pondered further.

Noticing her struggle to find a decent Derek-hose-size comparison, I lifted my hands and separated them approximately twenty centimetres wide, then quickly clasped them together as if clapping at absolutely nothing while smiling smugly at her. She gave me the 'not bad' face by pursing her lips together and nodding her head slowly. Then, putting her hand to her eye in a circular shape and pretending to look into it like a telescope, she inconspicuously asked for an indication of girth. *Uh huh.*

My hand shot out faster than lightning and picked up the candle.

Her jaw dropped.

I just grinned.

'Did you just explain to Alexis how big my cock is?' Derek asked, snapping me out of my how-big-is-my-boy-friend's-cock game. *Oh, shit! Think quick.*

'Um, no, I was just expressing my appreciation at the fact Bryce and Alexis use candles. Global warming is a serious issue, and cutting down on our greenhouse gas emissions is very important. Every little bit helps, you know,' I blurted out. *Save of the century.*

'Bullshit, you just sized my cock,' Derek bragged, not believing a word I just said and rightly so.

Lexi laughed and shrugged her shoulders.

'Na, you're wrong, mate. If she'd been sizing your cock, she would've held up her pinky,' Bryce goaded.

Derek shoved him. 'You're gonna force me to prove you wrong,' he said as he began to unbutton his jeans. *Oh yes, prove him wrong. And then maybe he will want to compare.*

'Um ... excuse me, Alexis,' a tall strawberry-blonde interrupted, her eyes falling to Derek's pants before quickly moving them back up to Alexis' face.

'Sam! I'm so glad you're here,' Lexi said happily, giving her a hug. 'Are you here with Gareth? Oh, that's wonderful —'

'I was here with Gareth, but that's what I wanted to talk to you about. Something happened and he left. He was furious and he kept muttering, "This ends here." I'm not sure if he meant us, or something else. I don't know what I did wrong.'

Bryce let go of Alexis' waist and grasped his chin with an expression of nervous contemplation. 'It's not you, Samantha, you did nothing wrong.'

The colour drained from Alexis's face, leaving her as pale as a ghost, her expression filling me with dread. She turned to Bryce and said in a shaky voice, 'I have a bad feeling about this. Something is wrong.'

'I know. I feel it too. I want you to stay away from Gareth. I have a feeling Scott has returned.' *Oh, shit! Scott, the bad alternate personality. The one Lexi is afraid of.*

'Bryce,' she said nervously, 'I think he never left.'

CHAPTER
22

Alexis instantly placed her hand across her stomach in a protective manner which made me nervous and inquisitive all at once. I had known my best friend practically all my life and could sense when something was not right. I had that feeling now.

'Come on, we'll go and look for him,' Derek suggested to Bryce, concern etched on his face.

'It's okay. I'll go look for him a little later on when everyone has gone home. I need to talk to him alone. Set some things straight,' Bryce explained with a long exhalation.

Derek nodded. 'Okay, you know where I am if needed.'

Closing his eyes for the smallest of moments, Bryce placed his thumb and forefinger on the bridge of his nose — the poor bastard was clearly distressed.

Noticing his unease, Alexis reached forward and took hold of that particular hand. She placed a quick kiss to it, her lips appearing to soothe his apprehension.

'I'm going to head off now, anyway,' Sam explained. 'If you find him, please tell him to call me. I'm worried.'

'We will, Sam,' Bryce answered, letting go of Alexis' hand and gesturing Sam back inside to accompany her to the door.

I watched as Lexi followed them both with her gaze until they were out of sight. 'You all right?' I asked, touching her arm gently.

She startled.

'Hey,' I said softly, stepping up to her and placing both of my hands on her shoulders for assurance. 'Talk to me.'

She shook her head dismissively. 'Sorry, I'm fine. I'm just tired and jet lagged, and I really need a decent night's sleep,' she explained, and took a deep breath.

'Well, we are just about to make tracks as well. So make sure you get some rest tonight, okay?' I gave her a quick hug and whispered into her ear. 'Congratulations. I'm so happy for you and Bryce, but please call me if you need to talk.'

She assured me that she would, but I got the feeling that particular phone call would never come. For the most part, Lexi liked to deal with things on her own. I understood that attribute as it was one we both shared. Regardless, I was confident that she knew I was ready to jump to her aid in any way, shape or form if ever she needed me to.

In the elevator on the way down to the car park, Derek pulled me to him and tucked my head under his chin. 'She'll be fine. They'll sort it out.'

I squeezed him tight, thankful for his reassuring arms. I needed them and his words, both making me feel at ease. 'I love y—' I said, stopping myself before I stupidly finished what I never meant to say. *Shit!*

He pulled back from me and searched my eyes and, before he could make up an excuse as to why it was too soon for him to say I love you back, I attempted to rectify my fucked-up slip of the tongue. 'I love your kindness, Derek,' I offered with a faux smile. 'Under all that badarse sexiness, you are very sweet.'

He furrowed his brow and went to say something but, thankfully, the elevator doors opened, allowing me to exit.

* * *

The drive back to Derek's house was deathly silent, so much so that I tuned out. *Fuck! What did I say that for? Stupid, stupid, stupid, stupid.* Knowing you love someone is one thing, but saying it to their face is entirely another. What was wrong with me? Was I becoming weak and dependant? Was I emotional over Alexis' pregnancy and her safety, or was it seeing Derek with Alexander, and subsequently, his paternal qualities? Whatever it was, it had rendered me temporarily foolish.

'Talk to me,' he said, turning off the ignition and bringing me back to the now. He undid his belt and shuffled in his seat to face me.

Slowly taking in the scene around me and discovering we were parked in his driveway, I turned to face him.

'What about?' I asked, opting to play dumb. Playing dumb was one of the best defences a person could possess.

'Don't play dumb with me,' he responded with an annoyed tone. *Okay, maybe not.*

'I'm not. What do you want to talk about? And wouldn't it be better if we did this inside?' I went to undo my belt but he placed his hand over it, preventing its release.

'What are you doing?'

'I want the truth,' he explained, annoyance rolling off him. 'No fucking lies or excuses.'

'Let go of the belt, Derek.'

'No.'

Taking in his determined stance, my eyes widened with shock. He was deadly serious. 'Remove your hand and let me out,' I said calmly but with enough bite to severe a finger.

His expression softened, but he did not move a muscle. 'Baby, I want the truth.'

'About what?' I said, exasperated.

'Do you love me?'

I gasped. Witnessing the pleading sincerity in his eyes made my heart pound rapidly and my breathing laboured. The time to be honest was now or never.

For some reason, I chose never. 'No,' I lied and turned away, tears welling in my eyes.

He lowered his voice. 'You're lying.'

Anger at his method of forcing me to open up bubbled over, and I wrenched at the seat belt. 'Let me out, now!'

'You do love me. You were going to say it back at the hotel, but you were too chickenshit to be honest, just like you are too chickenshit to be honest now,' he said, his expression one of disappointment.

Yanking on the belt, I couldn't stop the tears falling down my cheeks. Being honest and telling him that I love him was just too hard, for some reason.

'Fuck you,' I sobbed, opting to blame him, and therefore digging my fingernails into his hand. 'No, I don't love you. All right?'

As my nails pinned his skin, fury and something else that I couldn't quite put my finger on flamed in his eyes as he stared at me. 'Why?' he asked through gritted teeth.

More tears escaped the confines of my eyes and rolled down my cheeks. I watched as Derek's gaze followed their descent. 'Because loving someone means it will hurt like hell when they break your heart and leave. So, no, I refuse to love you.'

Looking down, I noticed blood pool on his hand and underneath my nails. I pulled my hand back with regret, which was when he let go of my belt. Without hesitation, I opened the car door and freed myself from his make-shift jail.

'Carly!' he called after me.

I ignored him and ran, unable to face him, it ... us. I couldn't face the truth that I had fallen in love with him. I couldn't face admitting it, because that made it real.

'Carly, stop!' he yelled, before capturing me in his arms and pinning my back to his front.

I struggled within his tight grip. 'Derek, let me go. Just let me go,' I cried.

He kissed the side of my head and whispered soothingly into my ear. 'Sh, baby. Why do you think I'm gonna break your heart?'

'Because that's what happens. You give someone your heart and they fucking break it. It's human nature,' I said, my body slumping in his hold.

'Give me your heart,' he pleaded, holding me tighter. 'I promise I won't break it.'

I pressed my eyelids together, shutting the world out. 'I want to, but I ... I can't.'

'You can,' he encouraged.

'Derek, please. You will break it. It's only a matter of time.'

'I love you,' he whispered, 'and I want you to love me back.'

My eyes shot open on an intake of breath. For a second, I wondered if I had in fact heard those words come out of his mouth.

Spinning me around to face him, he secured me to his front. 'How 'bout we come to a compromise. Give me your heart and I'll give you mine,' he offered with a small smile.

I couldn't say anything. I was stunned into immobility, unable to function, standing at a crossroads with a decision to make.

When I didn't respond he added sincerely, his face a stoic mask. 'I want to live in your socks, so I can be with you every step of the way.'

I tried not to laugh as he cracked my self-built shell. 'But they stink.'

He looked at my lips for a split second, then held my gaze. 'I thought happiness started with H. Why does mine start with U?'

'Because you can't spell,' I whispered, elevating to my tiptoes and creeping just a little bit closer to his mouth.

He leaned forward and stopped mere centimetres from my lips. 'You're so beautiful that you made me forget my pick-up line.'

Sealing his lips to mine, he kissed me with a soft reverence — by far our most sensual kiss to date — then bent down and lifted me into his arms, carrying me back to his house. Once we were inside, he headed straight for his bedroom and laid me down upon his bed.

Our actions weren't rushed, hungry or frenzied. They were soft, slow, exploratory and loving.

After we'd stripped one another bare and were skin to skin and breathing hard from our continuous kissing, he paused and positioned himself at my entrance. 'Do you love me?' he asked softly.

'Yes, Derek, I love you. I've loved you for a while and I'll love you a while longer. But don't break my heart. Because once it's broken, it'll stay that way.'

He pushed into me and sealed my mouth with a kiss. 'I won't.'

* * *

The next morning, we were up bright and early. Derek was on shift and I had to go home to get ready for work.

'Here, eat this,' he said while shoving a piece of Vegemite covered toast into my mouth right before he closed the passenger side door of his truck.

I hummed my appreciation. 'Mm ... nothing like a morning vegemgasm.'

'A what?' he asked as he secured himself into his seat and closed the door.

'A vegemgasm. A Vegemite-induced orgasm. They are almost as good as the real thing,' I added, giving him a cheeky wink. 'In fact, I'm thinking I'll need to add this condiment to my cock-tasting list, right under the mint sauce.'

'I thought we put that list of yours to rest when we bought the mint flavoured gel stuff.'

'No. I took a leaf out of your book and compromised by trying it and my verdict is that it was awful. In fact, I would've much preferred the taste of your cock without the gel. Sooooo, mint sauce is back on the menu.'

'I'll tell you what. You let me spread that tangy vinegar shit on your pussy first and then I'll let you spread it on my cock.'

A rather large and victorious smile spread across my face. 'You're on. How 'bout tonight?'

'No can do,' he smiled arrogantly. 'I'm on continuous shift for two days.'

I nodded my head at him, unconvinced. 'Wimp.'

'Don't fucking bait me, baby,' he smiled. 'You'll regret it.'

I let out a sinister laugh. 'Try me.'

Derek and I continued to make playful stabs at each other until he dropped me off at my house. It seemed openly expressing our love for one another had lifted an invisible weight from our shoulders. Well, it had from mine.

Before exiting the car, I leaned over the centre console and kissed him goodbye. 'Be careful,' I said softly, like I always did when he was due to go to work.

'I always am. I'll call you in a couple of days, okay?'

I nodded sadly and went to open the car door when he stopped me by pulling my hand to his chest, placing it across his heart. 'Remember, this is yours,' he said as he flexed his fingers over my hand. 'And this,' he explained as he gently teased the skin under the seam of my bra through the opening of my shirt, 'is mine.'

Derek's touch set me alight, which was kind of handy considering he was good at putting it out.

'Remember, don't break it,' I whispered, removing his hand and placing a swift kiss upon his knuckles.

Jumping out of the car, I turned back around and dismissively waved my hand in the air. 'Now go and rescue a cat or something.'

'Please don't mention cats, or I'll have your pussy on my mind all day.'

Laughing, I turned and walked to my door, sounding a 'meow'. Derek growled in response as he reversed out of my driveway before taking off down the street, leaving a ridiculously large smile on my face.

Moments later, as I was about to step into the shower, my phone beeped, indicating a text from Derek.

I hope you have pet insurance, because next time I see you, I'm going to destroy your pussy — Derek

Cheeky fucker. Feeling quite bold — as per usual — I positioned my phone in front of my snatch and took a photo. I then texted it to Derek with a message.

Are you sure you want to destroy this? — Carly

He replied instantly.

Jesus fucking Christ, baby. Are you trying to cause a car accident? — Derek

Oh shit! I decided not to text him any more.

* * *

Hours later, I was sitting at my desk going through the emails that had accumulated over the summer holidays and filtering the junk into the trash bin. School wasn't due to resume for another three days. However, there was a lot of paperwork and preparation to be done in order to ensure the smooth start to the new year.

Fuck off! I don't want to take care of your billions of dollars you Swahili fucktard, I inwardly cursed, pressing delete. *Would I like Viagra? I don't even own a dick.* Delete. *Ooh ... Novo has twenty percent off pumps. Awesome!*

Singing 'Clap Your Hands' by Sia, I made a mental note to go shopping after work when Libby walked in.

'Why are you so happy?' she asked suspiciously.

'I'm not.'

'Yes, you are.'

I fobbed her off. 'So I'm singing, big deal.'

'Carly, you are beaming so bright that you practically blinded me when I walked in.'

I shook my head and hid my face. 'Pfft. Am not.'

'Oh my god!' she squealed.

Ignoring her, I saved an email advertising laser hair removal.

'Either he has said the "L" word, or you have. Or both,' she said excitedly as she sat her arse on my desk, messing my paperwork piles.

How does she bloody do that? I swear she is a mentalist.

'You're an idiot,' I retorted grumpily, grabbing the documents that were poking out from underneath her arse.

'It was you!' she pointed. 'You said it!'

Continuing to ignore her, I bunched the paperwork in my hand and tapped it on the desktop. 'What was it that you wanted? I have so much work to do.'

She tapped her chin in a cocky knowing manner. 'He said it, didn't he? No, you both said it to each other.'

'Yes! All right,' I conceded. 'We both said the "L" word. So what?'

She patted me on the head in a condescending manner. 'Carly has finally become a grown-up. Congratulations. I am happy for you.'

Unsuccessfully trying to supress a smile — because ever since admitting to Derek that I loved him that's all my face wanted to do — I continued to act unfazed. 'Seriously, Lib, is there anything I can help you with? I'm kinda busy.'

Scrolling through her phone, she answered. 'Nope, I'm —'

I waited for her to continue and when she didn't, I looked up. 'Nope, you're what?'

She didn't answer me, instead concentrating quite deeply on whatever it was she was reading.

'Lib!'

'Carly, you might want to see this. It's breaking news. I don't know how true it is but —'

Seeing the panic on Lib's face, I took the phone from her hand and began to read the *Herald Sun* online breaking news.

CITY TOWERS PENTHOUSE EXPLOSION. ONE CONFIRMED DEAD.

'Oh, my god!' I shrieked. 'Oh no! Oh no.' Waves of terror rolled over me as my body began to tremble, causing me to drop her phone.

'Carly, honey, calm down. Let's ring Alexis' phone,' Lib suggested.

I nodded, fumbled for my phone, and dialled Lex. After many attempts, the call would not connect, which only added to my heightened terror. 'I've got to go. I've got to go there.'

Shooting up from my seat, I grabbed my phone and keys and headed for the door.

'Carly,' Libby called out, 'I'm coming with you.'

* * *

Libby ended up driving us both into the city, which was a good thing. My head was a mess — a jumble of anxious thoughts — and driving myself would have been a dangerous mistake. Traffic was crazy due to roads having been cordoned off by police. News crews and paparazzi were everywhere.

Looking up toward the top of City Tower before entering the entertainment precinct, I noticed smoke and a blackened exterior. The sight of it had me doubled over and feeling nauseated. 'I can't,' I said, gasping for air. 'I can't go any closer. I don't want to know.'

'Sweetie, you can't stay here. Come on, we'll see what we can find out.' Lib looped her arm around mine and led me toward the precinct.

Just shy of the building, we were stopped by a security officer.

'I'm sorry ladies, you can't go any further. It's not safe.'

'Alexis Summers, Mr Clark's fiancée, is my best friend. I need to know that she is all right. She won't answer her phone,' I pleaded.

'I'm sorry. I'm not at liberty to divulge any information at this stage,' he said impassively.

'Please!' I begged, tears now beckoning. 'I just need to know that she is okay.'

His demeanour softened just a little. 'I'm sorry ma'am, I —'

'Carly!' a voice sounded from behind him.

I peeked over the man's shoulder to find Liam walking briskly in our direction. 'Joey,' he said to the security officer, 'it's okay. Carly is Ms Summers' best friend.'

'I told him that,' I said crossly.

Liam patted Joey on the back. 'He's just following protocol, Carls.'

'Where's Lexi, Liam? Is she all right? I need to see her,' I begged.

'She's been taken to the hospital. She's fine, apart from smoke inhalation and, I dare say, shock. Bryce is with her.'

I sighed with relief and fell against Lib. 'Oh, thank goodness.' Another wave of terror washed over me. 'What about the kids?'

'I'm fairly sure they are with their father,' Liam said reassuringly.

Libby draped her arm over my shoulder and gave me a quick comforting squeeze. 'Come on, I'll take you to the hospital now. You can see for yourself that Lexi is fine.'

* * *

Libby drove me to The Alfred Hospital where we headed straight for the reception counter to find out what room Alexis was in. Upon my approach, I noticed Will heading for the exit.

'Will!' I called out.

Libby groaned with annoyance.

I turned and furrowed my eyebrows at her. 'What's your problem?'

'Nothing,' she muttered.

'Hey, Jaws. And nice to see you again, Labia,' he said suggestively, as his eyes raked her from top to toe.

'Hi, Will. You don't happen to know what room Lex is in, do you? It will save me the trouble of asking.'

'I know what room they are both in,' he answered with a smile, his eyes still roaming my redheaded friend.

'Yes, these are breasts, Will,' Lib explained with definitive poise. 'They are two protruding glands and their purpose is to secrete milk after childbirth.'

Will licked his lips. 'They have more purpose than just that, sweetheart.'

'You're a pig!' she chided and crossed her arms over her chest.

'What a minute,' I said, breaking up whatever it was the two of them were doing. 'You just said both, as in plural.'

He gave me an inquisitive look. 'Yeah, Alexis and Derek.'

'Derek!' I shrieked. 'Derek's here? Why is Derek here? What happened to Derek?' I asked, panic setting in once again.

'He mustn't have had time to call you yet. He was one of the first firefighters on the scene. He's just in for routine observation — mild smoke inhalation.'

'What?' I exclaimed. 'What room?'

'Level three, room eleven.'

I started for the elevator. 'Lib, do you mind waiting down here?' I called back.

'She'll be fine,' Will explained, draping his arm over her shoulder and pulling her to him. Libby pushed him away. 'I'll take good care of her. And by the way, Alexis is on level five, room eight.'

'Thanks,' I called back.

As I approached Derek's room, I heard a familiar female voice, one which had the power to pull on every jealous fibre I owned. *What is she doing here?* Deep down I knew what she was doing here, but it was more a question of why she was in the room with my injured boyfriend and I was not.

Knocking gently on the door, I walked in when invited, to find Lucy sitting in a guest chair next to Derek's bed and Alexander happily sitting on Derek's lap. They both looked up with shocked expressions when they saw me.

'Oh, I'm sorry,' I stuttered, their stunned demeanour causing me to feel unsettled. 'I'll come back.'

'No!' Lucy stated, standing up quickly. 'I was just leaving. I was just seeing how Derek was after visiting Alexis.'

'I can come back, it's fine,' I choked out, trying desperately not to show my betrayed feelings.

'No, no. Come on. Al, we have storytime at the library.' She picked up her son and waved his arm at Derek. 'Say bye.'

Derek smiled and waved in return, his affection for Al again causing the pit of my stomach to plummet into the abyss.

Lucy walked past and gave me a resigned yet guilt-ridden smile. 'Nice to see you again.'

I could only nod and follow her departing form and, when she was gone, I almost could not bring myself to turn around and look at Derek. I was hurt and angry that he did not think to call me. I was jealous and scared that Lucy seemed to always be his first point of call. I was so fucking confused. He made me confess my feelings, but then dismissed them by keeping me at an arm's-length. After everything, nothing had changed. My heart was now hurting and, as a result, my wall came up again, to protect and prevent any further battering of it. He may not have broken it one day after me giving it to him, but he sure as hell just gave it a good bruising. That was painful enough.

'Baby,' he said, sending an unwelcome chill up my spine, a feeling that word did not normally produce.

I spun around and took a seat, my body language uncontrollably rigid. 'Are you okay?' I asked flatly.

'I was going to call —'

I interrupted him, not wanting to hear his excuse. 'What happened at City Towers?'

He scrunched up his face and grabbed my hand, placing it upon his chest. 'I was going to call you right before Lucy popped in to see how I was. Prior to that, I had been subjected to routine tests and just never got the chance. I wanted enough time to explain what had happened so that you wouldn't worry.'

'I found out from Will,' I seethed, forcing back a tear and gritting my teeth, 'In the fucking lobby only moments ago where I was frantically trying to find my best friend to see if she was all right.' I removed my hand from his chest. 'I still have not done that yet.'

He dropped his gaze and stared at my hand which now sat on my lap. 'Physically, Alexis is fine. She suffered a little smoke inhalation. Lucy also mentioned that the baby is fine too.'

Swallowing heavily, I closed my eyes for the smallest of seconds and whispered, 'Thank god.'

'Gareth is dead,' he said quietly.

My eyes reopened with rapid speed, taking in his sad expression before he directed his gaze to the view outside his window.

'He tried to kill himself and Alexis by blowing up the apartment. She managed to get away in the nick of time, but was trapped in the elevator. No one knew she was there. Bryce thought she was dead and was beside himself with grief. Carly, I thought she was dead as well. I couldn't find her.'

A tear streamed down his cheek, prompting my own to overflow. Seeing his obvious pain, I pushed aside my own hurt and grabbed his hand, pressing it to my lips. 'She's okay. You're both okay.'

Derek continued to gaze forlornly out the window. 'I searched everywhere, but visibility from the smoke was next to zero. With every room I entered and found empty, my heart shattered. I'd promised Bryce I would find her. I promised him I would not come back unless I had her with me. Do you know how fucking hard it was for me to break my promise and leave that apartment without her?'

'Sh,' I hushed him, moving to sit on the bed and encase him in my arms. 'You did all you could. You didn't know she was in the elevator.'

Derek secured my arms to him and breathed deep to find composure. 'No, but seeing her in Bryce's arms when I finally made it back to where he was waiting was such a bloody relief. I'd already had confirmation of Gareth's death, so the last thing I wanted was to be the one to tell Bryce that Alexis was unaccounted for.'

I sat on the bed for a while longer with my arms around him, silence surrounding us. It was a suffocating torture. I loved him, that was unquestionable. But the day's events had put my heart on guard once again, and I couldn't stop returning to my safety bubble where my heart and I were safe.

CHAPTER

23

The emotional aftermath of the explosion was still felt over a month later. Alexis had retreated to her sanctuary, which was Bryce, her children and her family. This was how she coped. I checked in with her weekly via the phone, despite her reassurances that she was fine and in the process of picking up the broken pieces slowly. Things between Derek and I were also fine, if a little circumspect on my behalf. I couldn't help it. It was imprinted in my DNA.

Today being Alexander's first birthday, we were all to be together for the first time since the trauma of Gareth's death. To be honest, I wasn't looking forward to it. Not only would I be seeing Lucy there, but it was also a kid's party. With kids. Little kids. I'd much rather have each of my fingernails torn from my hands, scraped down a blackboard and then poked into my eyes.

For moral support, I'd asked Libby to come along. Well, truth be told, I'd bribed her. Okay, so I'd threatened her. Oh, and I lied to her. I'd mentioned that Will wasn't coming when he was. But I was willing to bear the brunt of the ear-drilling she would undoubtedly give me once we returned home.

Derek drove us to the park where the party was to be held. It was a stinking hot thirty-six degrees Celsius, but thank fuck for obscenely wealthy friends, because Bryce had organised for his nephew to have a kiddy wonderland in a fully air-conditioned marquee. It was basically a makeshift play centre for kids: all pits, slides, jumping castles, coloured foam mats ... and lots and lots of kids.

'Where in hell did all of these small humans come from?' I asked Derek as we stepped into the marquee. The high-pitched screams already had my head pounding.

Libby smiled and instantly went to the aid of one little girl who had managed to get the wheel of the trike she was pedalling stuck between two mats.

'I'm not quite sure. I think a lot of them belong to the mothers who are in Lucy's mother's group,' he answered with a shrug of his shoulders.

'Oh,' I nodded, surprised he knew the answer to that question.

We quickly said hello and gave Alexander his present. Derek had even gone shopping and made the effort to buy something suitable for a male toddler which I found adorable but, at the same time, felt guilty about.

Scanning the room, I spotted Alexis being lured onto the jumping castle by Charli. She looked up so I waved and blew her a kiss.

'Hey, guys,' Will said happily as he approached from out of nowhere. 'And if it isn't my favourite redheaded walking vagina,' he added, taking Libby's hand and kissing the back of it.

She screwed up her face and wiped her hand down the front of his top. 'Carly, a word. Now!' she fired in my direction.

Lib then turned around and headed for an empty table in one of the corners of the marquee. When we were out of everyone's hearing, she blasted me with her icy damnation. 'You little liar! You said he wasn't coming. This is a new low, even for you.'

'Don't get your labia in a knot,' I said in defence, unsuccessfully biting back a smile.

She pointed to her hilariously funny face. 'I'm not laughing. Is my face laughing?'

'No, but then again, it doesn't laugh often. You need to laugh more, starting with now. Laugh, this really is quite funny,' I goaded.

'Oh, I will be laughing. Mark my words. I'll be laughing like a hyena when I get my revenge.'

Taking a seat, I focussed my sights on the crowded room of people before me, spotting Derek talking with Lucy, Nic, Will and Matt. Alexander was desperately trying to lunge out of Nic's arms and into Derek's.

'I don't like hyenas,' I admitted solemnly. 'They are ugly looking, kind of like the by-product of sex between a dog and a clown.'

Libby sank into the seat next to me. 'What's wrong?'

Smiling at her perceptive skills, I shook my head. 'Am I forgiven already?'

'No. The best plots for revenge are not ones carried out hastily. Your time will come. In the meantime though, tell me why you look so deflated and no longer want to be here just as much as me.'

I nodded toward Lucy. 'I don't trust her.'

Lib followed my line of vision. 'Why? I thought the two of you got along well.'

'We do. She's lovely. I just don't trust her.'

'There's got to be a reason why, Carly.'

I shrugged my shoulders. 'Not really. Just call it a sixth sense. I feel as if I'm missing something.'

'Like what?' she queried with interest.

'I think Lucy and Derek dated before she turned lezzie. They have a history. That much is for certain.'

'So what, history is the operative word here. In the past. Yesteryear.'

I looked down at my fingers and fiddled with my aunt's ring. 'I get that. I just don't think it is entirely in the past.'

Lib gave me a sceptical look. 'What makes you say that?'

'God, I don't know, all right?' I answered frustratedly.

She stood up. 'Hey! I'm just trying to help. I'm going to get a drink. Do you want one ... or some fairy bread?'

I gave her an apologetic look and shook my head. 'No, thank you.'

'Ah ... I know, I saw some mini-pizzas and hot dogs,' she said enticingly.

I laughed mildly and tilted my head to the side. 'You had me at mini.'

'Thought as much. I'll be back in a minute.'

Once Lib was gone, I glanced back to where Derek had been, only to find him no longer there. I performed a quick scan of the room and couldn't find him anywhere. I also couldn't find Lucy.

I can't say what it was that propelled me to get up and look for them, or what it was that was saying to me that they were together. Regardless, I had to find him and discover for myself what I dreaded was the outcome.

As I was about to turn the corner to where a door lead into the kitchen, I heard Derek having a heated discussion with a woman, except the woman he was arguing with was not Lucy. It was Nic. My stomach tightened and I froze solid.

'Back the fuck off, Derek. I'm not going to warn you again,' Nic admonished.

'I'm sick of having this discussion with you. I'm not a fucking threat,' he hissed back.

'Bullshit, you aren't. You and I both know that Lucy will always love you.'

Hearing that Lucy loved Derek splintered my heart, yet I knew deep down it was true. It was obvious in the way she looked at him.

Derek groaned. 'It's not like that and you know it.'

'Just back off, Derek. Alexander may be your son, but he and Lucy are my family. Not yours.'

I gasped and took a step backward, bumping into someone behind me. Spinning around, I came face to face with Lucy.

'Carly, I —'

'Derek is Alexander's father?' I choked out.

By that stage, Derek and Nic had rounded the corner. 'Baby, let me expla—'

'Alexander is your son?' I shouted.

'Sh, Carly, please lower your voice,' Lucy pleaded with desperation.

'Lower my fucking voice? You lying pack of heart-less arseholes,' I spat out, before turning and making my escape.

'Baby, wait!' Derek called and caught my arm.

I spun around and slapped him forcefully on the cheek, the sting numbing my hand, the pain nowhere near as severe as the betrayed heart, torn in two, deep within my chest. Tears were streaming down my face. 'Don't touch me. Don't ever touch me again.' And with that, I wrenched my other arm free from his grasp and pushed past Lib and Alexis on my way out.

'Carly!' they both called after me, but I didn't stop.

I needed air.

I needed to vomit.

I needed to run far away.

CHAPTER
24

In the hours that followed, I'd cried more tears than I'd ever thought possible. I was shocked, hurt and angry. I felt betrayed, but more importantly, stupid. Stupid that I'd gone against everything I'd thought myself to be: independent and headstrong, free and unattached. I'd let one man infiltrate that protective wall and, in perfect arsehole-male fashion, he'd aimed straight for my heart and dismembered it. I was heartbroken because I'd allowed myself to love. I was accountable.

The hurt I was feeling had nothing to do with Derek being a dad. He'd made that choice — for whatever reason — long before I'd come along. What hurt beyond repair was that he never really loved me enough to let me into his life. He constantly held me at arm's-length where he felt comfortable having me, while telling me that we 'are'. Well, *we* 'are' something. *We* 'are' done.

Derek had tried calling and texting, but I wasn't interested. In fact, I went so far as to throw my phone in the bin. Apparently Lib didn't share my views, because she had retrieved it and placed it on my bed while I was in the shower. My redheaded fanta-pants friend was a pain in my arse, but little did she know that her actions were futile, because I had let the battery run flat and had not bothered to charge it.

'Carly, you have a visitor,' Libby called from the other side of my bedroom door.

I launched out of bed and hurled myself against it with a thump, leaning my entire sixty-one kilogram weight against it. 'If that's him, tell him to fuck off,' I yelled.

'It's not Derek, Carly. Please just come out,' she pleaded while turning the handle on my door.

I pushed harder against it and held the handle tight. 'Who is it then?'

'It's me, Carly.'

'Oh, no. No, no, no. I have nothing to say to you, Lucy. Absolutely fucking nothing.'

'Well I have something to say to you, so you can just listen.' *Fuck her!*

'La la la la la la la la laaaaaaaaaaaaaaaaaaaaaaaa,' I sang out repeatedly in an attempt to drown out what she wanted to say. Unfortunately, I was not an operatic singer and could not hold the notes for very long.

During a pause for breath, I heard Lucy ask Libby how old I was.

'She's thirty-five, although I know grade six students who act more maturely than she does at times,' Libby explained.

'I heard that,' I sulked. 'Look, Lucy, please just leave me alone. I don't want to hear anything you or Derek have to say. He had many chances to tell me about Alexander, and he chose not to. So it doesn't matter any more.'

'Alexander is not Derek's son, Carly. He is mine and Nic's. Derek was just a sperm donor. That's all. Please just let me in to explain, then I'll leave.'

I sucked in a deep breath and then let it out. 'No, Lucy, just leave. Lib, if you know what is good for you you'll show Lucy out.'

The next thing I knew, I was being pushed forward against my will.

'Keep pushing,' Libby said with a strained voice. 'Almost ...'

I fell to the floor with a thud.

'... There,' she finished and dusted her hands against each other.

Lucy stepped out from behind her. Sasha, too, prancing in to sit at Lucy's feet and wag her tale adoringly. *Oh, for fuck's sake. You can all go to hell.*

'Obviously you don't know what's good for you,' I said to Lib, glaring at her.

'Obviously,' she countered. 'But I do know what's good for you and listening to what Lucy has to say is just that. Come on, Sashy,' she said, patting her leg and coaxing Sasha from the room before closing the door behind her.

I stared at the panel of wood that was my bedroom door before noticing that Lucy had her hand out in order to help me stand.

'You've got one minute,' I explained, ignoring her offer of help.

She crossed her arms over her chest in a show of resilience. 'I won't need it.'

Fighting the desire to remove her confident expression, I walked over to Rico's tank and proceeded to feed him, giving an excuse to keep my back to her. 'You are so sure of yourself, aren't you?'

'Yes,' she stated categorically.

I tapped some food into the tank and reminded her of her dwindling time. 'Fifty seconds.'

'Derek loves you.'

'Pfft. No, he doesn't.'

'Yes, he does. A lot.'

I watched the salmon pellets sink to the bottom of the tank and answered nonchalantly. 'You don't keep secrets from the ones you love, Lucy.'

'Yes, you do if they are not your secrets to tell.'

I let out a frustrated breath and rolled my eyes. 'This was his secret to tell.'

'No, it wasn't,' she admonished, 'it was mine and Nic's and we didn't want it told.'

I turned to face her and walked back toward my bed. 'Really? Who else knows? Alexis?'

'No.' *Huh.*

'Bryce?'

She didn't say anything.

'So he knows and he hasn't told Lexi?' I asked, truly shocked.

'That's my point. It's not his secret to tell, Carly. He is loyal and the best brother you could ask for. He will tell Alexis when I'm ready for him to tell her. Derek is the same: loyal and the best friend a person could have. I swore him to secrecy and he adhered to it.'

I narrowed my eyes at her. 'Thirty seconds.'

'It's more like forty, actually.' *Argh! I want to bitch-slap this clever bitch.*

'Thirty-eight,' I said through gritted teeth.

'Carly, I love Nic with all my heart. She, Alexander and Bryce are all I have. You need to understand that I wouldn't have Alexander if it weren't for Derek. And because of that, he will always be special to me. He is such a kind, generous, giving man —'

'It would appear so,' I said, sarcastically.

She gave me a light shove on the shoulder, forcing me back onto the bed. 'Sit down, shut up and just listen,' she scolded. *Jesus, she's pushy.*

I sat there, dumbstruck, while she pointed at me.

'Derek is probably the best man you will ever come across in this lifetime. He loves you, and you love him. Don't take that for granted. You have no idea what it's like to love someone who the majority of society says you should not love. Just the simple fact that a man and a woman can love each other freely is something you heterosexual couples take for granted. You can say I love you to each other in public. You can hold hands, embrace and kiss without being ridiculed. Your love is recognised legally. Fucking legally, Carly.

'Love is uncontrollable. It's chaotic and disorganised, but it is what everyone seeks in life. When you find it, you fucking grab it and you don't let it go, no matter what or who gets in your way. Love is there right in front of you in the form of Derek, and I'll be damned if I'll stand by and let you close your eyes to it.'

I stood up, tears welling. 'Are you finished? Firstly, I wish we could all love freely. What a happy sunshiny world that would be,' I said with a hint of cynicism. 'But love is not free for a reason. If it were, *then* it would be taken for granted. Love is precious and rare and only bestowed when it's truly deserved.

'Secondly, I offered it to him. I wanted him to have it. But what I got in return was an illusion, a misconception. What Derek gave me was akin to a fake Louis Vuitton bag. It looked like the real thing, acted like it ... hell, it probably even smelled like it. But it wasn't genuine; it was forged. I don't do counterfeit, I never have and I never will.'

Walking over to my bedroom door, I opened it and gestured she leave. 'Your minute is up. You may go.'

Lucy smiled at me and it was almost evil ... almost. 'He won't give up, Carly,' she said as she walked up to me. Then, leaning forward, she added in a lower tone, 'I know him. And I think deep down in the pit of that stomach of yours, you know him too.'

* * *

After Lucy left, I threw on a pair of shorts and runners and took Sasha out for a walk. Lucy had riled me with her cunning assertiveness and pushy manner. But it was the sincerity in her delivery that had me pondering and, because of that, I had to clear my head with a walk.

'What about your phone?' Libby called out from her position at our letterbox, holding my iPhone in the air.

I turned and walked backward as Sasha pulled me, eager for her walk. 'It's dead. I let it run out of battery.'

She ran up to me and wedged it in my bra. 'I charged it.'

'I know what you are doing and I don't want it,' I said, thrusting it back at her.

'Take it. You may run into a murderer or a rapist, and if you do, you'll need it.'

'Right, and this murderer or rapist is going to let me make a call,' I said dryly, clearing my throat and sarcastically adding, 'Oh, excuse me, Mr Bad Man. Can you just hang on a minute while I call for a pizza?'

Looking past me, she sighed with defeat. 'I liked you better when you were in love,' she said sadly, and turned back to the house.

'I wasn't in love,' I shouted back. 'Love is reciprocated and that sure as hell wasn't the case.' I turned around to continue my walk and slammed straight into a man-wall.

'It fucking well was,' Derek bit out harshly.

I stumbled back in shock. Shock, because he was right there in front of me, and shock, because he just came out of nowhere.

After taking a few seconds to compose myself, I straightened my shoulders and summoned my inner bitch. 'Are you sure you don't have "actor" listed on that extensive résumé of yours? Because if you don't, you should, you're really good at it.'

Much to Sasha's disgust, I swung around and pulled her back toward the house, desperately wanting to get away from Derek. His presence was the most potent form of temptation I'd ever come across.

'Are you sure you don't have a doctorate in denial? Because you are really good at dismissing the facts,' he called out behind me.

'Just because you say they are facts doesn't mean they are. Facts need verification, you idiot. And you verified fuck all,' I yelled.

Derek jogged around me and blocked any further escape I had planned. 'I verified everything, baby. Each time I entered you, I fucking verified that we "are".'

I let go of Sasha's lead so that she could run into our yard and therefore free my hands to shove caramello con artist out of my way. 'We "are" nothing. Each time you entered me, all you did was verify our attraction ... and a fucking orgasm. That's it,' I shouted and shoved him.

Derek grabbed my hand and held it over his heart. 'Stop. Just stop with the bullshit, Carly,' he said softly. 'What we have is more than just attraction. You know it. I know it. Everyone knows it. And if you think I am just going to walk away because you want to protect your pride, then you have another think coming.'

'You are wrong. You think you love me, but you don't. You don't know what love is, Derek. Fuck, I don't know what it is either, but it's not this,' I said gesturing to the both of us with my free hand.

'Don't tell me what I do and don't know. I know what love is,' he said with hesitation as he glanced slightly to the side.

Curious as to why he was distracted, I also glanced sideways and spotted Sasha making her way toward us in a stealth-like fashion.

What happened next was a blur. Sasha's steps quickened until she was past us and stopped in the middle of the road, face to face with a cat. The screeching sound of tyres and the blare of a car horn pierced my body like a thousand bolts of lightning. But it was Derek I witnessed, rolling across the road in a haze of colour and moving body parts that had me frozen with profound terror.

'Derek!' I screamed.

The shrill sound of Sasha's yelps brutally churned my stomach as she stumbled around on the side of the road, before settling next to Derek who was lying motionless.

The car that hit them pulled to a stop and a middle-aged lady climbed out. 'Oh, my goodness. I couldn't stop in time. Oh my goodness, I'm sorry.'

'Call an ambulance,' I yelled as I ran across the road. 'Derek, are you okay? Oh my god, please be okay. Please be okay.'

He groaned then opened his eyes, squinting, pain evident on his face. 'I couldn't be better.'

'Oh thank god. Is anything broken?' I asked frantically, checking for visible protrusions that I honestly didn't want to find. 'Where does it hurt?'

'Here,' he answered, pointing to his chest.

'Please don't move. You could have internal bleeding or you could be having a heart attack or something,' I explained, anxiously.

He reached for my hand. 'Carly, if my heart is bleeding it's because of you. I love you, baby. Why can't you just accept that?' He went to sit up and winced, holding his arm in a nurturing manner.

'Don't move!' I yelled at him. 'Stay still.'

'I'm all right, but Sasha may not be. I hit the car, but when I rolled, I rolled on top of her.'

Scrambling to my feet, I walked around to where Sasha was sitting and panting profusely. I went to pat her, but she yelped in anticipation of my touch. 'Oh, Sashy, it's okay,' I said reassuringly.

'Here,' he winced again, turning to the side. 'Get my phone out of my pocket and dial Layla.'

* * *

The ambulance and a police car arrived minutes later, followed by Layla who had made an emergency dash from the surgery.

'Her leg is broken,' Layla informed me. 'I'll give her something for the pain, but I'm going to have to operate. I'll take her back to the surgery now. Okay?'

'Just put it back in,' Derek demanded quite harshly of the paramedic assessing him.

Standing with Layla and Libby alongside Layla's car, not too far from the ambulance, I glanced over at Derek, unsure as to what to do.

'Carls, you go and see Derek. I'll go with Layla to the surgery and stay with Sasha,' Libby said, as she placed her hand on my shoulder reassuringly.

'I'll take good care of Sasha,' Layla said. 'She'll be a perfect patient. Derek, on the other hand, will not. Go with him and keep him in check.'

I sighed. 'Okay, but please call me if anything changes. And, Layla ... once again, thank you so much.'

'No, I have to thank you. Since you and Derek have been together, I've seen more of him than in the past couple of years. So thanks,' she sadly replied.

I nodded and made my way over to where Derek was still arguing with the paramedic. 'Is he okay?' I asked timidly.

'I suspect he has a dislocated collarbone,' he explained. 'He'll need an X-ray before it can be reset.'

Derek huffed in annoyance. 'Just put it back in now and we'll be done with it.'

'Sorry, mate, but I'm not taking that risk.'

'I'm not riding in that thing,' Derek said with disgust as he surveyed the inside of the ambulance. 'Forget it.'

'Suit yourself,' the paramedic replied, unfazed.

'Thank you,' I said graciously. 'I'll take him to the hospital.'

After giving the police a report of the incident and apologising to the lady for Sasha running out in front of her car, I took Derek to the hospital. He tried to talk to me during the trip, but I shut him down. My emotions were all over the place. I was head-fucked beyond repair, not only due to our break-up, but because he risked his life to save my dog.

I needed time and space to clear my head.

Arriving at the hospital, he saw the triage nurse, who sat us both in a cubicle with the curtains drawn around us. He was sitting on the edge of a stretcher bed and I on the visitor's seat across from it. He'd had an X-ray taken which confirmed the paramedic's diagnosis and, because he was a professional firefighter who relied heavily on full movement of his body parts to do his job successfully, the doctor on call wanted a specialist to reset it. That specialist was not due to arrive for another thirty minutes.

'I've always wanted to fuck in a hospital,' Derek said quietly, abruptly snapping me out of my inner deliberations as I intently stared at the urine collection jug.

A smile threatened to creep across my face and betray my battle to remain indifferent in his presence. I knew exactly what he was up to. 'Why?' I asked, flatly.

'Because there are people everywhere,' he answered, clearly undressing me with his eyes. 'It's hot.'

His salacious appraisal of my features stirred the hunger between my legs and, uncontrollably, I shifted in my seat and crossed them.

Derek, in turn, adjusted his pants, letting his hand linger over his cock. 'You're getting wet thinking about it, aren't you?' he asked, amused.

I turned my head away and swallowed dryly. 'No. Don't flatter yourself.'

'Baby, you lie like a bucket of shit,' he said with a low, devious chuckle.

I watched from the corner of my eye as he slowly rubbed against the denim covering his groin, his rubbing actions creating an obvious bulge underneath his hand.

Powerless in the face of his seduction, I turned to meet his blazing eyes. 'Play with it all you like, because I won't be.'

'This is not something you *play* with,' he said pointing to his now cylindrical-shaped front.

At that moment the curtain was pulled aside and a young, pretty, brunette nurse entered the cubicle. 'Mr Ki—' she stuttered, as her eyes fell on Derek's evident erection.

I bit my lip to refrain from laughing.

'Yes,' he said with a flirtatious smile, choosing to boldly display his wood for her rather than concealing it.

She blushed and moved her stare to his face. 'How are you feeling?' she asked, emphasising the *feeling* part.

Her equally bold flirtatious manner removed my amused smile, replacing it with a scowl.

Derek noticed my transition and smiled smugly before using it to his advantage. 'I'm *feeling* a little *stiff*,' he explained.

She picked up his file and raised an eyebrow, glancing at his package one more time. 'I can see that.' *Um ... hello, ex-girlfriend here in the room with you.*

His eyes met mine and the challenge in them was profound. 'Can you give me something for it?' he asked, without removing his stare from me.

'Oh, I'd love to. But unfortunately, right now, I can't,' she responded.

There was silence in the cubicle for what seemed liked moments on end as Derek and I killed each other slowly with accusatory glares. I unleashed my anger-fuelled, jealousy-ridden, telepathic war on him and he seemed to revel in it.

'Right,' the slutsky nurse interrupted. 'Dr Wang will be here shortly to relieve that stiffness. Hopefully you will not have to endure it for much longer.' She opened the curtain and exited the cubicle and, the moment it swished shut behind her, I shot up from my seated position. Derek, too, straightened.

My heart was pounding like a jackhammer within my chest. I was so angry, furious, jealous and feeling wanton. I wanted nothing more than to claw at him, cause him grave pain, then wrap my arms around him and his around me. I wanted to get lost in him and never be found. I wanted to love him.

Fury surfacing in my pores, I strode toward him and smashed my lips to his, viciously delving my tongue into his mouth. My hand fell to his crotch where I clutched his hard cock, feeling its solidity in my grasp. He groaned harshly, thrust his pelvis toward me and pushed, making me stumble back just slightly and separate my lips from his.

He went to grab me and lead me back into his embrace, but I stepped away and covered my mouth with my hand before speaking. 'What we have isn't love, Derek. And that display with Nurse Slapper just proved it. I'll wait outside,' I said with disappointment, and turned to leave.

He grabbed my hand and pulled me to him, wincing when I slammed into his hard frame. 'Clearly, throwing myself in front of a car to save Sasha wasn't verification enough for you, huh?'

I closed my eyes, breathed in and then lowered my head to his chest, hugging him gently. 'Thank you. What you did was heroic and I will be forever grateful, but ...' I said raising my head and releasing myself from his hold, '... an act of kindness is not necessarily an act of love.'

Turning to leave for the final time, I stopped when he murmured my name. 'Carly, you want proof. You'll get it.'

CHAPTER
25

Derek's shoulder was reset and, as far as I knew, was healing nicely. He had been relentless with his quest to give me proof and had even sent me a recording of him singing 'Someday' by Nickelback. Hearing his voice, and the lyrics he chose to sing to me, spurred the emotion I had buried to rear its ugly head again. I wasn't sure I wanted him to 'make it all right' and I wasn't sure I wanted him to be relentless in his actions to win me back. The notion, of course, sounded nice. But winning me back meant that he could once again break my heart at some future point, and I couldn't let that happen. So despite the ache he kindled in my body, I refused to encourage him. And as much as that hurt, I ignored his attempts at contact.

I must admit that some attempts he made were a lot harder to ignore than others, like when I nearly tripped over a bottle of mint sauce that sat upon my front doorstep. I'd picked it up in my confusion and aggravation and found a note attached to it: *I'm ready when you are. Derek*

I had to give credit where credit was due — the mint sauce whet my appetite. But I had to remain strong, I had to remain smart and I had to remain free. I'd opted to place the bottle on the outdoor window ledge just in case he had plans to come back. It was my way of saying that mint sauce was off the menu for good. Well, off the cock-tasting menu anyway. *Pity.*

Oh, and he'd even sent a picture of the cock-moulding kit sitting on his bedside table with a message, again saying: *I'm ready when you are. Derek*

Seeing that pic had made me laugh, but then again, he'd always been able to make me laugh. When all was said and done, his actions, albeit cute and endearing, were far from 'proving' his claim that what we had was more than attraction.

It was now nearly a week since the accident. I'd taken annual leave from work to look after Sasha. My golden pup had fractured her ulna and it was tightly secured in a cast. Layla had given strict instructions for Sasha to rest, and for the first couple of days this request seemed easy enough to comply with. But Sasha — being an eight-month-old puppy — did not take kindly to being restricted and was getting her second wind and wanting to move more freely.

'Stay!' I warned, as I stood up from the couch to answer the door. She went to get up and perform her ritual over-enthusiastic greeting, but I cautioned her otherwise. 'Sasha, sit. Stay.'

Quickly opening the door in order to get rid my visitor so that I could get back to where Sasha was curled up on her bed in our lounge room, I found myself face to face with Derek. Even after what we'd been through, his presence still had the ability to steal my breath.

'Hey,' he said nervously as he stood there with his arm in a sling and presenting me with yet another bottle of mint sauce.

'Hey,' I answered, just as nervously, accepting the bottle from him. I leaned out the door and placed it on the window ledge next to the other bottle.

He let out a long, disappointed breath. 'You mind if I come in?'

Knowing I would regret my decision either way, I stood back and let him enter. He walked straight into my lounge room and dropped to his knees before a very happy Sasha.

'Hello, gorgeous girl,' he said adoringly as he stroked her golden fur. 'How's the patient?'

She rolled to her side, bared her belly and wagged her tail excitedly. The sight of his attentiveness toward Sasha was simply beautiful. If it weren't for him, there was a strong possibility Sasha would not be alive.

Sitting down on the sofa, I smiled at the two of them. 'She's doing well. Your sister-in-law is an angel.'

He tutted. 'Yeah, sometimes.'

Silence encircled us as he stroked Sasha, the invisible barrier both awkward and soothing.

'Carly, I'm sorry,' he said quietly, still patting Sasha. 'I fucked up. I know that.'

'Well, according to Lucy, it wasn't your secret to tell,' I said without so much as a hint of emotion, although my facade was hard to achieve.

He looked up at me. 'It doesn't matter what Lucy said. I should've told you. I owed you that much.'

I could see his remorse — it blanketed his expression, but as much as I wanted to give in and continue our relationship where we'd left off, I couldn't bring myself to concede. 'Yeah, well, it's too late for that now.'

Derek shuffled forward, until he was kneeling before me and could therefore grip my leg with his unrestricted hand. 'Don't say that,' he pleaded.

'Derek, I told you that if you broke my heart it would stay that way, and I meant it.'

'Baby, let —'

'Stop calling me baby,' I interrupted.

Rebellion flashed across his face. 'Baby, let me fix it. I'll fucking fix it.'

'You can't,' I explained, closing my eyes and shaking my head.

'Why?'

'Because I don't trust you.'

'You never fucking trusted me,' he said angrily, as he got to his feet.

His sudden change of mood took me by surprise. 'And rightly so, it seems,' I replied defensively.

Frustration clearly radiated from him as he began to pace back and forth while he ran his hand along his head. 'I offered my sperm to Luce and Nic so they could start a family. That's it!'

'How did the sperm find its way into Lucy's egg?' I asked, with a calm and almost emotionless composure.

He stopped pacing and stared at me in disbelief. I stared back and summoned all the strength I could, knowing that whatever he said next was going to hurt. If he denied it, or chose not to answer, it would just reinforce my inability to trust him. But if he confirmed my suspicion and admitted to sleeping with Lucy, then the knowledge would sting just as much.

'I fucked her,' he said coldly. 'I fucked her until she was pregnant.'

'Well, there you have it,' I choked, swallowing the lump that had formed in my throat.

'Why does it matter?' he asked beseechingly. 'You weren't in my life back then.'

'No, I wasn't. I get that. But tell me, why do I feel betrayed and deceived if it doesn't matter? Why does the admission of your and Lucy's relationship hurt so fucking much?'

He stepped up to me, leaned down and wiped the tear that had found its way onto my cheek. 'Isn't it obvious? Because you love me.'

'Loved, Derek,' I corrected him, wiping the tear for myself.

He shook his head and smiled sadly. 'Love, Carly.'

'No. Maybe it was back then for a split second, but not any more.'

'Fuck,' he growled and started pacing again. 'What do I have to do to fucking prove it to you?'

'You can't,' I yelled back. 'You can't prove something that is nonexistent.'

'Tell me what you want, Carly,' he said, gritting his teeth as he sat on the sofa next to me. 'What do you want me to do?'

I shuffled sideways until I was pressed against the arm of the chair and creating some distance between us. The last thing I wanted was to be physically close to him, for my body would betray my head. 'Nothing,' I said definitively. 'I don't want anything from you any more.'

Grabbing me with his free hand, he wrenched me to him. 'Nothing?' he queried with a bitter sneer as his hand gripped the skin of my arm. 'Do you just want to fuck? Is that it? Be fuck buddies.'

I tried to get free of his grip. 'Derek, stop it.'

'Do you want to *feel* nothing?' he asked before slamming his lips to mine, forcefully plunging his tongue into my mouth and pinning me to the couch.

The suffocating pressure of his weight, together with the shock of his desperation and aggressiveness, took a moment to wear off, but when it did I pushed against him and scrambled free, throwing myself onto the floor and scooting backward to get away from him. 'Get out!' I screamed.

He stared at me in disbelief. 'Shit, baby, I'm sorry. I didn't mean to frighten you. I —'

'Now! Just go,' I cried, unable to look at him any longer.

'Carly, I can't. I can't leave you like this. You're asking me to do the impossible. Baby, please don't push me away,' he pleaded sadly.

I got to my feet and wiped my nose with the back of my hand. 'If you don't leave, then I will.'

Derek stood up and moved tentatively toward me. 'Okay,' he said softly, gently grasping my chin and tilting my head so that I would look him in the eyes. 'I'm not giving up on us.' He placed a chaste kiss on my lips, causing a surge of emotions to envelop me completely. 'I love you and I know you love me. We "are" and we always will be.' He then placed his hand over his heart and stepped backward until he'd left my house.

When I heard the sound of the front door shutting behind him, I dropped to my knees and cried, sobs wracking my chest like never before. Love leads to immeasurable pain.

* * *

The following week I returned to work, and Derek — in true Derek form — followed through on his vow and continued his pursuit. The man never gave up. He sent texts every day, telling me how sorry he was for the way he acted and for frightening me as a result. He said the look on my face the last time we were together pierced his heart with a blunt knife. He vowed to never see that look again.

Honestly, it wasn't his aggression that had me fearful that day. It was the desperation he so clearly displayed, his anguish as he tried to break down my walls. That's what scared me the most, for I knew in that moment he would eventually succeed.

On the Monday that I returned to work, I'd found another bottle of mint sauce on the bonnet of my car, again displaying a message: *Ready and waiting. Derek*

Just like the times before, I placed it on the window ledge, adding it to my collection which now reminded me of the song '99 Bottles of Beer'.

On the Tuesday afternoon, upon returning from work, I found yet another bottle in my letterbox, this time the note saying: *When you are ready, so am I. Derek*

His persistence confounded me. It was both cute and delusional, and I wondered how long he would keep it up; there was only so much room on my window ledge.

On Wednesday, during my lunch hour, a courier delivered a box addressed to me. I didn't open it straight away, thinking it may have been stationery supplies. So when I eventually found the time to unseal the package after the final school bell sounded and all the children had gone home for the day, the ten bottles of mint sauce neatly packed inside had me falling down on my chair in resounding defeat. *You fucking tenacious tool.*

'What's that?' Libby asked as she peered into the box. 'You seriously have a problem, an obsession with that stuff. It's disgusting.'

'I didn't buy this,' I deadpanned.

She picked up the note which was poking out from underneath one of the bottles. 'Then who did?' she asked as she unfolded it. 'Oh!'

Snatching it from her, I bit the inside of my cheek as I read it to myself: *I couldn't wait any longer and tried it for myself. Baby, you are missing out. It glides on nicely. Derek*

'Is he suggesting what I think he is suggesting?' Libby asked, as she picked up a bottle and unscrewed the lid.

'If you're thinking that he wants me to suck it off his cock, then yes,' I answered.

'Are you going to?' she asked with a curious smile, dabbing some sauce onto her finger.

Grabbing the bottle from her, I dabbed some on my finger too and sucked at the tangy taste. 'Mm ... no.'

'You want to though,' she implied, grabbing the bottle back.

'I did. I don't any more.'

Lib smiled, this time greedily dabbing two fingers. 'When are you going to learn not to lie?'

I snatched it back and packed it away. 'I'm not. Are you ready? I want to get home to Sasha. Her boredom levels are increasing.'

* * *

As we pulled into the driveway, my eyes widened with shock.

'What the hell?' Libby shrieked. 'Are they —'

'Oh no! He didn't,' I exclaimed.

Libby laughed. 'Oh yes, he did.'

I turned the ignition off, climbed out of Suzi and stormed up the path, stopping and spinning 360°. Placed around the front of our house were easily one hundred bottles of mint sauce, with notes attached. They were on the front step, in the garden bed, lining the path. They were EVERYWHERE.

Snatching one up, I read the note: *I'm waiting. Derek*

'Grrr,' I growled and picked up another one: *Come and get it, baby. Derek*

Libby giggled and read out another. '"Two, four, six, eight, hurry up, I can't wait".'

Placing my hands on my hips, I tried not to smile. Proof of his determination was encircling me and decorating my front garden. I huffed and growled again when my phone beeped from within my pocket.

You look a little flustered — Derek

My head shot up and I surveyed my surroundings. Unsuccessful in my attempts to spot him, I quickly typed a response.

Where are you? This is not funny. Come and get all these bottles — Carly

A response came back instantly.

If I do, are you going to lick it off my cock? — Derek

'You arrogant arsehole,' I shouted to the street. 'No!'

Another message sounded from my phone.

You'll change your mind. And when you do, I'll be waiting — Derek

'Fuck you, Dik,' I shouted again and stormed up the path to my front door.

My phone beeped yet again, and I was almost of the mind to launch it into the garden. But I didn't, instead reading it because I just couldn't help myself.

I love you too — Derek

Pausing on the threshold to my house, I slumped against the wall and slid down it until I was sitting on my arse. 'I'm not giving in,' I said to myself.

Libby stepped over me and opened the front door. 'Yeah, good luck with that.'

CHAPTER
26

The following week started, as it did every week, with a school assembly. Our school co-captains, Katie Stahl and Matthew Banks — both aged ten — were delivering the announcements for the week while I stood and watched over the students who sat cross-legged on the floor. It was only 9.30 in the morning and already thirty degrees. Today was set to be a scorcher.

'This week's yard warrior is Jet Bradley from grade three,' Katie announced.

Jet sprang up from his seated position and voiced an enthusiastic, 'Yeah.'

During his journey to the front of the gymnasium where Katie and Matthew stood waiting to hand him his award, Jet performed some warrior-like moves, drawing a laugh from the students and faculty.

Libby — his teacher — shook her head with mild amusement, then applauded him on his efforts before he took his seat back amongst the rest of his class.

'We'd like to remind everyone that next week is Jump Rope for Heart Day. You will need to wear your sports uniform to school on that day. Please also remember to bring in any sponsorship money you have raised,' Matthew informed his peers. *Argh, I hate sorting money. Spending it ... yeah. Sorting it when it's not mine ... not so much.*

Katie and Matthew then took turns to inform everyone about the Easter Hat Parade and Easter Chocolate Drive that were scheduled in the coming weeks, when I noticed Samuel Carter — aged five — fishing for the world's most elusive booger. What was quite remarkable about his attempt was the angle at which he twisted and turned his finger in order to successfully secure it. Impressed with his skills or not, I shook my head at him when he caught my eye and indicated he remove his digit from his nostril. He blushed bright red then stuck his booger-encrusted finger directly into his mouth. *Eww! Feral little fucklets.*

'We would like to welcome Miss Hanson to speak to you about an exciting new music program,' Katie advised before handing Libby the microphone.

The mention of a new and exciting music program was news to me. So with curiosity, I listened intently.

'Good morning, Yellow Bark Primary School students,' Libby said in a chirpy tone.

'Good morning, Miss Hanson,' they replied in unison.

'Who enjoys singing and playing an instrument? Raise your hand for me,' she asked while surveying the room with her hand pressed to her forehead. 'Excellent, that's a lot of you. Well, it just so happens that I have some very exciting news to share with you. You see, I have a friend who sings and plays the guitar and he has agreed to come and visit the school once a week to give you some lessons,' Libby explained.

Many of the students clapped excitedly, but I stood perplexed and wondering what the fuck? These things were normally brought to my attention long before they were publicly announced.

Furrowing my brow, I continued to listen to her announcement, but caught Sally grinning at me like a deranged clown. 'What?' I mouthed, now even more confused.

She shook her head, her smile increasing, and mouthed the response, 'Nothing.'

Bullshit nothing.

'My special guest is part of a music ensemble, and he has kindly agreed to perform a song for you today so that you too can see just how much fun it is to sing and learn an instrument. Now, before I ask him out here, some of you may recognise him. Hmm ... I wonder who is smart enough to know why. Anyway, please make him feel very welcome, students. This is Mr King!' Libby announced and then locked eyes with me.

Holy fucking friend of the devil, she did not just say that.

I'm not sure if I blushed bright red or paled to a ghostly white — because I was without a mirror and couldn't see my reflection — regardless, I changed colour. I knew I did. I could feel it.

Looking around the room to try and pinpoint his whereabouts, I nearly jumped so high as to hit the roof when the twang of his guitar sounded behind me.

I turned around to find him casually dressed in jeans and a tight grey tee, his acoustic guitar hanging over his shoulder. He had on a microphone headpiece and was slowly walking toward me as he strummed his guitar.

I was rooted to the spot; stunned, unable to move any which way. I was also hell-bent on not making a scene or alluding to the fact that both Derek and I knew each other. The last thing I needed were students singing annoying love anthems every time I walked past them.

Watching him intently as he stopped beside me, my heart fluttered frantically within my chest. I honestly couldn't say what consumed me the most: fear, embarrassment or a realisation ...

Sucking in a deep breath, the scent that was Derek infiltrated my body, mind and soul. He was freshly showered and emitting a mixture of aftershave, deodorant and a hint of smokiness that all combined together to be purely Derek. Closing my eyes for the slightest of seconds, I quickly savoured the aroma and then reopened them.

He looked out over the students and gave them a confident grin right before he glanced in my direction and began to sing 'Unintended' by Muse. It floored me, because I recognised the song almost instantly. Alexis was a huge fan of that band and had dragged me to one or two of their concerts.

'That's firefighter Derek,' Tanner shouted and pointed toward him.

Derek smiled and chuckled through a lyric, then gave me another quick glance before continuing to walk through the centre of the gymnasium. Unfortunately, I was still in a state of astonishment and remained completely expressionless as he strode away.

The small walkway allowing movement through the two groups of students seated on the floor — what was referred to by the teachers and students as the catwalk — was an easy, clear and quick route for Derek to make his way to the front of the room. As he walked in between the children, my stare followed his retreating form as if it were invisibly glued to him, a part of him ... attracted to him.

Derek stopped every few steps and acknowledged a child with a smile or a wink and then continued until he was almost standing beside Libby at the front of the gym. His clear, flawless voice carried the ballad through the room beautifully, captivating everyone listening.

As he turned around to face the room, his eyes locked on mine, and the lyrics he then sang were undoubtedly directed at me. He was telling me through the song that I was his unintended, the one he chose to love. He was telling me that yes, he had a past, but that I was the one he wanted for his future. The sheer honesty and fragility of his public confession hit me so hard that a tear escaped my eye.

What is wrong with me? I don't cry. I don't do tears. I've never done tears. Wiping my cheek with my hand, I cursed the fact that this man had made me cry more in the eight months I had known him than I had at any other time in my life. He was a fucking human onion.

'Are you all right?' Brooke whispered as she stepped up beside me, inconspicuously covering her mouth.

'Mm-hmm,' I murmured, nodding a couple of times.

'Good. Just checking you weren't going to flee the room. I don't fancy tackling you in front of the student body,' she advised as she turned and made her way back to where her class was seated.

Directing her an astounded look, it went unnoticed as she didn't glance back at me. At that point, I looked up and found the faculty mesmerised by Derek's performance. My colleagues — even Vice Principal Sidebottom — were captivated and watching him with unwavering attention.

A smile broke through my tears as I returned my stare to him, finding that he had been watching me with what appeared to be a slight expression of trepidation. When he noticed my smile he beamed his own, which relit the fuse to my heart.

In that moment, I realised that he was the one. Mine ... my unintended. Derek and I just 'are'.

I wiped another tear and straightened my shoulders, mentally preparing myself for what lay ahead. I knew now — and probably had all along — that I wanted Derek in my life for good. I wanted Derek and everything that came along with him: his dangerous job, his unconventional family, his history where Lucy, Nic and Alexander were concerned. I realised that I could deal with it all if it meant that he and I were together.

Derek played the coda, slowing down the plucking of the strings to the very end. The room erupted into a round of applause, my own two hands frantically clapping as well.

'Thank you,' he said graciously. 'So how was that? Did you like it?'

The room's occupants said, 'Yes.'

'Would you like to learn how to do that?' he asked enthusiastically, his child-speaking-voice making me giggle.

Again the room's occupants said, 'Yes.'

'Great! Because I would really like to teach you.'

Libby raised the microphone to her mouth and addressed the room. 'Wasn't that cool? Thank you so much, Mr King. Now, I heard someone call out that they recognised our special guest.'

'Me,' Tanner shouted and stood up. 'That's firefighter Derek.'

'Tanner, yes it is, but please sit down, and next time raise your hand,' Libby instructed. 'Tanner is correct. Mr King is also firefighter Derek. He is a man of many talents.'

My eyebrows shot up, and I had to quickly cover my mouth with my hand to muffle my snort-outburst.

Brooke, Libby, Sally and Derek all glanced in my direction, Libby reddening in the cheeks at her slip of the tongue.

She cleared her throat and continued. 'You too can be good at many different things when you grow older. But first you have to be good in school. Do you think you can all do that?'

'Yes!' the children shouted happily.

'Excellent! Now, if you would like to learn to sing or play an instrument, make sure you take home today's newsletter and give it to your parents. Everyone please thank Mr King.'

The students said thank you to Derek in unison while Libby handed the microphone back to Katie, who then advised everyone that assembly was now over and for all to make their way back to class.

As the children — led by their teachers — filtered out of the gymnasium, I waited until Derek had politely accepted praise for his performance by passing staff and, in turn, expressed his gratitude.

The last of the room's occupants were leaving when Derek slowly strode toward me, stopping just shy of my position in the room. Silence ensued as we took each other in and waited to be left alone.

When the wooden door slammed and cemented our privacy, he spoke. 'Baby, you are my unintended and I am yours. Stop fighting it.'

'Okay,' I whispered, closing the distance between us and placing my hand on his cheek before pressing my lips to his.

Our kiss was quick, sweet and enough to relay the surrender within. I wanted it to be more, but I had control, and now was not the time or place for it to become what all kisses shared between Derek and I became.

Pulling away, I sucked in a breath. 'We have a few things to sort through.'

'I know, and we will. I promise to be more open with you. I want this, Carly. I want us to work.'

I nodded. 'How 'bout you come over tonight and —'

Derek's pager beeped continuously, interrupting our conversation. He pulled it from his pocket and grimaced with disappointment. 'Shit!'

'What's wrong?' I asked, noticing his unease.

'There's an out of control grass fire just past Wallan. It's a big one so I have to go,' he explained sorrowfully.

'Go, firefighter Derek. Go and put out fires,' I said as I placed my hands on his chest.

He chuckled, then kissed me once more. 'I'll call you later, as soon as I'm relieved from duty.'

I nodded. 'Okay.'

As Derek turned to leave the room, my stomach clenched tightly. 'Be careful,' I called out, almost desperately.

He stopped at the door and turned back. 'I always am,' then winked and left the room.

The extreme heat and strong winds that were forecast for the day were a major concern. Knowing the dangers, and knowing that Derek would be out there amongst it, left me feeling ill.

* * *

'Stop checking your watch,' Libby said from her lounging position on the couch. We were watching *Game of Thrones* but the telecast was forever being interrupted with updates of the grass fire in Wallan that had turned into an out of control bushfire, devastating over 10,000 hectares of land.

I couldn't function properly.

'I wasn't,' I lied in response. I'd been checking it constantly for the past three hours.

'He'll be busy, Carls. The fire flared up quickly, so he probably hasn't had a chance to ring in,' she offered for reassurance.

'I know. But it's been hours, Lib. Surely he'd get a break or something. To recharge and freshen up.' I leaned forward and placed my elbows on my knees, resting my head in my hands. 'I just want one text saying he's okay.'

Lib scooted over to where I was sitting and put her arm around my shoulder. 'This is what he does for a living. He fights fires. He saves people, animals and infrastructure. He's out there being a hero. Heroes don't have time to text their girlfriends.'

I rolled my eyes at her. 'Fine, but can we turn this off and watch something else. The constant newsflashes are making me crazy.'

Lib stood up and walked over to the DVD cabinet. 'Hmm ... how 'bout some Gosling?' she mused, pulling out *The Notebook*.

'Do you even need to ask?' I joked.

* * *

I woke the next morning and stretched uncomfortably, realising I had fallen asleep on the couch the night before.

Confusion washed over me: why hadn't I taken myself to bed? Then I remembered Derek hadn't called.

Dread filled my being, and I scrambled to find my phone in order to check whether he had left a message or tried to call while I was asleep.

'Where is it?' I groaned, wrenching the cushions from the couch to look underneath them.

'What are you doing?' Lib asked while sounding a simultaneous yawn.

'Trying to find my phone. Derek may have left a message or tried to call. And why didn't you wake me last night?'

'I did. You said you'd go to bed soon.'

'Was I even awake when I said that?' I asked, clearly annoyed. 'I slept out here all night.'

'Oh ... well, you slept and that's the whole point of sleeping, right?'

'Where is it?' I yelled, grabbing my hair and pulling frustratedly.

Lib walked up to me and pulled my top open. I was about to protest when she retrieved my phone from my bra.

'I don't know why you keep it there,' she said, a little bemused, as she walked into the kitchen.

Swiping my screen to activate it, I answered dismissively. 'Because pockets have no place in the world of fashion.'

Many emotions ran through my body when I realised Derek had not made contact: disappointment, fear, anxiety, and an overwhelming sense of dread that something was wrong.

Without a second thought, I dialled Derek's station, impatiently pacing while waiting for the call to connect.

'MFB Station 10. Can I help you?' a middle-aged woman answered.

'Yes, this is Carly, Officer King's girlfriend. I'm trying to get hold of him. I was wondering if he has called into the station?'

There was a pause before she answered. 'I'm sorry, Carly, but I'm not at liberty to release any information to anyone other than next of kin.'

'Next of kin,' I shrieked. 'Why? What's happened? Where's Derek? Is he okay?'

'I'm sorry, dear, but I cannot say anything further. You will need to get in contact with his family,' she said apologetically.

With a shaking hand I ended the call and stared blankly at my phone.

'Carly, what's wrong?' Lib asked, her voice etched with concern.

'Something has happened to Derek,' I explained, the words coming out of my mouth as if spoken by a robot.

She touched my shoulder and forced my gaze to hers. 'How do you know that?'

'Because the station receptionist said I should call his next of kin.'

Tears began to pool in my eyes. I tried blinking them away, but to no avail.

'That doesn't mean something is wrong, Carls. It's just a privacy thing. She can't tell you anything, good or bad.'

'I know him, Lib. He would've sent a text the second he could've. And if everything was okay, he would've had that second long before now,' I answered with absolute certainty.

As we stared at each other in indecision, the loud shrill of my ringing phone unexpectedly broke the silence and made me jump. I fumbled with it, nearly dropping it on the ground. After steadying my hand, Layla's name appeared on my screen and seeing it there stopped my heart's beat.

Frozen in fear, the constricting of my chest, and the inability to move, had me motionless, not wanting to answer it and be told what I could not even begin to fathom, yet I was desperate to hear that nothing was wrong and that he was all right. Never in my life had so much ridden on the simple touch of a finger to a screen.

Holding my breath, I swiped my phone to answer Layla's call. 'Hello,' I barely voiced.

'Carly? It's Layla. Have you heard from Derek?' she asked, her voice saturated with desperation.

Painfully — and slowly — I let my breath out. 'No. Have you?'

The sound of her masking a sob triggered an ache to develop in my heart. 'No ... he's ... he's MIA.'

CHAPTER
27

I didn't want to ask but had no power to stop the terrifying question from leaving my mouth.

'Yes. From what Sean and I have been told, he was with his tanker and crew on a property just past Kilmore. The wind changed direction and then communication was lost. Since then, the pilot of an air-crane who made a routine pass over the property reported that the house was completely destroyed, together with the tanker. Apparently the road into the property is still unsafe, so they cannot send additional crew,' she explained with resignation.

'Oh god, when ... when will the road be safe? They need to get more crew there. He could be hurt. They need to get someone there now!' I cried with desperation.

'Carly,' she sobbed. 'They are doing everything they can. Sean and I are about to head to a firefighting base camp they've set up in Wallan. Would you like to come with us?'

'Yes!' I answered with urgency. 'Yes, I would. I can't just sit here and wait.'

'Okay, we'll pick you up on the way. Give us twenty minutes.'

I disconnected the call and turned to Lib. 'Derek and his crew are unaccounted for,' I explained with a rush of breath as I made my way out of the room while continuing to talk.

'Oh no!' Libby gasped as she followed.

'Layla and Sean are heading to a base camp set up in Wallan. I'm going with them.'

'What can I do?'

'Nothing. I don't know. Nothing. Just hope for the best. Or pray. Or, I don't know,' I said, bursting into tears.

She wrapped her arms around me and squeezed me tight. 'He'll be fine. Everything is going to be okay.'

I hugged her back. 'I hope so. I don't want to think of the alternative.'

* * *

Roughly twenty minutes later, Layla and Sean arrived. Layla wasted no time in wrapping her arms around me and quietly stating that she believed Derek was fine. That he was smart and that he would return unharmed. I hugged her back in appreciation, finding her offering of reassurance comfortable. I liked Layla, there was just something about her I could relate to. I couldn't put my finger on it at that point in time, but I felt we shared somewhat of a mutual connection.

Sean was a suited-up, older-looking version of Derek, and the stresses of his job were clearly visible on his facial features. He had dark, neatly cut hair, and crow's feet feathered around the edges of his eyes. He certainly looked more worn down than his twin brother, and in assessing his aged appearance, I found myself wondering whether or not to respect and admire Derek for standing his ground and following his heart to become a fire-fighter. The alternative was to curse him for his decision, because if he hadn't followed his dream, he wouldn't be MIA and I wouldn't be scared fucking shitless as a result.

When we arrived at the base camp, the surrounding smoke hung heavy in the air, the thick suffocating by-product of fire reminding me of a lurking evil. It silently entered the space around you and mystified your senses, infiltrating your body uninvited and unwanted. Smoke was the perfect trespasser.

Not long after arriving, we were escorted to a tent, where Derek's fellow crew members' families and next of kin were waiting. The atmosphere was sombre yet bustling with activity and noise. It was both eerie and unnerving.

While enduring the maddening wait for information, it didn't take me long to figure out that Sean was a man of few words. However, when he did speak, he meant business. I'd almost go so far as to say he was arrogant and a little rude.

Since a brief introduction when I climbed into his Mercedes, he'd not said so much as five words to me. Well, actually, he'd said eight: 'Hi. Come on, we don't have much time'. He was tense, impatient and appeared to not like people, getting short-tempered with everyone around him.

'You'll have to excuse Sean,' Layla said quietly while leaning in my direction. 'He is extremely concerned about Derek.'

'Yeah, well we all are, but you don't see either of us biting everyone's heads off now, do you?' I answered just as quietly, regretting the words as soon as I had spoken them. 'Shit! I'm sorry. I understand he's worried about his brother. Of course he is.'

'Carly, I'm not sure what Derek has told you, but he and Sean have not spoken to one another for years. Their last exchange, shortly after Richard's stroke, was highly venomous. Sean said some horrible things to his brother that he has regretted ever since. Unfortunately, he is too proud a person to admit it ... and, I dare say, is now worried his time to do so has passed.'

Looking to where Sean stood staring blankly at the area map pinned to a noticeboard, I could see the worry and heartbreak behind his tough facade. It saddened me to think that some families had rifts so deep, they were perceived as irreparable. I guess it showed that obstinacy thwarted common sense. But then what would I know? I was an only child. Then again, maybe that's why I had the overwhelming desire to try and help resolve the conflict between the two siblings ... because I didn't have any.

'Well, I don't want to think that way. I don't want to think it is too late. Derek is fine. He is just waiting to be rescued. And you know what?' I declared, standing up and pulling out my phone. 'I don't want him to have to wait any longer. He has waited long enough.' I pressed Alexis' number and exited the tent, now on a mission of my own.

'I'm not sure I'm talking to you,' Lexi said, after answering her phone.

'Well, you don't have a choice —'

'I do have a choice,' she interrupted. 'You stormed out of Alexander's birthday party and you never told me why. I —'

'Lex, can we do this another time, please. I need your help. Actually, I need Bryce's help. Actually no, Derek needs Bryce's help. He's MIA, Lex, and I'm terrified —'

'Whoa, whoa, whoa,' she exclaimed, her voice growing louder with each word. 'What do you mean he's MIA?'

'He was working at the Kilmore front last night. The command centre lost contact with him and his crew shortly after a wind change. Reports say the property he was at, together with their tanker, was destroyed. Lex, they can't get any trucks in due to ground access being unsafe —'

'Oh my god! Carly, where are you?'

'I'm waiting at base camp in Wallan, but it's taking too long and —'

'Hang on a minute, the Crow!' Lexi offered, reading my mind. 'You want Bryce to fly the chopper to the property with a search and rescue team, don't you?'

'That's what I was hoping. Can he do it? Can he somehow get permission to arrange this?'

'Permission ... Bryce? Are you serious? Derek is his best friend. He's not going to give a shit about permission.'

Sighing with a small sense of relief, I whispered, 'Thank you.'

* * *

Just under an hour later, Bryce was landing the Crow on a nearby football oval. I, along with Sean, Layla and one of the chief ground officers, were there to greet him as he hurried from the helicopter, together with Lexi and Lucy.

While Lexi and I embraced, Bryce, Sean and the ground officer shook hands and then headed off to a nearby tent to prepare the rescue effort.

'Carly,' Lexi said as she pulled away. 'How are you, are you okay?'

'No,' I answered, wrapping my arms around myself. 'I just want him found.'

'Hey ... they'll find him. Bryce won't give up.'

I gave her a nod of acceptance, then turned to Layla. 'Sorry, Layla ... this is Alexis, my best friend. Lexi, this is Layla, Derek's sister-in-law. And this is Lucy,' I added in a clipped tone. Why she had to come along was beyond me.

After the quick introductions, we made our way toward the tent the others had disappeared into, which was a relief as I didn't like being outside. The smoke was invisibly choking me and the noise of the water bombers pierced my body like a deadly sting.

'Carly,' Lucy said, snagging my arm before entering. 'Can I have a quick word?'

I smiled politely at Layla and Alexis, Alexis furrowing her brow and giving me an unsure look. I alleviated her concern by nodding for her to go ahead.

After they entered the tent and we were alone, I turned to Lucy. 'What? What are you even doing here?'

'Back off,' she answered defensively. 'I'm here because I'm worried just as much as you are —'

'I doubt that,' I snapped.

'Carly, please, I just want to bury this rancour. I'm not a threat. And I'm sorry I asked Derek to keep something from you.'

'Lucy, now is not the time for this.'

'I know, I just don't want you anxious about me being here on top of everything else —'

'So why did you come?' I bit out, glaring at her.

She took a step back. 'I told you. I'm worried. I care about him too.'

'I think it's more than that,' I said quietly.

'You're wrong,' she said, lowering her voice. 'I've told you this before. Derek was just a sperm donor and a friend. That's all.'

'A sperm donor who fucked you until you were pregnant.'

Lucy gasped and covered her mouth, her eyes opening wide. 'He told you?'

'Yes, he told me.'

Fed up and turning away from her, I went to enter the tent for a second time when Lucy grabbed my arm and pulled me away. 'Carly, please,' she sobbed. 'You need to understand that what Derek and I share is nothing more than a deep friendship. I love him, yes, but not like you do. Please understand that.'

I could see the sincerity in her eyes as she stood there and begged me to understand. But my emotions were all over the place, and I didn't want to get into it with her at that point.

'Carly, he means so much to me, but for reasons that aren't romantic. Yes, we had sex in order for me to get pregnant. But it was emotionless sex. To be honest, it was horrible,' she said with a blush.

I raised my eyebrow questioningly at her. 'I find that hard to believe. I've had sex with Derek — many times — and it was far from horrible.'

'Trust me,' she smiled timidly. 'It was awkward as hell and we both hated it.'

Surrendering with a sigh, I scanned the surrounding racecourse turned base camp. 'Yeah, well I guess that doesn't matter right now. What matters is that Derek and his crew are found alive and safe.'

'You're right. He's going to be fine, Carly. You need to be positive. Bryce will find him.'

Dropping my head back and staring at the haze-ridden sky, I blinked back my tears. 'I hope so.'

Lucy rubbed her hands up and down my arms as if trying to warm me up, which was weird, the temperature was fucking nearly forty degrees Celsius. 'Come on. Let's find out what the plan of action is.'

We soon found out that the plan was for Bryce to land the chopper as close to the property as he could with a search and rescue team of three. Sean had demanded he go along, but there was no room for civilian passengers, the Crow only having the capacity to seat four.

As Bryce elevated his helicopter and headed off into the distance, I said a silent prayer, hoping that when it landed back on this very spot, Derek would climb out of the cockpit and bless me with his incredible smile. I longed for his smile.

* * *

'Have they radioed in yet?' I asked one of the ground officers for the umpteenth time.

It had been over an hour since the Crow had departed, and I was highly anxious. I just wanted the torturous wait to be over.

'Not yet, they —'

'Base camp, do you copy?' the radio sounded.

The middle-aged chubby man picked up the receiver. 'Yes, copy that,' he answered, wiping his brow with the back of his hand.

Layla and Sean stepped closer, as did the other family members in the room who were waiting just as anxiously as we were.

'Yes. Right. Okay. Copy that,' he finished and hung up the receiver.

'Well?' Sean asked, running his hands through his hair and gripping it tightly. 'Have they found my brother? Is he all right?'

'Yes, sir. Officer King and the rest of the crew are fine, together with three civilians and a cat.'

Oh, for the love of middle-aged men with beer guts and radio receivers.

Lexi wrapped her arms around me and rested her head on my shoulder. 'See? I told you Bryce would help find them. It's what he does.'

'Well, thank fuck for what he does,' I said with relief, resting my head against hers and smiling for the first time in over twenty-four hours.

* * *

Bryce touched the Crow to the ground not even fifty metres from where I was impatiently standing, my body tingling with nervous apprehension. He'd had to make additional trips to bring back the civilian family and crew members first. Derek, being the senior officer, took the last pass back to base camp.

As the rotor blades slowed, the cockpit door opened and bright yellow legs exited. I held my breath as Derek emerged in his protective suit, helmet in hand. He was covered in soot and looked extremely exhausted and dehydrated.

I began walking toward him, which turned into a slow jog, which then turned into a brisk run. Before I knew it, I'd slammed into him like an emotional tidal wave.

'Oh my god,' I cried, kissing his charcoal-covered face. 'For fuck's sake, don't ever do that again. Don't ever scare me like that again.'

'Baby, it's all right,' he reassured me between my frantic kisses. 'Sh ... I'm fine.'

I pulled away from him. 'No. You're not. Look at you. What happened?'

'The wind changed suddenly. We had no choice but to take cover in the property owner's bunker. We were very lucky they had one.'

'So why didn't you radio for help?'

'It's a long story,' he explained, his tone utterly exhausted. 'Come on, I need to debrief, hydrate and get the fuck home to shower.'

I kissed his cheek and wrapped my arm around his back. 'I can help you with one of those.'

'Excellent! I hate debriefing,' he admitted jokingly, making me laugh.

We began to walk toward the tent when Derek stopped in his tracks. 'Is that my brother, Sean?'

I stopped with him and took in his angry expression. 'Yeah, he's been worried sick.'

'I fucking doubt that,' he snapped and began walking again, his pace now quickened. I could barely keep up.

'He has. He's been —'

The sight of Derek's right hook, slamming into his brother's nose, stopped any further words exiting my mouth. Bloodspilled out almost instantly, peppering Sean's shirt.

Before I knew it, Bryce was holding Derek back. 'Hey, mate, now's not the time or place.'

'Why the fuck are you even here?' Derek barked out, furious but also looking sad and confused.

'I'm your brother. I was fucking worried,' Sean mumbled as he held his nose. 'Why else?'

'Let me go, Bryce. I'm all right. Let me go,' Derek demanded, his demeanour a little more subdued.

I stood frozen, my mouth covered with both my hands as Bryce released Derek's shoulders. Alexis and Lucy also looked shocked. Layla, not so much.

'You can leave now,' Derek spat out at Sean before he walked past him and into the tent.

Layla pulled a tissue out of her pocket and offered it to her husband. He took it from her, but refused to let her look at the damage. 'It's fine. Just leave it,' he instructed, clearly frustrated and annoyed.

'Sean, it's broken. You're going to have to go to the hospital,' she advised with a sad expression.

'Fuck,' he growled. Sean looked at the tent into which Derek had disappeared, a look of indecision on his battered and bloody face.

'Leave him. That was a long time in coming. You know that. And anyway, it was the most he's spoken to you in years. It's a start,' Layla added softly, as she placed her hand on her husband's arm reassuringly.

Sean shook his head and let out a surrendered breath. 'At least he's alive and safe.' Then, turning for their car, he added. 'Come on then. I guess I deserved that, at the very least.'

Layla mouthed the word 'Sorry', but I shook my head dismissively at her and mouthed 'Thank you' in return before she nodded and followed her husband's retreating form.

'What the hell was that about?' Alexis asked.

I shrugged my shoulders. 'I don't know the details.'

'I do,' both Bryce and Lucy said simultaneously.

Rolling my eyes, I placed my hand on my head. 'Why does that not surprise me?'

'Do you want to tell them or should I?' Lucy asked her brother.

'Be my guest,' he nodded to Lucy before wrapping his arms around Lex.

'Okay. Sean accused Derek of sleeping with Layla not long after their father had a stroke. His accusation was accompanied by the breaking of Derek's jaw,' Lucy confessed.

'What?' I shrieked.

'Apparently, Sean found out a little later on that his accusations were false, and therefore tried to rectify his mistake. But Derek wouldn't have a bar of it.'

'Why?' I asked, sadly.

'Because my brother is a worthless piece of shit and one I do not want in my life,' Derek interrupted.

He walked up to Bryce and gave him a hug. 'Mate, once again I can't thank you enough.'

'Don't mention it,' Bryce said with a slap on Derek's back. 'I'm just glad you are all right.'

Derek then turned to me and took hold of my hand. 'Baby, I want to go home. I want that shower and I want you in it.'

Wanting nothing more than to go home with the man I loved, I blew kisses of goodbye to everyone else and let him drag me away.

* * *

After Derek was given the necessary all-clear by the paramedics at base camp, we were driven to his house by another officer. For the entire hour it took to arrive in Richmond, I clung to him tightly, not wanting to let him go. I was an emotional mess, constantly fighting back tears every time I dwelled on what it had felt like when I thought I had lost him. The notion was making me ill — literally sick to my stomach.

By the time we pulled up to his house, he had drifted off to sleep.

'Baby,' I said softly into his ear. 'Wake up. We are home.'

'Sh ... I'm dreaming,' he groaned.

'No, you are not. We are really here.'

He opened one eye and squinted. 'Yes, I am. You just called me baby and said we were home. I have to be dreaming.'

I rolled my eyes. 'Don't push your luck,' I warned playfully while exiting the car.

He chuckled, said goodbye to the driver and then picked me up and threw me over his shoulder en route to the front door.

'Derek,' I squealed, 'put me down!' As I hung upside down, I took a moment to check out his arse. 'Actually, your arse from this angle is great. You have a great arse. It's nice and round and firm,' I explained as I happily squeezed it. 'It dips in all the right places.'

'Dips?' he questioned, fumbling with his keys.

'Yes, like a slide ... wheee!' I explained, sliding my finger down one of his dips.

Derek chuckled once again and entered the house, heading straight for his bathroom. He set me down on the basin and just stared intently into my eyes. He went to say something, but I stopped him by placing my finger over his lips and whispering. 'Sh.'

I kissed him softly and proceeded to undress him, pulling his polo t-shirt over his head while he manoeuvred his boots off with each foot.

Stopping again to just stare at each other, my heart filled with love. This man before me was a hero. He'd risked his life for people he did not know, saved them and stayed with them until they were safe. He was a gift and I planned on unwrapping and treasuring him.

Derek lifted me off the basin and pulled my singlet top over my head. I unbuckled his pants as he unclipped my bra. We stripped each other bare without so much as a word and then stepped into the shower.

When no words are spoken you can hear so much; the beating of a heart, the intake of a breath ... two people becoming one. There is no such thing as silence.

With soft touches and gentle kisses, I helped clean the soot and dirt from his body, washing the remnants of his terrible ordeal away. When they were no longer evident on his body and washed down the drain, I wrapped my arms around his neck and pressed my body to his.

'Derek,' I said, in a low but stern voice. 'I love you and can no longer deny it. I can live with your family problems and I can live with the fear of your job. I can even live knowing that Alexander is yours. But I cannot live without you. I just can't. I don't want to.'

A lone tear fell on my cheek and then travelled south until it formed part of the droplets of water cascading down my body.

He lifted me up and pressed my back against the tile wall. 'Then don't. Move in with me. Make us what we "are".'

The cool of the tiles made me gasp. 'And what "are" we again?' I asked with a smile.

'We just fucking "are",' he said, as he slid his erection inside me and pressed his lips to mine.

As Derek and I made love in the shower, I realised what we were. We were one; two people who made each other whole. Two people in search of each other without even knowing it, and two people brought together by an undeniable attraction that could not be ignored. Attraction is a force that acts between oppositely charged bodies, tending to draw them together. Attraction cannot be fought.

EPILOGUE

Just under two years later

'Hey! Get out!' I yelled at Bryce. 'No grooms allowed. Unless,' I suggested playfully, wiggling my body, 'you want to start removing your clothes.'

'You ...' he pointed his finger at me accusingly, 'you and I are gonna have some words later. 'And you ...' he pointed to the sexy-as-fuck stripper straddling Alexis's lap. 'Back the fuck off.'

Josh — also known as Mr Nude Australia — stepped aside with a knowing expression, as if this was not the first time an irate partner had stormed into the room during one of his performances.

I watched in disbelief as Bryce walked with purposeful strides toward Alexis' frozen frame, her expression extremely stunned. God, I don't know why she was so against seeing another man naked and having him dance and wipe his sweaty body over her. It was her hens' night, for fuck's sake. Not to mention it was hot and he was a stripper, so it was harmless.

She started to speak, seemingly to defend herself. 'I didn't know —'

Bryce reached out, took hold of her hand and pulled her to his chest, pressing a forceful kiss to her lips in a show of ownership. He pulled back and looked heatedly into her eyes. 'Want to go home?'

She smiled and nodded enthusiastically.

'Hey! No, you are not!' I protested. 'This is your hens' night. You can't leave with the groom. Who does that?'

They both ignored me.

Bryce bent down and hauled Alexis over his shoulder and, as he turned around and my eyes followed their retreating forms, I noticed Derek and Will. Derek was leaning against the wall with a sexy as hell grin on his face and Will was eyeing the stripper up and down with a look of disgust.

Watching as Bryce made his way to the exit, I called out in protest once again. 'You can't do this.'

'I can and I fucking well will,' he replied.

Lexi smiled with satisfaction and waved to me from her hung position over his shoulder.

I flipped her the bird, which inevitably made her smile grow wider.

Turning back toward Mr Nude Australia, I spied him beginning to pack up his shit.

'Hey, what do you think you are doing?' I asked angrily.

'I just figured the show was over,' he explained.

Slumping myself down on the seat like a stubborn child, I twitched my finger at him. 'It ain't fucking over.

I've paid for you to dance and remove your clothes. So dance and remove.'

He shrugged his shoulders and flipped the switch of his stereo, replaying JT's 'SexyBack'. 'If you say so.'

'I do,' I grumbled, crossing my arms conclusively.

As he began dry-humping my lap and placing my hands all over his oil-covered body, the music was cut off yet again.

'Off!' Derek growled.

I peeked over Josh's shoulder to where Derek was standing. 'What now?'

'I can't watch,' he said, shaking his head.

'Then don't. Haven't you got Miss Nude Australia in another suite? Go watch her,' I responded with a dismissive and haughty wave of my hand.

The thought of Derek watching a slutsky stripper did not sit well with me either, but I'd let it go for the sake of Alexis and Bryce's hens' and bucks' night celebrations. Now, I was just pissed off and getting my stubborn on.

Derek raised an eyebrow questioningly.

'What?' I sulked.

'Baby, do you really want to do this?'

Pouting and hanging my head, I groaned. 'No, all right. Are you happy?'

I gently slapped Josh's backside to indicate he stand up. Then, following him to my feet and grabbing my clutch from the coffee table, I walked past the rest of Alexis' friends. 'He's all yours, ladies.' I then turned to Derek. 'Fine. You win. Take me home.'

He slid his arm across my back, pulled me to him and whispered into my ear. 'With pleasure.'

* * *

The following evening, I was still sulking over Alexis' hens' night failure. Derek had even tried to cheer me up by attempting to bake a choc-mint pudding. To be honest, I was not sure why he bothered. Yes, the man could cook a mean satay, but baking was not Derek's thing. Plus, he hadn't let me eat it yet, saying it was for later on, which probably meant, 'I fucked it up and hope you will forget by then'. It did smell lovely though.

Sitting at our dining table and expelling my grumpiness by harshly flipping the pages of my *Cleo* magazine, I nearly had a heart attack when 'SexyBack' suddenly sounded through the room.

I shot my head up to where the iPad sat on the bench-top and found Derek standing next to it, fully kitted in his firefighter gear.

Confusion instantly hijacked my mind, but when I realised what he planned to do, I couldn't contain the smile that spread across my face.

'Apparently I owe you a striptease,' he said seductively.

Swallowing heavily as an overwhelming sense of excitement swept through my body, I pushed my seat back from the table and patted my lap. 'Giddy-up, officer.'

He chuckled, then started dancing toward me, rolling his body enticingly. I couldn't help it and laughed, tapping my feet in a running motion on the ground. Derek stopped in front of me with a grin that had the capacity to melt my underwear. The man — when in a cheeky mood — was a sight I would never get used to seeing. He lowered himself slowly and straddled my lap, taking off his helmet and placing it on my head before kissing my nose.

I leaned forward in an attempt to capture his lips with mine, but he shot up and spun around, slowly taking off his jacket to reveal his shirtless chest covered in nothing but tattoos and a pair of red braces.

My mouth went dry.

My vagina bats fluttered.

My Carly-cave collapsed. *Fuck. F.U.C.K. Fuck.*

Trying desperately to remain on the seat and not slide off in a pool of hormones on the ground before him, I gripped the table and firmly planted my feet on the floor.

Derek raised an eyebrow seductively and hooked his thumbs under both braces while singing about shackles and slaves. He slid his thumbs down his braces and back up again, stretching them away from his body. I made a grab for his pants, but he stepped back and turned around, taunting me by moving his hips in a figure eight.

'Argh,' I groaned, 'take it off.'

He spun back around and removed the braces then slowly undid his pants, one tormenting button at a time. Suddenly, he gave me a quick flash of his cock.

'Oh my god,' I laughed. 'You are commando under there.'

The devilish smile that crept across his face triggered an overwhelming sense of excitement and eager anticipation — it was a look that promised a huge reward.

Grabbing hold of my hand, he splayed it on his chest before sliding it down his body and slipping it into his pants while simultaneously gyrating his hips. *Oh. My. God. Oh, my god.*

The warmth of his hard erection beneath my hand was a fucking welcome delight, my fingers happily clasping around it and stroking with ardour.

'Carly,' he growled, 'I wouldn't if I were you.'

'Well, it's a good thing you are not me then,' I smiled, waggling my eyebrows and dipping forward to lick his delicious V muscle.

He removed my hand and lowered himself onto my lap then began to unbutton my shirt.

'Um ... apparently you are supposed to strip. Not strip me,' I explained with amusement as my nipples hardened at the slightest touch of his fingers against my bra.

'Shut the fuck up, baby. I'm in charge.'

Stripping my shirt from my shoulders and throwing it to the floor, he grasped my breasts with both hands and massaged them with exquisite force.

'Oh, fuck,' I moaned and threw my head back, causing the helmet to fall to the floor.

Instantly, his lips were on my neck, nipping, licking and sucking as he trailed them to my mouth. I grabbed him and ran my hands up his toned back, pressing him closer and wanting to feel as much of him as I could while our tongues stroked one another's.

Derek reached behind himself and took hold of my hands, removing them from his back so that he could stand up. I pouted at the loss.

'Suck that lip in or I'll bite it,' he warned.

Wanting to keep my pouty face and call his bluff, I struggled not to smile at his sexy threat.

He winked then hooked his thumbs into his pants and pulled them down, allowing his cock to spring free prominently when he stood back up. I smiled and bit my thumbnail.

Eye-fucking me intensely, he stepped up to me again and straddled my lap, thrusting his hips and rubbing his cock up and down my bare torso. I watched with sheer gratification as his crown glistened with pre-come while it slid along my skin. It was so fucking erotic, and I just wanted to grab it and impale myself on top like a god-damned human skewer.

I let out a guttural moan and tried to buck my hips in order to relieve some of the ache I was feeling in between my legs.

'You hungry, baby?' he asked, licking up my neck.

'Oh, yeah,' I murmured in response.

Derek pushed up from his seated position on my lap and made his way into the kitchen only to return with a cute little choc-mint pudding. *Oh ... that was not what I had in mind when I said I was hungry.*

Confused, I gave him an unsure grin.

He then knelt down and presented it to me. 'You once asked for proof. Well, the proof is in the pudding.'

'What?' I asked, giggling.

Displaying an adorably cocky grin, he indicated I take the pudding.

Tentatively taking it from his hands, my face flushed as his insinuation dawned on me.

'What?' I said again, staring back at him, wide-eyed.

'The proof is in the pudding, baby. Eat the fucking pudding.'

I shook my head from side to side at a rapid speed. 'I don't want to eat it.'

'Then just break the fucker open,' he said.

Slowly, I broke the small dome-shaped pudding in half to find a white gold and diamond ring nestled snugly inside.

My eyes popped.

My breath hitched.

My heart exploded.

Derek reached in and pulled it out, quickly dunking it in a glass of water to remove the pudding crumbs. He then held it in front of me and took a deep breath. 'Hey, is it just me, or are we destined to be married?'

A laugh mixed with an elated sob exited my mouth.

He shook his head. 'Na, that one was lame. What about this? I want a wife, so will you marry me?'

I giggled and wiped the tears that were pooling in my eyes so that I could see him more clearly.

'Na, I got it. How about ... baby, just fucking say yes?'

Offering my hand, I nodded excitedly. 'Yes, yes, I'll be your Mrs Dik.'

Derek hurriedly threaded the ring onto my finger then reached for my face, mashing his lips to mine.

'Yes?' he questioned, projecting a relieved happiness.

'Yes,' I replied through desperate kisses. Then, pulling away, I gave him a worried look. 'But we can't mention it yet.'

'Why?' he protested in exasperation.

'Because it's not fair to Bryce and Alexis. They are getting married in a few days. I don't want to steal any of their limelight. After what they have been through, they deserve it and have waited too long for it,' I answered.

Derek kissed my hand, which held proof of his love for me. 'Okay, we tell everyone after the wedding.'

An overwhelming sense of contentment washed over me. I grabbed his face in my hands and gazed at him with adoration. 'Boy, if you were a vegetable, you'd be a cutecumber.'

He growled playfully, wrapped his arms around me and stood up, lifting me with him. As he carried me to our room, I prepared to set sail on a new voyage.

Destination ... unknown.

And I couldn't have been happier.

EXTENDED EPILOGUE

Eight months later

'Mum, it's hideous. I'm not wearing this,' I said with disgust as I swiped her hands away from my head.

'Carly Josephine Henkley, you are my only daughter. You *are* wearing it.'

Slumping in defeat, I rolled my eyes. 'I'm your only *child*.'

'Exactly, which is why you have no choice. I wore it on my wedding day. Your grandmother wore it on hers, and your great-grandmother wore it on hers. It's tradition ... an honour,' she said proudly, as she secured the antique comb to my blonde hair.

'It's ugly,' I pouted, stepping away from her and the mirror. 'I'm ugly ... and fat. Look at me! That's it, I'm calling the wedding off,' I announced, reaching behind to try and unzip my dress.

Alexis stepped in front of me and placed her hands on my shoulders. 'Oh no you don't. Stop being a whiny little bitch. You are hormonal and pregnant. You're not fat. Carls, you're beautiful, and that baby bump of yours is beautiful too.'

I shook my head at her. 'I can't do this.'

Eight months ago, I said yes to marrying Derek. I took that leap. I'd wanted to. But back then I did not know that in a mere 243 days, I would not only be participating in the actual marrying that I'd agreed to, but that I'd also be five months pregnant with our baby.

Applying a light pressure to my shoulders, Alexis gently coaxed me into a sitting position on the bed. 'Yes, you can. You're just nervous. Call it wedding jitters if you must. Trust me, we all get them.'

'Ha! You didn't get them. You couldn't wait to become Mrs Clark,' I sulked.

Alexis raised her eyebrow. 'Um ... yeah I did, have you forgotten about my first marriage?'

I searched my memory, recalling the day she married Rick. She was a mess and the epitome of a bridezilla. Granted, she was only twenty-three years old.

'You were young, Lex. You had an excuse. I'm thirty-eight. I'm old.'

Alexis laughed and grabbed hold of my hand which was resting nervously on my lap. 'Well, I'm older ... and wiser. And I say you are stunning, glowing and a completely normal bride on her wedding day.'

My body bounced just slightly with the dip of the bed when Mum sat to my other side and placed her hand on top of mine and Lexi's. 'It's okay to be nervous, darling. So much has happened in such a short space of time. But you are ready.' Mum looked down at our hands and blinked a few times. 'I'm so proud of you. I'm proud of the both of you, actually,' she said, looking up at Alexis and I. 'Who would've thought thirty-four years ago when the two of you first met, that you'd both be sitting here now, hand in hand with families of your own. That in itself is rare and very special,' she said, before giving our hands a light tap and standing back up.

I watched Mum walk away and help Charli gather her rose petals as I deliberated what she'd just said. She was right. So much had happened to me and, surprisingly, I'd taken it well. Children of my own were never on the cards. I was too frightened. I still am.

Seeing Derek's excitement and love at the prospect of having his own family had eased that apprehension though. Don't get me wrong, I'm fully aware it can all go pear-shaped. But I've realised that fearing the 'what if' is pointless, 'what if' being solely a possibility. Avoiding aspects of life for fear of a dark outcome only leads to a life unfulfilled; a life not properly lived. I intended to live mine ... with my husband and child.

Looking down at my and Lexi's entwined fingers, they soon became blurred as my eyes filled with tears.

'No, no, no. No crying. You'll ruin your make-up,' Lexi said, attempting to retract her hand in order to wipe my tears.

I gripped it tightly and held it against my lap, blinking to clear my vision so that I could look upon her clearly. 'Thank you, for everything. For being here. For being my best friend and putting up with me. For being you.'

With a curious expression, she tilted her head to the side. 'Carls, you don't have to thank me. I wouldn't want to be anywhere else or with anyone else. And as for putting up with you? I have had years of practice,' she said with a wink. 'Now, enough of the waterworks. You have a man to marry.'

Lexi stood up and pulled me up with her. 'And boy, is that man keen to marry you.'

I let out a laugh-sob. 'No shit. Hence I'm wearing a maternity wedding dress. Who in their fucking right mind gets married when they are pregnant?'

'Two people who are too in love to wait, that's who. It's romantic,' she cooed as she brushed off my shoulders. 'And anyway, you are not wearing just any maternity wedding dress.'

'No, I'm not,' I answered while fluttering my hands in front of my face in order to compose myself.

Smiling back my hormonal tears, I glanced down at the Vera Wang gown that Alexis had gifted me. It was absolutely gorgeous: column-cut with Swarovski crystal embellished lace that covered my shoulders and continued over an ivory satin, full-length slip. The dress was snug but stretched comfortably across my tummy.

At first I had said no, that there was no way in hell I could accept it. But Lexi insisted and, let's face it, she's loaded now ... not to mention it's Vera-Fucking-Wang!

Just as I'd managed to gather my bearings, Lib barged through the door, quickly struggling to shut it behind her. 'Derek, I mean it, go away. You are not seeing her.'

'Baby, are you in there?' Derek called out, his arm jammed in the door, his hand frantically searching the wooden panel.

I broke away from Alexis and rushed to the door. 'Yes!'

'No!' Lib said, holding me at bay with her arm as she fought to keep Derek and I separated.

Reaching around her, I placed my hand in his, making sure I stayed out of his line of sight. 'What's wrong? Are you all right?'

'I am now,' he said softly as his fingers wrapped around mine. 'I wanted to make sure you were okay. I wanted to make sure both my girls had everything they needed.'

The adoration lacing his tone when he referred to me and our unborn daughter as 'his girls' was incredibly sweet. It was also an incredible turn-on. 'We are fine. Although, my cave could do with a quick exploration,' I stated with a hint of innuendo.

'Carly Josephine Henkley, I hope you are not insinuating what I think you are. Last time I checked, you were not the owner of a hollow space in the ground,' Mum questioned with a stern yet unperturbed tone.

Derek's grip tightened around my hand. 'Mrs Henkley, it would appear that I need to excuse your daughter for say ... ten minutes,' he implied. 'I'll bring her right back. I promise.'

'Derek, if you want to become my son-in-law today, you have exactly ten seconds to release Carly's hand and make your way to the marquee.'

He groaned painfully and let go of my hand. 'Fine, but you drive a hard bargain.' Quickly taking hold of it again, he gently caressed my engagement ring with his fingertips. 'I love you, baby. See you soon. Give her rub for me.'

Leaning forward, I kissed the back of his hand while rubbing my tummy like he'd asked. 'I will. Now go, or I'll be lat—'

'Derek, what the fuck are you doing?' a voice interrupted us. 'Get out of there.'

'Ease up, Sean. I'm just havin' a quick word,' Derek ground out.

'Well, your time is up. Step away from the door.'

'Hey, Sean?' I called out.

'Yeah?'

'Is Layla with you? We are nearly ready.'

'I'm here, I'm here,' she replied from the other side of the door, 'but I'm not coming in until Derek leaves.'

'Yeah, yeah. All right, I'm leaving,' Derek grumbled.

Seconds later, the door opened and Layla entered, a flurry of mint green chiffon whisking past me. 'Okay, everything is set. The boys are making their way to the marquee, the celebrant is ready and the guests are all seated,' she advised as Lex handed her a glass of champagne.

Just over two years ago, not too long after Derek and Sean came to blows at the firefighters base camp in Wallan, Layla and I conspired and decided it would be our mission to get the brothers on pleasant terms again. What we didn't bargain on was that they would not only reconcile their differences, but that they would become extremely close as a result. It was a fantastic outcome and a miracle to say the least, especially after how livid Derek was when he found out that I had gone behind his back to arrange for he and Sean to be stuck in an elevator together at City Towers.

My plan was brilliant, having made sure Bryce had absolutely nothing to do with it, as I did not want my actions jeopardising their friendship. Lucy, on the other hand, well ... she was all for it. And so it happened, she, together with Layla, ended up being my perfect accomplices. Admittedly, the plan was risky, because once the boys were stuck in the elevator, no one could pry them apart in a hurry if they went head to head, which they did. But luckily, I could communicate through the elevator's speaker system, and between Layla and I, we were able to keep their tempers neutral ... at least after they'd expelled their initial anger and testosterone. It really was perfect.

'Okay. I'm ready. I'm ready to become Mrs Dik,' I said eagerly, knowing that as soon as we got this whole process started, the sooner Derek and I could sneak away for some cave-diving.

My mother tutted before she hollered, 'Right! Lex, grab Carly's train. Lib, you look after the flowers. Layla, make sure everything is ready to go before she walks down the path, and Charli, sweetheart, you are with me.'

Everyone stood at Mum's orders, setting out to complete their tasks, when a knock at the door sounded and Dad entered the room. 'Ready when you are,' he said, blushing when he met my eyes.

'Dad, you totally just blushed!' I mocked endearingly.

He adjusted his tie and straightened his posture. 'Carly, I'm a grown man. I do not blush.'

'Sorry, Mr H, but you did indeed blush,' Lex stated, backing me up with a definitive smile.

Dad ignored us and wrestled with his tie once again, this time with more aggravation.

'Henry, what are you doing? You're making a mess of it,' Mum scolded as she made her way toward him.

His hand shot out to thwart her efforts. 'Back off, Joyce. I can fix my own tie.'

'Nonsense,' she replied, dismissing his hand by pushing it aside. 'Clearly, you can't.'

Watching Mum and Dad's exchange had me thinking of what Derek and I would be like in years to come. Would we be anything like my parents? I hoped so. My parents, although argumentative with each other at times, were the perfect couple. They knew what each other needed, even if it wasn't what they wanted. And they loved one another, and me, as much as humanly possible. If Derek's and my marriage could be anything remotely like theirs, then we were going to be fine.

As we all proceeded to exit the room — the girls in single file and looking stunning in their mint green Reem Acra knee-length strapless dresses — I felt a flutter in my lower abdomen. The sensation of my daughter's movements from within my womb was weird ... alien-like. Not that I thought my daughter was an alien or anything. She wasn't. She was an unplanned, unexpected shock to end all shocks. Yet she was also a living, breathing awakener and life-changer. Although she did kind of look like an alien the last time we saw her image on the ultrasound screen. My god was her head huge! Just the thought of that head coming out of my cave scared the absolute shit out of me. My cave is precious, unharmed and well looked after.

'Carly, you coming? Derek can't marry himself,' Dad announced, gaining my attention and holding his arm out for me.

I laughed. 'No, he can't. And I wouldn't want him to. Could you imagine the wedding night if he could?'

Shaking his head in amusement, he began to lead me down the stairs and out into the garden. 'I think it's about time I gave you away,' he joked.

I squeezed his arm tight and lay my head on his shoulder as we walked, smiling contentedly. 'Yes, I think you are right. I'm ready, Dad. I'm ready for you to give me to Derek.'

Derek

'Stop hopping around. You look like you need to take a piss,' Sean said from his position beside Will and Bryce.

'He probably does,' Will added, nodding his head to a beat that I knew from experience was playing silently in his mind.

I, too, was currently playing a song in my head, but mine was the one I'd written for Carls and planned on singing to her at our reception dinner.

'Drained the snake before we came out here. I'm all good. But thanks for thinking 'bout my junk. I'm flattered,' I responded, catching sight of a mint green dress near the entry to the marquee.

Bryce sniggered at my remark then lightly tapped me on the arm, indicating the ceremony was about to start. 'You ready?'

'You have no idea,' I answered, preening my neck to try and get a glimpse of Carls. I was beyond ready. I'd been ready ever since proposing, possibly even before that.

'Good to know, mate,' Bryce replied. 'Let's get you married, and then you can finally become a man.'

Fucking smartarse.

'Inevitable' — a Live Trepidation musical piece — started playing over the speaker as Charlotte, together with Alexander and Brayden, began to walk down the aisle, the two boys grabbing handfuls of petals from Charlotte's basket and throwing them all over the place. 'Inevitable' was the same song Alexis walked down the aisle to when she married Bryce. We decided that it would become the Live T marriage song, but we would alter the melody just slightly for each individual ceremony. At first I thought it was a stupid idea, but the girls seemed to like it, so the idea stuck. One thing I have learned is that you don't argue with a bride during the planning of a wedding. Especially a pregnant bride!

When the kids reached the end of the aisle, Lucy led the boys to their seats next to her and Nic while Charlotte held up a sign for me to read. It said:

LAST

I furrowed my brow, curious as to what the hell it was about. She turned and showed our guests and they, too, seemed a little puzzled.

Layla was not far behind Charlotte and the boys, she too stopping and displaying a sign. Hers read:

CHANCE

Again, I was fucking perplexed but also amused at the game Carly was playing. I shouldn't be surprised that she would orchestrate something like this.

After showing me the sign, Layla turned toward the rest of the room and shrugged her shoulders with a smile as she displayed it for them to read. There were a few whispers and mild laughs.

Libby made her way down the aisle soon after, her sign saying:

TO

'What the fuck?' I murmured and turned to Bryce who was now chuckling behind his hand. 'Did you know about this?'

He shook his head then averted his attention to his wife as she, too, made her way down the aisle. I knew not to probe any further, my attempt futile — Bryce's attention now locked on Alexis.

She stopped and winked at her pussy-whipped husband before holding up her sign which finished the sentence:

BACK OUT

What the fuck? Alexis gave me a stern but playful look which implied I really did not have a choice. Not that I needed one.

Letting out a loud laugh at Carly's antics, I raised both hands as if to say 'no way' as Alexis turned and showed everyone else the sign.

The room erupted into laughter as the final piece of this strange puzzle was revealed. I, on the other hand, rested my head in my hand.

Hearing the scraping of chairs and shuffling of feet, my head shot up, and my eyes searched the far end of the room until they fell on the most beautiful thing I had ever seen; Carly. The mother of my child. My wife to be. *Jesus fucking Christ.*

She was breathtaking. Her long blonde hair was curled and fell across her shoulders, a sprinkling of small flowers through it. She had lace covering her chest and a mint green ribbon, matching the other girl's dresses, wrapped around her tummy ... the place where my daughter grew bigger every day.

Jerking forward slightly, the result of Bryce slapping me across my back, he instructed me to 'Breathe.'

The sudden movement nearly had me choking, but he was right, I'd forgotten to exhale. You see, that's what a woman you love more than life itself can do to you ... still that life from your very lungs.

As she made her way closer, her hand dropped to her stomach and gave it a nurturing rub. *Fuuuck!* I couldn't possibly love her any more.

My heart pounded.

My temperature rose.

My peripheral vision vanished.

It was just me and her.

She stopped just out of my reach and turned to Henry for a quick hug. Then, like a fucking chameleon, her expression changed to one of don't-mess-with-me as she held up a sign that I only just noticed was in her other hand. It read:

DON'T EVEN THINK ABOUT BACKING OUT.
I OWN YOU, DIK.

I burst into laughter, as did the rest of the bridal party. Carly turned and curtsied while displaying her sign before handing it her father and taking my hand.

The feeling that shot through my fingers, up my arm and throughout my body as our skin connected, was pretty much indescribable. But I will say this: it's a feeling that happens once in a lifetime, a result of finding 'the one', of connecting with someone beyond attraction. It's the feeling of finding your soul mate.

Carly was it for me. She had been, years ago, the very moment that feeling first passed through me. She'd taught me to open up, to trust and to love.

Stepping up beside me, the glint of a seductive smile played across her face.

'If husbands are boogers, I pick you,' she said loudly.

I smiled the biggest fucking smile imaginable and turned to our celebrant. 'Marry us. Marry us now!'

THE END.

ACKNOWLEDGEMENTS

As always, and right off the bat, I need to thank my husband. This man, that I'm privileged to share my life with, is all kinds of wonderful. And, I think it's safe to say, if it weren't for him being the epitome of awesome, *Attraction* would not have been written or published.

Mum: you support me tirelessly, offering to help in whichever way you can. You spread the word as a genuine fan of my work and not only do you support me, but you also support the many other talented Aussie authors I call my friends. Go #AussiePimpMum

To my wonderful friends who beta read the first draft. Your comments and feedback were much appreciated. I'm so glad you were all there to calm my crazy head when I was uncertain as to how this book would be received.

Also, a special shout-out needs to be given to Melanie Sassymum, who was not only one of those wonderful friends who beta read for me, but who helped with promoting and spreading the word of *Attraction*'s release. Mel, your assistance has been instrumental. I flove you, my #pock.

To my editors Stephanie and Belinda, and to everyone at Harlequin Books Australia: thank you for your hard work and dedication to the series as a whole. I've thoroughly enjoyed working with you and seeing this novel be brought to life. Which brings me to Editor Extraordinaire, Annabel: I honestly can't say enough wonderful things about you. It has been an absolute joy working side by side during the editing of this book and the entire re-work of *Temptation, Satisfaction, Fulfilment & Attainment*. Some may assume the editing process to be daunting. But, with you at the helm, that assumption could not be further from the truth. It was such a pleasure to share this experience with you.

And lastly but certainly not the least, my fans: just quietly, I still cannot believe that I can say those two simple words together ... 'my fans'. It's just so surreal! However, you are all there and you make my writing journey all the more worth it. Thank you so very much. I hope you enjoyed Carly and Derek's story. After all, it was you who requested it.

Website:

http://www.kmgolland.com/

Goodreads:

http://www.goodreads.com/author/
show/6860161.K_M_Golland

Facebook:

https://www.facebook.com/temptationseries

Facebook:

https://www.facebook.com/profile.
php?id=100005897226649

Twitter:

https://twitter.com/KellyGolly

Make sure you visit my website and facebook pages. Bonus chapters will pop up every now and again ☺

More great titles
from International bestselling author

K.M. GOLLAND

AVAILABLE NOW